"I MERELY WANTED TO COMPLETE THE LESSON YOU STARTED."

He snorted. "You wanted to complete the task of throwing away your virginity?"

"It is mine to throw. Was mine," she corrected, not looking nearly so cool.

Martín studied her flushed face and sighed. "So, what do you want from me now, eh?"

Her already flushed face mottled. "Don't worry! I don't expect a declaration of everlasting love or marriage from someone like you."

Someone like him? What did she mean? Had she learned what he'd done in New Orleans? Was that why she'd come to him today?

"Somebody like me," he repeated, the words like broken glass in his mouth.

"What I meant was—"

He held up one hand. "So, you came to me for a lesson in bed sport. Now you know what somebody like *me* can do to someone like *you*."

Also by Minerva Spencer

Dangerous

Barbarous

Published by Kensington Publishing Corporation

Scandalous

Minerva Spencer

ZEBRA BOOKS
KENSINGTON PUBLISHING CORP.
www.kensingtonbooks.com

ZEBRA BOOKS are published by

Kensington Publishing Corp.
119 West 40th Street
New York, NY 10018

All Kensington titles, imprints, and distributed lines are available at special quantity discounts for bulk purchases for sales promotion, premiums, fund-raising, educational, or institutional use.

Special book excerpts or customized printings can also be created to fit specific needs. For details, write or phone the office of the Kensington Sales Manager: Attn.: Sales Department. Kensington Publishing Corp., 119 West 40th Street, New York, NY 10018. Phone: 1-800-221-2647.

Zebra and the Z logo Reg. U.S. Pat. & TM Off.

First Printing: October 2019
ISBN-13: 978-1-4201-4720-9
ISBN-10: 1-4201-4720-X

ISBN-13: 978-1-4201-4723-0 (eBook)
ISBN-10: 1-4201-4723-4 (eBook)

10 9 8 7 6 5 4 3 2 1

Printed in the United States of America

Dedicated to Brantly, my "hugsband"

Chapter One

1816, The Gold Coast of Africa,
Aboard the Golden Scythe

Martín drummed his fingers on the gleaming wooden railing and stared at the Dutch ship. The vessel was upwind and too far away to smell the stench, but Martín could imagine it. The pitiful cries of the slaves were another matter. Those he could hear even from this distance.

The dirty business of slaving was more lucrative than ever since the British and Americans had banned the importation of slaves in 1808. The American South paid well for smuggled slaves, as it could not function without their labor, a fact Martín knew all too well.

He turned to his first mate. "How many crew, Beauville?" he asked in English, rather than his native French. He'd begun speaking English after the British granted him his letter of marque, the document that made his profitable life as a privateer possible.

Beauville lowered his spyglass. "No more than forty, Captain, and most of those appear to be either drunk or incompetent."

Martín laughed at the man's dry assessment and strode

to where his second mate held the wheel. "Ready the men, Daniels, and then prepare to make the offer."

Although the Dutch ship had suffered some damage to its mast, it appeared to be a well-maintained ship and far cleaner than the usual run of slavers. Martín's own ship, the *Golden Scythe*, had been a slave ship before he'd captured her, but she'd cleaned up nicely. He regarded the immaculate deck with pride. With a crew of seventy men and fourteen cannon, the *Scythe* greatly outmatched the Dutch ship and was a force to be reckoned with.

Still, it was never wise to be too cocky. If the *Blue Bird* carried to capacity—five hundred souls—the money involved was great. Things would become ugly if the ship's captain was determined to fight for his cargo. Martín was confident he would triumph in such a struggle, but he knew it would not be without cost.

A flurry of activity broke out as he watched the other ship; the crew was flapping about like a flock of frightened hens. A dozen men stood near the main mast and gestured wildly to one another—a few with machetes. Martín shook his head; something odd was going on.

Daniels appeared beside him. "Everything is prepared, Captain, and we await your command."

Martín turned to Jenkins, his man of all work, who held out two pistols for his inspection. He checked the guns carefully before inserting them into a holster that kept both guns resting on his right hip while his rapier lay on his left. The holster was of Martín's design and allowed him to draw any of the three weapons quickly.

He glanced into the large mirror Jenkins held up before him and flicked an imaginary piece of lint from his immaculate coat. He took his time and made a minute adjustment to his cravat, careful to keep his movements languid and his expression bored. His crew was watching, their battered faces amused, yet proud. Martín knew they drew strength from his reputation as a cold, hard killer who was more concerned with his cravat than his life.

To be honest, Martín's stomach churned just as much, if not more, than that of any other man on the ship. If anyone died today, *he* would be to blame. While that might not bother his conscience—a hardened, shriveled thing—his pride was fat and healthy, and he could not bear to have poor decisions attributed to him.

Martín flicked his hand, and Jenkins took away the mirror. Daniels's mouth was pursed with disapproval. He knew the younger man still found his behavior shocking, even though he'd been Martín's second for over a year.

Martín found his irritation amusing. "Make the offer, Mr. Daniels."

"Aye, Captain!" Daniels turned and gave the midshipman a hand signal. A second later a loud crack issued from one of the *Scythe*'s cannons. The smoke had barely cleared before a black flag crept up the Dutch ship's pole.

Martín exhaled; they would parley.

"Excellent shot, gentlemen, and very persuasive. Beauville, please escort their captain to the wardroom when he arrives." Martín unfastened his weapon belt and handed it to Jenkins. "Don't unload these just yet," he advised before going below deck.

Once inside his cabin, he cast his hat onto the desk and collapsed in a high-backed chair, careful not to crush the tails of his coat. His excessive concern for his appearance was only partly feigned. He loved fine clothing. As a young slave in New Orleans he'd envied the wealthy, well-dressed men who'd frequented Madam Sonia's establishment, vowing he would dress even better one day. Now he was rich enough to dress however he pleased, and what pleased him was the best.

He idly studied his reflection in the glass that hung over his desk, frowning at the man who looked back. Nobody would ever mistake him for a European, no matter the color of his eyes, skin, and hair. Even though his skin was lighter than that of anyone imprisoned on the Dutch ship, Martín could be bought and sold just as readily were he to step foot on American soil. Actually, he would face death if he returned home, death being the punishment for a runaway slave.

Martín pushed the thought away and absently picked up a book and opened it. He immediately wished he hadn't. The black marks danced on the pages before him, inscrutable and taunting. It was a criminal offense to teach a slave to read in America, and Martín had been far too old to learn after he'd escaped.

The only three words he could read or write were those that comprised his name: Martín Etienne Bouchard—a name that wasn't even his, but one he'd cobbled together for himself.

The name Martín he had taken from a story an old woman had once told him: the tale of Martín Garatuza, the legendary Mexican trickster.

And Etienne Bouchard he'd added some time later, taking it from the old man who'd taught him everything he knew about horses. And why not? Old Bouchard had been dead by then; he no longer needed the name.

Martín shut the book with a snap and replaced it on the shelf. Most of the books had been on the *Scythe* when he'd taken her, but his friend and mentor One-Eyed Standish had given him some of the others, mercifully unaware his protégé did not know how to read.

Martín frowned. Thoughts of his humiliating past only came to him when he was too tired to control his memories. Or too restless. And he was always restless when it came to seizing another man's ship. But soon it would be over.

He stood and unfastened the gold buttons of his navy wool coat before draping it over the back of the chair. Once he was finished with the parley he would return to Freetown, set the captives free, turn the offenders over to His Majesty's government, and collect his reward. In other words: he'd do the same thing he always did, and there was no reason to feel restless.

Martín looked at the ornate gold clock that sat on his desk; there was at least an hour before the other captain would arrive to parley. He could rest and catch up on the sleep he had missed while they'd followed the slaver.

Calmed by his comfortable vision of the future, Martín stretched out on his luxurious bed, closed his eyes, and imagined amusing ways in which to spend the money he would get from capturing this ship.

Meanwhile, on the Blue Bird . . .

Sarah was finishing setting a little boy's broken arm using a filthy strip of skirt and a stiff piece of leather from her battered medical bag when the hatch to the slave hold opened and a ladder was lowered into the gloom.

"Woman!" The guttural voice came from the narrow opening high above.

Sarah squinted up, but the light was too bright to see the speaker's face.

"Captain want, now," the man ordered in English so guttural she could barely understand him.

"There is a woman in need of burying," Sarah called back in French, glancing at the new mother she had been unable to save, who now lay packed between two of the ship's ribs in the bilge and waste.

"Come *now*!"

Sarah shut her mouth, said a silent prayer, and crawled across the splintered wood and over the tightly packed bodies toward the ladder. What was left of her wet skirts dragged behind her, snagging and tearing, making the short journey twice as long. Just before she made it to the swaying ladder a hand caught her arm; it was Femi, a captive she had met on the hellish three-week journey from the inland to the coastal settlement of Ouidah.

Sarah paused, and Femi leaned close and whispered in Yoruba, "If there is some way for you to get the doors open, even for only a few moments, we will be waiting." He looked up at the opening—squinting against the light. "Maybe at night you will be able to sneak away—after." He gave her a grim, humorless smile and shrugged his massive shoulders. They both knew what he meant. Why else would these monsters take a woman from the hold?

He gave her arm a brief squeeze. "But if not . . ."

They stared at each other in the gloom, more words unnecessary.

Two other women had disappeared in the days they'd spent in this hell; neither woman had returned.

She gave him an abrupt nod and commenced the torturous climb. The muscles in her shoulders and wrists burned hotter with each rung. She'd begun to think she wouldn't make it to the top when rough hands closed around her arms. The men cursed her smell and grunted under the weight of her soaking clothing as they lifted her into the blazing sunshine.

A scarred, unshaven face was pushed up against hers. "You fix captain."

Sarah reeled back from the alcohol fumes and stench of rotting teeth, noticeable even after the horrid smell of the hold. She would have fallen had he not given her arm a vicious yank and dragged her down a short flight of steps into a dim, narrow corridor.

They led her to the last door, and the leader rapped. "Kapiten!"

A much softer answer came from behind the handsome mahogany and brass door, and her captor wrenched it open.

He muttered something in Dutch before thrusting Sarah inside and slamming the door behind her.

Sarah's first glimpse of the captain was both a shock and a relief. He was young, perhaps five-and-twenty. His build was slight—almost delicate—and he was very fair, bearing more than a passing resemblance to the angels in her father's religious books.

But the thing that left her weak with relief was the fact he was ill—far too ill to have even the slightest amorous glint in his watery blue eyes.

He stood and gestured to a chair across from him. "Please have a seat," he said in almost unaccented English.

Sarah moved past him, and he covered his mouth, his nostrils quivering as the smell hit him. She dropped into the chair and crossed her arms.

"Thank you so much for joining me."

Sarah snorted.

His smile wavered at the rude noise. "I am Mies Graaf; my family owns the *Blue Bird*. My men tell me you are a medical person and—" A ferocious bout of coughing doubled him over.

Grim satisfaction trickled through Sarah as she watched his suffering; it was only fair that this architect of human misery should receive his own share of pain.

An image of her father's kind, worn face appeared in Sarah's mind and froze her smile. Reverend Michael Fisher would have argued that a man depraved enough to deal in human flesh deserved her pity rather than scorn.

Always remember we are not on Earth to judge, Sarah.

The memory of her father's words drove the vengeful thoughts from her head and left shame in their wake. She was behaving like a fool. Instead of letting rage consume her, she needed to harness her anger and use it to figure out a way to get the doors to the hold open.

She eyed the sick man. He was all she had to work with, and there was no point antagonizing him.

The Dutchman's coughing diminished, and he straightened in his chair, his movements slow and deliberate, like those of a very old man. "I apologize, Miss, er—"

"Fisher. Sarah Fisher."

He frowned at whatever he saw on her face. "I was not aware of your presence in the hold until a short time ago. I am sorry you have been subjected to such indignity. You will be given a cabin and treated as my guest."

"What of the others?"

His handsome brow wrinkled. "Excuse me?"

"The other *people* in your hold—what about *them*?"

He flinched back from the violence in her tone, his eyes flickering about the room, as if searching for answers, a dark red stain creeping over his already flushed cheeks. "Ah . . . that. Buying these people was not my doing—nor was it my intention to—" His voice broke, and, when he drew in a ragged breath to speak, he was wracked by more coughing.

Sarah made an irritated noise and stood. "Give me your wrist."

Still coughing, he regarded her grimy hand with apprehension.

"Do you wish for my help or not?"

He held out one pale, slim, *clean* hand.

Sarah snatched up the proffered limb. His pulse was irregular and fast, and his skin hot and damp.

She dropped his arm. "I will need to look in your ears and mouth."

He leaned forward, and she took his angelic, clean face with her filthy hands and tilted him toward the light streaming through the porthole window. "Open your mouth and depress your tongue with your finger." He did so, and Sarah looked her fill before resuming her seat and meeting his frightened gaze.

"You have the choking fever," she lied, adding a silent prayer.

"The choking fever," he repeated, as if in a trance. "And the cure?" The hope in his eyes was painful to witness, no matter how much he deserved his suffering.

"Only the thorn of Christ will cure it." Sarah offered more prayers for forgiveness of the lies pouring from her mouth. Surely the dire circumstances would excuse her dishonesty?

"Thorn of Christ?" he repeated.

"Yes, a rare herb." *So rare as to be nonexistent.*

"Where can we procure this herb?"

It was the question Sarah had been hoping for.

"It only grows near coastal marshes." It was imperative she convince him to take the ship back to shore. It was the only chance for her and the people in the hold—*if* she could get the door open.

Sarah pushed the thought away. First things first.

She examined the room while the captain pondered her words. A pair of dueling pistols hung over the desk, the guns so ornate Sarah could hardly believe they were real. She was imagining ways to get her hands on one when a deafening *crack* shook the room.

She jumped to her feet. "What was that?"

The Dutch captain gave her a grim look. "That, Miss Fisher, was the sound of cannon fire."

Chapter Two

"Cannon fire?" Sarah repeated, the words hanging in the air between them like so much smoke.

Graaf uttered several uncivil-sounding words in Dutch and made for the door. "I will return directly." He slammed the door, and a key scraped in the lock; so, he was not distracted enough to forget to lock the cabin door behind him.

Sarah waited until his footsteps receded before lunging for one of the pistols. She tripped over her sodden skirts and banged into the captain's heavy teak chair in the process.

"Blast," she muttered, standing on tiptoe to pluck the ornate pistol from the wall. She broke open the breech and almost sobbed—the gun was real.

"Thank you, thank you, thank you," she whispered frantically beneath her breath.

She jammed a gun in each of her tattered skirt pockets and commenced to riffle drawers and cabinets, her hands shaking so badly, she dropped clothing, books, and other items all over the cabin floor. Just when she thought the search was fruitless, she spied a polished wooden box. It contained powder, lead balls, and pistol-shaped indentations lined with red silk.

"Oh, *thank you!*" she said with a sob, dropping to the floor and beginning the process of loading the guns. Her father had owned an ancient pistol and had taught her to load and clean the weapon one year when three lions had menaced their village. This gun, although far fancier, was, in all important aspects, the same.

When she'd finished loading the second gun, she secured it in the waistband of her skirt and placed the remaining powder and balls into the pocket of her tattered petticoat. She'd just taken up a position behind the door and pulled back the hammer when a key clicked in the lock.

The squawk of surprise that tore from Graaf's mouth when the barrel of his own pistol touched his temple was more than a little satisfying.

"This pistol is loaded, and I will not hesitate to use it." Sarah was proud of her steady hand and voice. "Now, sit down."

The captain sat, his shoulders sagging with defeat. "Whatever it is you want, you probably will not get it. That cannon was fired by the privateer who has been following us."

"Privateer?" Her fingers tightened on the pistol, and the Dutchman grimaced, his eyes wide as he stared at her hand.

"Yes, a privateer, a man who has been empowered by the British government to capture ships on behalf of their king. Not only are we outgunned by the privateer vessel, but I am certain the first mate began to incite mutiny among my crew when I told him we would parley." The Dutchman closed his eyes and shook his head. "The men are angry. None of them wanted to crew on a slaver ship—it was de Heeckeren, the first mate, who got us into this. But now that we are . . ." Graaf opened his eyes and must have seen the lack of sympathy on her face. He held up his hands in a gesture that was both placating and beseeching. "Please, Miss Fisher, you must believe me when I tell you dealing in slaves was *not* my idea."

"I. Don't. Care." She had to force the words through clenched jaws, and it was all she could do not to shoot him for wallowing in self-pity while people died beneath his feet. "I don't care *whose* idea it was," she repeated. "Do you have any idea what happened to our lives? People are suffering and dying because of you," she said, her voice rising. "This is a chance for you to help stop this nightmare. It will not redeem you—not even close—but it will be a start. Now, here is what you will do: you will take the ship back to shore and release everyone from the hold, or I will *shoot* you."

He snorted. "You would be doing me a favor. I think you have a mistaken notion about what is going on, Miss Fisher. While I and many of my crew did not want to run this cargo—"

"Cargo? These are *people*, Captain Graaf—I want to hear you say it."

His jaw tightened, and he swayed a little, sweat pouring down his temples. "While I and many of my crew did not want to buy and sell *people*, I think *you* do not understand the situation. I am merely a token, a representative of the Graaf family—I'm not even a captain, although I am using the title. The real person in charge is de Heeckeren." Graaf grimaced. "He is an experienced sailor and greatly feared— and not just by *me*."

Sarah frowned, confused. "*He* is the captain?"

"In everything except name. He is also the reason we left Ouidah with a hold full of . . . people. The men didn't realize they were signing on to crew a slave ship, but they know there will be no pay if they turn back. Some of them will not let that happen and will follow my first mate." He shook his head. "I cannot say how many." He suffered another coughing spell.

Sarah stared at him, trying to gain his measure. What was the Dutchman trying to get at? Was he saying *he* might be agreeable to returning to shore—for the mythical thorn of Christ, if for nothing else? Just how much did he regret his decision to allow his first mate to fill his hold with human cargo? Enough to risk his life to let them go?

Graaf regained his breath and continued in a hoarse voice. "The men know the privateer will bring the captain and crew before the Vice-Admiralty Court once we reach Freetown—and some of them do not view this threat lightly. Without the proper leadership, they will follow de Heeckeren and fight the privateer vessel rather than parley. And then we will all most likely die."

"I'm afraid I don't understand your position in all this, Captain. What are you trying to say?"

"I propose we join forces."

His words surprised a laugh out of her. "And what do you have that I might want? A mutinous crew? The imminent arrival of a shipload of marauding privateers? Please, I am curious to know what you bring to the bargain."

He sighed, the grooves that bracketed his mouth deepening. "If all my crew was on the side of my first mate, then I would be bobbing in the ocean, and you and I would not be having this conversation, Miss Fisher. I'm telling you that if we act before it is too late, we may be able to gain the support we need." He stopped and pulled a handkerchief from his pocket, wiping sweat from his brow and staring at her through red-rimmed, watery eyes.

Sarah examined his face for any trace of deceit, but all she saw was exhaustion and illness.

"We do not have much time," he prodded.

Sarah drew in a deep breath before speaking. "What about the privateers?"

"Once we have control of the ship, we parley. The privateer will attack us if we do not. Either way, I will be boarded, and the ship will be confiscated for violation of a recent Anglo-Dutch treaty. I would prefer to surrender without any damage to my ship or loss of life."

Sarah chewed her lip so hard the metallic tang of blood

flooded her mouth. Could she trust him? She snorted at the thought. What other choice did she have? She stared, not seeing him but the faces in the hold. The only way people got out of the hold was when the crew threw their bodies over the side of the ship. This might be everyone's only chance.

"If I agree to help you, how will we go about it, Captain?"

His shoulders sagged with relief, as if she'd already agreed.

Well, he could think whatever he wanted. Sarah had no qualms about using him, at least until she had the backing of the only people on the ship she trusted: those imprisoned in the hold.

"I will summon my first mate with an offer to capitulate. If we can capture him, I believe the mutiny will die quickly. You wait behind the door as you did with me. I will take the other pistol and confront him when he enters."

"What if he is more suspicious than you and sends someone else? What if he brings a pistol of his own?"

He flushed at her not-so-subtle mockery of his own easy capture. "De Heeckeren is overconfident and not expecting any resistance from me. He will come. Also, I possess the only pistols on this ship, and he would not bring a musket to such a close space."

"And once we have the first mate, you will unlock the hold and free everyone?"

He nodded. "I daresay they will prove loyal to our cause, which is more than I can say for many of my crew."

"And then we will parley?"

Again he nodded.

Sarah hesitated.

"This is no trick. The privateers are now our best hope. But we must hurry."

What else could she do? She could not single-handedly capture the ship. She could—

"Miss Fisher, we must—"

She raised the gun. "Let me *think*."

His mouth snapped shut, and he slumped in his chair.

What did she have? A pair of guns and herself. She grimaced. She needed help to get past the sailors and to reach the hold and Femi. She bit back a groan as the thoughts chased one another around and around inside her exhausted brain.

She *had* to trust somebody. There was no other way. She studied the captain from beneath her lashes. His skin was sheened with sweat, and his hands shook. He might not even stay conscious long enough to take back his ship.

Something slammed hard on the deck above them, and Sarah jumped.

"What are they doing?" she demanded.

"Probably preparing the cannons to fight the privateers."

Cannons! The people in the hold would be the first to die if the ships exchanged cannon fire.

Sarah said a silent prayer and pulled the second pistol from her waistband. "It is loaded."

He took the gun and checked it.

"Extra ammunition?" he asked, ignoring the weapon she still had leveled at his chest.

Sarah struggled with her wet, heavy clothing to pull out the little bag of powder and balls. After an interminable time digging about, she located both and handed them over. He looked at her for a moment, opened his mouth as if to say something, but then closed it again.

"What?"

"It is only . . . Well, if you will forgive me, I was going to say we may need to move quickly. Will you be able to do so in your wet garments?" The captain flushed under her suspicious stare and shrugged. "Should you desire it, there is dry clothing in the wardrobe behind you. It is men's clothing, but we are of a similar height, and you will be able to move faster."

He was right—her clothing was a hindrance. Besides,

she stank and was cold. Sarah could discern no sly intent or cunning in his face. All the same, she backed toward the wardrobe without lowering her gun. She jerked open the door and glanced inside.

"For the love of God." He plunked down the pistol on the desk. "There, keep it. Although how you plan to change your clothing and shoot me at the same time I cannot guess." He moved his chair so his back was toward her and collapsed into it.

Sarah tore off several buttons in her haste to get out of her garments. She yanked one of his fine linen shirts over her worn chemise before stepping out of her tattered skirt and into a pair of breeches, all the while keeping her eyes on Graaf's back. After she'd donned a waistcoat and a blue woolen frock coat, she picked up the second gun and handed it over his shoulder.

The captain looked at her outfit and snorted, his barely suppressed amusement triggering a coughing fit.

"That serves you right for laughing." Sarah cocked her pistol and took her place behind the door. "Now, are you ready to take back your ship?"

Chapter Three

When Martín opened the door to the wardroom he found two similarly dressed people sitting across from Beauville and Daniels. Both people were fair-skinned and slim, their pale faces wan beneath their hats. One of them was female.

"*Bonjour,* Captain. *Bonjour, madam? Mademoiselle?*" He cocked an inquiring eyebrow at the woman. The gasps that escaped Beauville and Daniels told Martín his men had been fooled by her male clothing.

He turned to his first mate and made a *tsk-tsk* sound. "For shame, Beauville. How is it you could fail to notice a beautiful woman even when she is dressed as a man?"

The woman inhaled sharply at Martín's inaccurate description. Her thin, pale face was, in fact, not particularly handsome. And, judging by the way she had fooled his crew, she must have a figure to match.

She glared at him. "My name is Sarah Fisher. *Miss* Sarah Fisher. And this"—she gestured to the man beside her—"is Mies Graaf, captain of the *Blue Bird.*" The blond man gave Martín a tired smile and lifted his shoulders, as if to say he was merely along on a whim.

Martín eyed the weak-looking slaver with scorn. It would be far more entertaining, not to mention humiliating, to

Minerva Spencer

deal with the captain's excitable woman rather than the man himself.

Martín turned to her and bowed with a flourish. "Welcome to my ship, *Miss* Fisher. I am Captain Martín Bouchard. I take it by your presence here that you are going to turn yourselves and your ship over without any fuss, eh?"

She crossed her arms. "By what right do you claim Captain Graaf's ship and cargo?"

Martín leaned across the table, both to get a closer look under her hat and to let her know he was not a man to be held at arm's length by frigid looks. "By the power of the letter of marque granted to me by the British government, *Miss* Fisher."

She glanced at the Dutchman, clearly hoping for assistance.

She received none.

Her eyes slid back to Martín's face, but she let slip no indication of what she was thinking.

He smiled; such cool behavior was intriguing. Women usually flung themselves at him, or, at the very least, giggled and behaved foolishly in his company. Who was this plain woman with such self-possession and calm? And what was she to the mute, pitiful lump of man beside her? His sister? His wife? His whore? She flushed under his stare, as if he'd spoken the words out loud.

"The *Blue Bird* was in the process of returning to Ouidah when you stopped us, Captain. The people on the ship are going home. There is no need for you to interfere; nobody on that ship will be sold into slavery."

Martín laughed and threw his hands in the air. "*Enfin, mademoiselle,* I see now that I have made a terrible mistake. You are free to go."

The woman's lips parted, and she looked sideways at the Dutchman. Neither spoke as they rose hesitantly to their feet.

Martín waited until they were standing before leaning

across the table, no longer smiling. "*You* may go, but I will retain your ship, crew, and human cargo."

The captain slumped back into his seat, but the woman flushed a deep red and planted both hands on the table. She glared down at him. "I am not interested in playing your games, Captain Bouchard," she said, her words soft and menacing.

By God, she was a treat!

Martín leaned toward her until the brims of their hats touched.

"Oh? Whose games *would* you like to play, *mademoiselle*?"

Her eyes narrowed to slits. "We have one hundred armed men and twenty loaded cannon. You would be well-advised to let us be on our way or face the consequences."

This time, Beauville joined Martín when he burst out laughing.

When they were able to stop, it was Captain Graaf who spoke. "They know we have fewer than forty men and only two guns," he told the woman before turning to Martín. "I am in no position to fight, nor do I wish to. I daresay you can see I am not an experienced seaman or even a captain. This is my first voyage—I'm sure you have guessed I was put on this ship as a figurehead for my family. We were to have picked up an entirely different cargo in Ouidah, but something happened, and we would have left port empty. That was when my first mate took matters into his own hands." Graaf frowned. "But I am not without blame—I'm afraid I was ill and not aware until we were well under way, or I should have stopped him from buying slaves. I—"

Martín snorted.

The Dutchman flushed, but doggedly continued. "I accept responsibility for all of it. I'd ask that you hold me on the slaving charge and my first mate for his role in the mutiny, but guarantee the rest of my crew will go free once we reach Freetown."

Martín sneered at the apparently selfless demand. "Why should your crew not be punished? Did they not know they were engaged in slaving?"

"Yes, they knew, but they had no say in the matter."

"They had no say? How is that, Captain? Do you employ slaves for a crew? Were they not free to decline to work when they saw what it was—*who* it was—you put into your hold?"

"Of course I do not employ slaves, but—"

"Then they had a *choice*!" Martín slammed his fist on the table, and everyone jumped. He looked from the captain to the woman, their shocked expressions enraging him even further. "I tell you what, *Captain*, I will give your crew the same choice they gave the people in your hold. You know what choice I mean, eh? They can get into the ship's hold, or they can *die*."

Both the Dutchman and the woman stared back at him in wide-eyed, open-jawed amazement.

Martín fought to get a grip on his frayed temper as he looked from the pale blond man to his feisty companion, both so eager to tell *him* about choices while hundreds of people suffered on their ship. "That is your choice, as well, Captain Graaf. If you do not like it?" Martín shrugged. "I will throw the whole damn lot of you to the sharks, you and your whore included."

Martín was not surprised when the woman shot to her feet at the word "whore."

He sat back and savored her reaction. He did not believe her to be a whore—she had neither the look nor the demeanor of a woman who earned her living pleasuring men. In fact, she had the look of an innocent, which made him very curious as to what the hell she was doing on a slaver's ship.

"How dare you? I am no . . . *whore*." She trembled with the force of her emotions. "Have you no decency?"

"None at all," he admitted, grinning.

Her eyes spit fire, and her pale cheeks bore twin flags of color. She was quite attractive in her anger. Also, her hips stretched her snug breeches in a most intriguing manner.

He gestured to her clothing. "Do you always dress so?"

Her smooth brow furrowed. "What has that to do with anything?"

Martín shrugged.

"I donned these clothes to stop the mutineers." She enunciated each word as if speaking to a lackwit, and Martín frowned. But before he could contrive a suitable response, she jabbed a finger at the Dutchman. "This man risked his life so that we might return home. Can you not forgo money just this once?"

"Home?" Martín repeated, perplexed.

"Yes, *home*. I live in the village of N'goe, not far from Bantè. At least it *used* to be a village before the entire population was captured and sold to slavers, which was how I ended up on the *Blue Bird*." She glared down at the Dutchman, forgetting she'd been his champion only a moment before.

Martín looked from the Dutchman to the woman, and then back again. She was his captive? His slave? He shifted irritably in the too-small wardroom chair, tired and short-tempered from a lack of sleep. When he stretched out his legs to get more comfortable, he noticed an unsightly mark on the toe of one boot. He stared in disbelief at the hideous smudge; Jenkins had missed a spot. Just wait until—

"Captain? *Captain? Are you listening?*"

"Eh?" Martín pulled his eyes away from his blemished boot and tried to recall what she'd just said. "Are you telling me Graaf *purchased* you, *mademoiselle*?"

She gave the Dutchman a speculative look. "Not precisely."

"But he kept you in the hold?"

"Well, yes—"

Martín held up a hand, not wanting to lose the thread. "But then he took you *out* of the hold?"

She made a huffing noise and crossed her arms. "Yes."

He looked from her to the Dutchman and back. "Are you wearing his clothing?"

She sneered. "I refuse to discuss my clothing with you, Captain Bouchard." She raked her eyes across him, an unpleasant twist to her lips. "Although *you* certainly look as if you think of nothing else."

Martín frowned and sat up. "You think my clothing is not, eh, how do you say it?" He snapped his fingers to summon the words. "*Comme il faut?*" he asked when the English words refused to come.

Her eyes narrowed to slits. "*Will you*, or will you *not*, let our ship go?"

Martín blinked at this unexpected change of subject and threw up his hands. "*Voyons,* of course I will not release your ship." He looked from the infuriating woman to the fool beside her. The Dutchman coughed, an expression of abject misery in his hazy blue eyes.

"What is wrong with you?" Martín asked, all of a sudden noticing the man's complexion had a somewhat greenish cast.

"I have the choking fever."

Martín squinted. "You have the *what*?"

The woman fluttered her hand, as if to catch Martín's attention.

"The choking fever," the Dutchman repeated. "Mademoiselle Fisher assured me the thorn of Christ, which only grows in coastal marshes, will cure it."

Martín looked from the sick man to the furiously blushing woman. She gave a minute shake of her head, and mouthed the word *please.*

What was this? She did not wish him to pursue the matter? Why not?

Martín shrugged away the questions. He would find out later. But for now . . .

"Ah," he said, as if in dawning comprehension. "You have the *choking fever.* Yes, yes, I *see.* Well, that is indeed unfortunate."

The woman glared at Martín's mocking and exaggerated tone, while the Dutchman looked confused.

Martín smirked at both. But, as amusing as this was, he did not have either the time or the patience to get to the bottom of whatever was going on. He would question the woman later, perhaps over dinner in his cabin. Just the two of them—alone.

After she had taken a bath.

Martín stood. "Beauville will take you to our cook," he told the Dutchman. "He is a good enough doctor. As for the ringleader of the mutiny, you brought him with you and he is on deck with my men?"

Graaf nodded.

"*Bien.* I will deal with him, and then we can make plans to be on our way."

Martín's hand was on the brass door handle when the woman's ringing voice stopped him.

"What will you do with him, Captain?"

He pivoted on his heel. "Pardon?" He used his most discouraging tone, the one that made grown men feel for their weapons or look for cover.

"The first mate, de Heeckeren, what will you do with him?"

"I will do what is always done with mutineers. I will cut off his head and throw his body overboard."

Her jaw dropped. "But, that is . . . *barbaric*," she gasped.

Martín studied her with no small amount of bewilderment. "What else would you have me do? Invite him to tea and crumpets?" All the men, even the sickly captain, chuckled, and the woman flushed.

Martín gentled his voice. "A mutineer is like a mad dog

that has bitten its master, *mademoiselle*. It will always bite again."

"Could you not turn him over to the authorities in Freetown?"

"I can do many things. Anything I choose, in point of fact. What I *will* do is cut off his head and throw him overboard." Martín sketched a brief bow and left the boardroom before she could say anything else.

His second mate followed hard on his heels.

"What do you want, Mr. Daniels?"

"What shall you do with the woman, Captain?"

Martín stopped so suddenly Daniels almost slammed into him. He pivoted to face the younger man, arrested. "*Do* with her? Are you asking me if you may have her, Daniels?"

The Englishman turned the color of a brick. "Of course not, Captain."

Martín frowned at the man's chiding tone, but decided to overlook it this once. "What the devil is it, then?" He turned away and took the stairs two at a time, leaving the other man to trot behind him.

"What will you do with her, sir?"

"Have you suffered some manner of head injury, Daniels?" Martín demanded, not pausing to wait for an answer. "I'm not going to *do* anything *with* her."

"You cannot just leave her in Freetown, sir."

Martín crossed the deck and stopped in front of the mutineer, who was bound and surrounded by a cluster of Martín's men, glaring at him with seething hatred. "She can do whatever she likes once I release her."

"But it will be dangerous for her on shore, Captain."

Martín ground his teeth and turned away from the hostile Dutchman, back to his second mate. "I weary of your obscure babbling. Either express yourself with sense or have done with this subject."

"She is English, sir. Perhaps we could take her back to England? Are we not headed home after we leave Freetown?"

Martín stared at the younger man, mystified. Was it chivalry—a concept he was only vaguely aware of—that motivated Daniels? Martín's sole interest in women was whether or not he wanted to bed them and then how to get rid of them once he'd done so.

Thinking about beds gave him an idea. "I tell you what, Daniels, I shall carefully consider the woman's future," he lied. "But while I do so, she should stay in your cabin. You will bunk with the men."

Rather than protest violently, as any normal man would do, Daniels smiled, as if Martín had given him a gold coin instead of condemning him to miserable nights in a hammock surrounded by stinking sailors.

"Thank you, sir." Daniels nodded and scuttled off without another word.

"Fool," Martín muttered before turning back to the mutineer.

The Dutchman was a stocky man and as tall as Martín. Anger and hostility flowed from him in almost tangible waves. "You are de Heeckeren, the leader of the mutiny?"

The Dutchman glowered, and Martín repeated the question in French.

"*Oui.*"

"How do you plead to the charges of mutiny?" Martín continued in the same language.

The mutineer scowled. "*Coupable!*"

"You know the punishment for mutiny is death?"

De Heeckeren stared sullenly.

"Answer me."

"*Je comprends.*"

Martín gestured to the men standing beside de Heeckeren and one withdrew a razor-sharp scimitar from its sheath, while two others dragged the prisoner toward a huge block of wood and commenced to stretch his neck across it.

"*Stop!*"

Martín gritted his teeth and whipped around. "*Mademoiselle Fisher*. Why am I not surprised? Are you trying to make me lose my temper?"

She faltered under his glare, but came closer. "Please, Captain, can you not show Christian kindness?"

"I am not a Christian, *mademoiselle*."

His shocking admission did not stop her. She laid a hand on his sleeve, the gesture oddly compelling. "Please, do not do this barbaric thing," she begged in a whisper.

Up close, Martín saw that her brown eyes were flecked with green and gold. They were actually quite pretty. He flinched away from the pointless observation and forced his lips into a sneer. "You would plead mercy for men who have captured, imprisoned, and sold the people of your village into slavery?"

"I am a Christian, Captain. I strive to forgive those who would do me violence."

"That is an admirable sentiment, *mademoiselle*. Unfortunately, I am not motivated by such elevated notions. Besides, what if my crew viewed such forgiveness as a sign of weakness? I might soon find myself in the same situation as Graaf."

"It is not weakness, but mercy. Have you no mercy?"

"Mercy is bad for business, *mademoiselle*."

"Is business all you think about?" Her voice broke on the last word.

The question made him smile. "Now and then I think of other things," he admitted, sweeping her body with a lingering, suggestive look. "I might be persuaded to show mercy if I received something in return."

"Something from me?" Her sandy brows arched.

Martín closed the distance between them, standing close enough to see the freckles sprinkled across the bridge of her nose. "Yes, *mademoiselle,* something from *you.*"

"I . . . I don't understand. What could you want from me?"

Martín chuckled, and she flushed, dropping her gaze. "Oh."

He took her chin and tilted her face until she could not avoid his eyes. "Oh, indeed, *mademoiselle.* Something for something, eh?"

The moment stretched. Just when Martín believed she would back down, she surprised him.

"Very well, I offer my . . . my . . . person in exchange for your mercy." Her voice was firm, but so quiet only he could hear her.

His mouth twisted with contempt—contempt for himself. When had he become the kind of man who extorted favors from women?

He ignored the irritating thought. "We have a bargain," he agreed, running his thumb lightly across her jaw before turning back to the mutineer.

"Today is not your last day, after all, de Heeckeren. This lady has bought you a reprieve—"

"And the other mutineers, too," she broke in.

Martín smiled, but inclined his head. "And your cohorts, as well. Every moment until we reach Freetown is a gift from Mademoiselle Fisher. Perhaps you would like to thank her?"

The hostile Dutchman gave the woman who'd just saved his life a look of pure hate, curled his tongue, and spat. Martín stepped quickly in front of the projectile, stopping it from reaching its intended target with his foot.

"*Merde!*" He looked from his phlegm-spattered boot to the woman. "There." He flung a hand toward his soiled footwear. "You see the kind of man you saved with your sacrifice?"

For once, she appeared speechless.

Martín glared at Daniels, who hurried up beside her.

"Take her below and see that she cleans herself up. You, *mademoiselle*"—he fixed her with a hard look—"will prepare for dinner in my cabin." He eyed her outfit. "I will have appropriate clothing brought to you. Now go," he barked.

Once the two had fled, Martín turned to Beauville. "Put the Dutchman in the hold and make sure he is secure. We wouldn't want him running amok and spitting on any more of my footwear, eh?" Martín's men laughed appreciatively before dispersing.

He leaned against the railing and stared at the *Blue Bird*. Hundreds of dark heads milled about on her deck—the captives. If they were lucky, this brief incarceration would be the closest they came to slavery. Martín had not been so lucky. He'd been born a slave, answering to the name of "boy" until the man who owned him—the same man who'd fathered him, he suspected—fell on hard times and sold all his possessions, including his own son.

The brand on his arm itched, and Martín scratched at it, annoyed to be thinking of such long-ago things. He was a wealthy, powerful man now, not a runaway slave at the wrong end of a branding iron. He shook away the unpleasant memories and thought instead of the woman awaiting him below. Had she realized yet the full extent of the bargain she'd made? He recalled the virtuous expression she'd worn as she'd pleaded for the mutineers' lives and doubted it. She was an innocent. A better man would release her from the ill-conceived bargain and dine alone tonight.

Martín snorted. It was too bad for her that she'd made her bargain with him.

Chapter Four

Sarah followed the kind-faced Englishman below deck, numbed by what she had just done—what she had just promised.

"This way, miss." Daniels led her toward a door at the end of the corridor. "It's small, but it's clean and private." He ushered her into a room the size of Captain Graaf's wardrobe.

"Am I putting somebody out?" she asked.

He flushed. "It's no bother, miss. I've bunked with the lads before. Anyhow, you being the only lady on board, you'll need space for your . . . er . . . business."

Her eyes blurred with tears at the unexpected kindness—and from exhaustion. "You are very kind, Mr. Daniels," she said, a wobble in her voice.

"It's no bother, miss." He turned away and began pointing out the features of her cabin, his reddened face and abrupt manner proclaiming his discomfort louder than words.

He'd just finished showing her how to work the fold-out table when three men arrived with a compact hip-bath.

"Ah, here is your bath, miss. I'll just go and see to some other matters while the men fill the tub."

Within a short time the tub was full of steaming water, and there were several thick, fluffy towels piled on the bunk.

The men were just leaving when Daniels returned with an armload of garments, his homely face a fiery red.

"The Captain sent these, miss."

Sarah took the pile of clothing and laid it on the bunk. She wanted to ask why Captain Bouchard possessed such garments, but knew it would just agitate the second mate.

Instead, she gave him a reassuring smile. "Thank you, Mr. Daniels."

He nodded, his eyes on anything but her. "Lock the door when I leave, miss."

Sarah locked the door and turned to the steaming tub of water. She'd never had a bath in a real tub before. It was an unthinkable luxury, and she forced herself to stop worrying about the evening ahead and enjoy this singular experience. After all, she was a prisoner; who knew what might happen to her tomorrow? This might be the first and only bath she would ever have.

She stripped off her clothing, eager to get into the water before it cooled. Once she submerged as much of herself as possible, she closed her eyes and mulled over the events of the last few hectic hours.

The mutiny had died quickly after they'd lured de Heeckeren to Graaf's cabin and captured him. Apparently many of the mutineers had already started drinking to celebrate their control of the ship and were slow-moving and clumsy when it came time to fight.

Speaking in Yoruba, Sarah had told the people they were free before opening the hold. It would not go well for them if Femi burst out and began laying waste—they were still dreadfully outnumbered and unarmed. She added that they should send up the strongest men first to ensure their freedom.

The sickening stench that billowed from the hold when the sailors opened the hatch drove everyone back, and eight huge men emerged from the stinking hole, with Femi in the lead.

Sarah handed him the pistol. "I am sorry—this is the only gun I could take, but there are also some knives and machetes." She pointed to the small pile of weapons they'd taken from the mutineers. "Are you familiar with this kind of gun?"

Femi quickly examined the pistol before giving her an abrupt nod. "I have not used one, but I have seen them used often enough."

Sarah handed him her extra ammunition. "This is all I have." She gestured to the remaining sailors, all of whom were red-faced and looking anywhere but at the people they'd held captive, and then she gave Femi a grim smile. "I know you wish to shoot them; so do I. Unfortunately, we need them to get our ship to safety."

"I will not hurt them." He jerked his chin at the other men, all of whom vibrated with barely tethered rage. "I will tell the others."

Before long the entire back half of the deck was filled with people, many too sick or weak to stand. Sarah found the husband of the young mother who'd died, protecting his newborn and the woman who'd agreed to nurse the baby.

"These three will need someplace private and quiet to rest."

Graaf hastened to translate her orders into Dutch, his cheeks flushed. Sarah knew that if not for the mutiny, he would have sailed halfway round the world and never contemplated the hell right below his feet. That a human being would consider causing such devastating misery to others for money was so befuddling, Sarah could not get her mind to accept it. Hate for Graaf and his crew threatened to overwhelm her common sense, and it was a constant struggle to remind herself that she was a Christian, and Christians believed in forgiveness. Besides, she needed Graaf to deal with the privateers, whomever they were.

It hadn't been until later, when Sarah was setting foot

onto the privateer vessel, that she had questioned the wisdom of accompanying the Dutchman to the parley. She had just escaped one boatload of slave-trading filth; what was to say she was not giving herself to another? Well, it had been too late by then. And when they'd found themselves sitting in the wardroom—waiting for Bouchard—she'd asked Graaf, "If slaving is so lucrative, why would these privateers return the people to Ouidah?"

"Most likely they will take them to Freetown. That is where they will hand me over to the authorities." The Dutchman had been shivering and sweating, his eyes dull with self-pity and suffering.

"Might these privateers take the slaves and sell them themselves?"

The captain had shrugged, as if he were too consumed with his own fate to care about anyone else. "Anything is possible, I suppose."

Sarah considered the Dutchman as she soaped her hair in the cooling bath water. It had been wrong to lie to him about a cure, but she couldn't feel much guilt about what she'd done. Her lie had made all the difference in the world to her and the people in the hold. Besides, only time and rest would cure most of the jungle fevers that ravaged the area, and Graaf was better off in Bouchard's custody than on his mutinous ship. Her lies might have actually saved the man's life.

Cheered by the thought, she stood and used the water from the pitcher to rinse the soap from her head and body. She wrung out her hair before stepping out of the tub and toweling her hair dry. She glanced at the remaining towels and hesitated.

"Oh, why not?" she muttered, snatching up a fresh towel for her body.

Once she was dry and wrapped in a towel she took up the comb the second mate had left and began the unpleasant task of removing tangles.

She examined the clothing Bouchard had sent while she combed. Sarah knew very little about fashion, but even she could see the garments were not the kind a proper woman would wear. One of the gowns was made of nothing but black lace, and she blushed to think what such a thing would look like on her. It was positively scandalous.

She settled on the least revealing article, a beautiful robe of heavy black silk, embroidered with silver dragons. The robe covered her from neck to feet and was large enough that she could wrap it around herself before belting it. A pair of plain black slippers completed her outfit and hid her large, battered and sunburned feet from view.

Bathed, dressed, and ready, she sat on the bed and stared at nothing in particular. She was left breathless and bemused by the bargain she'd made with the most beautiful person— male or female—she'd ever seen.

Captain Graaf was attractive, but he paled in every sense of the word when compared to the exotic Captain Bouchard. Sarah blushed just thinking the man's name. It had taken all her strength not to begin gibbering when he'd entered the small wardroom.

His eyes alone were enough to make him breathtaking. They were deep-set and heavy-lidded, fringed with lashes that looked in danger of tangling. But it was their molten gold color that was most striking. Sarah had looked into those liquid depths and seen no sign of his thoughts.

But if his eyes were unreadable, his mouth betrayed him. His full, sensual lips—the only soft thing about him—had shifted from amused to displeased to mocking all in a matter of seconds, just like a willful child's.

Sarah had taunted him about his clothing because he'd blinded her with his masculine elegance. His coat, breeches, and boots were tailored so intimately to his muscular frame that her own body had responded in unnerving ways when she looked at him. His clothes were those of a gentleman, but they could not hide the powerful physique they covered. He was broad-shouldered and brawny, and his fingers had been calloused when he'd touched her chin, demonstrating that he was no stranger to work. His hands were big and scarred, completely unlike those of Graaf, whose slim white hands were so soft they could have belonged to a woman. Sarah glanced down at her own hands and frowned.

Well, any woman's but hers, which were as scarred and rough as Bouchard's.

The two captains were a fascinating contrast. Graaf had the face of an angel, but was willing to traffic in human misery. Bouchard was sin in human form, but became enraged at the mere mention of slavery. Sarah tried to convince herself his refusal to tolerate slavery was merely expediency—after all, he made his living confiscating slave ships—but she knew that wasn't true. No, Martín Bouchard would not enslave and sell the people on Graaf's ship. He had turned savage in an instant, his veneer of amused arrogance dropping away to reveal the rage inside him: a rage that strained like a provoked and maddened beast against its tether.

And she'd bartered herself to such a man.

"Dear God," she whispered.

Her hands shook as she pulled the sash of her robe tighter.

Well, if Captain Bouchard wanted physical coupling, at least Sarah would not be entirely ignorant. She did have eyes, after all, and the people in her village had not been prudish. She had always envied her neighbors their spouses and children, but no young man had ever looked at *her* with yearning, a fact that had become increasingly difficult to bear after first her parents and then Abena had died, leaving her on her own.

The sickness that killed Abena and Sarah's parents had killed many others in the village. Anyone who could leave had done so. Less than two dozen remained and many of them old or infirm. The thought of years of loneliness stretching before her had made Sarah chafe against the promises she'd given her parents two years before.

How could they have asked such things of her? How could they expect her to fill *both* their shoes with no help-mate, no husband?

Sarah shied away from the anger and guilt that always accompanied the memory of her last words with both her parents and steered her mind to the evening ahead—to Captain Bouchard and what he wanted from her.

Just because she knew what occurred between men and women, it didn't mean she wasn't frightened. Even so, she could not regret the deal she'd made. It was ridiculous to value virtue above human life.

Sarah knew her mother would not have agreed, but she suspected her father would have. She had saved dozens of men's lives by giving Bouchard the thing he had asked for—a thing nobody else seemed to want from her.

But why did he want such things from *her?* She'd seen the way he'd looked at her, and it had not been admiration or lust in his gaze. His gaze had been dismissive more than anything else. That was not surprising. After all, a man with his physical beauty was probably accustomed to coupling with women as attractive as he was. Sarah was not such a woman.

She was tall and spare with no soft curves to speak of. Her chest was woefully flat when compared to those of most of the young women in her village. Her skin had freckled in the harsh tropical sun, and her straight hair was thick but dirty blond in color. Her best feature was her eyes, which were large with long lashes, although an indeterminate shade of brown. Sarah could only suppose Bouchard was bored to want her.

She was four and twenty and had never even kissed a man. She'd long ago accepted that she was not attractive, but she'd never stopped yearning to know love or have children. Not that Captain Bouchard was offering her either of those choices, of course.

She recalled his amused response to her choking fever lie and smiled. If the man had been attractive in repose, he was stunning when he smiled.

Sarah shook her head at the foolish observation. What did it matter how beautiful he was?

Instead of fantasizing about the arrogant captain, she should be considering her future. Unfortunately, that, too, led back to Bouchard. What would happen to her? Would he give her to the authorities along with all the others?

Sarah grimaced as she realized how much her life, as well as everyone else's on this ship, depended on one capricious man.

A knock on the door made her jump, and she swallowed. It was time for dinner.

Chapter Five

Mr. Daniels's lips parted and his eyes widened as he took in Sarah's altered appearance. It was by far the most flattering reaction she'd ever elicited from a man.

"You look beautiful, miss."

Sarah laughed. "Well, hardly that, Mr. Daniels. But thank you."

He led her a short distance down the corridor before halting in front of a door that was larger and more ornate than any of the others. He raised his hand to knock, but paused. "The captain is . . ." He flushed. "Well, I know he can seem a bit harsh, but—"

The door swung inward to reveal the exquisitely dressed Captain Bouchard.

He filled the doorway, his disconcerting yellow eyes flickering between Daniels and Sarah.

"That will be all, Daniels," he said, his intense gaze finally settling on her. "Come in, Miss Fisher." He ushered her inside and closed the door in his second mate's face.

Bouchard's lair was as sensual and lush as the man himself. It was nothing like Graaf's, which had been elegant, but spare. An ornate, carved desk stood against the wall just inside the door. Above the desk was a built-in mahogany bookshelf that contained dozens of books. Sarah's breath quickened at the sight of such riches and her hands twitched to browse their contents. She'd had only a half-dozen well-used books in her possession and those had been destroyed when the slavers burned down the small mission school. She restrained the impulse to gorge on books and looked around the rest of the room.

A huge bed occupied the entire right side of the cabin, the masculine lines of the dark wood softened by layer upon layer of brown and gold bedding. It was a bed designed for something other than sleeping. Wicked, unbidden images of the man behind her leapt into her head and Sarah flushed and turned away.

A table surrounded by wooden benches took up most of the other side of the cabin. Brown leather cushions padded the benches, and the table was covered with a fine linen cloth and set for two, complete with a small pair of brass candle holders and tapered white candles. Sarah reached out and fingered one of the snowy linen napkins, marveling at the beauty of the scene.

"Wine?" Bouchard asked.

Sarah turned, no longer able to avoid looking at him. Like her, he had bathed and changed clothes. His robe was a dull gold and tied loosely over a sand-colored tunic and trousers. Sarah's gaze fixed on the flesh that was exposed by his collarless shirt. His smooth brown skin was still damp, and she could smell the clean, fresh scent of soap, the same as the cake she'd used.

She looked up to find him watching her, his full lips pulled into a knowing smile. He oozed an arrogant confidence that told her he was used to female adulation and viewed it as his due. He was indeed a perfect physical specimen, but Sarah forced herself to recall the man who occupied the body: a man who would cut off another person's head as easily as he would smash a fly.

He placed a glass in her hand and took a drink from his own vessel, his eyes watchful.

Sarah had never tasted wine before and took only the smallest of sips. The dry, tangy taste was not unpleasant, but it was not what she'd expected. She put down the glass, refusing to allow alcohol to turn her into a babbling fool.

"You have a fine selection of books, Captain." She inched around him and went to the bookshelf. "May I?" she asked, unable to keep the excitement from her voice.

"My cabin is your cabin." Bouchard managed to imbue the innocent words with a carnality that made her blush.

Sarah ignored the innuendo and motioned to a volume by Pope. "Tell me, Captain, why do you keep some of your books upside down?" She turned around when he didn't answer.

Bouchard's eyes flickered over the shelf, and an odd expression crossed his face. He shrugged. "Perhaps Daniels or Beauville borrowed one and put it back that way. You like to read?"

Sarah turned back to the selection, more than one of which was upside-down. "Yes, I do," she murmured, her attention on the books. "Oh, you have Herodotus in Greek." She skimmed past it and plucked a different volume from the shelf, a book she'd not heard of, *Clarissa*.

Bouchard came to stand beside her, looking at the book she held in her hands.

"I do not read Greek. That one was here when I took the ship." He stared somewhat fixedly at the book she held, his jaw tense.

Sarah frowned and turned the book's spine toward him, so the title, *Clarissa*, was clear. "I should like to borrow this—do you mind?"

He glared at the book, a small line of annoyance forming between his eyes. "I already said I do not read Greek. Take it and keep it—consider it a gift."

He turned away, as if tired of the subject of books. "Come, let us sit and enjoy the food my cook has prepared for us."

Sarah's jaw sagged and she stared at his broad back as the realization struck her.

He could not read and was trying to hide it.

An almost suffocating wave of pity welled up inside her for the handsome, arrogant man. How terrible it would be not to be able to read. How did he manage to function as captain of this fine ship? Did he have a man of affairs to manage his business? Why had he never learned to read?

Bouchard gestured to a plate arrayed with unrecognizable foods, and Sarah decided it would be wise to dismiss such questions from her mind. The matter did not concern her. She had plenty of her own problems—many caused by the man in question.

She took a seat and pointed to some hard-looking yellow slabs. "What are these?"

His brows rose. "You have not had cheese before?"

"I have heard of it, but never tasted any."

"That is a type of cheddar."

"Before I eat, Captain, the people who were in the hold—"

"Luckily we resupplied only ten days ago, so Mr. Beauville was able to bring ample food, water, and supplies from my ship to make sure the captives have what they need." He frowned. "Understandably, most have chosen to sleep on deck. They are crowded, but it does not make sense to transport people onto this ship, where there is actually less available room given the number of my crew. The weather is pleasant and should stay so for the next few days. Also, our ship's surgeon has gone over and examined a few of the captives who were very weak and ill. Those have been put in crew cabins and are being treated."

"I should like to go over tomorrow and see if I am needed—to translate, if nothing else."

He nodded. "That can be arranged."

"I wonder, did your man happen to mention a newborn? She is not quite—"

"I know of the child. She and the father and nursemaid are in a cabin of their own."

Sarah exhaled, so relieved she felt weak. Yesterday at this same time she'd been certain they would all perish in the hold of that ship. "Thank you for your kindness. I am very—"

He made a dismissive gesture. "Eat," he ordered, turning to the table and filling a small plate with delicacies.

She looked at the top of his head, her mouth open.

Was he . . . embarrassed?

Sarah realized she was hungry, too, and dropped the matter. She picked up a piece of cheese and took a small bite.

"This is delicious," she said, forcing herself to eat slowly.

The smile he gave her was the first genuine one she'd seen on his face. She'd not thought he could look more attractive. She'd been wrong.

"How is it that you do not know cheese?"

"We had nothing like this in our village. Perhaps the closest thing would be a type of paste we sometimes received in trade from a neighboring village. The people with whom we lived were quite poor. My father said they were poor even in comparison to the other villages in the area."

"Your father? Where is he now?"

"He died almost two years ago, shortly after my mother."

"And you have been living in this village alone since that time?" His frown showed what he thought of such an idea.

"I was born there. It is the only home I've ever known. Well, until the last few weeks." She nibbled on something that looked like meat, but was dry and quite salty. "This is very good, also."

"That is cured meat from Italy."

"Oh, have you been to Italy? Is it wonderful?"

Bouchard smiled tolerantly at her enthusiasm. "Yes, Italy

is quite beautiful, at least what I saw of it. Tell me, why were your parents in such a remote place?"

"They were missionaries and came to the area over twenty years ago. The church that funded them was among the first to send people to Africa. They used to send us supplies four times a year; then it dropped to twice a year. Three years ago we received one shipment, and the following year, nothing."

She took a sip of wine. It was actually quite delightful when paired with the salted meat and cheese.

"Your father did not think to leave when this happened?"

"My parents sickened and died shortly afterward. They died within weeks of each other. By that time there was no way to leave even if I had had someplace else to go."

"How did you come to be on the Dutch ship?" Bouchard refilled both their glasses before leaning back and crossing his arms over his chest. The movement did distracting things to the front of his robe.

Sarah tried not to stare. She looked at her plate and told herself to be calm and take this opportunity to befriend him. Perhaps she could find out what his plans for her might be.

"The slavers came to my village—N'goe—and captured everyone who was left." She shrugged. "I went with them."

Bouchard's jaw dropped, and his lips parted in shock. "Graaf *bought* you?"

Sarah bristled. "Along with hundreds of others—or are they not worthy of mention because of the color of their skin?"

Bouchard held up a hand. "Sheath your claws, Miss Fisher—you will get no argument from me on the issues of slavery and skin color. I was simply making a point that his behavior was rather odd. Enslaving whites is not unheard of, of course, but he was likely headed for Spanish Florida, and it would be difficult to sell a white woman there." His eyes flickered over her in a way that said *especially one as homely as you.*

Her face heated at the thought, but she shrugged it away. What did she care if he found her attractive or not?

"I don't believe Graaf knew anything about it."

His expression remained skeptical.

"Besides, I'm not even sure he *paid* for me. The slavers seemed to think my presence was something of a jest."

His eyebrows shot up. "They are not the kind of men who like to jest—they are the type of men who like to rape, enslave, or kill."

Sarah's face was hot, and she knew it would be glowing like a coal. "Yes, well, two of them tried the first of those things on the long journey from my village. But one of the slavers, a Dutchman, was apparently a very devout Christian, and he saw me with my father's Bible." She shrugged, not wishing to tell Bouchard just how terrified she had been the night the big slaver fought the two other men until they were bloody pulps. But neither they—nor any other man—had bothered her again.

Bouchard gave an ugly laugh, and Sarah looked up.

"So, this Dutch slaver was a religious man—but he could still buy and sell human beings, eh?"

"Sheath your claws, Captain. You'll get no argument from me on the subject."

His eyes went wide at her sarcasm, and she thought, for an instant, that perhaps she had gone too far. But then he threw his head back and laughed.

He grinned at her when he could finally stop, his beautiful face robbing her of breath. "Go on with your story, Miss Fisher. I have not been so diverted in ages."

"When we arrived in Ouidah—" She shuddered, memories of that nightmarish day coming back vividly.

"I know what you found in Ouidah," he said grimly. "The slave market."

She nodded. "In the middle of all the agony and chaos, a young woman went into labor. I was the only one in our small group who had medical knowledge so I—"

"How is it that you have medical knowledge?"

He looked so interested that Sarah forgave him his rude interruption. "My father was a doctor and my closest friend in the village was the healer. Unlike my father, Abena knew of many remedies that could be made from local plants. She taught me only a fraction of what she knew before she died." Sarah blinked rapidly, ashamed that she mourned the loss of Abena more than her parents. But the clever, quiet, and loving woman had been Sarah's best friend since the two could barely toddle. Abena had learned medicine at the knee of her grandmother, and then had generously shared that gift with Sarah.

Sarah looked up to find his expression had turned embarrassed. She wiped the tears from her eyes and went on. "I think Graaf's crew was content to leave me alone as long as I was seeing to the birth of the child. No doubt they did not wish to lose a valuable piece of cargo."

Bouchard met her eyes, and she flinched at the raw fury she saw on his face.

"I knew they would come for me once the girl gave birth, and they did. But when I was finally brought before Graaf, he wanted medical help and not . . . well, not the other," she finished lamely.

Bouchard snorted. "No, he does not look like a man too interested in *the other* right now."

"Where is Captain Graaf?" Her face had heated at having to mention such a scandalous topic, and she wished to change the subject.

Bouchard's smile was wry, as if he was aware of her discomfort and enjoyed it. "He is receiving the best treatment available, which is to say not much other than rest and food. He is not, I think, very happy about your tales of choking fever and promises of a cure." He laughed and took a big drink of wine. "I, on the other hand, have not been so entertained in years. The fool actually believed you would lead him to some secret remedy for a jungle fever?"

"I deeply regret lying to him, but—"

"He also says you held him at the end of his own pistol and threatened to shoot him if he did not release the slaves? His *own* pistol," Bouchard repeated gleefully. "I would shoot myself before admitting that to another man."

Sarah had deliberately left that part out of the story she'd told to Bouchard. It seemed she needn't have bothered.

"I would never have shot him, but it was important he believe I would. He was not so difficult to convince because I think he *wanted* to turn back. He said the cargo he was supposed to collect in Ouidah hadn't shown up and that his first mate was the one who arranged for the purchase of people while Graaf was too ill with fever to know what de Heeckeren was doing. Graaf did not want to traffic in slaves."

Bouchard's expression shifted from amused to ice-cold in a heartbeat. "The Dutchman is a man full grown, *mademoiselle.* And he is either a liar or a fool—what other *cargo* had he expected from such a port?" He shook his head, his mouth twisted with disgust. "Even if what he said is the truth, he went along with his first mate's decision because he is a coward and would rather buy and sell people than stand up for himself. He will certainly get the opportunity to stand up for himself once I turn him over to the English." He looked through her, as if he were imagining Graaf's trial.

Sarah was spared responding by a knock on the door.

Two men entered, both laden with platters and covered bowls. They placed the food on the table under the watchful eye of Captain Bouchard before he dismissed them and turned to a platter that held a large cooked fish stuffed with something amazingly fragrant.

Sarah's stomach rumbled audibly and she cringed.

Oh, please, don't let Bouchard have heard that.

A slow grin spread across his face. "I hope we have made enough for you, *mademoiselle.*"

He cut off a large portion of fish and placed it on a plate, adding a healthy serving from each of the other bowls. "Flame blackened whitefish stuffed with rice and herbs. Potatoes cooked with butter and shallots, and a ground corn dish favored by the Italians, called polenta. Please"—he inclined his head—"enjoy."

Sarah speared a piece of fish and popped it into her mouth. It was delicious and flaky and melted on her tongue. She bit back a moan. She'd never tasted anything so delicious in her entire life. "The polenta is from Italy; are the other dishes French?"

"These dishes are from the mind of my cook, whom I pay more than I should so that I may eat like this even at the outskirts of civilization."

"Am I mistaken in thinking you are from France, Captain?"

"I am from the United States, *mademoiselle.* From New Orleans, to be precise. You have heard of it?" He took a mouthful of food and chewed, an odd glitter in his eyes.

"That is in the portion purchased some years back by your President Jefferson. I have not met an American before." She put a forkful of potatoes in her mouth and froze as the flavor exploded. She closed her eyes at the sheer bliss of it.

"I do not call myself an American." His knife clattered against his plate, and she opened her eyes.

"Oh, why is that?"

"Let's just say I would not be welcomed with open arms should I ever wish to return to that country." His frigid tone told her the subject was closed.

Sarah busied herself with her meal while she considered his response. She could only suppose his inability to read and his hostile attitude toward his origins were the result of an unpleasant past.

She chose another topic. "Where do you live when you are not at sea?"

"I have spent some time in England, but mainly I live at sea. Now that Napoleon is safely restrained, I may settle in France."

"Did you live in London?"

"The south coast. A friend of mine has a house there and I have stayed with him from time to time. But country living is too parochial for my taste." He pushed aside his half-eaten plate of food.

Sarah's own plate was almost empty. She'd been eating like a starving baboon. She grimaced and put down her fork before lowering her hands to her lap. Looking at the lovely robe brought another topic to mind. "Thank you for the beautiful garments you sent, Captain."

His eyes dropped to her chest and Sarah instantly wished she'd kept her mouth shut.

"While you look delightful in it, I must say I am disappointed you made the most prosaic choice from my offerings."

Sarah stared at his darkening eyes. Was it possible he was imagining her in the black lace confection? She saw his lips twitch, and heat surged up her neck. No, he was merely tormenting her. How could a man who looked like *him* respond otherwise to a woman who looked like her? She glared, thrusting out her chin. What did it matter if he made his disparaging thoughts so obvious?

"Tell me, Mademoiselle Fisher, what are your plans after I return you to Freetown?"

Sarah frowned at the unexpected change of subject. "I suppose I will see if any of the others wish to return to our village."

"There are many others on Graaf's ship from your village?"

"No, but there are people from nearby villages."

"How many?"

"There are two men, well, boys, really. And there is also one older woman—"

"Bah! Four people? Two children and two women? You would do best to stay in Freetown and forget about returning to the jungle, *mademoiselle*."

"Why do you say that?"

He shrugged, the movement sinuous yet controlled. He reminded Sarah of one of the large snakes that lay in wait in the trees around the village. His body was pure muscle, coiled and dangerous.

"What is there for them in Freetown?" she asked, annoyed by his certainty.

"Safety from slavers, for one. They would be fools to return to their village. So would you. Why would you go back to burned-out ruins? You said all your people had fled. How would you live there all alone? Do you know how to grow your own food? Hunt your own meat?"

"Have you any suggestions, Captain, as you appear to find my own ideas so diverting? Where else should I go? Perhaps there's a position on board your ship you would like to offer?" She regretted her words even as they left her mouth.

He ignored her suggestion and eyed her lazily, as if her fate were of little concern to him. "My second mate has it in his mind that you should return to England."

Sarah hesitated before answering. Was he offering her passage? She yearned for guidance as to what she should do, but hated that she must seek it from such an obnoxious source.

"I have considered approaching the missionary society in Freetown—if there is one. Perhaps they would send me to England so that I might seek help to rebuild our village."

The captain watched from beneath lowered lids, the thick fringe of lashes hiding whatever was in his eyes. "You have no family you can go to in England?"

Sarah thought back to the small, yellowed scrap of paper

she'd found in her father's possessions that had held a single name and address. "My father broke away from his family after becoming a Nonconformist. His family was Lutheran and never forgave him. My mother was the only daughter of a vicar. I suppose my grandparents might still be alive." She shrugged. "All this is pointless speculation as I have no money to purchase passage to England."

When Sarah raised the glass of wine to her lips, she was surprised to find it empty.

Martín refilled the woman's empty glass. Was she becoming drunk? She was obviously unused to wine; he should give her no more. He blinked at the solicitous thought. So what if she was unaccustomed to wine? Since when did he worry about a woman he meant to bed and how much she'd had to drink?

He folded his arms across his chest and leaned back. And that was all she was to him: a night's entertainment, a tumble in his bed. This meal was about getting her into his bed. Not that he needed to exert any effort to do so. She'd made a bargain with him, and he could see she was a woman with a most stringent—and probably uncomfortable—moral code.

No, he did not need to court her to get what she had already promised. Yet here he was, wasting time over food and pointless talk. He frowned; he must be bored to want to bed such a skinny wench. Although he had to admit she looked far more appealing after a bath. Her features were chiseled and spare, but he thought a month of plentiful food would take the sharpness from them. She had thick, honey-brown hair and eyes that changed color with her moods—from a tranquil green to a snapping golden-brown.

Not only that, but she was charming and interesting to talk to, which he found more than a little surprising. He rarely spoke to women; he'd never really seen the point. His closest friend, Hugh Ramsay, had argued more than once that a smart woman was the very best company. Martín had always believed the big Englishman was crazy. Yet here he sat: talking.

He suspected Sarah Fisher was a clever woman—perhaps too clever. He couldn't put his finger on it, but she'd given him an odd look when they'd discussed his book collection.

He looked at her body and smiled. She'd wrapped the robe almost twice around her, vainly attempting to hide herself. If there was one thing Martín knew well, it was women. Or at least women's bodies.

She flushed under his scrutiny and lurched to her feet, taking slow, careful steps toward his desk. Her slim form shifted enticingly beneath the heavy silk, and he began to harden. His body's response both surprised and pleased him. Perhaps the evening would be more interesting than he'd hoped.

"What a lovely chessboard." She was stroking the inlaid ivory board on the desk in a distracting fashion. "Do you play, Captain?"

It was a struggle to wrench his eyes off her long slim hand and its caressing motions. His body had begun to heat and pulse. Sexual anticipation was something to be savored and enjoyed. He was in no hurry.

"Do you wish for a game?" he asked.

Her brown eyes sparkled with mischief, and her delicate lips curved in a way that made his breath catch.

"That would be lovely. I have not played since well before my father died. Are you *very* good?"

Martín saw no reason to tell her he'd won very few games against Ramsay, the man who'd taught him. He also saw no reason to tell her how he had dashed many a piece against the wall when the big man had beaten him. Why bother telling her those things? He had no intention of losing to her.

And there would be plenty of time for bedding her after he'd mastered her at chess. He looked into her smiling face and felt his own lips curve in response.

"Let us have a game."

He brought the board and pieces to their table and pushed aside the food. She took a pawn of each color and placed her hands behind her back. Martín gestured to her left arm, and she produced the white pawn.

"First move to you, Captain." She moved the board until the correct corner was before him. They set up their pieces in silence, but before they began to play she looked up at him.

"What are the stakes?" she asked.

Something about the glint in her eyes made his groin tighten. "Stakes? You wish to play for money?"

"I have no money. We must play for something else." She paused. "I know. Whoever wins can ask anything of the other that is within their power to give."

Martín laughed. "I have already won everything you have to give."

Her eyes narrowed at his ungentlemanly reminder. "Very well, I have already traded *that,* so we will play for something else—the truth. One question to be answered honestly."

Martín squinted, confused. The truth? The truth about what? What could she possibly wish to ask him? When had anyone ever wanted to know something about him enough to make it a stake in a game? Martín looked at her smiling face and frowned. Why did he feel as if he were stepping into a snare? He hesitated, and then was annoyed by his hesitation. *This* was what came of speaking to smart women.

"Done," he snapped, irked that she might mistake his hesitation for fear.

The play was quick and quiet, neither of them speaking during the first tense minutes. He'd just taken one of her bishops and was feeling quite confident when her queen swept across the board and he became aware of her knights. He looked from the board to her, but her face was unreadable. He studied the board, mentally playing out the game.

Bloody hell.

He played out the game again, and again came up with the same result: checkmate in five moves, no matter what he did. He looked down at his hand and saw he still held her bishop and was squeezing it. Hard. He set the piece down, unwilling to look at her. His hands clenched and unclenched with the urge to break something. He hated to lose. And losing to a woman?

He reached out and set his king on its side with exaggerated care. "I concede." He refused to give her the satisfaction of a slow slaughter. He snatched his pieces off the side of the table and began to reset the board. "I want another game."

She laughed. "Not so hasty, Captain. I thought you were a man of your word."

"Word? What word?"

"We had a wager."

Martín gritted his teeth. "What the devil do you want?"

"Just one question."

He crossed his arms to keep from grabbing the board and throwing it out the small cabin window. "Get on with it."

Her smile dimmed as the seconds crawled past. "How is it that you cannot read?"

Martín's jaw dropped. "Read?"

"The book I showed you earlier was not written in Greek, yet you did not recognize that. You cannot read," she explained carefully, just in case he was stupid as well as illiterate.

A scorching sensation caused the edges of his vision to tinge with red, as if his eyes were cooking. He could not make his jaws form words; he could only stare, watching as her expression turned from curiosity to something else. . . . Pity?

"You needn't answer." She turned away to place the pieces

back on the board, the dull red flush on her face telling him that she felt his humiliation keenly.

Something inside him cracked and released a reservoir of rage. He only realized what he'd done when he saw pieces of delicate ivory bouncing against the wall and the girl jumping to her feet at the sudden explosion. Martín was on her in an instant. He pressed her long, slim body against the door of his cabin, not stopping until his face was less than an inch from hers.

"I'm so sorry," she blurted. "I did not mean to offend you." Her heart pounded like a small, insistent drum against his chest. Her eyes were wide, and the pitying look in them was the last straw.

He captured her mouth with his, not bothering with finesse, stabbing with his tongue as though it were a sword. Her lips were soft and cool, and they parted easily beneath his onslaught.

Her yielding sweetness was like a dousing of cold water, and Martín closed his eyes against her startled expression and wrenched himself back, drawing a shaking hand across his mouth.

Bloody hell! He had never come so close to doing violence to one weaker than he.

He turned away from her, as if he could turn away from the vision she had forced him to look at: that of an illiterate brute only aping his betters with fine clothes, rich trappings, and books he could not read.

Martín felt a light touch on his arm and whipped around.

"I'm sorry if my question was impertinent. I was merely surprised. You must have worked very hard to achieve your position without being able to read. It is not difficult to learn, you know. Reading, that is." Her expression was no longer pitying, but tentative and gentle. "I have taught many people to read."

Martín's eyes shifted away from hers. He could not look

at her and think at the same time. Was she offering to teach him to read? He bristled. Who was she to think he needed her help to do anything? He let his eyes slide back to hers, hoping to find something to fuel his anger. Instead he found those inexplicably kind eyes. It was not the desire he usually saw in women's eyes. It was something different. It was, he realized with a shock, the same look she'd worn when she fought to save the lives of the mutineers. She viewed him as an object for her mercy, somebody she wished to save.

He felt an unpleasant smile take possession of his face, and he gave in to his baser instincts and inclination to exploit any weakness he encountered. He planted a hand on either side of her body, his palms flat on the mahogany wood paneling, trapping her between his arms. Her eyes were no longer so sure.

"I believe you are engaged in yet another negotiation, *mademoiselle*." He didn't wait for an answer before darting forward to nuzzle her neck. She quivered beneath him, and he felt a surge of pleasure that he could disconcert *her* the way she had *him*. "It does not seem right to commence bargaining when you have not repaid your last debt, does it?"

Her throat moved beneath his lips as she swallowed. "I am prepared to honor the bargain I made."

He took her small earlobe into his mouth and rolled it between his teeth and tongue, nipping her hard, smiling against her neck at her sharp intake of breath.

"Do you even know what bargain you made?"

"I am not ignorant in such matters. I know what I have agreed to." Her voice was low and breathy and made him throb.

He chuckled at her bravado. "Oh, I doubt that, *mademoiselle*." He tongued the tender flesh between her neck and collarbone before stopping over the pulse that pounded at the base of her throat. She was so fine-grained and smooth;

he had a burning need to consume her. He took a mouthful of soft flesh and sucked. A gasp of pleasure made the skin vibrate beneath his mouth and he sucked harder, until he was certain he'd given her a love bite. He pulled back to examine his work. A small oval of bruised flesh rose and fell with the pulsing vein below it.

Her hands, as soft as the wings of a moth, fluttered along the side of his body before settling at his waist. The feather-light sensation caused a hard spike of desire to shoot through him, and he pressed closer, enflamed by the way her body yielded beneath him.

He looked from his mark to her face. Her eyes were half-closed, her lips parted, and her head rested limply against the wall. Up close he could see the pale blond hairs and freckles that dusted her skin. His fingers looked obscenely large as he explored the delicate bones of her face, tracing over her finely drawn lower lip. The rough pad of his thumb rested against the satin seam of her mouth, and her lids flickered open, her eyes wide and confused. He pressed and her lips parted. Her chest rose and fell in ragged jerks, and her eyes became almost black. Martín held his breath as he waited, wondering what she would do.

The first touch of her tongue was so light he barely felt it, but the slight graze of her teeth as she took him into the incredible softness of her mouth made him gasp. Her eyes never left his, and the sight of her fragile pink lips stretched around him made him so hard it hurt.

He swooped down and replaced his thumb with his mouth, capturing her lips, stroking and caressing into her silken mouth while he held her head motionless for his penetration. He flicked and probed and teased until he'd lured her tongue into his mouth. Once she was inside him, he wrapped his lips around her and sucked until she shivered beneath him, her hips pushing into his as her hands clutched at his chest.

He pulled away, and she made a small sound and grasped his robe, as if to pull him back.

Martín smiled. It seemed he'd been mistaken about her; perhaps she was not the helpless innocent he'd believed. The realization aroused him even more; he had not wanted a virgin. He scooped her into his arms, momentarily thrown off-balance by the scarce weight of her. She was tall but delicate like spun glass. He held her against his chest while plundering her mouth. When she was as pliable as a reed he laid her across the velvet and silk bed.

He stood back and pulled off his robe and tunic. Her already flushed skin darkened even more as her eyes roamed his torso and fastened on the erection his silk trousers could not hide. Martín smiled at her wide-eyed look and parted lips and took her hand, kissing each finger and then her palm before placing it on the front of his trousers.

Her hand tightened as if in reflex.

Martín groaned, reveling in her touch for a moment before gritting his teeth and gently removing her hand. "Too much of that and I won't be any good to you, *mademoiselle*." He lowered himself onto the bed, straddling her body, her slim hips warm between his knees.

Her eyes grew even bigger, and her body trembled.

"Shh," he murmured, stretching over her, their bodies barely touching. He lowered his hips against her taut stomach and kissed her brow, breathing in the scent of clean, aroused woman. Her hands came up to rest on his sides, and he stroked himself against the silk barrier that separated their bodies. He froze, the sensation so erotic he feared he would spend if he continued. He laid a trail of kisses from her jaw to the mark he'd left on her throat, propping himself up with one arm while untying her robe with his free hand.

He tongued and nibbled, his fingers slowly teasing the folds of silk apart until he could feel smooth, hot skin.

When he'd finished, he sat back on his heels and stared at what he'd unwrapped.

"*Mon Dieu.*" His eyes flickered from her body to her face.

She watched him, her expression unreadable.

Martín swallowed hard at the sight of her small, pink-tipped mounds, a stab of desire almost doubling him over. She looked like a painting he'd watched men looting from a palace in Alexandria. The massive panel had depicted a tall, slim woman—some ancient empress, no doubt—garbed in a thigh-length skirt and magnificent headdress, a serpent encircling her naked torso. He could still recall the look of contempt on that starkly beautiful face as her captors toted her away from her past, away from her home, and off to some foreign land. This skinny missionary's daughter possessed the same body as some bygone Egyptian queen. She was delicate, sleek, and strangely potent.

Martín stroked his hands up her slender ribcage until he held a perfect breast in each hand. She hissed in a breath and arched against him, pushing herself into his palms, the thin skin of her breasts so sensitive she cried out when he grazed their stiff peaks.

His mouth flooded with want, and he leaned lower to take a taut bud between his lips.

"Captain!"

The woman screamed, and Martín almost fell off the bed.

"Captain?" Daniels called again, pounding on the door so hard it shuddered in the frame.

"*Merde!*" Martín snatched up his discarded robe and handed it to the wide-eyed woman before stalking to the door and almost tearing it from its hinges.

"The ship better be on fire, Daniels," he yelled, his voice still hoarse with arousal.

Daniels took a step back, his mouth ajar, and his eyes anywhere but on Martín's obscenely tented silk trousers.

"Speak, you fool!"

"It seems that the, er, the Dutch mutineer is, um, well, he's gone, sir."

Chapter Six

For a moment Martín was too shocked to speak. "How long?"

Daniels shrugged, his face a study in shame, mortification, and misery.

Martín swore in three different languages. "Get every man on deck. If de Heeckeren gets to the other ship and frees the crew, there will be hell to pay."

Daniels scurried off, and Martín slammed the door and turned around, his eyes settling on the woman he had just been preparing to bed and now wanted to strangle.

"Your damned de Heeckeren has escaped the brig," he shouted, yanking open his wardrobe and pulling out a pair of breeches. He didn't bother to turn away as he stepped out of his silk trousers and pulled on his oldest buckskins, tucking his still rigid cock behind the fall.

She sat bolt upright, apparently speechless, whether at the sight of his naked body or the surprising news, Martín could not have said.

He snatched up a battered leather jerkin before pulling on his boots and grabbing his still-holstered weapons from the hook on which Jenkins had hung them earlier in the day.

Martín pointed a finger at her. "You stay here." He didn't

wait for an answer and strode from the cabin, slamming the door behind him.

The deck was ablaze with a dozen torches, and Salier, the loudest man onboard, was yelling across to the Dutch ship.

Martín snatched up his glass and opened it, peering through the darkness. Of course it would be a night with almost no moon. He cursed.

Salier continued to yell while Martín gave the order to bring them closer. He kept his eyes fastened on the dim ship. Only because he was staring so intently did he see the small flare of light.

"Incoming!" he yelled, just before the blast of a cannon filled the night and the dull *whoosh* of a large ball of iron cut through air. The ball landed in the water mere feet from their bow.

"Prime and load numbers four, six, seven, and nine." He snapped the glass closed and felt for his pistols while he moved toward a torch. He checked one gun and handed the other to Jenkins, who'd materialized beside him, disheveled but awake and aware. Martín heard the clatter of feet behind him and turned to find the Englishwoman, breathless, wearing only his dressing gown.

Martín's mouth opened at the sight, but he didn't have any words available.

"What has happened?" she demanded.

"Go back down below, *now.*"

"You cannot mean to fire on their ship?"

Martín thought his head might explode before his cannons did. He turned away from the infuriating woman, afraid he might do her bodily harm.

"Daniels," he shouted at the top of his lungs.

"Captain Bouchard," Sarah shouted behind him, her voice almost as loud as his. He ignored her. A hand gripped his arm, and Martín whirled around.

"*Assez!*" he bellowed, his entire body shaking. "You will

go below deck with Daniels or I will have you bound and gagged and thrown into the hold. Do you hear me?"

She planted her fists on her slim hips. "There are innocent people on that ship. You cannot fire on them. If you will stop and think a minute, you will agree. You wanted to *save* those people, Captain, not kill them."

Daniels appeared and laid a hand on her shoulder.

She brushed Daniels's hand away and took a step toward Martín. "Captain?"

Martín's eyes threatened to bulge out of his head at her chastising tone. He gave her a look that should have reduced her to a smoking pile of rubble before turning to Daniels.

"Get her out of my sight or I will." He turned away, ignoring the sounds of a scuffle from behind him; Daniels could manage one skinny woman on his own.

"Captain!" The word was like the crack from a pistol. The faces of the men in front of Martín were almost laughable; to a man, they stared in open-mouthed horror at something behind him. Martín did not want to turn, but his body acted without consulting him.

The woman was ten feet away, pointing Martín's own pistol at him.

He let out a string of vile curse words and looked at Jenkins, who stood empty-handed with a terrified expression on his face. Martín shook his head. "I will deal with *you* later, Jenkins."

"If you fire those cannons, I shall shoot you, Captain Bouchard." Her voice was loud enough to be heard on the other ship.

Martín did not hesitate before striding toward her.

"I'm warning you, Captain." Her voice was louder, but less assured.

"*Mademoiselle,* you will have to shoot me before I take orders from you or anyone else while standing on the deck of my own ship." He closed the distance between them in a few long strides, only stopping when the barrel of the gun touched his chest, the metal tip against bare skin where his jerkin gaped open. He watched with genuine interest as she looked from his face to the end of the pistol and back again. The moment seemed to stretch forever. Her mouth twitched; her nostrils quivered. If she fired at such close range it would be the end for him. He smiled. Would she?

Her entire body shuddered, and she closed her eyes.

Martín took the pistol from her limp fingers and handed it to Jenkins with a withering glare that made the small man flinch. Daniels came forward and led the unresisting woman away, murmuring to her as he guided her below deck.

Martín thrust the woman from his mind just as a shout broke through the gloom, accompanied by the flaring of a torch on the *Blue Bird*'s deck. Men boiled from below deck, many armed with swords or clubs. Those already on deck—mainly former captives—scrambled to repel them. The entire ship erupted into hand-to-hand combat within seconds.

More torches blazed to life, and Martín saw that one of the *Blue Bird*'s sails was flapping uselessly in the mild breeze. An African stood below the billowing canvas, a large knife held at the ready, mute evidence of who had halted the *Blue Bird*'s progress. Dozens of freed slaves, as well as the men Martín had left onboard, grappled with the mutinous sailors they'd locked in the ship's hold earlier that day.

The same mutineers he had pardoned for the woman who had just threatened to shoot him.

Martín shook his head, both at the bargain he'd made and his own stupidity. He'd been foolishly confident to leave only a half-dozen of his crew on board the *Blue Bird*, and he was *very* lucky both the freed slaves and loyal members of Graaf's crew were making short and brutal work of the mutineers. He swept the *Blue Bird*'s deck for Beauville, holding his breath until he spotted him. His first mate was bleeding from a cut on his forehead, but otherwise looked unharmed.

Martín heaved a sigh of relief. "It appears Beauville is taking matters in hand. Salier, Truesdale, and Marx, prepare to take us over." He turned to find Jenkins beside him, clutching his pistol. Martín gestured for the gun and slid it into his second holster.

"Go below and make sure the woman has not located more of my weapons."

Jenkins turned a dull red, but kept his mouth shut before scuttling away.

Martín turned back to stare at the other ship. The night had been exciting, but not in the way he had hoped.

Sarah huddled on the small, hard bunk in her cabin and hugged her knees tightly to her chest, appalled at what she had just done. By drawing a weapon on the captain—his own pistol, of all things—in front of his men, she had surely signed her own death warrant. Bouchard was not like Graaf. The Dutch captain had seemed almost grateful when Sarah took him hostage and made his decisions for him at the parley.

Bouchard was something completely different.

Everything she'd learned about him thus far screamed of his pride and his obsession with appearances. She had attacked both in full view of his men. It wouldn't matter to him that he had easily disarmed her.

She winced as she recalled how quickly he had done so. His face had been as hard as a stone wall when he put himself at the end of a loaded and cocked pistol. He did not fear dying. No, what he feared was looking weak or foolish. Twice in one night she had found the gap in his carefully constructed armor and shoved something sharp inside. She shook her head at her own idiocy. Why had she goaded him about his inability to read? His look of murderous rage when she'd exposed him had been even more frightening than when she had held him at gunpoint.

But what he'd been doing to her in the cabin before Daniels interrupted them had been even more terrifying.

The place between her legs—a place she'd given little thought until tonight—tightened with a frustrating combination of intense pleasure and nagging want as she remembered what he'd been doing.

Sarah covered her hot face with her hands, embarrassment vying with desire at the memory of his eyes and hands and mouth on her skin. She'd thought she knew what would happen tonight, but nothing the captain had done was like anything she'd seen village boys doing. His hands were so clever and wicked, and it had felt as though he had ten of them instead of just two. She would dare any woman to get that close to the gorgeous man and keep her wits. She refused to feel guilty about giving in to his practiced wiles. The physical sensations he'd evoked had been impossible to ignore or rise above. She'd wanted something so badly—*still* wanted it—that she would have given anything to get it. Was that how it was for everyone? Was that what her parents had always preached against?

The memory of his arousal and how it had felt in her hand made her throb and tingle. She knew what his hardness meant. He'd wanted her. He wanted to put himself inside her. Her entire body thrummed at the mere thought, and she pressed her thighs together, mortified. She must be some kind of deviant; she'd not felt ashamed or embarrassed, just *hungry*. How could she be so wicked? So wanton? What would her mother and father have thought?

Sarah tried to summon her parents' faces, but couldn't. The desire in her body overwhelmed any shame. She couldn't stop wondering if he would come back and finish what he'd started.

The memory of what she'd done on deck came crashing

down on her, and she groaned. If he came to her now, it would be to throw her in the brig—or even overboard. Sarah would not be surprised to find out that she would be joining the rest of the mutineers, her severed head bobbing among theirs on the open water.

Beauville was waiting for Martín when he stepped on board the *Blue Bird*. A pile of unmoving bodies lay on the deck behind his first mate.

"De Heeckeren?" Martín asked.

"He is dead, Captain, along with five others."

Martín looked at the bleeding cut on his first mate's forehead and frowned. "What happened?"

Beauville's hand moved to the goose egg on his forehead, and he winced. "I was sleeping when he sneaked aboard. He knew this ship like the back of his hand and was able to get down to the brig unmolested. He knocked out the guards who were standing watch and jammed several crew cabin doors shut, but not mine. And then he led his men to take back the ship.

"The commotion of so many feet woke me, and I came on deck and was attacked at the top of the stairs. It was lucky for me that several of the Africans jumped on the man who hit me and subdued him. The mutineers took many of the sleeping crew by surprise," Beauville admitted. "Without the assistance of the Africans, we would have been done for."

Martín looked around at the silent faces watching their interaction.

"You've done well tonight, and I will see you are rewarded for your help," he said to a huge young man who held a large, bloody sword and appeared to be the leader.

The man merely blinked at him.

"The only one who understands and speaks a little French is Ubu, the man with the infant. I have tried French, English,

Portuguese, and Dutch on the others to no avail. They speak a number of dialects, but the only one who can speak Yoruba is the woman."

Martín grimaced. Of course it would be the woman. He glanced at what was left of de Heeckeren's men. They were a sorry-looking bunch, several of them wounded so badly they would not make it through the night. He considered putting them all to the sword, but he'd given the woman his word. "Shackle and tie them all and then lock them in the hold. And keep them in there this time, Mr. Beauville."

The Frenchman flushed and nodded.

"Set up enough lanterns to begin mending the damaged sails. I am sick of waiting."

By the time Martín returned to his ship it was almost daylight. He halted for a moment outside of Daniels's cabin, toying with the idea of confronting the missionary woman. He decided he was too tired to deal with an infuriating female. In fact, he would steer clear of her until they reached Freetown and he'd gotten her off his ship. He'd be glad to be rid of the whole damned mess: the irritating woman, the sick, ineffectual captain, and the troublesome Dutch crew.

He pushed it all from his mind and marched to his cabin, where he slammed the door. He was pleased to see Jenkins had cleared away all signs of the evening. He'd also had the foresight to have a basin of hot water waiting for Martín.

After washing and changing into his dressing gown, Martín collapsed onto his bed and massaged his aching temples. He could not stop his mind from going back to the last time he'd lain on this bed, with the woman beneath him, half-naked and ready. The memory of her body caused his cock to harden. There was no denying she had a deliciously responsive body and he should have buried himself inside it when he'd had the opportunity.

He dismissed the thought with a muttered curse. She was a menace. He would release her from their ridiculous bargain and do so happily. She'd been in his cabin less than an hour before she'd discerned he was illiterate. Who knew what she would weasel out of him if he spent any more time in her company?

No, the longer she stayed on his ship, the greater the chances she might end up its damned captain. He laughed grudgingly as he recalled the sight of her with his gun pointed at his chest. For the second time in one day she had held a captain at the point of his own pistol on his own ship. The poor dumb Dutch bastard had lost his command, his ship, and might even lose his life as a result of her work. Martín would be damned if he'd join the man.

He sighed and closed his eyes. Sleep. He just needed some sleep. It would all be over and done with soon. They would take care of their business in Freetown and journey back to England. He could forget the entire unfortunate incident.

Chapter Seven

Martín slept only a few hours before bright sunlight slanted through the porthole windows and woke him. He'd come awake for a moment earlier in the morning when the ship began moving, the subtle creaking alerting him to the fact that they were again on their way.

He was lounging comfortably in his robe and enjoying a hearty breakfast a short time later when somebody rapped on his door.

"Come," he said, slathering a thick slice of bread with preserves. He had a bottomless craving for sweets and often consumed an entire jar at one sitting. He took an enormous mouthful of the still hot bread.

Daniels opened the door just wide enough to slip inside, his pale face even paler than usual.

Martín chewed at his own damn pace before he swallowed and said, "What?"

"Er, Captain, the uh, that is—"

The door flew open, and Mademoiselle Fisher stepped inside.

Martín rolled his eyes. It should be no surprise that Daniels couldn't control her; *Martín* could not control her, either.

Still, he refused to let the woman annoy him this morning. The weather was clear, the ships were moving along at a goodly clip, and he had a delicious cup of coffee and fresh bread and jam.

"*Mademoiselle,* what a delightful surprise," he lied, not bothering to hide his sarcasm. "Won't you join me?" He gestured to the opposite seat. Martín could see his pleasant demeanor was not what she'd expected. He would swear she was disappointed that he hadn't begun yelling at or threatening her.

"Er, no thank you, Captain Bouchard. I have already eaten breakfast. Hours ago," she added, as if in criticism of his late breakfasting habits.

Martín felt a twinge of annoyance, but refused to offer any explanation for his late morning—as if it were any business of hers what he did or when he did it. He raised an eyebrow at his hovering second mate. "It would seem you are no longer necessary, Daniels. Close the door behind you." Martín waited until she'd seated herself before resuming his breakfast.

She was again wearing Graaf's clothing. He gave a mental shrug. What did he care that she'd rather take clothing from a degenerate slaver than from him? Her eyes went from his face to his bare chest, and he could see by her deepening flush and averted eyes that she realized he was naked beneath his dressing gown and it made her uncomfortable. Good, he hoped it made her so uncomfortable she would leave.

"What can I do for you, *mademoiselle*?" he asked, not that he had any intention of doing anything for her other than depositing her in Freetown. He buttered another slice of bread.

"Mr. Daniels just informed me the ships are headed toward Freetown even though Ouidah is far closer. Is that true?"

Martín made a mental note to tell Daniels to keep his trap shut around the nosy woman. He took a mouthful of coffee and paused to wipe his mouth with a linen napkin before leaning back, enjoying her look of impatience. He could see his state of undress was distracting her concentration from the object of her visit, which appeared to be bossing him about.

He smiled at her obvious irritation. He should have thanked Daniels for providing him with entertainment before he'd dismissed him.

"Yes, that is true."

"But it can be no problem for you to deposit the captives at Ouidah. You said as much during our parley." Her voice was at least an octave higher than usual.

"I said no such thing, *mademoiselle.*" He crossed his arms and made himself comfortable.

"When I told you Captain Graaf had turned back the ship, you said—" She stopped and searched her memory. Not finding what she was seeking, she tried a different tack. "You didn't actually *disagree.* Freetown is a great distance from where most of the captives were taken. How will they ever make their way back to their people?"

"That, *mademoiselle,* is not my concern." She opened her mouth and stared, looking very much like a fish gasping for air. Martín relented, but only slightly. "As I said last night, Freetown is a much safer place for them. If they return to their villages, they will be taken again. I have seen it happen over and over."

Her jaw worked as if she wanted to argue but could not come up with anything persuasive. "What of me?" she finally asked.

Martín didn't try to stop the evil smile that spread across his face. "What of you?" He paused to savor the moment. "As you are a British citizen, I will personally escort you to the British authorities so they can determine what to do with you. You can tell them whatever story you wish, but I would advise you not to hold *them* at gunpoint if they refuse to do as you like."

She bit her lip, making him curious as to what devious

plans were going through her clever mind. He did not have to wait long.

"You mentioned last night you might be willing to take me back to England." Her face turned a dark red at the reference to the night before.

"Actually, I said *Daniels* thought you should return—not that you should do so on my ship. Besides, that was last night, before you stole my pistol and held me at gunpoint."

She lowered her eyes to the table, which she was gripping with white-knuckled fingers. "I . . . I am very sorry for that, Captain." The honest regret in her eyes made him feel like a bully.

"I accept your apology," he said shortly, no longer interested in toying with her. "You must take my word when I tell you the authorities in Freetown will take better care of you than anyone else. They will know whom to contact on your behalf." Martín realized he had no idea whether his assurance was true or not. *That* realization angered him. So what if he didn't know? It was no concern of his—*she* was no concern of his.

She looked at him for a long moment before nodding. "Very well, Captain."

Martín moved to the door, eager to get her out of his cabin. He felt uneasy, rather than pleased, now that he had triumphed over her. He opened the door and looked down at her, experiencing an odd shortness of breath when he met her clear-eyed gaze.

"Would it be possible to see Captain Graaf?"

Her reference to the slaver sent a jolt of annoyance through him and brought him back to his senses.

He sneered. "By all means, *mademoiselle*. Be sure to take Daniels with you—we wouldn't want Graaf getting any *ideas*." He nudged her out of the cabin and shut the door on her affronted expression. He stood with his back against the door, his hand still clasping the doorknob, as if she might try to force her way back inside.

What was it about this woman? Why did he suffer such bizarre thoughts while in her presence? Martín had bedded hundreds of women, and most of them were far more beautiful or desirable than she; *all* of them had certainly been less trouble. He shook his head in mute exasperation at his strange reaction to her. His problem could only be that he hadn't had a woman in too long. After all, she had worked him into a passion last night, and he had had no release. And again this morning.

Martín knew the frustration that came from a lack of sexual release was detrimental to a man's mental processes. His current state was proof of that.

He would drop off the woman, the sick captain, and the rest of them and then immediately find a whore, preferably more than one, and then he could begin to think sensibly again.

Sarah bit back her disappointment at the captain's refusal to return the captives to Ouidah or her to England. She supposed she should be grateful he hadn't thrown her in the hold after last night.

Daniels was waiting for her just down the corridor.

"Miss Fisher." He sounded relieved and surprised in equal measures. Sarah wondered if he'd expected Bouchard to ravish her rather than kick her out of his cabin. Frankly, Sarah had been wondering the same thing. If she was honest with herself—which she strove to be, no matter how uncomfortable her thoughts might be—she'd have to admit that part of her had looked forward to a resumption of last night's fascinating activities. The captain must not have found the experience as captivating. He'd barely tolerated her presence in his cabin and had all but shoved her out the door.

"Captain Bouchard said that I may see Captain Graaf, but that you should accompany me."

"Very good, miss. Would you like to see him now?"

"If you think he will be awake." She was in no hurry to find the Dutch captain in the same state of undress as Bouchard. She flushed again just thinking of his muscular, tanned chest.

"I'll just nip into his room and speak to him first." Daniels paused and looked at her, his expression tense. "Please, Miss Fisher, will you promise me that you won't—"

"I promise not to seize any guns or to accost Captain Bouchard, Mr. Daniels." She smiled to show him she took no offense.

He gave her a boyish grin. "Very good, miss. I'll be back in a jiffy," he said.

Sarah looked down at her clothing as she listened to the murmur of voices beyond the door. She was wearing the slippers Captain Bouchard had given her, but otherwise was dressed in Graaf's clothing. Well, her options for clothing were rather limited right now. She could hardly wear the satin robe or either of the other scandalous gowns.

The door opened, interrupting her thoughts. "He'll see you now. I'll wait for you out here, Miss Fisher."

Graaf's cabin was much like Sarah's, except for a glass-fronted cabinet that was filled with simple medical supplies. He began to stand, and she held up a hand.

"Please, you need to be resting." Sarah took the only chair in the room. "You are looking much better, Captain." That was not a lie. He was pale, but no longer the shade of yellow-gray he'd been a mere day before.

"I feel much better, although not as a result of any medicine, but rather because of the weight that has been lifted from my conscience. I must thank you for that. If you hadn't come along, most likely I would have either died or wished that I had. I have no excuse for what I did to you and the people of your village." His was a pale pink when he finished.

Sarah was nonplussed by his apology. She suddenly realized it had been easier to despise him than it was to forgive him. The thought shamed her. She'd been preaching forgiveness and mercy to Captain Bouchard and not practicing it herself. She should start forgiving Graaf now, even though she had little hope of succeeding.

"Can you forgive me for lying to you about your illness?"

He gave a low chuckle that turned into a cough. When he was able to speak, he was smiling. "I'd like to think I would not have been so credulous had I not been so ill. Thank you for helping yesterday. You would make an excellent captain, Miss Fisher, much better than I could ever be." He no longer looked so amused. Sarah thought he was imagining his father's reaction to the news of his son's capture and the loss of a ship.

"I'm sorry for what you will have to undergo, but I don't believe you are the type of person who could have sold other human beings and lived comfortably with yourself afterward. I know you will face reprisals, but it is better for everyone this way."

He grimaced. "Nobody should be comfortable with such a thing. Unfortunately, we all tell ourselves the lies we need to hear. You are an exception, Miss Fisher. You had the courage of your convictions even when you could have saved yourself and left everyone else to fend for themselves."

Sarah brushed away his praise. "Let us talk of something else, Captain Graaf. Although I gave your sickness a spurious name, it is an illness I have seen many times. There is usually very little anyone can do, but if a person can make it through the fever stage, they recover. You are no longer feverish?"

"Bouchard's man assured me I am within a normal range.

I think I may have suffered the worst of the sickness before we left Ouidah. I was fortunate, I suppose, that we were at anchor and my lack of wits was less obvious to my crew."

"You are fortunate you did not die. Every year such sicknesses carry away dozens in my village."

His enormous blue eyes were less watery, although the white portion was still discolored. "I never learned how you came to be in such a place. Are you from the British fort? I had thought the fort in Ouidah abandoned?"

"My village was in the jungle a few days from Ouidah. My father was a doctor, and my parents were missionaries. I was born in Africa. I am English, but African, too."

"Where are your parents? How is it that you were taken with the, er, other captives?" he asked, carefully avoiding the word "slave."

"My parents died two years ago."

"*Two years?* How have you survived?"

She was amused by his shocked expression. "I continued to live as I always did. The people in my village are the only people I have ever known. They fed me and, in exchange, I tended to their illnesses. First I was the helper of my father and the village healer; later I was the only healer. I was content."

Graaf shook his head, a look of wonder on his face. Again Sarah changed the subject, not interested in trying to make him understand her life.

"And you, Captain, what were you doing before your father pressed you into his business?"

"I was in Leiden, at the university."

"You must be very clever. Tell me, what did you study?"

"Mathematics. My father told me on my last visit home that he needed me to join my two elder brothers in our family business, shipping. When father began to suffer difficulties, he refused to seek help from his family, no matter that they are very wealthy." Two spots of color appeared on his pale cheeks. "Now he will have to approach my uncles for aid, and they will help him because they could not bear the scandal of the Graaf name being associated with bankruptcy."

"What do you think will happen in Freetown?"

"The British will seize my ship and compensate Bouchard for his efforts. They will most likely hang those involved in the mutiny. As for me?" He shrugged. "Perhaps they will transport me for breaking the law. But what about you? Will you return to your village?"

"Captain Bouchard made the point—a good one, I daresay—that the captives would be in danger of recapture if they went back. He believes they will be safer in Freetown. I don't like it, but I think he is probably correct."

"So you will stay in Freetown?"

"It will depend on what the British representative decides. After what I did last night, I may be transported along with you."

"What happened last night?"

Sarah realized Graaf must have slept through the excitement. She sighed and quickly explained the events of the last day, leaving out both the bargain and the fact that she'd been mostly naked when de Heeckeren escaped.

He burst out laughing before she even finished, unable to speak for several minutes as he alternately laughed and coughed, tears spilling down his cheeks. Well, in this one way, at least, he was like Bouchard.

Sarah crossed her arms and waited for him to regain control of himself.

"I apologize for my behavior, Miss Fisher, but what I wouldn't give to have seen Bouchard's expression. How grateful I am not to be the only man on this ship to find himself at the wrong end of his own pistol."

"I'm so glad to have been of service, Captain Graaf."

He ignored her sarcasm and chuckled again. "The great Bouchard, held at the point of his own pistol."

"Why do you call him the great Bouchard?"

"You have not heard of him before?"

"Not until yesterday."

"I assumed everyone had heard of the *Golden Scythe* and its famous captain, a former slave himself."

His words stunned her, flooding her brain with so many questions, she didn't know which to ask first.

Graaf nodded slowly, as if relishing her shock. "Yes, our captain is a famous man. He started off as a lowly mate under the gentleman pirate One-Eyed Standish, the privateer who was really an English lord, Baron Ramsay. Surely you've heard of *him?*"

She shook her head. "I have spent my life in a jungle, Captain."

"Baron Ramsay was famous in the Mediterranean for almost twenty years. He was taken by Barbary corsairs and made a slave. He somehow broke free, stole a corsair ship, and spent years as a privateer for the British government. He encountered our Captain Bouchard, a mere slave at the time, somewhere along the way. I don't know the details, only what my brother Per told me when he learned where our father was sending me.

"My brother saw Bouchard in Alexandria once, in a water-front bar of the worst kind. Bouchard approached a table of five men, all slave traders, and started a fight with his bare fists. He put one man down before the other four rushed him with swords. He knocked down three of them before others intervened. My brother swears he's never seen a man deadlier with his bare hands. The man doesn't adhere to any rules of pugilism that a true gentleman would. How could he? Imagine, an ex-slave? It is no wonder he hates me, is it?" His handsome face was more than a little anxious.

No, Sarah thought, it was not a wonder. She considered

Graaf's story. How much of it was true? She certainly believed the part about Bouchard's being a fierce fighter. His body, which she'd felt with her own hands, had been solid muscle without an ounce of fat. Bouchard could break the fragile Dutch captain into little pieces with one hand.

But Bouchard a slave? How?

"How could he have been a slave? He looks nothing like the people of my village. His skin is hardly darker than mine, and his hair is actually lighter."

Graaf shrugged. "That is how it is in America. A man is considered to be a slave even with only a small portion of African blood. I understand some slaves are blue-eyed and fair-skinned, like me."

They stared at each other silently as they considered the implications.

They were still contemplating their futures, and the man who controlled them, when the door to the sickroom swung open, and Bouchard himself entered. He smiled at their undoubtedly guilty-looking faces, his sly look making Sarah wonder if he'd heard their conversation. She dismissed the silly notion. Bouchard was not the type to listen at doors.

"Good morning, *Captain* Graaf." Bouchard's beautiful lips curved in a cruel smile. "You are feeling much better, I see? Well enough to entertain visitors?"

Graaf colored under Bouchard's mocking gaze. Sarah looked from one to the other and again marveled at the two different examples of male beauty. The Dutchman looked like a fairy-tale prince with eyes as blue as the sea and patrician features to go with his elegant, gentleman's body.

Bouchard looked like Lucifer come to Earth, well pleased with the exchange of his eternal status for an opportunity to indulge in endless carnal delights.

The Dutchman inclined his head stiffly, clearly feeling the disadvantage of lying on his back before his vital adversary. "Miss Fisher came to inquire about my health."

"And stayed to discuss other, more interesting matters, I think?" Bouchard mocked. He leaned against the doorframe, taking up a position that required Sarah to turn back and forth if she wanted to look at both men. "You will excuse us, *mademoiselle,*" Bouchard said, not bothering to look at her. "I need to speak in private with *Captain* Graaf."

Sarah stood at his obvious dismissal and looked at Graaf. "I am glad you are feeling better, Captain." She turned to the door, which was blocked by Bouchard's big body. He let the moment stretch before taking a small step back. Even so, Sarah was forced to brush against him.

Back inside her cabin, she found the book *Clarissa* on her bed. It was the book she'd used to trap Bouchard the night before. She'd forgotten all about it when her attention had been claimed by more interesting matters, namely Bouchard's clever hands and lips.

He must have placed it in her room. Sarah picked up the book and stared at it, as though it could tell her something. She didn't understand the kind gesture any more than she understood the man.

Chapter Eight

Martín led his two companions toward the Vice-Admiralty Court, forcing himself to maintain a dignified pace and not sprint. He couldn't wait to get rid of his charges. The past few days onboard the ship with them had been beyond aggravating, and he'd been humiliated to realize that he'd been avoiding the woman—on his own bloody ship.

The building they were looking for was at the end of a scruffy street not too far from the harbor. It had been a while since he'd last been to the frontier town, and time had not improved it much. Like every other structure in the ramshackle town, Admiral Keeton's office was made of irregular planks of raw wood, which gave it the appearance of having been designed by a drunken architect and then built by drunken sailors—which was probably not far from the truth. A limp-looking flag dangled from a tall bamboo pole, and a single soldier stood beside the entrance. The soldier bulged out of his uniform in more than one place and did not look like much of a threat. He sized up the approaching visitors with an insolent smirk that made Martín's hands curl into fists.

"We are here to speak to Admiral Keeton."

"And who are *you*?" His eyes slid over Martín's two companions and then snapped back again, when he realized one of them was a woman wearing men's clothing.

"Captain Bouchard of the *Golden Scythe*," Martín barked,

unaccountably annoyed by the way the man's eyes were traveling over the missionary woman's body.

The soldier stiffened and looked at him with an expression that was no longer slack and disrespectful. "Captain Bouchard?"

Martín frowned. "As you see."

"*The* Captain Bouchard?"

Martín glared, and the man jolted into action and yanked open the door.

"I'll be back right smartly, sir," he said, before darting into the house.

"It would seem your reputation precedes you, Captain Bouchard," Graaf said.

"Perhaps I should have mentioned your name instead, *Captain*?" Martín retorted, sneering at the flush that crept up the blond man's throat.

The soldier returned before the seething Dutchman could answer. "The admiral will see you at once, Captain Bouchard."

The admiral's office was everything Martín had expected: a dreary little room in a dreary little house. The admiral himself was a dreary little man, and he looked well past his prime. Martín was not surprised. Freetown would not be considered a plum posting.

Keeton rose as Martín entered the muggy, dingy office. "Captain Bouchard, what a pleasure to meet you. I have heard much about you."

That was more than Martín could say about Keeton. He'd never heard the man's name before today. Still, an admiral was not a person to trifle with. Besides, why behave churlishly when the man was so obviously pleased to see him?

"Thank you for agreeing to see me so quickly, Admiral."

"I have heard much about your exploits—and Captain Standish's too, of course. Some of those stories came from Admiral Nelson himself." The red-faced man had an unhealthy sheen of sweat on his face. Living in the tropics was not something that tended to improve one's constitution.

Martín indulged the man in a few minutes of chatter before steering the conversation to the point and launching into a succinct explanation of the past few days.

Keeton's bloodshot eyes moved from Martín to the Dutchman and narrowed, as if he were trying to recall something.

"So," Martín concluded a few minutes later, "I've taken the liberty of releasing those of Graaf's crew who assisted me against the mutineers. Captain Graaf, the rest of the mutineers, and his ship, however, I relinquish to your possession."

The admiral had not stopped staring at Graaf.

"Graaf?" The admiral cleared his throat. "Are you any relation to Hertog Graaf, er, that is, His Grace of Orange?"

Graaf sighed, as though the weight of the world had just been lowered onto his spindly shoulders. "Yes, he is my grandfather."

Keeton seemed to shrink to half his size before Martín's eyes. He swallowed audibly. "Ah, yes, very good, my . . . ?"

"Captain Graaf will do, Admiral."

Martín stared at the younger man as comprehension slowly dawned. He had captured a bloody Dutch *peer?* He had to clamp his jaw tight to hold back his yell. He *knew* he should have thrown the useless, slaving, effete-looking fool off his ship when he'd had the chance. Now it was too late. It would take years to get his reward with a member of the peerage involved.

The admiral interrupted Martín's internal raging. "And who is this, Captain Bouchard?" He motioned to the woman.

Martín tore his eyes away from the dithering functionary. "This is Mademoiselle Fisher, the daughter of English missionaries. She found herself in the hold of the *Blue Bird* after the people of her village were enslaved." Martín wanted to make certain the irritatingly merciful and forgiving woman never, *ever* forgot how it was that she'd come into contact with the slaving Dutch peer.

The admiral's eyebrows climbed to where his hairline would have been if he'd had any hair.

Martín continued when the other man did not speak. "She requires the help of the British government to return to England. She is, after all, British."

The admiral nodded at the woman, but quickly looked back at Graaf, as though the sight of the younger man was causing him physical pain.

Martín took advantage of the lull in conversation to further explain. "My first mate is awaiting a member of your staff so that he might turn over the Dutch ship." He paused, but the admiral was still staring at Graaf.

Martín refused to think about what the admiral's expression meant. He also refused to stay in the man's presence any longer. He was worried he might cut off the admiral's head or shoot him if he remained. He lunged to his feet.

"I'm afraid I must be going as I have rather pressing business in town. I beg your pardon for my haste." Martín nodded to the bewildered man before turning to the other two. "Mademoiselle Fisher, I bid you good-bye and good luck." He inclined his head to the woman without meeting her eyes and left without speaking to the Dutchman.

He almost made it out the front door before Keeton caught up to him. The man must be fitter than he looked.

"Please wait, Captain Bouchard, I beg of you."

Bouchard pasted a smile on his face and turned. "Yes, Admiral?"

"Do you know who that man *is*?"

"No." Martín was only half lying. Even an ignorant oaf such as he could see Graaf was some sort of Dutch aristocrat. "I don't know who he is, and, furthermore, it has nothing to do with me. I can see you hope it has nothing to do with you, either. However, Admiral, *you* are the ranking official here, and it is usual in these cases for me to turn over the ship, crew, and cargo. The letter I carry grants me no more power than that, nor am I required to do anything more. I bid you good day, Admiral." He bowed, clapped his hat on his head with more force than was necessary, and stepped out of the house, shutting the door on whatever the man had been about to say next.

Martín exhaled and straightened his cuffs. When he looked up, it was to find the fat soldier watching him. Martín nodded dismissively at the man, and then thought of something. "Tell me—" He paused and looked for any insignia on the man's uniform that might indicate rank. He saw none.

"Watch Captain Kettle, sir!" The rotund man threw out his chest and snapped to attention.

"Tell me, Captain Kettle—it has been a while since my last visit. Where might I find the most attractive whores in Freetown?"

The man squinted at Martín and then cocked his head as if he were hard of hearing.

"Beggin' your pardon, did you say . . . whores, sir?"

"Yes, whores. Ladies of the evening? The muslin crowd? Daughters of Eve? Prostitutes."

The man reddened. "Aye, sir. Whores."

"The best in town, Captain."

"That would be at the Magnolia House. Just follow this street until you can't go any farther and take a left. You can't miss it, sir."

"Excellent, Watch Captain." Martín nodded and headed in the direction the fellow had indicated. There was no time like the present to take care of his "pressing business."

Chapter Nine

A loud pounding noise jolted him awake. "Captain? Captain Bouchard?"

"Eh?" Martín turned away from the door and rolled over onto a small body in the process. The woman beneath him grunted.

"Captain Bouchard!" the German woman—Bettina?—repeated before pounding even harder, the sound causing his head to throb.

"*Mon Dieu,*" Martín swore softly, so as not to cause himself unnecessary pain. He turned back the other way and came up against yet another body. He opened his eyes a crack and saw a soundly sleeping woman.

The pounding ceased, and the door opened. "Are you awake, Captain? There is a man from Admiral Keeton's office to see you."

"What does he want?" he croaked.

"I don't know, but I don't want any trouble. You must get dressed and go with him. He says he won't leave without you. He is standing in the hallway and will not move. Captain? Captain! *Macht schnell!*" She came all the way into the room and yanked the blankets off him.

Martín groaned. "*Merde.* What time is it?"

"Eight o'clock."

Martín hesitated. "At night?"

She muttered something in German. "Eight in the morning."

Mere hours before, Martín had thought the woman's heavy accent charming, but now he couldn't recall why. Perhaps it had been the three bottles of her best wine?

She bustled around the room, yanking open the heavy drapes and letting in the bright morning light, piling crockery onto a tray—noisily—and generally making a racket. There would be no more sleeping. Well, he probably couldn't have stayed much longer in any case. He'd hoped to leave immediately after Beauville finished his business with the *Blue Bird.*

After coming to Madam Bettina's, Martín had sent a messenger to Beauville, instructing him to fetch Martín as soon as the ship was ready to leave. He had then proceeded to enjoy a lazy afternoon, an excellent dinner, and an exceptionally disappointing evening.

Martín was in no mood to tackle thoughts of last night. He climbed over a sleeping body and picked his breeches off the floor, struggling with the five buttons as though they were five hundred. His shirt hung from the corner of a portrait of George III, a flattering representation of the monarch before he'd become a recluse. Martín hunted everywhere for his waistcoat before realizing one of the women in bed was wearing it.

He patted her plump behind. "*Chérie,* you must give me back my clothes." She muttered something as he prized the waistcoat free, but never woke up. Martín slumped on the edge of the bed and pulled on his boots, grunting at the effort. His neckcloth was tied around the other woman's waist. He shrugged and immediately regretted the movement. He would leave the neckcloth. He was in no condition to tie it on his person, and he doubted it was in any condition to be worn.

He located his coat on a hook beside the door and took a generous handful of coins from his pocket, tossing them onto the table by the door. The women who'd raised him had taught him to always leave something extra. Especially if he wanted to purchase some discretion, a thing he'd never needed to do before last night.

"*Merde*," he muttered, his face heating with shame.

Bettina was waiting beside the soldier from Keeton's office, who was holding a cup of coffee. Martín took the coffee from the man's unresisting fingers and swallowed the scalding beverage in one long gulp.

"Excellent coffee, madam." He gave her a pained smile along with the empty cup. "You will remember the conversation we had last night?" Martín was surprised *he* remembered it after three bottles.

Her businesslike smile bore no resemblance to the ones she'd lavished on him the previous day and night. "I thought you wanted me to forget that conversation, Captain Bouchard."

He rolled his eyes—which hurt—and reached for his purse, then placed what remained into her outstretched hand.

Her broad, pretty face creased into a sly smile. "*Danke*. This will help us *all* forget." She stood on her toes and kissed him on the cheek before turning away.

Martín turned to the gawking sailor. "Come, let us go see what the admiral wants of me." The man's bulging eyes were on the voluptuous madam. "Or perhaps you would like to stay here, Kettle?"

"What? Oh, no, Captain, I'd best come with you," he said with obvious regret.

"You are a frequent visitor of Madam Bettina's?" Martín asked as they began the short journey to Admiral Keeton's chambers-cum-office.

"A bit above my touch, sir. But there's no shortage of much cheaper places. Every day more and more of them.

Some come here because they ain't got any other place to go. But a fair number, like Madam Bettina, come all the way from back home to ply their trade."

Martín knew it was the same the world over, yet somehow he felt depressed by what the soldier said. Freetown was the creation of idealistic people who'd believed they could offer freed slaves a new and better life. As he looked around at the ragged town and desperate people, he realized it wasn't the kind of life most people would desire.

It certainly wasn't the life he wanted. Last night had been a dismal affair, no matter how much he'd tried to tell himself otherwise. Martín had needed to drown himself in wine just to get through the evening. For the first time in his life, he'd felt a twinge of shame at bedding whores. It didn't matter that the women were free agents and not slaves; he would never go to someone who was compelled to service him. Still, the evening had felt sordid. Maybe that was why he'd not been able to . . . perform.

He scrubbed one hand over his face and pinched the bridge of his nose, shaking his head. Perhaps it had been because of all the wine he'd consumed. It had been a long time since he'd been the worse for drink. That must have been why . . .

Martín pushed the entire dreadful ordeal from his mind. He could only hope the whores would keep his secret.

He found not only the admiral, but also Captain Graaf and Sarah Fisher waiting for him in the rickety building. Martín groaned out loud, not realizing until that moment just how much he'd wanted to leave without seeing either one of them ever again.

Keeton's smile looked rather strained. "Captain Bouchard, thank you for coming so quickly."

Martín squinted at the man, wondering if he was making some kind of jest. He'd sent a damned soldier for him—what else was Martín supposed to have done?

"Please, have a seat, Captain." The admiral gestured to the remaining chair, refusing to meet Martín's eyes.

A cold sweat began to build on his forehead, in spite of the warmness of the morning. He put a hand on the chair back to prop himself up. "Thank you, Admiral, but I'm afraid I cannot stay too long. My crew is even now making my ship ready for departure." Martín had no idea what either his crew or his ship were doing.

"Actually, they are awaiting my permission before they do anything. Please take a seat and enjoy some coffee, the best—from Java, one of ours now." He was referring to the 1811 British capture of the Dutch possession. Martín shot a quick look at the captive Dutchman to see how he viewed the admiral's comment. As usual, Graaf looked ill more than anything else. In fact, he looked worse than yesterday. He appeared to have found Freetown as exhausting as Martín had, albeit probably for other reasons.

Martín took the cup of coffee and sat.

"I'm afraid I am going to have to impose on you on behalf of His Majesty's government, Captain." Keeton stopped, as if to gauge the effect of his words so far. Whatever he saw on Martín's face caused him to continue somewhat hastily. "I need you to transport, er, Captain Graaf back to England. I conferred with our Chief Justice, who is in charge of such matters at the Vice-Admiralty Court, and we both agree that we simply do not have the authority to dispose of this matter here."

Martín stared, blood pulsing louder and louder in his ears like insistent pounding from a club. It took a long, excruciating moment to find enough spit in his mouth to squeeze out the words.

"Excuse me, Admiral, but am I to understand you want *me* to take Graaf to England because *you* lack the authority to prosecute him for trading in slaves?"

The older man fiddled with the handle of his cup.

It was the woman who answered. Naturally.

"It would seem Captain Graaf is related to some rather important people, Captain Bouchard. So important, the admiral does not feel he is the person to determine the outcome of this matter." Martín could hear something in her voice that sounded like anger. He met her eyes and saw that he was right. She was angry. At the slaving Dutch captain? The pounding in his skull seemed to ease up.

"And the *Blue Bird*?" Martín turned from the woman to the admiral, his heart sinking even before he heard the answer.

"I'm afraid I cannot make any firm decision on that right now, either. I will hold her, of course, and await word from London."

Martín resisted the urge to hurl his cup at the man's head. Instead, he took a deep breath and looked at the other two people in the room. Only the woman met his eyes, her face an unreadable mask.

The admiral cleared his throat, and Martín turned back to him.

"Miss Fisher has explained her circumstances to me. I have informed her that we can offer her no assistance at this time regarding her village. I have also informed her that I cannot, in good conscience, allow her to leave Freetown by herself." Martín could feel the woman's anger without even looking. "We have agreed England is the best place for her right now. Your ship is returning to England, Captain. Surely there is no good reason you cannot accommodate her?" For the first time Martín heard steel in the man's voice. Keeton might feel shame for caving under the pressure of foreign dignitaries, but he wasn't bending when it came to what was due an English gentlewoman.

Martín squeezed the cup as he worked his mouth, biting his tongue both literally and figuratively.

"I'm sure you will receive recompense for her passage," Keeton added, knowing nothing of the sort.

Martín jerked out a nod and stood. "When can we depart?"

"You are free to shove off as soon as the captain and Miss Fisher are ready. I've taken the liberty of having their personal items transferred to your ship."

Martín turned on the pair, who'd also risen. "May I have your permission to depart?" His voice was raw with the strain of not yelling.

"I am ready," the woman said.

Captain Graaf inclined his head.

"Excellent!" The admiral rubbed his hands together as if he were looking forward to a journey himself. "Let me escort you to the door."

The trip back to the ship was quick and silent, both the woman and the sick man too busy keeping up with Martín's savage pace to attempt any conversation.

Beauville met him as soon as he stepped off the gangplank, his silent stare and compressed lips proof he already knew the reason for the presence of the two people behind him.

Martín turned to his unwanted passengers. "Captain, please retire to the sick bay; it is the only spare cabin. Mademoiselle Fisher, you might as well tell Daniels to remove his possessions from his cabin." He turned on his heel before she could open her mouth. "Beauville, with me."

Martín found Jenkins in his cabin. "A bath and breakfast, in that order." Once the little man had left, he turned to Beauville. "Speak," he said, taking off his wrinkled coat and waistcoat and throwing them over a chair.

"I was told the disposition of the ship was a matter to be determined in England. I was given the opportunity to make a complete inventory of the *Blue Bird*. By my calculations we are owed a great deal. The ship is in excellent shape and appointed with nothing but the best. The admiral's factotum would tell me nothing other than that all crew members were to be released, mutineers included, and the ship was to be held indefinitely."

Martín collapsed onto the padded bench as Jenkins came into the room bearing a pot of coffee.

"I have nothing to add," Martín said, raising one foot so Jenkins could remove his boot. "Except that we *must* bring Graaf back to England. I would hazard a guess the good captain has some rather powerful connections and is too valuable to squander out here in the middle of nowhere. I would not be at all surprised if we end up with empty hands at the end of all this." He shot his first mate a hard look. "Keep that to yourself, Beauville."

The laconic Frenchman nodded. Beauville knew Martín could afford to pay his men out of his own pocket and would do so if necessary.

The money Martín had earned working for Captain Standish—or Lord Ramsay, as he was now known—had been equal to the wealth of kings. Martín had plenty of money, more than he could ever spend. He'd learned his methods from Standish and had been wise about choosing and keeping his men. The division of property on his ship was much more equitable than on any other privateer. As a result, sailors fought to crew his ship.

That didn't mean Martín planned to let the Dutch ship go without a struggle. He boiled to think Graaf might escape all punishment. Martín stripped off his breeches and tossed them to Jenkins before shrugging into the robe he held open.

"Get us the hell out of here, Beauville. I want to be gone before Keeton comes up with something else for me to do."

Beauville left without another word.

Martín absently watched as Jenkins dragged in the hip-bath and then assembled his shaving equipment. He drank two mugs of coffee before allowing Jenkins to wrap a steaming strip of linen around his face and neck. For some reason

Martín felt desperate for his bath, even more so than usual. He'd always been an obsessive bather, something else he'd learned from the whores who'd raised him. Martín closed his eyes and relaxed as Jenkins shaved him.

He knew what he felt about Graaf's presence on his ship, but he couldn't say the same about the woman. He couldn't tell if the feelings that stirred in his stomach when he thought about her were ones of anger, annoyance, or anticipation. What he did know was that it would be next to impossible to avoid her in the coming months.

Chapter Ten

Sarah was disappointed, but not surprised when Daniels delivered a meal to her cabin that evening. She'd seen by Bouchard's expression how displeased he was to be saddled with her—perhaps even angrier than he was about being stuck with Graaf.

She'd passed the prior twenty-four hours in a daze. Graaf, a Dutch aristocrat? A member of the House of Orange-Nassau and in line to inherit the throne, albeit quite a way down the list?

Even though he behaved toward her as he had from the beginning, Sarah felt different around the young captain. She could see Captain Bouchard regarded him differently, as well. She'd seen the wheels turning in the handsome captain's head as he realized what Graaf's connections meant to him and his rights to the *Blue Bird*. She could imagine Bouchard deciding sometime during the long journey that the aristocrat wouldn't recover from his sickness. The Dutchman's death would be viewed as just another tragic outcome of an ill-fated journey to deepest Africa.

Sarah frowned at the thought. She would need to make sure that didn't happen. Her frown deepened as she thought back to this morning. Admiral Keeton had tried to keep the conversation with his man quiet, but Sarah had heard enough to know Bouchard had spent the previous day and evening in a bordello.

The feelings this information evoked had discountenanced her. She'd tried to examine her emotions honestly. Disgust wasn't the only, or even strongest, one she felt. She'd also been hit by a breathtaking wave of jealousy. That had led her to a disappointing, but not wholly surprising, revelation: she was infatuated with Captain Bouchard. Indeed, how could she not be attracted to him? She'd known very few men in her life who'd evinced any curiosity about her at all and certainly none who looked like him. Sarah doubted there *were* many men who were as handsome or virile as Bouchard. It was natural, albeit unfortunate, that she'd quickly succumbed to him.

It was also no secret how he felt about her after she'd held him at gunpoint. She told herself it was all to the good. After all, what had she hoped for? A tempestuous liaison resulting in love, marriage, and children? There was no future with a man like him. The fact that he sought prostitutes at the first opportunity only proved what he was and what he wanted. She fumed. It was clear he was willing to take satisfaction from any woman available. Except her, of course.

Sarah groaned and pushed away her half-eaten tray of food. She looked at the heavy book Bouchard had given her. It was tragic he had such a wonderful collection of books and would never know what they contained.

She smoothed the serviceable brown cloth of the gown the admiral had procured for her and considered her position on the ship and the long weeks ahead. It was unlikely Captain Bouchard would ever receive payment for her passage. The thought caused her cheeks to burn. It was charity. She'd accepted the admiral's charity—a few items of clothing that had belonged to his deceased wife—with gratitude, rather than anger. So why did she feel so hostile when thinking of Bouchard's charity?

Because he despised her. So much so that he didn't even want to touch her.

She recalled how she'd offered herself to him and reveled in his touch. And then she thought of his cool rejection. No, Sarah would *not* be a charitable case where he was concerned.

She needed to pay him for her cabin and food if it was the last thing she did. She chewed her lip. There was only one way she could pay him. Well, only one *other* way. She would teach him to read. If he refused her offer, which was likely given his arrogance, then she would find a way to force him, even if she had to threaten him.

She stood. It was best to take action before she lost heart. She returned her dinner tray to a surprised galley hand and then rapped on Bouchard's door.

There was no answer. She knocked louder. Again there was no answer. Before she could change her mind, she turned the handle. It was unlocked. She pushed open the door and peered inside. The bed was empty, as was the chair in front of his desk. She peeked around the door to the small dining area. It, too, was unoccupied. She stepped inside and closed the door behind her.

Stop it! Are you insane? Get out of here now.

Sarah ignored the voice of caution and looked at the books on the shelf, slowly dragging her finger across their spines, the simple act of touching them enough to make her happy.

You are courting disaster. You will be thrown from the ship, made to walk the plank.

She ignored the hysterical babbling and pulled a book from the shelf, *Gargantua* by Rabelais.

Leave now. Leave now! Now! Before it's too late!

Sarah had read *Pantagruel* in French several years ago. It had taken her weeks to finish the book, but it had been most rewarding. She would need to ask the captain if she could borrow this volume. She was replacing the book on the shelf when the door swung open.

Bouchard's eyebrows shot up. "Mademoiselle Fisher, what a surprise. Are you looking for my pistols? They are behind you in my wardrobe. Would you like me to load one for you?" He crossed his arms and leaned against the door-frame, his expression mocking rather than shocked, almost as if he'd expected to find her riffling his possessions.

Sarah's face flamed. "I came looking for you, and when you didn't answer I couldn't resist looking at your library. I shouldn't have. I apologize."

"You are a prodigious reader to have already finished the book I gave you."

"I have not finished *Clarissa*. I just wanted to see what you had."

He pushed away from the door and closed the distance between them, stopping a fraction of an inch away from her. He was only a few inches taller than she, but his heavily muscled body was very broad. His aggressive personality made him seem even larger.

"Now that you have seen what *I have* perhaps you can tell me how I can be of service to you?" He reached up and tucked a strand of hair behind her ear. Sarah jumped and took a step back. His mocking smile grew, but he did not pursue her.

Her throat had constricted at his touch, and she gave a slight cough to clear it. "I came to offer you payment for my passage."

He cocked one eyebrow.

"Not that kind of payment," she snapped. "Besides, I should think you would be well and good in that department after last night." Sarah instantly wished she could retract the words.

"Ah, *mademoiselle,* how little you know of men. We are never so 'well and good'—as you so charmingly put it—

to decline further offers in that department. If the offer is attractive enough."

Her hand itched to slap the smug, insulting smirk from his face. "Do not worry, Captain; I am not offering my body in payment. I am repeating my offer to teach you to read and write."

The amusement drained from his face, and he raked her with a hostile look that took her breath away. "Thank you, *mademoiselle,* but *no thank you.* The only payment I require from you is that you stay out of my business. And my cabin." He turned and marched to the door.

"I, however, am not satisfied to be in your debt. You will agree to my form of payment or I will tell every member of your crew that you are illiterate."

His hand froze in the act of reaching for the doorknob, and he turned around slowly and raised one hand to the side of his head. He tapped his ear. "I must have misheard you, *mademoiselle.* Surely you weren't threatening me?"

Sarah flinched, even though his voice had not risen. "No, Captain, you did not mishear me. You will either submit to my teaching, or I will expose you."

He was across the room in a heartbeat, not stopping until her nose touched his throat, forcing her to take a step back. He continued walking until she felt the wall at her back. And still he kept coming, until his hard thighs and chest pinned her, his body like warm stone.

"What is to stop me from simply throwing you overboard, *mademoiselle*?" His voice rumbled from his chest to hers like distant thunder.

"Very little." She spoke into the muscular column of his throat, which was dotted with tiny dark hairs. She was momentarily distracted by the observation. She was also distracted by the smell of him. It reminded her of the last time their bodies had been this close. For a long moment there was only the feeling of his breath on her hair and the regular rise and fall of his chest against hers. And then he was gone, quicker than should have been possible.

He jerked open the door. "Come to me tomorrow after I have had my breakfast. I will give you an hour to convince me."

Sarah bolted for the open door. It was not until she was back in her cabin that she stopped expecting to be struck in the back of the head and dumped from the ship. She had *threatened* him. His cabin had all but pulsed with menace. Would she even make it until tomorrow?

What had she been thinking?

What the devil had he been thinking?

The woman was an interfering menace, and he'd condemned himself to days spent in her presence.

Martín poured a glass of brandy, tossed it back in one swallow, and poured another.

It had taken Sarah Fisher less than one day to disturb his peace and attempt to take control of him. This time she'd done it more surely than if she'd put him at the point of his pistol.

But he knew a thing or two she did not. Her audacious threat had not scared him; it had liberated him. He would have cut off his own tongue before admitting how much he yearned to read and write. And now he could keep that precious organ because *she* believed she'd blackmailed *him*.

He knew he should have been disgusted by his pitiful subterfuge. He was too afraid to tell a mere girl what he wanted? The enormity of his own pride stunned him, but he ruthlessly shoved his surprise into a hole that was filled with other, far darker thoughts and fears.

Besides, why the hell should he tell her what he wanted or why he wanted it? She'd been correct in saying she owed him. Only a fool would expect payment from the British government for transporting her to England. Martín might as well derive some benefit from her annoying presence on his ship.

It was too damn bad he could not say the same about Graaf. He fiddled with the glass as he toyed with the idea of throwing the Dutch nobleman overboard. After all, it would be very easy to say he'd died of his fever. In fact, Graaf might die of his sickness anyway; it happened all the time.

He grinned, enjoying the thought for a few moments before dismissing it. If Martín threw Graaf overboard, he would have to throw the woman right behind him. Or right before him, if he wanted to be on the safe side.

Martín snorted. God only knew what she would do to him and his crew if she got wind that he was considering disposing of the Dutch peer.

No, he couldn't get rid of Graaf because he couldn't get rid of the woman. He needed her. Martín considered what he had just committed himself to: hours—no, days—in her company. Was he insane? The woman was a menace to any man's peace. Thank God he'd never actually bedded her. He recalled her reaction to the news that he'd visited a whorehouse and smiled. Good! He wanted her to know she meant *nothing* to him, certainly no more than any other woman. He would keep his hands off her. She was too much trouble, and learning to read and write was more important than a quick fuck. Particularly given his pitiful performance in Freetown.

He snorted again and scratched at the brand on his shoulder. He did not hold much hope she could teach him anything. At thirty years of age—or even more, for all he knew—he was probably beyond the point of learning such things.

His arm itched like the devil, and he pulled off his jacket to scratch it. It didn't seem to matter how hard he rubbed the hateful brand. Was it trying to tell him something? To remind him that teaching a slave to read and write was a crime in the United States? That it was even illegal for a slave to possess a book—or at least a damned bad idea. The brand on his arm was nothing compared to the brand of ignorance his owners had burnt into his brain.

The men who relied on slave labor knew well the need to keep their chattel under control.

He picked up his glass and stared into the amber liquid. For years he'd allowed the situation to stand—enabled the men who'd striven to keep him ignorant and vulnerable. Tomorrow he would change that, and all those men could go to hell. He threw back the rest of his brandy and bared his teeth as it burned down his throat. He was free, wealthy, and the master of his own destiny; he could do anything he wished.

His arm itched, and he scratched until it bled.

Chapter Eleven

Sarah crawled around the cabin floor on her hands and knees and collected the scattered paper, broken quill, and empty ink well, grimacing at the stain spattered across the lovely silk bedding.

"Miss Fisher? Are you all right?" Daniels stood in the open doorway, his boyish features compressed with anxiety.

Bouchard hadn't bothered to close the door after flinging it open and stomping off, cursing furiously in French and a collection of other languages.

"Yes, thank you, Mr. Daniels." She accepted his hand up and held out the damaged quill. "I'm afraid I've been rather clumsy." It was easier to claim the effects of the captain's tantrums as her own, as she'd been doing almost every day for weeks.

Sarah had guessed Captain Bouchard might be a challenging pupil, but nothing had prepared her for the difficulties she faced. He was the most impatient, arrogant, and excitable person she'd ever known. If he did not grasp a concept immediately—which he did often, as his mind was agile and hungry—he became enraged. If he wasn't flinging the contents of the table across the room, he was accusing her of toying with him, as he'd done today. She must be failing

Bouchard somehow; otherwise he wouldn't react with such frustrated anger.

"You should be more careful, Miss Fisher. This is the fourth quill I've fixed for you this week," Daniels chided, examining the splayed tip.

"I'm afraid I have rather a heavy hand, Mr. Daniels."

Daniels closed the door to the captain's cabin.

"Miss Fisher? Is that you?" Captain Graaf's voice came from behind his cabin door as they passed and stopped both her and the second mate in their tracks. Sarah considered ignoring the bored aristocrat, but knew Daniels was watching her. It would be rude to ignore the man under such circumstances.

"Coming, Captain Graaf." She nodded to the second mate and turned to walk the short distance to the Dutchman's cabin.

His face lit up at the sight of her, and Sarah couldn't help feeling flattered, even though she could not entirely like the man.

"Good afternoon, Captain. What can I do for you?"

"Please, won't you sit and talk with me? Or read to me? Or play chess with me?"

Sarah made herself smile, although who he was and what he'd done was never far from her mind. Practicing forgiveness was proving to be more of a challenge than she had anticipated. "Very well, which do you prefer?"

"Perhaps a little talking and then a game of chess? Or maybe cards? Have you any cards?"

"No, I do not. I'm afraid I've never even seen a deck of cards."

"Then I must procure some immediately. I will teach you piquet, and maybe I'll be able to beat you at something. I am quite exhausted from all the beatings I have endured in chess. Can you not let me win every fifth or sixth time?" He importuned her with eyes that were a clear, celestial blue. As his health improved, his demands on her attention increased. His growing infatuation was not surprising; Sarah was the only person onboard who would interact with him.

She gave a little snort of contempt. She could captivate a nobleman she privately despised, and could befriend several of Bouchard's crew, but not the frustrating Frenchman himself. A man who made it no secret that he preferred whores to her.

"You look so sad. What are you thinking, Miss Fisher?"

Sarah sat down. "I am merely tired."

He made a *tsk*ing sound. "I told you helping Bouchard with his bookwork would not be a pleasant task."

Doing bookwork to pay for her passage was a myth she'd concocted to explain why she spent so much time in Bouchard's cabin. She doubted the pretense would be necessary for much longer.

She chewed her lower lip. If she couldn't find some way to break through whatever was stopping Bouchard from progressing, he would call a halt to her efforts. She'd wracked her brain for weeks over what the problem was. He was quick at writing and reading the sample exercise she drew up every day, but when it came to reading an actual book, he became sullen and angry. Perhaps she wasn't offering him items that interested him enough to learn? Maybe he would prefer ship records?

Graaf's voice intruded on her thoughts. "Come, you are very distracted today, Miss Fisher. What is it?"

Sarah looked at his earnest, hopeful face and felt a pang. She forced the more interesting topic of Captain Bouchard from her mind and tried to concentrate on the man across from her. "Please, won't you call me Sarah? We have been on this ship for several weeks, and there are still many to go."

His pale cheeks tinted. "I would like that very much, Sarah. You must call me Mies. Captain Graaf is not only a mouthful, it is also not a title I've earned."

Sarah ignored the last part of his comment. "Your cough seems to have gone away. How are you feeling otherwise?"

"Better each day. No doubt I will be ready to get on a ship and make the journey home when we reach England."

Not if Bouchard had anything to say about it.

Sarah frowned at the thought. Was there no topic of discussion that did not lead her back to the aggravating captain? "Tell me about your home—what is it like?"

Graaf's expression lightened at her invitation, and soon he was painting a vivid image of the life he'd left behind at his father's bidding. As she listened to stories of his indulgent older siblings and parents, Sarah realized he was not evil, but rather a weak-willed man who had done something evil. The realization made it easier to forgive him, but she could never respect such a man, nor could she forget he'd been willing to trade in other human beings.

"And you, Sarah, what of your childhood? It is always I who talk. But your life must have been unusual indeed, living in the jungle among savages."

Sarah flinched at his characterization of her friends and neighbors, but he didn't seem to notice. She bit her tongue. Why try to make him see the error of his thoughts when she did not care what he thought?

"There must have been many different and dangerous animals. Tell me, did you ever see a lion or tiger?"

The ridiculous question made her laugh. "Tigers do not live in Africa."

She was still teasing him for his ignorance when Captain Bouchard appeared in the doorway. Sarah always left the door to the Dutchman's cabin open when she was with him.

"Ah, Captain Bouchard," Graaf said. "I am glad you are here. Sarah has been abusing me. You must remind her that I am an ill man."

Bouchard's eyebrows rose at the nobleman's use of her Christian name, and Sarah flushed under his disconcerting yellow gaze. "*Sarah* is quite skilled at finding a man's weaknesses, Graaf. I hesitate to draw her attention to mine."

Sarah glared at him. "I didn't think you had any weaknesses, Captain Bouchard."

"You should not work her so hard, Bouchard. Surely you have someone else who can serve as your steward. Too much reading is bad for a lady's eyes."

Bouchard's lids lowered. Sarah hoped he did not think the Dutchman's comment meant she had been complaining. The bitter twist of his lips and his next words disabused her of that hope.

"I believe I am almost out of work for Mademoiselle Fisher."

"Excellent. I plan to teach her to play cards. Can you believe she does not know any card games, Captain?"

Bouchard turned away. "Mademoiselle Fisher is good at games. I'm sure she will be a quick learner," he tossed over his shoulder, closing the door behind him.

That night, for the first time since leaving N'goe, Sarah dreamt of her parents.

She was in the rickety two-room building that had been her family's home since before she'd been born. Her father lay in the room that doubled as master bedroom and dining room. It was either the eleventh or twelfth of June; she was never sure afterward. In any event, it was the peak of the wet season, and everything was coated with a layer of fine, slimy mist. The air was so heavy it was like breathing water. Insects the size of saucers buzzed and bombarded the heavy netting that surrounded her parents' bed. Well, it was her father's bed, as her mother had died a few weeks before.

It was nighttime, and Michael Fisher was finally dozing after a day of coughing up blood and writhing in agony. Abena had been needed by other sick villagers that night, so

Sarah had been alone. She'd done the best she could without the help of her friend—who was a far more skilled healer than Sarah could ever hope to be.

"Your father is dying, Sarah," Abena had said, her dark brown eyes flooded with sympathy. "I have given him a very big dose of my pain-killing powder, which will make him sleep. It is the best we can do to ease his passing."

If not for Abena and the compounds she made, Sarah's father would have died in screaming agony.

Sarah's mother had always been dismissive of folk remedies. "It is foolish to put your faith in a people who believe tying a bone to one's leg will be sufficient to heal a break," she had said on more than one occasion.

Sarah had loved her mother, but never understood her. To Sarah, English and African medicine and culture were more alike than not. While the Africans might put their faith in an animal or plant spirit, Christians did the same with their belief in the saints and the Holy Trinity. Both groups relied on faith.

She must have been twelve the first time she spoke this observation out loud. She'd been helping her father patch a corner of their thatched roof.

He'd paused to wipe his forehead with a frayed handkerchief. "That is the observation of a natural philosopher, Sarah." His eyes had drifted to where her mother labored over a tub of laundry. "While I find your comment thought provoking, I'm afraid your mother might not appreciate such speculation."

Even then, Sarah had known what her father meant. Her mother clung to her beliefs with a rigidity that never bent or gave, even after a quarter of a century of hard, ceaseless labor. Clara Fisher viewed herself as a bulwark of Christianity between her family and the dangerous vastness that threatened to overwhelm them. Her mother would have given her last mouthful of food to another, but she would never believe the people of the small village of N'goe were not in need of saving.

Even on her deathbed she'd pursued her life's goal. "I was a young woman once—I know you are torn by conflicting desires."

Sarah had been stunned to hear her mother admit such a thing.

Clara had seen her surprise. "You want excitement, amusement, and all the other furbelows you read about in the books you sneak from the missionary barrel." She nodded knowingly at Sarah's flushed face. "Those are the temptations of the flesh, Sarah. You must fight them. You must continue our good work here. Your father will need you now more than ever. We have not done as well as we'd hoped spreading God's Grace, but the English School must go on."

The name was a rather grand appellation for the one-room shack where both her parents spent their days and where they had undoubtedly picked up their sickness from one of their students. Her mother had become sick first. Her father had caught the jungle fever from his wife while he, Abena, and Sarah nursed her. Sarah couldn't understand why she'd been spared the sickness when so many in their village had succumbed. Her father had struggled on for over two weeks after his wife. By the end, his skin was almost translucent, his narrow face wasted. The powder Abena had given him had bought him some peace, but his body still raged like a furnace in the humid heat.

Sarah must have fallen asleep because she woke to a gentle tugging sensation on her hand.

"Sarah?" her father croaked, his claw-like hand around hers.

"I'm here, Father."

"The village, you must—"

"Shh," she soothed, passing the clean, cool cloth over the boiling skin on his forehead. "I will continue with the school, Father. I gave Mother my word, remember?" Her father had been ill the night Clara died, but he'd been at her bedside and would have heard Sarah's pledge.

He shook his head back and forth, wincing at the jerky movement as if it caused him more pain. "I want you to know—"

"What, Father? You want me to know what? What—"

Sarah's own voice woke her at this point, just as it always did. She lay in the narrow bunk, shaking and sweating with frustration and shame as she listened to the now-familiar sound of the waves on the hull of the *Golden Scythe* as the ship flew through the night.

What had her father wanted to tell her? Was he on the brink of asking for some new, even weightier commitment or would his words have been a reprieve—an absolution— from the deathbed promise she'd given her mother? Guilt joined frustration, and she groaned and turned toward the small porthole window. The light from a partial moon silvered the room and somehow soothed her churning emotions.

She calmly made a mental list of what her father might have said if he'd lived. Should she approach the missionary society and see why they'd stopped sending supplies? Try to find another benefactor altogether? Should she build a school in a neighboring village? Find a male missionary in need of a wife and cleave unto him?

This last thought gave her pause. She'd thought of it almost every day since her father had died. She needed a helpmate.

The people of her village had been kind and had helped her just as they had any other villager. Even so, Sarah had gradually realized she was not one of them. When her parents were alive—particularly her mother—Sarah had assumed the young men had given her a wide berth to avoid her parents' disapproval. But in the almost two years since her father's death not a single young man in the village had shown any interest in her.

At first she'd believed it a residual worry, but, as more and more time passed, she had to face the truth: she simply did not fit in. But she'd also not fit in with her own family. Oh, her parents had loved her, of course, but she'd seen the looks they'd exchanged when she'd said or done something the way a villager would.

Of course that begged the question—where *would* she fit in?

She turned onto her back and closed her eyes against the disturbing vision her question summoned. Her wicked mind moved stealthily to her most private thoughts via a very, very circuitous path. As usual, Martín Bouchard awaited her. He was clothed in the same silk tunic and trousers he'd worn that night. He was also aroused. However, his face wore a welcoming smile rather than a sneer of contempt. When he opened his arms, she did not hesitate to step into his warm embrace.

It was not cold, but she shivered.

Martín Bouchard was not the answer to her problem. Martín Bouchard was an entirely new set of problems.

Chapter Twelve

When Sarah showed up at Bouchard's cabin the following morning, he wasn't there. She toyed with the idea of tracking him down. How hard could it be to find him on a ship? But she decided to let him be. After all, his message was clear: he was finished with her.

Without those daily lessons, the days crawled. She spent far too much time with Graaf learning to play piquet and cribbage, arguing with him about a variety of subjects, or reading to him, which he claimed to enjoy.

"I prefer to listen to you read rather than do so myself. I cannot seem to stay awake for long when I read anything other than math books."

Sarah did not point out that he slept more often than not when she read to him.

"I'm afraid I was a poor student of anything other than numbers," he told her one day, when she'd paused during her reading so that she might take some tea and soothe her throat. "If it wasn't mathematics, I paid little attention." He took a sip of tea and then grimaced. "Bouchard's man does not care for tea, I'm afraid." He pushed his cup away. "I am spoiled, I know, but the Dutch are accustomed to the finest tea in the world." He sighed, shifting restlessly. "Tell me,

what do you think will happen when we reach England?"
It was a question he'd asked her more than once.

"You are related to royalty, Mies, in line for the crown itself. You should know of such things better than I, a mere savage from Africa."

He appeared not to hear the sarcasm in her voice. "While it is true I am related to King William and the House of Orange, we have little contact with him or any others on my father's side of the family. I was not raised with any expectation of ever having the connection acknowledged, and none of us ever thought he would end up where he is now, not after his grandfather was driven out at sword point. From stadtholder to exile to king in the course of only a few years." Graaf sighed. "All I ever wanted was to be left to my studies. I am only suited to understanding calculus." He turned a speculative look on her. "You are learned, Sarah. Have you made a study of mathematics?"

"Only the most rudimentary. My father was exposed to the work of Newton at university, but I believe he'd forgotten much of what he knew by the time I was old enough to learn."

Graaf's face had become flushed, and he didn't appear to be listening. "Will you open that trunk?" He gestured to the lovely brass-bound trunk that sat in one corner of his small room.

Sarah tugged the trunk away from the wall and unfastened the three straps. She swung open the lid. It contained a few items of clothing and some other personal items, but was mostly full of books.

"I would like the book bound in brown calfskin. There is also a small walnut box. Could you bring me a pair of spectacles? I'm afraid I need them for reading very fine print."

The box contained three pairs of spectacles. "Which pair?"

"They are all the same. I ruined my eyes when I was a boy by too much reading in the dark. It is most maddening how the functions dance on the page, and I soon get a terrible headache if I try to read without them."

Sarah stared at the spectacles, a thought in her mind. "May I borrow a pair? I've noticed lately it is something of a strain to read for very long."

"Take a pair and keep them. I find selfish comfort in the fact that I am not the only one on board with an old person's vision." He opened the book and placed the silver-framed spectacles on the bridge of his fine, aquiline nose. "See here," he said, pointing to a page filled with inexplicable figures and numbers.

Sarah listened to his enthusiastic chatter with only part of her mind. Instead she thought of the small circles of glass and fine metal, trying not to hope.

Martín was in the process of cleaning his pistols—an activity he enjoyed attending to himself—when there was a knock on the door. He squinted at the ornate timepiece on the desk. It was half past nine.

"Come," he said, expecting Beauville or Daniels. Instead it was the woman. Sarah, as he now thought of her. Which he did more often than he would have preferred, even though he was no longer closeted with her for several hours each morning.

He put the oiled pistol back in the case, watching her face as he did so. A flush spread across her cheekbones as she looked at the guns.

"Have you come looking for my pistols, *mademoiselle*?"

She cocked her head at his mocking tone and cut him a look that caused a powerful pounding in his chest. When had she begun to appear so attractive to him?

"What can I do for you, Mademoiselle Fisher?" he asked, sounding rather sharper than he'd intended.

She closed the door behind her, and Martín's eyebrows

rose. They had never been in his cabin with the door closed all the way. Except for that first night.

She reached into the pocket of her hideous brown frock and extracted something wrapped in a bit of gauze. "Here, put these on."

Martín glanced at the object in her palm and then up at her. "Spectacles?"

"Yes, it came to me this morning when Mies, that is Captain Graaf," she corrected, coloring up, "said he'd ruined his vision by straining his eyes. I thought maybe you might have strained yours at some point. Perhaps being at sea so much? I have noticed I get a headache when I am on deck and stare at the water too long." She unfolded the delicate metal and held the spectacles out. "Go ahead, try them on."

Martín looked from her face to the spectacles, several times. When he was certain she was not offering him the glasses in jest, he took them from her, hesitant to put them on. He'd always thought spectacles were hideously disfiguring.

"Put them on," she repeated, snatching a book from the shelf and placing it before him, tapping her toe with impatience.

He frowned at her. What was she up to?

She rolled her eyes and laughed. "You are as vain as a peacock."

Warmth crawled up his neck as he realized the truth of her words. He was, indeed, worried how he would appear.

"It is only I who will see you. Please, just for a moment."

He sighed irritably and placed the glasses on his face, having to push the frame all the way up the bridge of his nose so the earpieces would clasp behind his ears. He blinked at her blurry face.

"Not me, the page."

Martín glanced down at the book she'd placed on the desk

and gasped. "*Merde*," he muttered without thinking. He could see them! The individual letters, the ones she'd been forcing him to write and learn but which he could never see in the pages of a book. There they all were, arrayed on the pages before him—*m*'s and *d*'s and *s*'s and *a*'s—*all* of them. He traced a wondering finger over the page and looked over the top rim of the spectacles and met her un-blurry face. She was holding her breath, her eyebrows arched, her eyes wide and expectant.

Martín fought the urge to grab and squeeze her. And kiss her. "I can see them all," he admitted gruffly, fighting the grin that was threatening to take over his face.

She gave an ear-piercing scream and jumped up and down like a little girl. "I knew it! I knew it! I knew it!" She grabbed him in an awkward embrace, still jumping up and down as she held onto his shoulders.

Martín closed his eyes at the feel and smell of her, rocked to the core by something he could not immediately identify. A warm, soothing sensation that made him feel cherished and secure.

It was a feeling he'd experienced only once before in his life, the night he'd jumped from the second-story window of Madam Sonia's brothel. The same night he'd killed his master.

He'd been knocked almost senseless when he fell to the cobblestone courtyard, his yelp drawing the attention of the men who kept watch at the brothel entrance. He'd not gotten far before they caught him. They'd been dragging him back inside the house when an enormous shadow had loomed ahead of them.

"Well, well, well."

The doormen had stopped in their tracks at the sight of the one-eyed giant.

Even at such a moment as that, Martín hadn't been able

to help noticing the details of the man's clothing. His garments had been simple yet exquisite. And enormous.

"What have we here?" The man had examined them through the gaudiest quizzing glass Martín had ever seen. He'd looked like a golden god as he towered above them, the black patch that covered one eye the only thing that marred his otherwise perfect appearance.

"He's one of the whores, sir. Trying to escape again," the head doorman explained, giving the big man an apprehensive look.

"Escape?" the giant repeated, lowering the ridiculously ornate quizzing glass.

"He's a slave, sir, even though he don't look like one. He belongs to Madam Sonia. Or he did—she just sold him."

The man's expression didn't change, but Martín would have sworn the very air around him became colder, thicker. He wasn't the only one who noticed the change. The men tightened their grip.

"He looks most unwilling to go with you," the stranger pointed out, as if that were unusual behavior in a slave who'd been trying to escape.

"He was trying to *escape*." The doorman began to move toward the door, but the big man stepped into their path, no longer holding his quizzing glass.

"I know Madam. Quite well, in fact." His mouth twisted, as if he were enjoying a private joke. He cocked an inquiring eyebrow at Martín. "What is your name?" asked the man Martín would soon come to know as One-Eyed Standish.

Martín had muttered his name through clenched jaws, mortified he might cry out from the pain in his leg if he opened his mouth any wider.

"Unhand Martín and let him go with my crew, gentlemen." It was not a request. The giant gestured to the shadows.

"Delacroix, Van Ries, Wustenfalke, please help Martín back to the ship."

Three rough-looking men materialized from the gloom.

"Come with me," the shortest of them said, his face crosshatched with hundreds of scars.

Martín tried to move, but his captors tightened their grip.

"Let him go," the shorter man barked, far less amused than the giant who employed him. The tense silence filled with the hiss of swords leaving their scabbards.

Martín's captors released him.

"Excellent!" Standish beamed down at them, as though he'd just been dealt a particularly satisfying hand of cards. He spoke to Martín, but his solitary eye settled on the two doormen. "Run along with Delacroix. I shall take care of Madam Sonia. Come, gentlemen."

And then he'd turned and sauntered off.

"Come, you are safe, boy. The captain will deal with your mistress," Delacroix assured Martín, his face so calm and confident, Martín had been overcome by a crippling wave of an emotion he'd never felt before. And then he'd taken a step on his damaged leg and fainted dead away.

The emotion, he'd decided in the years that followed, was gratitude.

Gratitude swamped him now just as it had done all those years ago. This time he did not plunge into blessed darkness, but had to face the unnerving emotion head-on.

Sarah must have seen something on his face because she stopped squeezing him and released his arms, her own face registering shock at what she had just done. They stared at each other as she backed away.

"Tomorrow we resume our lessons?" Her voice was as shaky as his breathing.

Martín cleared his throat, stalling for time, worried his voice would come out a mere squeak if he tried to use it.

She opened the door a crack. "I shall see you first thing tomorrow." The door clicked shut on the last word.

"Tomorrow," he repeated to the empty room. He took off the glasses and stared at the cabin door, his entire being pulsing with gratitude—and something even more foreign. An emotion he had no name for and one he'd never experienced before.

Chapter Thirteen

The lessons sped past quickly and pleasurably, if not necessarily quietly. Sarah and Bouchard still squabbled several times a day, but usually over minor matters, and quills and inkwells no longer ended up on the floor.

Sarah rejoiced at Bouchard's nimble, hungry mind. When she came into his cabin each morning it was to find books and paper scattered over not only his desk but also the dining table and small nightstand. Watching him discover the joy of books was like rediscovering them herself, all over again.

His progress was doubly amazing given that he was learning in English, rather than his native French. She could not believe that he'd managed so long without books. With a mind as sharp as his, he must have suffered without the stimulation words and language offered. It broke her heart to know that most of his crew could not read either and would probably never have the chance to learn. An idea began to form in her head, and she resolved to tell him of it when he was in a receptive frame of mind.

The opportunity came one morning after they'd just finished a satisfying lesson about verbs. His mood was uncharacteristically placid, and Sarah decided the time was as good as any.

"Do you have a few minutes, Captain?"

"Hmm?" He glanced up from his writing, his golden eyes magnified by the delicate spectacles.

Even after hours and hours together, the sight of his beautiful face was able to rob her of breath.

"You wish to speak to me, *mademoiselle*?" He laid down his quill and carefully removed his glasses before looking up at her. A small line formed between his stunning eyes as he waited.

Sarah ignored her body's inconvenient reaction. "Yes, just for a few minutes, if you don't mind."

"I am at your service, *mademoiselle.*"

"I was wondering if you would permit me to read to your men."

His dark blond brows arched. "Read to my men?"

"Yes. I've noticed there are large parts of the day when they are busy with tasks that would be more pleasant with a little distraction."

"You wish to give my men a distraction?" His piercing eyes flickered down over her neck and bodice before returning to her face.

Her anger flared. "I want to *read* to them, Captain."

He laughed and held up his hands. "Please, do not bite off my head. What would you like to . . . distract them with?"

Sarah turned to his bookshelf and pulled *Gulliver's Travels* from it. He put on his glasses and looked at the cover.

"Gull . . . Gull 'I'?" He stopped and looked at her, confused.

"Gulliver. The 'I' is soft."

"What is this book?"

"It's an adventure novel."

He opened the cover and squinted at something on the flyleaf.

"What is it?"

He showed her the book. There was something written in

a lovely, bold hand on the flyleaf. "What does it say? It is too difficult to read," he said.

"It says: To my friend Martín, who occasionally makes me glad I did not kill him on our own long voyages. Signed—"

Bouchard laughed. "It is my friend One-Eyed Standish. You do not need to tell me that," he said, still chuckling.

"He has signed it 'Hugh Redvers.'" She handed the book back to him.

"Yes, he is the Baron Ramsay, Hugh Redvers, *and* One-Eyed Standish. He is a big man and carries many names with ease."

"He must know you very well."

Bouchard looked up from the book at her not-so-subtle comment and waved a chiding finger at her. "Oh, *mademoiselle,* that was very ill done of you."

"Perhaps, but that does not make it any less true. I'm glad to know I'm not the only one who has considered grievous bodily harm from time to time."

He grinned and looked down at the book.

"You were on his ship before you acquired the *Scythe?*" she asked.

"I was on the *Batavia's Ghost* for almost seven years. I started out peeling potatoes and cleaning the head. But not at the same time," he added with a playful look that made her heart thrash like an animal in a snare. "I was his second mate by the time we captured the *Scythe*."

"He is a great friend of yours?"

He nodded slowly, his eyes still on the copperplate writing, as if he saw something else in the inscription. "There is nobody else quite like him." He looked up, his eyes distant. "He saved me."

"Oh?" She wondered how far she could pry. "How did he do that?"

Bouchard's eyes sharpened, and he snapped the book

shut, his face closing just as quickly. "You may read to the men so long as they work. If I see they are neglecting their chores, the reading will stop."

Sarah sighed and took the book. "Thank you, Captain."

He opened the door for her, shutting it quickly behind her.

The man was a mystery Sarah burned to solve. She flopped down on her hard bunk and closed her eyes. Why was she such a fool? He'd showed her in every way possible that he had no interest in her as a woman or a person. She suspected Bouchard didn't actually think of women as people. The thought should enrage or disgust her, but it only made her more curious. Why couldn't she transfer her affections to somebody more worthy? Somebody like Daniels, who respected her and cared about her comfort and well-being? The answer to that question was easy: she was a weak, besotted, heartsick fool.

The men performed their less taxing jobs during the heat of the day. That afternoon Sarah told Mr. Daniels what she'd planned, assuring him that she had Bouchard's approval. He located a chair and placed it beside a group of men who were repairing rope and sails, which seemed to be never-ending chores.

They clambered to their feet when Sarah approached. "Please, do not get up." She held up the book. "I thought I would read to you while you worked. I have found listening to a story makes doing tedious tasks more enjoyable."

The men gaped, as if she'd just told them she'd come to instruct them in needlepoint and ballroom dancing.

Sarah lowered her head and fumbled with the book. What impulse had possessed her to think a bunch of hardened sailors would enjoy a children's book?

She began to read.

The next time she looked up, a quarter of an hour later, several others had drifted over. One man was dismantling and cleaning a large piece of machinery, while one of the galley hands was peeling potatoes.

Daniels hovered off to one side to ensure nobody offered her any discourtesy. Sarah looked around at the collection of hardened, interested faces and smiled. She doubted she would have to worry about a lack of courtesy.

Between teaching Bouchard, reading to the crew, and entertaining the recovering Graaf, Sarah had little time to brood about her situation. It was not until they approached Tenerife, where they would stop to resupply and make some repairs, that she realized time was flying. She needed to give some thought to her plans.

She longed to talk to Bouchard about the matter, but she was still less than comfortable with him even though they no longer spent their daily lessons fighting. Unlike Mies, who was almost lighthearted in spite of his situation, Bouchard seemed determined to maintain a distance between them.

When he wasn't ignoring her, he behaved like an arrogant, conceited beast. He was easily the vainest person she'd ever met. And rude, she mustn't forget rudeness. He reveled in being rude. The only good thing she could say was that he didn't limit his obnoxious treatment to her. He took particular delight in tormenting Mies. Sarah was ashamed to admit she took a certain degree of satisfaction from his mocking persecution of the Dutchman. Yet another reason to dislike Bouchard—the ease with which he managed to bring her down to his childish, unchristian, and vindictive level.

Sarah sighed as she tied the end of her plait with a frayed piece of ribbon, grateful she didn't have a glass in her small cabin. Not that she needed a mirror with Bouchard around.

After their lesson had finished yesterday, she'd expressed her eagerness to explore her first port of call today. Bouchard had responded with his usual insensitivity.

"There are several dressmakers there. I trust you will be able to acquire something less hideous to wear."

Sarah had stopped what she'd been doing—mending yet another quill for him, because he was too clumsy and rough on them—and gaped at him in disbelief.

It had taken at least a full moment of frigid silence before he'd noticed her glare.

"What?" he demanded, looking annoyingly clueless.

"Why must you say such hurtful things?"

He lifted his hands and shrugged his shoulders. "What hurtful things? About your frock, you mean?"

"Yes, 'about my frock.'" She mimicked his accent and perplexed tone even though she knew it was childish.

He laughed. "That is a very good imitation of me, *mademoiselle*. Are you trying to say something hurtful?" he asked, mimicking her in return. Sarah couldn't help laughing at his pursed lips and artificially high voice.

"I do not sound like that. You are a vile beast." She shook her head, annoyed at her inability to stay angry with him.

"Why? Because I would have you wear something less"—his brow wrinkled as he searched for the correct word—"unattractive?" His eyes swept up and down her body in a way calculated to make her temperature rise.

"Why should you care what I wear?" She finished the quill and slammed the small knife down on his desk, barely missing his hand. "Here is your quill, your highness. Next time *you* may fix your own."

He moved the knife out of her reach. "I don't understand what I have said that is so insulting. You should want to look more attractive for those around you. Why wear such a horrible gown when you can have something that makes you look nicer?"

It hurt beyond reason that he thought she needed a new gown to make her attractive. "I don't have any money to buy a gown with, you idiot!" She sprang up, eager to leave him before she said or did something she regretted.

He was on his feet and at the door before her, blocking her exit.

"Stop a minute," he said, taking her gently by the shoulders. "Why are you so angry? Is it because I have insulted you? Or because you have no money to buy yourself something pretty?" He didn't wait for an answer. "You should not be foolish. I am very happy to buy you something to wear—any dresses you desire, in fact." His glorious eyes were gentle, almost pitying, as they roamed her face. Knowing what he was seeing—her plain face and skinny body—was like a kick to her stomach. A cruel vision of him embracing a woman equal in beauty to his own flashed through her mind, and she stiffened, recalling how this man preferred to take his pleasure.

"Thank you, but I am not some . . . *whore* to be purchased by pretty baubles. I'll not take any charity from you, Captain."

Bouchard flinched as though she'd struck him. His full lips thinned, and his eyes narrowed to slits. He reached an arm around her, the motion bringing their faces close. "Oh, *mademoiselle,* trust me," he said in a voice that was like silk over iron, "you would not be taking charity. You would be doing us *all* a favor by making yourself more attractive." He opened the door. "Please, don't let me keep you."

His smirking face blurred, and she blinked rapidly.

"You are odious beyond belief." She had shoved past him and stormed toward her cabin, grinding her teeth at the sound of his laughter behind her. He was nothing but a vain, arrogant *whore-mongering* swine.

Sarah's jaw firmed as she recalled his humiliating treatment yesterday, and she yanked on the worn cotton gloves that had come in the admiral's small bundle of used clothes. Yesterday was the last time she would be kind to Bouchard. Oh, she would continue his lessons; she owed him that much. But yesterday would be the last time she allowed him to get under her skin.

The next time anyone's skin was invaded, it would be *his*.

Chapter Fourteen

Martín was conferring with Beauville when they came into the harbor at Tenerife. They would be stopping for a few days, and there was the usual business of determining shore leave and arranging for repairs. By the time Martín went below deck, Sarah was not in her cabin. He pushed back his hat and scratched his head. Clearly she was still angry from yesterday.

He leaned against the doorframe and chewed the inside of his cheek. Her comment about whores hadn't been directed against him or his sordid past, of course, but that hadn't seemed to matter. He'd responded to her expression of distaste like a maddened dog, snapping and snarling. It was not until he was tossing and turning and failing to find sleep that he'd finally admitted the truth. He didn't know why or when it had happened, but the plain missionary woman's opinion of him mattered. When he thought about his past, and what she'd do if she knew about it, his chest became heavy with a toxic blend of fear, anger, and apprehension.

He closed the door to her empty cabin, wishing he could do the same with his thoughts. The Dutchman's door was closed. Was she in there? He was at the door before he even knew he'd moved. He pressed his ear against the thick wood. No sound came from the other side. Were they in there together? Were they—

He yanked open the door.

The Dutchman yelped and dropped the book he'd been reading. Fear, surprise, resignation, and finally humor settled on his face. "Captain Bouchard, what a pleasure," he said flatly. He picked up his book and looked at Martín over a pair of spectacles that were identical to the ones Martín wore—something that had irked him almost beyond reason when he'd found out. His first stop today would be a shop he'd visited often over the years. The last time he'd been on the island he'd brought his spyglass for repair. He could only hope the man also sold spectacles so he could return the pair he'd been using to the Dutch slaver.

Martín raked the blond man with a look that held all the contempt he felt. "I see you are dressed. Are you going someplace?"

The Dutchman smiled easily in return, far more confident now that he was not in danger of dying at any moment—at least not from his illness. "I'd hoped I might be allowed a little time on shore."

"You hoped that, did you? And why should I let a prisoner have shore leave?"

The Dutchman flushed, but refused to rise to the bait. "Oh, come, Captain. What harm can it do? You have my word as a gentleman I will not try to escape. In fact, why may I not go with you? Or had you other plans? Perhaps you'd hoped to accompany Sarah?" His grin was sly, as if he knew something Martín did not. Martín wrestled with the same desire that threatened to overtake him whenever he was in the Dutch nobleman's presence: the desire to toss him overboard.

Graaf smirked at him. "I'm afraid you are too late. Sarah has gone off with Daniels. That would be your fault, Captain. You gave him shore leave, I believe?" He shrugged one of his slim shoulders. "Of course you can always leave me here. I shall be glad to pass along any message you have for Sarah when she returns."

It galled Martín to succumb to such an obvious ploy, but the thought of Sarah spending time alone with the idiot Dutchman galled him even more. It was better to take the fool with him. He certainly was not concerned about Graaf's slipping off to freedom. That would actually be a bloody godsend, as Martín could then sail off and leave him here.

"I am leaving in five minutes. If you are not ready, you can stay in your cabin."

Graaf sprang to his feet. "I am ready right now, Captain." He snatched up his coat and shrugged himself into it easily.

The Dutchman had lost weight, but Martín grudgingly admitted the man still looked well in his impeccably tailored garments, a realization that made him want to murder him even more.

He strode from the cabin, not caring whether Graaf kept up or not. "I have several errands," he flung over his shoulder. "So you'd best reconcile yourself to the fact that this won't be a pleasure journey."

"Any time not spent in my cabin will be a pleasure journey, Captain," Graaf contradicted, breathing heavily as he all but sprinted to keep pace.

"Beauville!" Martín's bellow drew his first mate's attention away from the cluster of men awaiting their shore leave assignments.

"Yes, Captain?"

"I'm taking Captain Graaf out of his kennel for a little walk. Give me one of those men to accompany us. I'd hate to find myself suddenly overpowered and thrown into the bay by the good captain." The men roared, and even the somber Beauville cracked a smile.

Martín left the ship with Graaf and a large, quiet black man known only as Banks. All Martín knew about Banks was that he was an escaped slave. The only reason he knew even that much was because Banks had volunteered the information to Beauville before he'd been hired. Martín didn't know whom he'd escaped from or how he'd done it, and he didn't care. As he knew only too well, the last thing an escaped slave enjoyed was questions about his life as another man's chattel.

The three men made their way through the crush of people who milled between the harbor and the small town.

"What is our first destination, Captain?" The Dutchman's voice was breathy as he tried to keep pace with Martín's aggressive stride. Banks kept up the rear, his eyes on the prisoner. Martín was not worried Graaf would try to escape; he'd just wanted to humiliate the man by assigning him a guard as if he were a common prisoner. Graaf seemed unaware of Martín's intention and looked around with open curiosity, clearly pleased at having gotten off the ship.

"We are going to an optical shop."

"Are you purchasing something or having something repaired?"

Martín stopped suddenly, and Graaf careened into him. "If you plan on babbling like a woman the entire time, I'll have Mr. Banks gag you or take you back to the ship." Martín secretly wished to see the former scenario.

Graaf smiled, as if there were nothing he liked better than being threatened. "My apologies, Captain. I didn't realize we were engaged in a mission requiring secrecy."

Martín resumed his journey without comment, more than a little disappointed the Dutchman was proving so difficult to provoke.

The optics shop was in a small building at the very end of the main commercial street. Martín had been coming here for years and had purchased his first sextant from the old Scotsman who owned the shop.

A small, stooped man came out of a back room to greet

them as soon as they opened the door. His gnomish face broke into a genuine smile. "Ah, Captain Bouchard, what a pleasure to see you again. It has been too long." He extended a small, bent hand.

"*Bonjour,* Monsieur Farquhar. And how is your business?" The old man's fingers felt like a bundle of dry, fragile twigs, and Martín was glad when he could let go of them.

"Oh, excellent, excellent. You've brought friends, I see?" The Scotsman peered up at the spindly Dutchman and hulking black man.

"This is Captain Graaf and Mr. Banks, one of my crew."

"Welcome, gentlemen. Feel free to look around and ask me any questions."

A long pause followed as Graaf and Banks stared at Martín.

He sighed, realizing he couldn't keep the object of his visit a secret. He was also cheered by the fact that the old man was wearing glasses. "I am here to inquire about a pair of spectacles."

Farquhar nodded. "You have developed a problem seeing things up close?" Martín's surprise must have shown on his face. "Oh, it is nothing unusual, I assure you. All the greatest men wear them if they are lucky to live so long. Even your Mr. Jefferson wears spectacles," he added, as if Martín would be comforted by the knowledge that an American slave owner was similarly afflicted with poor vision. Martín let the comment pass, for the moment more interested in the issue of his vision than a disputation on slavery.

"This is a common problem, then?"

"Oh yes. Come with me."

Martín scowled at Graaf when he made to follow, and the Dutchman held up his hands and turned away to look at a display of spyglasses.

Farquhar led Martín to an ornate glass case at the back of his shop. Inside the case were dozens of pairs of glasses. The old Scotsman opened the cabinet and extracted four pairs from different trays, setting them out on a piece of velvet.

"There are different strengths. You are young, almost too young to need them, but a person never knows. Take me for instance—I have worn spectacles all my life. These I have on were invented by the brilliant Doctor Franklin." He gestured to his glasses, which had a curious split across the middle. "These are for people who need help seeing both close and far. That is not what you need, I think. Here try these first." He opened a pair and handed them to Martín, and they proceeded to narrow the choices with a series of simple reading tests.

When Martín saw the vision charts he almost wept with relief. Thank God—or Sarah—he was able to recognize the letters Farquhar set before him. It would have been most embarrassing if he'd had to confess he was unable to read.

After Farquhar had determined which pair best suited him, Martín bought three pairs, hating to think he would ever again not be able to see well enough to read. The old Scotsman was well pleased with the sale and escorted the men to the door while thanking Martín profusely the entire way.

Graaf turned to Martín as they descended the shop steps. "I am famished. Could we stop and eat or do you need to finish your errands first?"

Martín's first impulse was to argue with Graaf, but he was also hungry. Nor did he have any pressing errands. The truth was, he had looked forward to showing Sarah the first town of any size she'd ever visited. He'd hoped to spend the day with her, perhaps taking her to dine.

He frowned as yesterday's unpleasant and confusing interaction replayed itself yet again in his mind. Why did his offering to purchase her something to wear make her so angry? Did not *all* women enjoy gifts, or was it really only whores who liked to receive presents? The disdain in her voice when she'd spoken the word "whore" echoed through him and made his stomach clench. It was better this way, even if it meant he was stuck with the idiot Graaf as a dinner companion.

"The Hotel Saint Frances offers excellent food," Martín said abruptly, turning in the direction of the elegant establishment where he'd last dined with Standish and several other men from the crew of the *Batavia's Ghost*.

"You are a well-traveled man, Captain Bouchard. How long have you been at sea?"

Was the Dutchman getting at something? Martín gave the shorter man a hard look.

No, Graaf appeared as vapid as he normally did.

"I've been at sea since I was sixteen, more or less."

"More or less?"

"Yes, more or less, Captain Graaf. As I'm sure you know, I began my life as a slave. Nobody cares what year a slave was born—or at least nobody ever bothered to inform me. While that adds a degree of mystery to my past that charms the ladies, it does make it difficult for me to truthfully state my age."

Graaf's mouth snapped shut, and the rest of the short walk took place in silence.

The Hotel Saint Frances was the only establishment of its kind on the island. It had been in business for perhaps fifteen years and catered to the wealthier element on the island as well as the officers of various navies. Even English vessels frequented the Canaries during the war, something of a miracle considering the fact that Nelson had left the island in disgrace—and minus one arm—the last time the British had tried to capture it.

Herr Dietzel, the rotund, rosy-cheeked proprietor, bustled over to greet them, his face beaming. "Captain Bouchard, what a pleasure to see you again!"

"*Bonjour,* Monsieur Dietzel. It has been a long time, my friend. Do you have any food left for me and my companions?"

Dietzel chortled. "Always! You are here for a while perhaps?" The older man shuffled ahead of them into the dining room.

"Only a few days. I'm afraid I have urgent business in England. Would you mind holding this package for me while we dine?" Martín handed him the box that held his new spectacles.

"It will be a pleasure, Captain. So, you are off to England, yes? Perhaps you will see Captain Standish? I understand he lives there now and has given up his mistress for a wife, eh?"

Martín sat in one of the ornate gilt chairs. "Yes, Standish is married and rather settled. I daresay he will not be making this journey anytime soon."

"Please give him my best when you next see him. Now, shall I send you a bottle of something wonderful that I have recently procured?"

"Yes, I leave the selection entirely up to you; the food as well." Martín breathed a sigh of relief when the garrulous Prussian left.

"You are a popular man here, Captain Bouchard," Graaf noted.

Martín snapped the white linen napkin and laid it across his lap. "Here in the uncivilized wilderness, a man's actions are far more important than his lineage, Graaf."

"Touché, Captain. Perhaps we could call a truce to our sparring for the time being? Maybe only so long as we share a meal together?"

Martín shrugged. He was tired of baiting the man in any case. Graaf was far too easy game. "Very well, a truce. I gather you have not been in the Canaries before?"

"No, I have actually been to very few places. This was my first voyage. My eldest brother captained the *Blue Bird* until we stopped at Gibraltar, where another of my father's ships was in for repairs."

Herr Dietzel appeared with a bottle of red wine and poured a sample into Martín's glass. Martín took a sip and nodded, and the Prussian filled the other men's glasses.

Graaf's eyes lingered on Banks, as if sharing a bottle of wine with a black man made him uneasy. The Dutchman wasn't the only one. Patrons at a nearby table were muttering and giving their table angry looks.

Banks turned to Martín and began to stand. "I'll go wait outside, Captain."

"Nonsense, Mr. Banks. We came here to eat. We will eat, all of us."

Banks sat, his face impassive, but concern rolling off him in waves.

For his part, Martín was beginning to get the light, almost dizzy sensation he usually experienced right before he engaged in violence.

Graaf looked from Banks to Martín, his angelic features equal parts worry and confusion. Martín smiled at the Dutchman's discomfort. It was clear he'd never experienced the invigorating sensation currently flooding Martín's body.

The only other man Martín had met who'd understand his blind fury on the issue of slavery was Standish. It had always intrigued Martín that such a cultured and well-bred man could suffer from the same uncontrollable anger as an ex-slave whore.

Unfortunately, a major difference between Martín and his mentor was Ramsay's ability to recognize the feeling and stop it. Well, at least some of the time.

Martín sipped his wine and chatted with Graaf, nodding at whatever he said without listening. The four men at the other table were becoming increasingly agitated by the presence of a black man in the dining room. Too bad they didn't realize there were really *two* black men polluting the dining room.

Martín was close to coming apart at the seams when one of the men stood, his friends muttering angry encouragement as he stalked over to their table.

"What's he doing in here?" the man demanded, interrupting something Graaf had been saying.

Martín glanced up as if he'd only just then noticed the man. He was as big as Martín, but perhaps a few years older. He had the brown, battered face of a sailor, but wore expensive, if tasteless clothing. Martín raised his eyebrows. "I beg your pardon?"

"I *said*, what makes you think you can bring him in here?" he repeated, his face darkening at having to repeat himself.

"I did not bring him in here; he brought himself in here."

The man's face contorted. "You know what I mean. His kind isn't allowed in here."

"His kind?" Martín set down his glass and scratched his forehead.

Herr Dietzel appeared, his cherubic face tense. "Excuse me, gentlemen. Is there a problem?" His protuberant blue eyes swung from Martín to the man hovering over him.

"This gentleman says my friend is not allowed in here." Martín turned to the Dutchman. "It appears he does not care for Dutchmen, Captain Graaf. I think he wants you to leave."

Graaf's jaw dropped.

"You know damn well I don't mean him. Do you think I'm some kind of fool?" The thug's face was dangerously red.

Martín shoved back his chair and stood. The other man took a step back as Martín shrugged out of his coat.

"Will you please hold this?"

The stunned Prussian took the garment without speaking.

Martín turned to face his aggressor, who'd swelled up like a poison-spitting toad. "No," Martín said, giving his shirt cuff a minute adjustment. "I do not *think* you are a fool. I *know* you are one."

Martín saw the punch coming before the man even knew he'd swung his arm. He ducked the roundhouse swing and jabbed the sluggish man twice in his side, doubling him over and then capping him off with a powerful left to his jaw. The big man's body hit the floor so hard that dust puffed up from the gaps in the wood flooring, and cutlery, china, and crystal jumped on tables twenty feet in any direction.

Martín looked down at the groaning lump at his feet, adjusting his cuffs again as he waited for the man's three friends to make up their minds.

They did not disappoint.

The men rose up like a single organism and clambered toward him, knocking aside chairs and tables in their clumsy fury, leaving shattered glass and clattering silverware in their wake.

Martín turned to the horrified Prussian. "Please take my coat somewhere safe, Herr Dietzel," he murmured, as Banks rushed to greet the first of the aggressors. "I should hate for it to get soiled."

The big ex-slave punched the closest man in the face with a fist as large and heavy as a twelve-pound shot. The man was teetering drunkenly when Banks hit him with a full-body slam that threw him back a good ten feet to his now empty dinner table.

Banks straightened and turned just in time to dodge a chair and then marched implacably toward the next man.

Martín's new opponent was smaller and lighter than he, but exceptionally quick. He danced and bobbed in a manner that told Martín he'd done his share of sparring, if not actual fighting.

They exchanged a few jabs while Martín took his measure. It didn't take him long to assess his opponent. His moves were predictable, obviously learned in some gentleman's salon.

He displayed a fundamental knowledge of pugilism, but he lacked cunning, something Martín possessed in abundance.

Still, it was enjoyable to have such a sparring partner, and Martín took his time, harrying the man with small, quick jabs rather than laying him out. He realized he'd toyed with him too long when the sound of a breaking glass came from behind him.

He turned to find Graaf holding a broken bottle, his gaze fixed on the prone figure of the first man who'd attacked Martín. The fellow had clearly been about to rejoin the fray before the Dutchman intervened. Graaf looked up at Martín and his opponent, both of whom had frozen.

"I am hungry, Captain Bouchard. Would you please conclude your business?" Graaf asked coolly. He laid the broken bottle carefully on the table and picked up his glass of wine. Only the slight shaking of the glass gave away what his violent action had cost him.

Martín laughed and turned back just in time to take a punishing blow to his chin rather than the side of his head. He staggered and hit the table before bouncing back up, his mouth filling with the metallic taste of blood. He swallowed and shook his head to clear it.

He smiled at the other man with genuine admiration. "That was a damned good hit."

The other man reacted to his praise by roaring and charging, his blind rage robbing him of any science.

"I'm sorry, my friend," Martín apologized before ducking under the other man's slack guard and punching him so hard in the side he heard the crack of a rib. The man yowled and clutched his side, the action giving Martín wide-open access to his face.

Martín obliged him with the requisite blow and watched him fall.

"We should leave, Captain," Banks said from behind him.

Martín turned around, seeing for the first time the room full of horrified diners.

He needed to catch his breath before he could speak. He smiled up at the bigger man, who was breathing normally. "We have yet to eat, Mr. Banks. If there is one thing you should know about me, it is that I become irritable when I am hungry." He waved to Dietzel, who scurried over still holding his jacket.

Martín donned the garment and dropped into his chair. "Herr Dietzel, pray add any damages to my bill. Before you do so, however, could you remove these men so we might eat in peace?" He gestured to the bodies of the four men; two of the men were moaning loudly.

Dietzel was a wizard. Bodies were removed, their table was reset, and a fresh bottle delivered in a remarkably short time. While they waited for their food to arrive, Martín looked at the Dutchman.

"I give you my thanks, Captain Graaf. You behaved with remarkable aplomb. I gather this is not a common experience for you?"

Graaf laughed, the sound as shaky as his hands. His thin nostrils were pinched, and the flags of color on his pale cheeks told louder than words how much the action had cost him. "I daresay the same cannot be said for you, Captain Bouchard."

Martín shrugged. "I've been known to get my hands dirty when the occasion demands it." He glanced at Banks. The only sign he'd just engaged in a fight was the torn knuckles on the big hand that rested on the table.

Although Banks didn't show it, Martín knew he was probably as upset as the Dutchman and would have preferred to avoid the scuffle altogether. Martín would wager Banks was a member of the "turn the other cheek" school of thought, a group Martín had never been able to understand.

Graaf suddenly shot to his feet, his eyes on something over Martín's shoulder.

Martín sighed. What now? More friends of the four men they'd just put down? It was going to be a long afternoon.

He was about to turn around when a familiar voice rang out behind him.

"What in the world has happened here?"

Chapter Fifteen

Sarah entered the most beautiful building she'd seen in her life only to find Bouchard and Graaf and the sailor named Banks sitting in the midst of a dining room that looked as if it had been attacked by a small army.

Mies's open mouth and round eyes gave Sarah a moment of gratification, but the expression on Captain Bouchard's face was beyond price. His golden eyes swept over her not once or even twice, but three times. Most satisfying of all was the way his mouth hung open before he recalled himself and shut it.

"May we join you?" She glanced around at the sea of destruction. "That is, if there are any chairs left that are not broken."

Graaf leapt up. "Take mine."

Bouchard eyed the Dutchman as if he were a noxious smell.

"Here you go, Miss Fisher." Daniels seized a chair from a nearby table and hovered, an uncertain look on his boyish features when he realized she'd already taken the Dutchman's chair.

"Give Graaf the chair and get another for yourself, Daniels," Bouchard ordered, not looking at her.

Sarah smirked. It no longer mattered to her *what* he said

or did. The memory of his earlier reaction would be with her for a long, long time.

She was not a vain person, but even she had had a difficult time looking away from her reflection in the small dress shop mirror.

Daniels had located the shop for her and then escorted her there first thing when they came ashore. Sarah had been the only customer that early in the day, and the two French sisters who owned the shop had both come out to greet her and take her back for a fitting.

"I'll wait for you out here, Miss Fisher." Daniels had motioned to a small waiting room, complete with reading material, a platter of biscuits, and a comfortable chair.

"No, you must leave her with us," one of the women said. They were identical twins, or at least near enough. "This is no place for a man," the other added, escorting Daniels to the door. "Come back for her just before luncheon," she said, shutting the door in his surprised face.

When the women learned Sarah had arrived on Captain Bouchard's ship, they'd hung the *Closed* sign in the window, ordered a full tea from their servant, and pulled Sarah into the back room. "We must know everything about you and the delectable captain."

They'd proceeded to extract every detail about Sarah's life to date, including the little she knew of Captain Bouchard. The sisters, like everyone else in the world, had heard of Bouchard even though they'd only seen him from afar.

"He is beautiful, that one, eh, Arlette?" the one named Adele asked.

"*Oui!* So exotic! So virile!" She nudged Sarah in the ribs. "You will need something special to keep that one's attention, I think."

"His attention is not mine to keep," Sarah protested. "Nor is any other part of him."

The sisters ignored her, instead rooting through the large

rack of ready-made garments. "You have a beautiful figure—so tall and thin—no corset for you, eh?" Arlette had a remarkably ribald laugh for such a small woman.

Sarah's ears burned. "I've only borrowed enough money for one dress," she said, watching in dismay as the women began creating a huge pile of garments.

Adele waved away her words as if they were a bothersome fly. "Don't be a silly girl. You cannot live with only one dress. Especially not on a ship filled with men. You can send us payment after you reach your family."

"But I told you, I don't know if I *have* any family left. Even if I do, I cannot assume they will be in a position to give me money. Really, I—"

"You belong to a wealthy family—I know it." Adele closed her eyes as she spoke, as if prognosticating. "They will be delighted to have you back."

Arlette nodded. "Yes, you must have several dresses. It is a shame you are not here longer. We will have to alter what we have instead of making something just for you."

Sarah had protested over and over, but they had ignored her.

"We are giving you these dresses because we wish to do so. If you cannot pay?" Arlette flicked her wrist in a gesture that was richly dismissive. "Bah! It is nothing to us. We have no daughters or nieces of our own, and our father left us well provided for. We have never needed to take a man as husband. Only to bed, eh, Adele?"

They cackled and then went on to list their multiple lovers and describe them in fascinating, but excruciating detail. Both of them offered unsolicited advice on how to capture Captain Bouchard and what to do with him once she had him.

Sarah learned more in a few hours about men and their various uses than she'd learned in all her previous years. She was convinced her face was a permanent shade of red.

Instead, when she gazed in the mirror, she looked almost pretty. They'd trimmed, curled, crimped, and arranged her hair high on her head and forced a string of pearls on her, complete with matching bracelet.

"It's only paste, my dear. Besides, neither of us are the type who can wear pearls," Adele had explained when Sarah demurred.

"We are too wicked," Arlette had agreed through a mouthful of pins, which she was using to mark the dress Sarah was wearing.

The women had compensated for her above-average height by quickly adding several flounces to the hem. Oh, and the fabric—it was delectable enough to eat. It was a peachy pink muslin that made Sarah's hair look tawny rather than mousy brown. The ensemble also made her very small breasts seem prominent, if not actually larger. In fact, they looked so prominent she was concerned. The women had waved away her concerns.

"You do not need stays for your very slim waist, but a corset is helpful in other ways." They'd cinched her into a beautiful pink undergarment that pushed up her small breasts until they were two creamy swells.

After seeing the reactions of Daniels, Bouchard, Graaf, and even the usually shy and retiring Mr. Banks, Sarah could not feel sorry she'd allowed herself to be laced into the tight corset. For the first time in her life, she felt pretty.

The meal passed far too quickly. Even with the dining room in shambles, it was still the most elegant experience she'd ever had. Graaf was amusing and engaging, Daniels sweet and friendly, and even the reticent Banks spoke a word or two, coming out of his shell for a brief time. Everyone looked happy except for Bouchard, who maintained a grim silence throughout the meal. Sarah refused to let his sullenness dampen her excitement about dining in a hotel and wearing a new dress. And it wasn't her *only* new dress, either.

"We will work like women possessed and send the other gowns to the ship before it departs."

"Are you sure I can't—"

Arlette made a firm chopping motion with one hand. "I'm sure you can hem a straight seam, but you will not do so on these dresses. You are only here for a short while. You must see the island and enjoy yourself."

"You can join us for tea tomorrow if you find yourself with some time."

"But your evenings you should reserve for the delicious Bouchard." Arlette placed the back of her hand on her forehead and feigned a swoon.

Sarah had quickly made her first adult female friends since leaving her village and would just as quickly have to leave them.

Sarah was in her cabin unpacking several other items the French women had pressed upon her as well as a small leather-bound dictionary she'd found at the tiny island bookstore, when the door to the cabin flew open. Bouchard swept inside without asking permission and slammed the door behind him.

"What is it?" she asked, alarmed.

"What is it? What *is* it?" Scornful disbelief disfigured his handsome face. "Did Daniels buy you that dress?"

If not the last thing she'd expected him to say, it was a close second. "What?"

"That dress you are wearing—those pearls, did Daniels buy them for you?"

"No, he did not," she stammered before she could help it.

"Where did you get the money?"

She frowned. "Not that it is any of your business, but Mies—"

"Mies? *Mies!*" His voice shook the room, and his eyes went wide like those of a crazy person.

Sarah held up her hands. "Goodness, Captain Bouchard, would you please lower your voice before the entire ship discovers you are in my cabin."

His eyes narrowed until they were yellow slits. "Oh, and that would concern you, would it? Who do you want in here, eh? *Mies*, perhaps?"

She gasped. "Are you demented?"

He was on her in an instant, moving in the quick, silent manner she'd seen several times before. He pinned her in the narrow space between the cot and wardrobe. "So, you are thinking to capture yourself a nobleman?"

She had to replay the words several times before she understood. "You . . . you . . . odious, arrogant—"

His mouth crushed, and his tongue stabbed. It was not a kiss, but rather a declaration of war, an all-out offensive with one objective: domination.

Her body rejoiced at his touch.

But her mind was still stunned by his anger. What had he meant? Why had he been so furious? Something told her she needed to find out.

She somehow dredged up the will to resist; she clamped her lips shut and pushed as hard as she could on his chest. His body didn't budge, but his head jerked back, an odd look in his eyes. His breaths came in short blasts, and his jaw worked, as if he were chewing something indigestible. Before Sarah could think of something to say or do, his lids dropped, and he lowered his mouth again.

She assumed the same defensive posture, but the onslaught never came. Instead, her traitorous body swayed toward him and met his halfway, as if pulled by an invisible string.

His lips were soft and teasing, the light flick of his tongue on the seam of her mouth tantalizing rather than assaulting.

His body was heavy and hard against her, but his hands—oh, they held her head so very lightly, as if she were breakable.

She opened to him, unable to resist the invitation in his kisses. Her entire body began to melt, a slow, warm collapse of resistance that left her too weak to move.

Don't do this, her mind shrieked. But the warning voice faded without any echo as his tongue slid between her lips. Sarah sighed at the gentle, inexorable invasion and pressed her body against his, opening her mouth to take him deeper. She stroked the side of his face, marveling at the flexing of muscles beneath smooth, warm skin as he angled his head and delved deeper. He murmured at her stroking and pressed his hips against her stomach. Sarah shivered against his hardness. He was aroused for her—only her. She slid her hands around his neck and pulled him closer, rubbing against him as if she could merge their bodies by pressing hard enough.

His hands roamed the sides of her torso, hot even through the fabric of her gown. He grazed the tops of her exposed breasts with a maddeningly light touch. She pushed herself into his hands and grew bolder, exploring the wet heat of his mouth more deeply, her tongue tangling with his before she captured him and sucked.

A low, animal growl rumbled in his chest, the sound primitive and intense. Her body responded with a hot pounding need that turned her bones to water.

A hand grazed the bare skin of her thighs, and Sarah startled. The voice that had been muffled by desire rose again to the surface. He'd managed to insinuate himself beneath her skirts without her even noticing.

"Captain—"

"Martín," he murmured, taking her lower lip in his mouth and gently sucking it before running a path of kisses across her cheek, stopping at her ear. "Say it," he ordered softly.

The name fit him perfectly—exotic and beautiful. "Martín."

Her voice was so throaty and low she wasn't sure it was really her speaking.

"I want to give you pleasure, Sarah, and your body needs release. Tell me, do you want me to stop? You only need to say stop, and I will." His hands drifted up and down her thighs, as light as a feather.

"Martín," she said again, as if it were the only word she knew any longer.

"Yes, *chérie?* Tell me what you want—I am yours to command." His hands swept over the front of her shaking legs, perilously close to the spot that had been tormenting her for weeks. His fingers brushed over her chemise, his touch softer than silk.

Her hips jerked against his hand. "Please don't stop."

He cupped her sex over the fine fabric, the touch of his hand shocking yet somehow right. Sarah dropped her forehead on his shoulder, a sob of pleasure breaking from her.

"Shh, *ma belle*, I will give you what you need." He gently stroked a single finger into her.

Sarah bucked violently and bit his shoulder to keep from crying out.

"You are drenched." His voice was hoarse, as if he were having trouble speaking.

Sarah felt the same, incapable of saying anything, incapable of thinking anything, incapable of doing anything other than shuddering each time he stroked. Her hips jerked, and her legs shook, and she *wanted*.

He stroked harder, this time parting the slick, swollen folds and touching something exquisitely sensitive. "I will not hurt you." The words were a low, hot rumble against her neck while his thumb circled and circled, coming close to the center of her pleasure but never touching it.

"Sarah, I want to give you an orgasm." He spoke the words into the base of her throat as his hand drove her toward madness. "Tell me you want it. I want to hear you say it—please give me an orgasm, Martín." Smiling lips curved against her skin, and his hand stopped. "Tell me what you want and you can have it." A quick flick of his finger illustrated the pleasure he could bestow so easily.

Sarah squirmed against his elusive hand, unable to form the mortifying word he demanded. He pulled away so he could look at her, his flushed skin and enormous pupils proof he was far from unmoved.

"Sarah," he whispered, his eyes almost black.

The sight of his passion made her brave. "I want you to give me an . . . an . . . orgasm. Please, Martín." The last word was only a sigh as his hand resumed its magic, his expression a mixture of hunger and triumph and something else she was too distracted to identify.

She watched his beautiful, intent face until an almost suffocating surge of pleasure forced her eyes shut, and every particle of her being focused on one tiny, demanding spot. The intense—almost excruciating—pleasure began to unfurl slowly, and her body stiffened, as if to protect itself against something too powerful to endure. She distantly heard her own voice cry out as another, even more powerful, wave engulfed the first, and another. Until she lost track, shuddering in his arms.

He held her tight while she came apart, murmuring sweet words in her ear. She wrapped her arms around his narrow waist and collapsed against the broad expanse of his chest, sighing with a contentment so deep it must have come from her bones.

A soft laugh rumbled through her. "That was good, eh?" He stroked her hair gently before pulling away to look at her face. His smile was oddly twisted as he tucked a loose strand of hair behind her ear, brushing the curve of her cheek with the back of his hand as he studied her, his fingers running up and down her jaw. "It is the least I can give you since you won't take a dress or anything else from me. Consider it my contribution to your bride's dowry, something you can bring to the marriage bed. If he cannot make you climax, it will be no fault of your responsive body." He smiled mockingly and chucked her under the chin as if she were a child.

Sarah flinched back as if he'd struck her, her arms slipping from around his body as she sagged back against the wall.

He straightened his cuffs and cravat while giving her a slight smile and bowing. "I hope you will excuse me, *mademoiselle,* but I have some business I must attend to on shore."

Sarah watched him leave without saying a word. What could she say? She stared at the door. Surely he would come back through it and say it had been a jest, or explain what had happened, or why he had done it, or say *anything*.

She slid down the wall to the floor. He wasn't coming back. Her temples pounded, and her eyes hurt. What in God's name had just happened? She flushed. She knew *what* had happened, but she had no reason *why*. Because she wouldn't take a dress from him? Because she wouldn't take his charity?

The memory of what he'd done—how he'd made her beg—was like a spike through her chest. She couldn't face the words head on; they were too bright, too painful.

What else had he said? She couldn't recall everything, but she knew it made no sense. He'd yelled accusations about both Daniels and Graaf, his eyes almost insane with anger—or something else. If Sarah didn't know better, she would have called it jealousy.

But she *did* know better. He wasn't jealous; he was insulted—or rather his pride was insulted. He couldn't bear the thought she might prefer to rely on some other man, even to borrow money. She laughed, but it came out a sob. How could he be so stupid? And so cruel. He acted like a vicious, vindictive child, lashing out and inflicting pain whenever he felt threatened.

Sarah swallowed back another sob. She refused to cry over him. There was something very wrong with him, and she would not feel shame about what she'd allowed him to do to her. It was clear that making her feel bad—and cheap—had been his object. Sarah refused to grant him that satisfaction. He was hateful. The most hateful person she'd ever known. She'd not felt this much hate since the day she'd been packed in the hold of Graaf's ship.

A wave of fury coursed through her, almost as strong as the passion she'd felt only moments before. Bouchard hadn't hurt her; she wouldn't give him that much power.

Chapter Sixteen

Martín thought he might have to shoot any member of his crew who either approached him or spoke to him. Perhaps they sensed as much from his face, because he left the ship unmolested. He headed toward the north end of town, toward the only place he could think to go when his mind was disordered: a whorehouse.

He snorted. Once a whore, always a whore, apparently. Sarah's shocked face rose up in his mind, and he stumbled like a drunk, drawing looks from the few people still out and about. He paused by a sturdy hitching post, taking several deep breaths, refusing to think of what he'd just done. Not that he *could* think in his current state. His brain was not functioning properly, the result of his persistent state of arousal. It was enough to drive him mad. He'd been hard for days—weeks! He became aroused every time she stood close to him while explaining some concept or other. In fact, he found himself frequently *pretending* ignorance so she would be forced to come closer—to spend more time with him. He *thirsted* to hear her voice, to smell her, to feel the heat of her body beside his, to—he groaned and snatched his hat from his head, staring blindly at it as he turned it round and round.

It was a well-known fact: a man could not think straight

with a hard cock. His brain was permanently befogged. She had turned him into a pitiful wreck of a man, and he would put a stop to it right now. He would take care of his scattered wits the only way he knew how, at the fine brothel he knew was nearby. It was imperative he achieve release with a woman. He jammed his hat on his head and was about to turn down the side street he wanted when he heard his name. He turned to find two small, identical women approaching.

"Did you hail me?" he asked, struggling to keep the impatience out of his voice.

"I daresay we are shockingly forward, but we couldn't help introducing ourselves to you. After all, we feel as if we know you." The woman spoke French with the accent of the islands. The other woman, obviously her twin, smiled and nodded her head.

Martín was struck speechless, his mind racing over the possibilities. They were unusual looking to say the least, garbed in colorful dresses that seemed to have been designed with whimsy, rather than fashion, in mind. He couldn't imagine they were whores; he certainly would not have forgotten them. The one who'd spoken had sounded far too well-bred to work in a bordello.

"We met Miss Fisher today," the second one explained after enjoying his look of confusion for a moment. "She came to us for new dresses."

"Ah." Martín nodded his understanding, clear as to who they were but not what they wanted. "I am pleased to meet you." He looked inquiringly at the woman who stood nearest.

"Oh, how silly. Yes, I am Arlette DuValle, and this is my sister, Adele."

"It is a pleasure to make your acquaintance," Martín said again, taking each lady's hand and bowing, still perplexed.

"Miss Fisher told us all about you, Captain," said one of the sisters, he'd already forgotten which one. She was eying him with a look he could only call provocative—a look he was accustomed to receiving, although not from such elderly women.

"Oh, er, is that so, Mademoiselle DuValle?" Her smile told him he had judged correctly that she was a spinster.

"We were quite taken with Sarah. We were so happy to do what we could for her, even though she argued fiercely against taking charity."

Martín felt a strange falling sensation in his stomach. "She did not pay for her dress?"

"Oh, goodness, no. We told her it was not charity, but a loan, and she could send us payment when she returned to her family."

"I see."

The two women regarded him with their sharp dark eyes, like two small birds.

"You *will* see that she is safely returned to her family, Captain?" The woman's words were pleasant, but her eyes hard.

He nodded, unable to speak.

"We have several more frocks to send with her. Our girls are working late into the evening, but we'll have them to your ship before you depart."

Martín blinked, uncertain which woman had just spoken. "Please excuse me. I have an appointment." He lurched away without waiting for a response. He could feel their eyes on his back, no doubt guessing where he was headed. He turned the corner and then slumped against the nearest shop front, staring at the ground before him. She had not taken gifts from Graaf or Daniels. And for that Martín had treated her like a whore. *Worse* than a whore. He had never behaved so disrespectfully—so cruelly—to any woman he'd paid.

He stood against the cool stone wall, his mind racing.

"Can I help you, *monsieur*?"

Martín looked up to find a man—a shopkeeper, Martín guessed—staring at him. He waved the man away and continued down the street. He needed to be someplace where he could think. Or *not* think.

The two-story pitch pine house looked almost uninhabited from the street. He knew from experience that large windows overlooked the back courtyard, a delightful, hidden garden that was protected from prying eyes.

The door opened before he knocked. "Captain Bouchard," a tiny woman with almond-shaped eyes said. "I'd heard you'd returned to our little island. Welcome back." She ushered him inside, and Martín entered the cool dimness of the house, leaving the hot chaos of his thoughts behind him.

Chapter Seventeen

Beauville watched without comment as Bouchard stalked across the deck of the *Scythe*. Judging by his stiff gait, the Captain had spent the prior two nights—and days—with more than one bottle. And probably with more than one woman.

He shook his head as the captain descended to his cabin. Beauville had known two days ago that the captain would not be back for the tide. He hadn't been surprised when the time to leave had come and gone. And he most certainly had not been foolish enough to send somebody ashore to find him.

Bouchard's whoring had always been legendary, even among sailors, a group who were notorious for their sexual appetites. That said, Beauville could not recall the last time he had seen his captain so deep inside the bottle, and certainly not twice in one journey. It was as if Bouchard needed to ply himself with drink before he could engage in his usual pursuits.

Beauville was not entirely without thoughts on the matter. He'd seen the way the captain stared at Miss Fisher when he thought nobody was watching. A smile pulled at his mouth. As smart as Bouchard was in most matters, he certainly seemed to be stupid when it came to his own heart. That didn't surprise Beauville. He would never deny Martín Bouchard was a loyal friend and generous master, but he'd long suspected the man didn't have a heart when it came to the fairer sex. No, Bouchard was a true menace to a woman's peace of mind and virtue.

Beauville could not count the number of times women had come seeking Bouchard, crying, begging and—on one memorable occasion—brandishing a gun.

The striking ex-slave was more skilled at attracting the opposite sex than any man Beauville had ever known. He was also colder and more ruthless than any when it came to discarding them. The first mate believed he knew his captain as well as anyone could know such a proud, arrogant man and doubted Bouchard ever completely opened his budget with anyone. Well, perhaps he was honest with his mentor, One-Eyed Standish, a man as inscrutable as himself.

The captain was as scarred by life as any man could be, and for good reason. Beauville himself had been a slave on a corsair galley for a little over a year before his ship was captured and he was freed by One-Eyed Standish.

Bouchard had been born a slave, chattel since the day he came into the world. Beauville shuddered at the thought of his captain's brutal past. The man could hardly have ended up any differently than he had.

But lately the captain had been stranger than usual. His behavior around the plain missionary woman was different from anything Beauville had seen before. If he had been forced to guess, he would have said Bouchard was acting like a jealous lover. Beauville had found him more than once lurking outside the Dutchman's cabin, always when Miss Fisher was inside.

Beauville chuckled to think of the hardened captain finally losing his heart to a woman or even discovering that he *had* a heart. And to such a woman as the missionary. Not that Sarah Fisher was ugly, far from it. But she was nothing compared to the women Bouchard had always attracted in droves—not just whores, but beautiful women, rich women. Women who would do anything for him.

As far as Beauville could tell, Sarah Fisher treated Bouchard the same way she did Daniels or Graaf, both of whom also seemed besotted by the kind, rather plain woman.

He shrugged. It was one of life's mysteries. Who knew why a person's heart made the choices it did? Certainly not he. After all, Beauville was besotted with a mere slip of a girl he had seen only twice in the town of Eastbourne. He'd never even spoken to her, and he was as lovelorn as his captain. He could not stop thinking of her and would have to make her an honest offer when he returned to England. She was not the type of woman who would accept anything less.

Beauville sighed with contentment; the idea of taking a wife and settling down held more than a little appeal. For most of his life he'd lived on a ship and rubbed shoulders with both the best and the worst of men. Like most sailors he knew few females other than whores or the promiscuous wives of men who did not take care of their women. When it came to women of virtue, he was without a clue. Maybe the dark-haired little serving wench would not want an older, battered French husband. All he could do was ask.

He did not think his arrogant captain would allow the capture of his heart with such a sanguine attitude. Bouchard had the look of a man who would go down fighting, all the way to the bitter end.

Chapter Eighteen

A sharp rapping sound shook Martín from his restless slumber. Before he could find his voice to tell whomever it was to go away, Sarah Fisher entered his cabin, slamming the door with unnecessary force. He winced, closed his eyes, and pushed his head under a large, soft pillow.

"Why are you still abed, Captain Bouchard? I believe we have three lessons this morning since you *missed* the last two."

The pillow did nothing to muffle her piercing voice.

"Captain?"

She would not go away. That much was plain. Martín inhaled deeply and squinted through eyes that were swollen and watery with drink.

And pain.

He carefully cleared his throat, but even that hurt his head. "Ah—"

"You may view my teaching as a frivolous waste of time, but I see it as the only way to pay my debts. I see you are incapacitated. The result of alcohol and prostitutes, no doubt. Be that as it may"—her voice went up an octave—"I can only answer for my own behavior. I will complete our arrangement as agreed. I can work around your indisposition. I will return in an hour." She stomped to the door and then stopped, swinging around. "Oh, I purchased this in town, mistakenly believing you would enjoy it."

Martín barely dodged the missile she hurled at his head.

She did not wait for a response before slamming the door behind her. He could feel the thud of her feet as she stomped down the corridor.

Martín picked up the brown paper-wrapped package, curiosity overwhelming the pain in his head. A gift? He had received very few gifts in his life. His hands shook as he unwrapped the package; it was a book. His hand scrabbled blindly on the nightstand for Graaf's spectacles, which he had not yet returned. He put them on and looked at the book. It was a dictionary. Inside, on the flyleaf, was her neat, careful writing: *For my friend Captain Bouchard, may you never be at a loss for words, Sarah Fisher.*

He dropped his head back on the pillow, moaning in pain at the sudden movement.

Martín was a jackass, but it hurt too much to think about it right now. He'd barely closed his eyes when he realized somebody was at his door again. This time it was a soft scratching sound, rather than pounding.

"Yes," he called weakly, not bothering to sit up for fear he would vomit. He cracked an eyelid and watched through a watery, red haze as Jenkins entered the room, not making a sound.

The little man held a tray, his shifty eyes darting from Martín to the table and back to the bed. "I've brought you some hot coffee. I'll go and fetch your hot water while you drink it. Miss Fisher sent me, Captain," he added, when Martín failed to move or respond.

"Miss Fisher?"

Martín could hear his wiry servant swallow from across the room. The soft clink of a spoon on china filled the long pause. "I'll just put your coffee here, sir." He cleared his throat. "Miss Fisher says you're to be ready for a meeting in an hour, sir."

The door latch clicked shut, telling him Jenkins had departed without waiting for an answer.

That was just as well, as Martín seemed incapable of giving one. A rich, dark aroma teased his nostrils, and he propped himself up and took the steaming cup in his shaking hands, clutching it tightly before putting it to his lips.

"Ahhhh." He clenched his jaws as hot liquid scorched his throat. Any pain was better than that in his head.

Martín drained his cup before he knew it and reached for the pot.

The second cup jarred loose the memories of the last few days. Well, some of them.

As was his practice in a brothel, he'd engaged for a meal, drink, and the best-looking woman in the house. The food had been excellent, as had the wine. The woman, also, was much finer than those in most port towns. She'd also been eager and skilled.

Not, apparently, skilled enough.

Martín groaned and immediately regretted it. His last memory had been of paying the madam three times the amount she usually charged in exchange for her promise to keep the *lack* of activities to herself. At the rate he was going, there wouldn't be a whore in existence who wasn't privy to his embarrassing secret.

Martín had sent the woman from his room and proceeded to get drunk, as if that would help him forget that his cock had refused to function for an unprecedented second time in a row—at least it wouldn't in the presence of a whore.

Once he was alone, his treacherous brain had replayed the episode with Sarah over and over again. Just recalling her powerful orgasm had given him an erection of raging proportions. Instead of feeling relief that his breeding organ still functioned—after all, his cock had been the center of his existence his entire life—he'd felt only anger. What good was it that it did so in response to only one woman? A woman who was not available, and never would be after the way he'd treated her.

It had been a good thing he was alone and nobody else had witnessed the ensuing orgy of self-pity. Not to mention that the only way he'd been able to vanquish his insistent arousal had been to satisfy his own urges, something he'd not been forced to do since he was a boy. And certainly never while in a building filled with dozens of perfectly good whores. Martín's face heated with shame at the memory.

After two pots of coffee, a hot bath, and a larger breakfast than he had believed he could eat, he was ready for Sarah when she showed up precisely one hour later.

He wouldn't have thought it possible, but the two hours that followed were even more humiliating than the previous two nights. She treated him like a stranger she'd been engaged to teach. She was polite yet distant, gentle, yet firm. The lesson was nothing more than a business transaction. Gone were the small personal asides she'd previously included while teaching him. Gone were the warm smiles and uninhibited praise.

It was misery. And it was all he could do not to push her from the room and go back to bed.

But Martín survived the lesson, his body becoming almost weak with relief when she stacked up her books and papers and left. He'd survived today, but he did not know how he could tolerate such treatment for the remainder of the journey.

Apologize.

The errant thought hit him like a stray piece of shot.

Apologize? Where had *that* come from? It was not a thought of his making; perhaps he was still drunk?

Martín looked down at the desk to the page he'd been

working on, a sheet of practice words and sentences. His large loopy handwriting looked nothing like Sarah's, which was consistent and uniform. Just like she was. She'd been consistently open and caring from the beginning, even while holding him at gunpoint.

She had behaved the same way with him while he had been . . . Martín stopped. Why go in that well-trammeled direction? He'd done what he'd done, and nothing could undo it. Apologize? He snorted and crossed his arms. He would not apologize, and nobody could make him.

Nobody.

He grasped the quill and signed his name with a flourish on the blank paper in front of him, as if he had just struck a deal and made his mark to seal it.

Nobody.

When Martín later reflected on the weeks that followed Tenerife, he could say, in all honesty, they were some of the worst of his life. True, they were nothing compared to being a slave, so they were not *the* most terrible days of his life.

Sarah treated him with a politeness that made him recall his boorish behavior every second they were together. Not a single personal comment or discussion occurred during the weeks of tutoring that followed. If he made a joke, she ignored it. If he smiled at her, she ignored it. When he thanked her for the dictionary, she ignored him.

All she allowed were the same businesslike transactions Martín had with any other member of his crew.

Her cool behavior was even more jarring when he walked past Graaf's cabin—which he admittedly did more often than was necessary—and heard laughter coming from behind the closed door. It was all Martín could do not to smash through that door and pull the Dutchman's head from his shoulders.

Every time he saw her strolling the deck with Daniels, it was like a boot to his groin.

Each afternoon she spent reading to the men who gathered before her on deck was like having a treat dangled before him that was *just* out of reach.

Her reading was miraculous, her voice changing with each and every character. Martín lingered on deck just like all the others while she spun a web of magic over his men. Over him. He hated that he held his breath in suspense as he braved the world's perils with Gulliver. Really, it was agonizing, and he'd brought it all on himself.

Martín stared at her face while she read, his rage enough to choke him. He wrenched his eyes away from her profile and looked up. Beauville was watching him. His first mate's face was impassive, but Martín swore he saw a flicker of amusement in the other man's eyes.

"Have you nothing better to do?" Martín snapped, ignoring the fact that he, too, was lounging and listening instead of working.

Beauville moved along, his lack of argument making Martín even more irascible. He repressed the urge to yell at the other lounging men and instead stalked below deck. He was about to enter his cabin when he noticed the Dutchman's door was open. Why wasn't the fool up on deck with the rest of the fools? Martín strode to the open door and looked inside.

Graaf was hunched over his miniscule desk, concentrating so hard he didn't hear Martín's approach.

"What are you working on? A letter to your cousin the king?"

The other man jumped and gave a startled yelp. "No," Graaf said once he'd collected himself. "I am working on a letter to a missionary society in Amsterdam."

"Oh?" Martín was disgusted by the curiosity he heard in the single syllable.

"Yes, I told Sarah I would write to them. When my mother was alive she had connections with the brother and sister who operated the mission."

Martín glared, frustrated by his inability to find anything to scorn in the man's words. The Dutchman continued to regard him with his wide blue eyes, the hint of superiority in his smile raising Martín's hackles. He snorted and left the room. The temptation to choke the life out of Graaf seemed to get stronger the closer they got to England.

Martín slammed the door to his cabin and flung himself into his chair, staring blankly at the books and papers left on his desk from the morning's lesson. There would not be too many more lessons, he realized, taking up the quill he had split yet again with his heavy-handed use.

Heavy-handed. Martín laughed. That was a perfect description of him, especially when it came to Sarah Fisher. His feelings toward her were so frustrating, they made him wish he could tear off his *own* head and throw it overboard.

Right after Graaf's, of course.

Writing to missionaries? The man was obviously engaged in ingratiating himself with Sarah, dangling promises of aid for her ridiculous scheme of returning to the burnt-out village and rebuilding it.

Still, he couldn't honestly blame Graaf for trying. At least the man knew how to gain a woman's attention with something other than his cock. That was pretty much the limit of Martín's abilities in that regard. And even that had been less than impressive lately.

But how could Sarah be taken in by the Dutchman's efforts? How could she care for a man who'd bought her people and stowed them in the hold of his ship like so many head of beef or crates of fruit? Graaf's claim that he'd been unaware of the people his first mate had purchased—even if it were true—did not excuse the man. Nothing could.

Oh, Martín knew what Sarah *said*. She was a Christian. Christians practiced forgiveness.

He could not begin to countenance forgiveness of such a matter. Slavery and the willingness to engage in it merited only one response: vengeance. Well, and perhaps death.

Martín chewed at his cheek and twirled the splintered quill between his fingers. He'd repeatedly tried to use Sarah's forgiveness of Graaf to work up a dislike for her, but never succeeded. Her propensity to forgive anyone for anything—except *him,* of course—aggravated, annoyed, and angered him, but it didn't make him dislike her.

But he disliked *intensely* her effect on him. He hated how she dominated his mind and ruined all other women for him. And it drove him mad to see her laughing and talking with his crew. It drove him even crazier when he realized he was displaying his craziness to either her or his men.

Her attitude toward Graaf was infuriating, but at least she showed him no preference. Daniels, on the other hand . . . The younger man seemed determined to assume the role of Sarah's protector. He'd even had the effrontery to linger around her when she was near Martín, as if Martín were some vile, corrupting influence that should be kept at bay. What made it worse was Martín agreed with Daniels. He *was* a corrupting influence. All Martín could think about was getting her into his bed and corrupting her. Again and again.

He dropped his head into his hands. "*Merde.*" Why couldn't he ignore the traitorous thoughts his mind seemed increasingly bent on generating? He yearned for the time before Sarah Fisher dominated his every waking—and sleeping—hour, when he'd been happy, or at least ignorant of anything other than fulfilling his appetites for pleasure and vengeance in equal measures.

What had happened to him? Perhaps it was some fever of the brain? He would speak to Ramsay when he reached Eastbourne. The man had a far greater knowledge of mental and emotional workings, subjects Martín had always considered irrelevant in the past.

In any case, it was Martín's plan to bring his two "guests" to the baron's hall near Eastbourne. It was rude to make such plans without asking Ramsay, but where else could Martín keep the king of the Netherlands' bloody cousin while making arrangements to haul him to London?

Martín could put Sarah at Ramsay's, along with the Dutchman. Ramsay's wife would know what to do with Sarah. While Martín didn't entirely trust the baron's reserved, clever wife, he did think she was unusually practical for a woman. He respected her, which was something he didn't feel for many females. She handled her husband—a man whose name still struck terror in savage killers all over the globe—with impressive ease. Martín had initially made the mistake of underestimating Lady Ramsay and would never do so again. She was the perfect person to assist Sarah with her foray into British society.

He could leave Sarah in the baroness's capable hands, take Graaf to London, and deposit him with British officials. There would be no point in lingering and waiting for resolution of the Dutchman's case, which he doubted would ever come to anything. Martín would be lucky if he even received reimbursement for transporting and feeding the man.

After he'd disposed of Graaf? Well, Martín could do whatever he wanted. He could go to Paris, something he'd never been able to do because of the damned war.

He looked down at the desk, at the sheet of paper Sarah had left for him. The page was filled with her neat writing, sentences, word problems, and other exercises. Suddenly, it struck him like an axe between the eyes: he could read. Not quickly or easily, of course, but he got better every day. Now, with his dictionary—yet another thing she'd given him—he could read anything he wanted.

What had he given her? Passage back to England, a thing that cost him almost nothing? That night in her cabin? Yes, he had certainly given her something then. Pleasure, followed by humiliation.

Martín dropped his head into his hands. *Merde.* He couldn't wait for this endless journey to be over.

Chapter Nineteen

Sarah closed the book she'd been reading, a history of the Roman Empire, and placed it on the pile with the rest of the books she'd borrowed. She needed to return them. Tomorrow they would reach England, and she would be in a homeland she knew nothing about. Terror simmered in her stomach at the thought of leaving the ship.

The thought of leaving Bouchard was even worse.

Sarah closed her eyes and dropped her head back against the wall with a thud. Why could she not love Daniels, who had asked for her hand in marriage two days earlier? Why must she love the only man on this ship who took pleasure in showing her he preferred the company of prostitutes to her?

The thought of him with other women made her entire body tense with fury. Even worse than that was the painful knowledge that she had fallen for him just like every other woman. How she wished she'd thrown him out of her cabin the last time he'd entered it. It was agonizing to recall how easily he'd demonstrated his mastery over her body.

But it was even more agonizing when she realized it would never happen again.

Sarah looked at the pile of books and chewed her lip. She'd used his books, but had had nothing to do with the man himself, outside of lessons, for weeks. She'd ignored every overture and comment he'd made that was not related to reading or writing. Not that he'd appeared to notice any difference in her behavior.

Sarah sighed. Really, what was the point? He barely noticed her existence; why should she expect him to consider her feelings and how he'd hurt them? He behaved like a child, and it was up to her to be the adult. She picked up the books and made her way to his cabin.

She knocked on the door and waited so long she thought he might not be in. She'd just turned away when he answered. He wore only his shirtsleeves and a pair of old, worn breeches. His curly hair stood at odd angles, as if he'd been running his hands through it, and his spectacles were still perched on his nose.

"*Mademoiselle?*" he asked, distracted. Sarah glanced behind him and saw his desk piled high with ledgers.

"What are you working on?"

For a minute Sarah thought he was going to tell her to mind her own business. Instead, he opened the door wider and stepped back, closing it behind her before going to his desk and staring down at the open books.

"I am trying to follow the bookkeeping and see if we are carrying as effectively as we could." He scrubbed his hand roughly through his hair and shook his head. "I cannot understand what Beauville means by using all these short words." He pointed to one of the pages, and Sarah leaned closer to look. "They are on every page. I have searched for them in the dictionary, but they are not there."

"These are abbreviations."

"Abbreviations? I do not know that word." He frowned at the page and leaned closer, the action bringing his shoulder next to hers, close enough that she could smell him. He smelled of soap, sweat, and Martín Bouchard. She took a deep breath and held it.

He glanced at her, his look questioning.

Sarah exhaled. "Oh, yes. Abbreviations are shortened forms of words. For example, this one means gross." She turned and found the side of his face only inches from hers. He was staring at the page, his brow furrowed in concentration. Small lines bracketed his full lips, and tiny bits of hair glinted on his jaw. He must shave twice daily if his beard grew so quickly.

"And this?" He pointed to something else on the page.

His hair was made up of hundreds of shades of gold, each strand so thick she could see the hairs individually.

He turned when she didn't answer, and Sarah found herself staring into eyes the color of old gold. She would later tell herself that she leaned closer to get a better look at those eyes and he misunderstood the action.

His arms snaked around her, and he bent her body into an almost painful arch with the force of his embrace. He captured her mouth, parted her lips, and stroked into her in one fluid motion. She sucked his tongue deeper and he moaned before tightening his grip on her body until she gasped.

He pulled away roughly and put her at arm's length, his grip on her shoulders almost painful. "What do you mean by coming here?" His voice was ragged and husky, but his eyes had gone as hard as two guineas.

It was no use lying; she hadn't come to return books. She wanted him. She couldn't bear the thought of never seeing him again without ever having . . . Well, without ever experiencing at least a physical joining with him. It didn't matter that it would never go any further than a bed. It didn't matter that her parents would spin in their graves. She'd fought herself for months, but nothing worked to loosen the hold he had. Each time she came up with a new argument to resist him, her brain offered ways around it. The truth was, she would most likely find a place with a missionary group and return to Africa and live out her days as a spinster. Was it so bad to want *one* experience to treasure over the decades to come?

"I want to make love with you."

His mouth hardened. "You don't know what you are asking, Sarah." The sound of her name in his mouth made the place between her thighs tighten, which in turn sent waves of pleasure spiraling from her womb. "You have come here without thinking." He spoke with certitude, rather than smugness. His hands loosened their grip. It was her chance to step away, but she ignored it.

"I know more than you think."

A slow smile curved his lips, and Sarah realized she'd turned down a road that soon would allow no return. "Are you telling me you wish to give me your virginity?"

His superior smile jarred her into recklessness. "Whatever made you think I was a virgin?" Something flickered across his face at her words: Surprise? Disappointment? Relief?

"Are you saying you aren't?"

She snorted. "My parents died two years ago, Captain. I've had plenty of experiences since then."

His eyelids dropped low, concealing his thoughts. For a moment Sarah thought he would put her away from him, push her out the door, crush what was left of her pride and her heart. And then his expression shifted. A taut sensuality shaped his lips as his eyes swept up and down her body, making her very aware of her old muslin dress and how thin and worn it was.

"Unbutton my breeches." The sound of his voice shocked her almost as much as his words.

"What—"

"You may stay, or you may go. If you stay, you will do as

I tell you." He wore the same cool, expectant look she'd seen on his face when he'd given his crew an order and knew it would be obeyed.

Sarah willed her shaking hands to steady. The old buckskins were butter soft and tight, and there was no hiding what was inside them. She fumbled with the catches before the fall opened and exposed a short row of buttons. She worked the first button, and he inhaled sharply at the pressure of her hand against him. The sound gave her strength. He was not as indifferent as he chose to appear.

When the last button had been freed, the breeches slid down his compact hips. He wore no smallclothes.

She stopped breathing, her eyes riveted to the long, hard length of him. She had seen naked bodies—naked penises, even—more than once. But she had never seen one so . . . aroused, so . . . angry.

"Sarah."

She looked up at the sound of her name.

"Take me in your hand."

She wrapped her palm around him, and they both gasped.

"Bloody hell." He slumped back against the wardrobe door with a thump. One of his hands closed around hers, making her fingers into a tight fist, far tighter than she would have believed pleasant. He guided her, demonstrating how to pleasure him. A low growl broke from him when he released her and she continued her stroking, her eyes riveted to the sight of so much masculine arousal in her hand. His breathing became labored, and she looked up to see him watching her, his face slack. His hips pumped with controlled thrusts, and her hand became slick.

Sarah's body began shaking, odd, sharp tremors that originated at the juncture of her legs and made it hard to stand.

His hand went around hers, holding her motionless. "Enough." He took her arms and held her away. "Unfasten your dress."

She looked from her damp, trembling hand to his hard face, dazed by the demanding pulse between her legs.

He raised his brows. "The dress, Sarah."

Sarah worked the fastenings as if in a trance. Fortunately her old brown dress had buttons that ran from neck to navel. When she'd gone halfway he leaned forward and pushed the shoulders down, exposing the fine muslin of her chemise. She was not wearing stays.

He looked at her for a long moment, then took the chemise straps and pulled them over her shoulders. When her hands went to cover herself, he shook his head. "Show me how you would like me to touch you."

Her mouth fell open. "You want—"

"I want you to touch yourself."

She heard the words, but her brain could make no sense of them.

He shrugged and moved as if to pull up his breeches.

"No."

The sharp word stopped him, and he straightened, crossing his arms.

Sarah tentatively lifted her hands and cupped a breast in each hand, something she'd never done before.

His chest rose and fell faster beneath his linen shirt. "Go on."

Sarah wanted to run from the cabin at his words, but his eyes held her in place. She let her thumb drift over one nipple, and it hardened instantly. She gasped at the unexpected sensation of pleasure.

He muttered something and closed the distance between them in a blur. His hot, soft mouth covered the stiff peak, his hands replacing hers. He commenced stroking her far more skillfully than she had with her awkward fumbling, using his tongue and fingers to tease, his teeth to nip, his lips to suck, until she was floating somewhere outside her body.

Her eyes were closed when his hands undid her petticoat. The fabric slid to the floor in a soft *whoosh,* leaving her standing in only her stockings. He held her hand as she stepped out of the clothing and then walked her backward toward the desk.

"Rest your bottom on the desk and spread your legs," he ordered in French, his voice so ragged she could barely understand him. She gripped the desk with a hand on either side of her hips, her face on fire as his knee nudged apart her legs, pushing her into a wicked position that left her open and exposed. Sarah swallowed hard and closed her eyes. She only realized where he'd gone when she felt his breath on her belly, inches from her sex.

"Wider, Sarah." His words were hot puffs of air against her skin and his gentle but firm hands rested on her thighs.

The muscles in her legs jumped and twitched, but did not respond to his pressure. "Is this . . . is this . . . normal?"

"Not the way I do it. Open."

She was suddenly weak, as if she might expire from sheer embarrassment, but she spread her feet. Her sex clenched in anticipation of his touch, but nothing happened.

"You are beautiful." His voice sounded unlike him— almost reverent. A hand slid up her thigh to her cleft, and a finger nudged between her swollen folds. "Wet," he whispered, planting an open-mouthed kiss over her hipbone while he stroked, grazing a place that made her cry out. Sarah's head fell back and her feet slid farther apart.

His throaty laughter feathered against her skin, and gentle, insistent fingers parted her and something indescribably soft touched her and she shivered. When the next probing flick caressed her, she realized it was his tongue. She bucked against him, and he gripped her hips to hold her steady. His tongue was wickedly skillful but oddly . . . elusive. He stroked and stroked but the need she felt, the nagging, demanding, maddening itch, never receded. Instead, it only got worse. Why didn't he understand? She wanted *more, harder, faster, deeper*.

Sarah pushed against him, but he held her firm. And then suddenly, the sensations that surged from his touch were overwhelming—blinding. She froze as her body seized with that familiar pleasure, the one that drove all thoughts from her head. Wave after wave after wave battered her body, weakening her until her knees felt ready to buckle.

He stood and caught her in his arms, kissing her temple. "So beautiful," he murmured in her ear. His arm slid around her waist, and he held her against him while his hand went between them and he guided himself to the entrance to her body. She felt him press against her—hot, slick, and hard— and then he pushed, entering her in one long, smooth thrust.

Sarah bit back a scream. *Oh dear God! Could a person die from this?*

He froze, motionless but for the exhale of hot, damp breath against the side of her neck.

"You lied to me, Sarah."

She swallowed and gave a tiny nod.

He made a noise of profound frustration and began to pull away.

"No!" The violence of her command stunned them both. "No. Do not stop." She felt him hesitate, only part-way inside her as his body and mind engaged in an argument she could almost hear. "Please, don't stop."

The initial pain had disappeared quickly, and the feel of his body inside hers was no longer shocking.

He took a deep breath and exhaled slowly. "Relax your body."

Sarah tried, but instead she contracted around him, and a ragged gasp tore from his throat. He bit her shoulder, held her still, and muttered something in French before saying, "Breathe, Sarah."

Sarah took slow, deep breaths as her body submitted to his invasion. He filled her slowly, but inexorably, not stopping until he was fully seated. Or so she hoped. He held her still, shaking with leashed need as he waited for her body to become accustomed to his.

"Sarah." It was a sigh, a question.

Her body knew the answer and she tilted her hips and took him deeper. His low groan signaled the end of his already fraying control, and she gasped, somewhere between pleasure and pain as he pulled out and then thrust again and again, each time harder and deeper than the last, his breathing harsh as he worked toward his climax.

"I can't stop now, Sarah," he gritted, his hands digging into the flesh of her hips. She pushed herself against him, thrilling at the effect she had on his body.

The raw power of his climax was unlike anything she could have imagined. He held her hips in an unbreakable grip, shouting her name before abruptly leaving her body and spending himself in hot ribbons across her belly.

He finally collapsed, covering her with his heaving body and holding her in his arms as the waves of his receding climax rocked their entwined bodies.

It was the most joyous and the loneliest moment in Sarah's life.

She had let him inside of her, and now she would never get him out.

Martín swam toward consciousness with slow, lazy strokes, in no hurry to leave the dark, warm comfort of his release. But when he noticed he still had her pinned to the desk, he stood, giving her slim, sleek, body a last admiring glance.

Martín had never bedded a maiden and had not been sure what to expect. She had bled, but it was not as much as he had feared. He stooped to pick up her clothes, laying them across the chair.

"There is water in the pitcher beside the basin, also a cloth," he said gruffly, turning his back so that she might have some privacy.

He pulled on his discarded breeches and pushed his arms into his coat. Sounds came from behind him, and when he turned she was composed, if somewhat less neatly attired than before.

He gestured to the chair. "Sit." To his surprise, she sat. Martín poured them each a glass of brandy. When she demurred he put the glass on the desk beside her and took a seat at the table, grateful to have some distance between himself and the enigma of Sarah Fisher.

"Did I hurt you?" he asked.

She shook her head, a flush on her cheeks.

"Perhaps you could explain why you lied to me."

The look she gave him was surprisingly cool—especially as she was a virgin, or at least had been. "I merely wanted to complete the lesson you started."

He snorted. "You wanted to complete the task of throwing away your virginity?"

"It is mine to throw. Was mine," she corrected, not looking nearly so cool.

Martín studied her flushed face and sighed. "So, what do you want from me now, eh?"

Her already flushed face mottled. "Don't worry! I don't expect a declaration of everlasting love or marriage from someone like you."

Someone like him? What did she mean? Had she learned

what he'd done in New Orleans? Was that why she'd come to him today?

"Somebody like me," he repeated, the words like broken glass in his mouth.

"What I meant was—"

He held up one hand. "So, you came to me for a lesson in bed sport. Now you know what somebody like *me* can do to someone like *you*."

"I did not mean it the way it sounded."

"How did you mean it?"

"I have lived in a jungle my entire life. I wanted to know more about . . . things . . . before I reached England. I am tired of being ignorant in such matters. I will be twenty-five on my next birthday and am no longer a girl."

"Why didn't you have Mies teach you about *things*?"

"Mies is a gentleman. He would never—" She stopped, her eyes widening. "I did not mean that the way it sounded. What I meant was—"

"Please, don't apologize for something that does not bother me," he lied. "I know I am no gentleman." He forced an expression of tolerant amusement onto his face. He'd cut off his own damned head before he'd show how much her words rankled. "How do you think your slave-trading *gentleman* will feel when he learns what you have let me do to you? Begged me to do to you, in point of fact."

Her face tightened, but she was honest enough not to argue with his assessment. "How would Mies ever find out about this?"

"Husbands usually learn such things on their wedding night."

She gave an unladylike snort. "Mies has not asked me to marry him."

"What will you tell him if he does?"

"That is hardly your affair, is it?" She stood and looked

down her nose at him, smoothing her hideous dress across her hips. "I daresay I shan't see you again after tomorrow."

Martín felt as though he'd been kicked in the stomach by a horse. He lunged to his feet. "Well then, I am very pleased I could be of service to you before we parted ways. It was the least I could do after you answered my bookkeeping questions." He flung a hand toward the cabin door. "I would like to return to what I was doing before you interrupted me."

Her eyes widened in shock, and Martín could only hope he'd hurt her. He could only hope that she felt cheapened by the fact that she'd used him as a stud service since Graaf was too much of a bloody gentleman.

She touched his sleeve, and he jerked his arm away. "What is it *now,* Miss Fisher?"

"This is all a mistake. I've made a dreadful hash of things."

"What? You regret begging me to take your virginity? Don't worry, I will not tell *Mies*, or Daniels either," he sneered.

She stamped her foot. "Why do you keep bringing Mies into this? Or Daniels? Are you jealous of my relationships with them? Why can't you see that—"

Martín's head buzzed at the word "jealous," and he raised one hand, cutting off whatever she'd been about to say. "One last piece of advice, *mademoiselle.* When it comes to bed sport, men are not interested in exhaustive discussion after they've had their fuck."

She recoiled at the vulgar word, her mouth a shocked O and her face as pale as the sheets of paper scattered across his desk. Martín flung open the cabin door and turned his back on her.

She left without a sound.

Sarah stumbled to her cabin, grateful nobody was in the corridor to witness the tears streaming down her face. She locked the door and collapsed on the narrow bunk, her body shaking with silent sobs.

Why had she done it? It was as though she'd been seized by some insane tempest when she'd knocked on his door. She'd thought that the weeks since Tenerife had served to eradicate the hold he had over her. Why had she suffered such a horrifying relapse just as freedom was within her sights?

Why had she thought that giving herself to him would make anything between them any different? He might lie with her, but he was not the kind of man to offer more. Why would he? He was beautiful, rich, and coveted. She was penniless and plain and had begged him to take her virginity. He'd never even claimed his rights to her body from the bargain they'd made so many weeks ago. She'd needed to throw herself at him before he had taken her.

He'd made love to countless women. Sarah knew that—she'd heard stories about his conquests during their months at sea. Even so, some part of her, some hopeful little ember, had continued to burn. She'd hoped his behavior at Tenerife, inexcusable though it was, had shown he had some feelings for her. Feelings he was too emotionally stunted to understand. She hadn't wanted to believe his feelings were only thwarted pride, but now she knew she'd been fooling herself. Not for a moment after their lovemaking had he shown even a shred of affection for her. He'd been far more interested in taunting her about Mies than in examining whatever might be between them. He'd made love to her—the most emotionally and physically powerful experience of Sarah's life—and then had gone back to his ledgers.

Sarah lowered her head onto her bunk and cried.

Chapter Twenty

A surprising number of ships dotted the waters off Eastbourne. Although Napoleon had been vanquished, Martín had still been forced to show his papers more times than seemed necessary. He was left with the distinct impression that the coastal authorities merely wished to speak to him. He knew he should have been flattered, but he was far too irritated for such an emotion.

Sarah and Graaf were leaning against the railing, chatting to each other with the ease of longtime companions. Martín realized it was too late to shove the man overboard now.

"Beauville!" He didn't know what he wanted to say; he just felt the need to yell.

"Aye, Captain?" The man popped up behind him so soundlessly, Martín almost leapt out of his skin.

"Good God, man, must you lurk so?"

"I'm sorry, Captain." Beauville's gaze drifted toward the couple at the rail and back to Martín.

Martín narrowed his eyes at the gesture. "I'd like you to acquire suitable transportation to take our guests to Baron Ramsay's hall. Send word to the baron letting him know of our arrival. We shall have something to eat at the Pig and

Whistle while we wait. You will join us when you've carried out my orders."

"Aye, Captain." Beauville had an annoying gleam in his eyes as he turned away to do Martín's bidding. Martín had noticed the first mate's sly looks often over the past weeks.

He realized Sarah and the Dutchman had stopped chattering and were looking at him.

"What?" he demanded nastily.

Sarah shrugged. "Nothing."

"What are you two discussing so earnestly? Plans for your new mission?"

Rather than look offended, she gave him a sweet smile. "Yes, we thought we'd leave the plans for a bordello in your capable hands."

Her unorthodox reply drew a shocked gasp from Graaf.

Martín laughed, genuinely amused by her display of fire. "Yes, *mademoiselle,* you had best leave things neither of you understand in wiser, less *gentlemanly* hands." He smirked at Graaf. "We will be reaching Eastbourne shortly. Are you both ready to disembark?"

"Mr. Daniels has kindly given me a box for my possessions and brought it up on deck."

Martín rolled his eyes and turned to Graaf, gesturing to two small trunks. "Is this all there is for you, Your Highness?"

"Yes, Mr. Daniels has brought all my possessions up for me, as well."

"It would appear Mr. Daniels is better suited to the position of stevedore than second mate," Martín snapped, turning on his heel.

Daniels had been getting on his nerves more with every passing day, and Martín would be glad to have some time away from him and the rest of his crew—many of whom seemed suddenly disapproving of him and overprotective of Sarah Fisher. It was time they all recalled who paid them, especially when that payment was likely to come from Martín's own pocket.

As Martín led his guests toward the Pig, he saw several people he knew from his time at Lessing Hall, Baron Ramsay's ancestral seat. He received few welcoming smiles, and those only from women. Most of the townspeople turned away or pointedly ignored him.

One man hustled out of his shop and snatched a girl—his daughter?—out of Martín's path and dragged her inside.

"It seems you are well-known here, Captain Bouchard," Sarah commented.

"Perhaps it is not me, but Captain Graaf's fearsome reputation that precedes him." Martín chuckled at his ludicrous suggestion.

Sarah ignored him, and the Dutchman glared.

Martín had sent ahead for a private parlor. "Some tea for the lady, porter for me, and whatever you serve to visiting royalty for the prince here." Martín gestured to Graaf.

"Porter will be fine," the Dutchman assured the gaping innkeeper. He turned to Martín after the man had gone. "Tell me, Captain, do you intend to mock me all the way to London?"

Martín shrugged, his eyes on Sarah rather than the blond man and his too pretty looks. "I will if it pleases me, *Captain.* And I will not consult you before doing so, either."

What was Sarah thinking behind her well-shuttered eyes? About yesterday? Did she wonder if her Dutch gentleman would be able to do the things to her that the barbaric ex-slave had done? Did it even matter to her that the man she'd chosen to ally herself with would sell other humans if told to do so?

The entrance of his first mate checked Martín's building

fury. "Ah, Mr. Beauville, welcome. A porter for my first mate, innkeeper."

"Very good, Captain. And will Mr. Beauville be joining your party?" the innkeeper asked, his eyes sliding nervously toward Graaf. He was clearly uncomfortable with the presence of silent royalty.

"Yes, he will. Bring us your best for four." The man hastened away, and Martín turned back to Beauville. "Has Mr. Wilson arrived?"

Beauville opened his mouth, but then paused when the door opened and a dark-haired wench entered with a serving tray. The Frenchman's eyes were riveted to the chit until the door closed behind her and he turned to Martín, as if waking from a daze.

Martín's eyebrows rose. Beauville reddened, but ignored Martín's inquiring look.

"Wilson is certain we can dispose of most of the items quickly and at a good profit."

"What items?" Sarah asked.

"Do you work for English customs, *mademoiselle*?" Martín teased. "Don't worry," he said, giving Graaf a mocking smile. "We aren't hiding anything *illegal* in our hold."

Sarah clamped her lips shut, and the Dutchman gnawed the inside of his cheek, as if he'd very much like to say something. Martín wished to God he would dare.

The innkeeper returned shortly with the little wench, and Martín amused himself by scrutinizing the young woman, his attention creating a charming flush on her plump cheeks. He was equally pleased by the daggers he saw in Beauville's eyes. So, his first mate fancied the wench? She was a pretty little thing. . . . Martín realized three sets of eyes were regarding him with varying degrees of hostility and grinned back at his guests.

The meal passed largely in silence, moved along only by his occasional comments and observations.

As much as he enjoyed baiting his companions, he was impatient to be off once he'd finished eating. He stood as the serving girl entered the room, catching her hand and pressing a coin into her small palm, keeping it longer than was proper.

"This is for your excellent service, *mademoiselle*." She'd frozen at his touch, her large blue eyes wide. Martín reached out on instinct to stroke the slight down on the curve of her jaw. "*Enchanté*."

Beauville's chair scraped noisily beside him. "The coach is waiting for you, Captain. I shall report to you later this evening," he said harshly, regarding Martín with a grimness that made him release the young girl's hand. Once freed, she moved away like a frightened deer.

Sarah had long believed Martín Bouchard to be the most trying and obnoxious person she'd ever met, but today he was outdoing even himself.

For a moment she'd thought Mr. Beauville, a man who was usually a pillar of calm, might strike his captain. Even a fool could see he was deeply in love with the young serving girl. And any fool, other than Bouchard apparently, could see she was not the kind of girl to sell her favors.

Sarah's hand itched to slap his snidely handsome face. What was *wrong* with the man? What on earth drove him to behave in such a universally insulting and reprehensible manner?

Once seated in the coach, Sarah fumed and stared across the short distance at him. He appeared oblivious, gazing out the window with a slight smile on his face as if contemplating something amusing. No doubt imagining himself bedding the serving wench.

The swine!

Graaf, who was seated beside her, must have sensed her anger. He patted her hand as it lay on her knee.

The intimate action drew a scowl from Bouchard, and Sarah extracted her hand, using it to point out the window. "Is that Lessing Hall?"

Mies leaned across her to look out the window toward the enormous white manor house that lay at the end of the long drive. "Hmmm, I should guess the bulk of it is fourteenth, perhaps fifteenth century."

Bouchard's eyes narrowed even further, and he leaned toward the Dutchman, his hands clenched, as if he were about to begin pounding the slighter man.

Thankfully, the carriage drew to a halt before fisticuffs broke out. A host of elegantly clad servants swarmed down the steps toward them. Sarah was so desperate to escape the hostile environment inside the carriage that she pushed open the door. She would have stumbled if not for Bouchard's steadying hand on her arm.

"Don't worry, I won't hurt him," he muttered in her ear before passing her hand to one of the footmen.

Before Sarah could respond, her attention was captured by the enormous man coming down the steps. He was the tallest person she'd ever seen, well over six feet. Not only was he physically imposing, but he was also incredibly handsome. He was dressed less formally than Captain Bouchard, his clothing immaculate but more suited to the pursuits of a country gentleman. All that marred his perfection was a scar that cut across his attractive face and a black patch over one eye.

"Welcome to Lessing Hall, Miss Fisher. I am Hugh Redvers." The giant took Sarah's hand in his enormous one and bowed over it, pressing his lips to her fingers.

Sarah grew hot at the old-fashioned yet somehow sensual gesture. She could tell by the amused glint in his single eye, he knew what he was doing. Up close she could see he was older than she'd first thought, closer to forty than thirty. He turned from her toward the carriage.

"Ah, Martín! Greetings, brother." He dwarfed Captain Bouchard as they embraced in a way she'd seen the men use on the ship: a handshake that included the entire forearm while they gripped each other's shoulders.

Bouchard grinned, looking like a boy happy to see his father or elder brother. It was the first time she'd seen any sign of affection on his face. Naturally it made him even more gorgeous.

"It is always good to see you, Lord Ramsay," Martín answered, his use of the honorific another sign of his esteem.

The baron turned to Mies. "Welcome to Lessing Hall, Captain Graaf." He made Mies look like a child as he towered above him. "Come inside. My wife is very eager to meet you."

"What a lovely house you have, my lord," Sarah said, gazing about the enormous hall in wonder.

"It's an imposing old pile, but it is home." He waited until they'd given their various possessions to a servant before leading them up a sweeping stone staircase and halfway down a long hallway. The door he opened led to the room of Sarah's dreams. Books, books, and more books. She stood just inside the doorway, her jaw hanging open in wonder.

The baron recoiled. "Oh no, not another bookish woman."

"Don't be such a beast, Hugh." The soft voice came from the corner of the large room. Sarah had been too busy staring at the books to notice the person in the room.

If the room was beautiful, then the woman who walked toward her was its perfect complement. Like Sarah she was tall, but that was where the resemblance ended.

Sarah felt a combination of awe and envy as she took in the Baroness Ramsay. No matter what kind of frock she wore, Sarah would never look half as lovely as this woman did dressed in a simple dress of yellow muslin.

She shared the same coloring as the Dutch nobleman, her pale skin and golden hair a perfect foil for a pair of blue eyes so perfect they looked as if they belonged on a canvas. Her manner, however, was warm and welcoming. "Don't listen to my husband, Miss Fisher. He is teasing me. I am the reason you are being received in a library rather than the drawing room, as is proper."

"I cannot imagine any room more welcoming than this, Lady Ramsay."

The blond woman smiled and turned to her other two guests. "Captain Graaf, what a pleasure. I understand you are from Amsterdam? I am currently reading a work by one of your master philosophers, Mr. Spinoza." She paused.

Everyone looked at the Dutchman, who flushed darkly under so much attention. "Er, Spinoza. Why, yes, I've heard of him."

"Perhaps you will help me with some of the translation? My grasp of Dutch is quite rudimentary."

Mies gaped.

"Darling! Let the poor man catch his breath before you start tampering with his brain," the baron chided, his pride showing through his teasing.

"You are correct, of course. I daresay we shall have plenty of time to discuss the matter later," Lady Ramsay promised the goggling Dutchman. She turned to the third member of their party and her mouth tightened. "Captain Bouchard."

"Lady Ramsay, it is always a pleasure." The handsome captain bowed mockingly over her hand before she pulled it away.

"Martín, still charming the ladies, I see," the baron said, laughing. He turned to Sarah and Mies after they'd seated themselves. "I understand we are all going to make a trip to London?"

"I would not want to put you out, my lord," Mies said. "I give you my word I would take myself to London without supervision."

"I'm sure nobody doubts your honor, Captain." Ramsay cut Bouchard an amused glance. "Besides, a trip to London will not be an inconvenience. We shall be in good time to catch a part of the Season, and I had already decided to take Lady Ramsay. She's looking a bit hagged, and I'm hoping to give her a little town polish."

Lady Ramsay was clearly accustomed to her husband's teasing ways and ignored his levity. "I understand you have relatives in London, Miss Fisher?" She saw Sarah's confused look. "Captain Bouchard explained your circumstances in the letter he sent with the messenger."

Bouchard had written a letter? Sarah grinned at him; what a fine student he'd turned out to be!

He responded to her smug look with a scowl.

"We'll give you a few days to rest while we organize our trip," Ramsay said, his sharp eye on their interaction.

Just then the door to the library flew open, and three bodies hurtled into the room. One of them, a boy of perhaps fourteen, stopped in front of Lady Ramsay. "Mama, you must make Antonia stop following us." The other boy stood silent, and Sarah saw he was absolutely identical to the first.

Lady Ramsay lifted her brows and gave them both a very significant look.

They turned, their young faces flushing when they noticed Sarah and Graaf, who sat on the settee. And then they noticed Bouchard.

"Martín!" they both yelled, launching themselves across the room.

The third child was a very dirty little girl. Sarah thought she was perhaps four years of age.

"Uncle Martín, Lucien is being beastly," the little girl lisped, pushing past her brothers and crawling into Bouchard's lap, covering him with mud in the process.

Bouchard's expression was priceless as he looked from the little girl to his no longer spotless coat and pantaloons.

"Antonia, what have you been doing? You are a *petite cochon*."

Antonia ignored him and burrowed into his arms, her small filthy hand worming itself into his previously white cravat.

Martín stared at the ceiling with a look of resignation, but Sarah noticed his arm had snaked around the little girl and he was cradling her gently against his chest as he turned to the boy beside him. "Lucien, why do you keep your little sister in a pig sty?"

The boy snorted. "She followed us down to the river and then fell in and cried. We had to stop everything and bring her back home."

Martín turned to the other boy.

"Hello, Captain Bouchard." The second boy's face was identical to his brother's but his expression was as calm as Lady Ramsay's; Lady Ramsay was obviously the mother of all three blond children.

"Hello, Richard," Bouchard greeted him, nodding with equal seriousness while cuddling the little girl, who was poking her tongue out at her brother Lucien.

Martín smirked at Sarah, perfectly aware of how adorable he looked holding the beautiful child in his arms.

Sarah scowled at him.

"That is the look of somebody who has been closeted with Martín for too long," Ramsay observed, chuckling.

"I've seen that look on your face before, Hugh," Lady Ramsay told her spouse.

Martín rose to his feet. "It is my cue to leave when people discuss me as if I am not here. I will return you to your father, you dirty little girl." He kissed the top of her golden head before thrusting her into the baron's arms.

"You will come back for dinner, I trust?" The baron held his filthy daughter at a safe distance.

"With pleasure. Mademoiselle Fisher." Martín bowed to her and then left without another word, ignoring Mies as usual.

An awkward silence was cut short by the appearance of a servant looking for her charges. All three grumbled, but left with the woman.

Lady Ramsay stood. "Miss Fisher, let me show you to your chambers."

"Thank you for your kind hospitality, Lady Ramsay," Sarah said as the woman led her through a confusing collection of turns.

"Please, call me Daphne. Also, promise me this will be the last time you thank me."

Sarah laughed at the blunt words. "Very well, and will you call me Sarah?"

"Here are your chambers, Sarah." The tall blonde opened a door to an enormous room furnished in a delightful buttery yellow.

Sarah's jaw sagged. "What a beautiful room." The suite had a sitting room, a dressing room, and a room for bathing. "Oh my, what an enormous tub."

"My husband comes from a family of tall men." The baroness paused. "Your journey with Captains Bouchard and Graaf must have been most interesting."

"It was . . . unusual. I believe I deserve the bulk of the praise for Captain Graaf arriving in one piece."

"Yes, I daresay Bouchard would not find it easy to have another captain on his ship."

"It was not so much that, as it was the issue of slaving."

Lady Ramsay's pale eyebrows arched. "Oh, so that's the

case. No, Captain Bouchard would not go easy on such a man. Neither would my husband."

Sarah cursed her loose lips and hoped she hadn't just damned Graaf's chances for help from the big man.

"Don't worry," the blond woman assured her, reading Sarah's expression with an ease that left her unnerved. "Ramsay will stand by his word. He is less . . . barbaric in his methods than he used to be."

"I've heard stories of your husband from several people. He is still very much respected and not a little feared, I think."

"Yes. I believe he misses those days, particularly when the children fail to obey him as his crew was used to doing."

The women laughed, and the tense moment passed.

Sarah lay in the enormous tub long after the water had cooled, until her fingers and toes wrinkled, and she began to shiver from the cold. She bundled up in thick towels that had been heated with hot bricks and padded into her dressing room.

A small, aged woman with a dour expression was riffling through her dresses. She gave Sarah a quick, unsmiling glance before turning back to the garments.

"My name is Rowena. My lady sent me to help you with your toilette."

Sarah felt odd having somebody help her dress, but Rowena looked unwilling to take no for an answer.

She pushed Sarah down in front of the mirror and proceeded to work on her hair with all the care of a farmer hoeing a field. Sarah gritted her teeth to hold back agonized screams as the woman drew out the tangles. Rowena left her tormented hair to dry and then helped Sarah into a chemise and drawers before cinching her into a corset with a ruthlessness that would have done a general proud.

The little termagant had selected the fanciest dress Arlette and Adele had given her, a jade green silk embroidered with tiny jet beads. Once Sarah was dressed, Rowena pushed her back onto the yellow silk padded bench and resumed working on her hair. She only spoke to tell Sarah to move one way or the other.

It was deeply uncomfortable to be the beneficiary of such intense, silent care.

"Have you been with Lady Ramsay long?" Sarah asked, for lack of anything else to say.

"All her life." Rowena spoke around the pins she held in her lips as she created an artful crown of ringlets from Sarah's straight hair. "Tilt your face down."

It was like watching a miracle in progress. Sarah would not have believed she could look so elegant. When Rowena finished with her hair, she opened a small casket and rooted around before pulling out a triple strand of pearls with a single emerald cabochon in the middle. She clasped it around Sarah's neck and stood back to admire her work. She grunted.

Sarah just stared.

The woman in the mirror was still Sarah, but not as she'd ever seen herself before. Not even a gown as fine as the green silk could make her beautiful, of course, but it somehow made her eyes look larger and more green than brown. And her hair? Well, that was beyond amazing.

"Thank you, Rowena. I have never looked so splendid."

"My lady said to bring you to the drawing room." Rowena opened the door and went through it, not waiting to see if Sarah followed.

The only person in the drawing room was Baron Ramsay, looking enormous and elegant in his black-and-white dinner clothes.

"Good evening, Miss Fisher, Rowena."

Rowena turned and left the room without a word.

The baron winked at Sarah. "She adores me."

Sarah laughed, and the baron raised an ornate gold quizzing glass. "You look lovely, Miss Fisher," he said, and then frowned.

"What is it, my lord?" She looked down at her gloved hands and examined her skirt. Had she managed to rip or stain her gown?

He tapped the glass against his chin, a wry look on his face. "Perhaps you look *too* lovely. I'm afraid Martín and Graaf will be engaged in fisticuffs before the first course has finished."

Sarah rolled her eyes. "You are cruel to tease me, my lord. I have already coped with the two of them for weeks on end. I'm lucky to be sane."

The baron's booming laugh filled the room. "Yes, I could see how it was this afternoon. Martín is like a bear with a sore head. He wasn't even interested in looking at my new horses before he stormed back to the *Scythe*. Whatever have you done to him?"

Sarah didn't have to answer the baron's question as the man himself entered just then.

"Good God, Martín, how fine you've become." The baron eyed the other man through his quizzing glass.

Ramsay was not exaggerating. Even Sarah could see Bouchard's clothing was cut far more fashionably than their host's.

The points of his collar brushed his jaw, and the white of his linen contrasted starkly with his dark skin. His waistcoat was a shade of antique gold that matched his eyes too closely to be an accident. His black coat was as snug as a second skin, and he wore black pantaloons rather than the more traditional breeches. The thin fabric stretched over his sculpted hips and thighs in a manner that caused her to blush and look away.

"You look lovely, Mademoiselle Fisher," Martín murmured, coming to stand before her.

"Yes, doesn't she?" The baron was watching his friend with open fascination. Sarah realized Lord Ramsay's mischievous sense of humor was even more dangerous than his reputation as a privateer.

Martín ignored his host, his face expressionless as his eyes swept her, lingering speculatively on the jewels. Did he think they were from Mies? Sarah hoped so. He bowed over her hand, and she felt the heat of his breath through her glove. For a moment she thought her knees might buckle.

But then she reminded herself that he was only interested in her to the extent that he believed Mies wanted her. His predatory nature made such a competition impossible to resist. He did not want her, but he did not want Mies to have her either.

She was seized by an overwhelming desire to kick him.

She was saved from making a fool of herself and hurting her foot by Lady Ramsay's entrance, on Mies's arm. The baroness was truly flawless, her simple gown the same shade of blue as her eyes, her only ornament a diamond pendant. Sarah was shocked by the wave of envy that swept her. Was this how she would be from now on? Dreading the fact that just about every woman she encountered would be more attractive than she was?

Sarah could not bear to look at Martín's face and see his reaction to Daphne.

Instead she turned to Mies. He looked reassuringly the same, and Sarah realized the clothing he wore, the same outfit he'd worn in Tenerife, was probably the only evening attire he'd brought with him from home. In his dark gray jacket and breeches he could not compete with the elegance of the other two men, but the waistcoat he wore was one she had not seen before, sky-blue embroidered with tiny silver birds. His flaxen hair was still damp, the loose curls falling over his collar. His eyes were openly admiring as they took in her hair and dress.

Sarah looked away from his warm gaze, not wishing to encourage him, the fact that he'd been willing to engage in slavery never far from her mind. She frowned, realizing that Christian forgiveness—along with purity and chastity—seemed determined to elude her.

The dining room at the hall was an ancient room with a flagstone floor that appeared to have been here since the dawn of time. The table and chairs had all been constructed on a massive scale, as if they'd been built during an age when people were far larger. A footman waited behind each chair to move the weighty-looking pieces of furniture.

Three massive chandeliers hung from heavy chains, each holding dozens of candles that cast long shadows across the almost Teutonic room. The table glittered with more crystal, silver, and dishes than she'd ever seen in one place. Sarah tried not to gape like a bumpkin at the service, the food, and the innumerable footmen who swarmed around the five diners. There was a place set for a sixth, but neither Lord nor Lady Ramsay seemed inclined to wait for the absent party.

Sarah was kept busy with the array of cutlery and new dishes and watched Mies for cues on which to use before attacking each dish. She looked up at one point and saw Martín's eyes on her, his amusement at her nervousness apparent. Sarah narrowed her eyes at him and turned back to their host, who was discussing the plans for their journey.

"I hope leaving three days hence will inconvenience nobody?" The baron glanced around and, upon meeting no demur, he continued. "Miss Fisher, my wife tells me the only information you have about your father is that he belonged to a Dutch merchant family in London?"

Mies jolted, his cutlery clattering against his plate. "Why have you not told me before that your father was Dutch?"

Why hadn't she told him? They had, after all, talked about their families and childhoods many times in the months they were at sea. "I suppose I didn't think it mattered. I know nothing of his family, and they disowned my father when he decided to marry my mother."

Mies continued to look wounded, and Sarah darted a look at Martín and then wished she hadn't. He was staring at them both with an expression of sardonic superiority that made her feel violent.

The baron's single eye darted among the three of them as if he were enjoying a particularly amusing play and didn't want to miss anything.

"In any event," the baroness said, apparently unaware of the currents swirling around the table, "Hugh will look into the matter when we arrive in London."

The rest of the conversation followed more conventional lines. It seemed Napoleon's treatment on Saint Helena was the most talked about subject at the moment. Articles in the London *Times* claimed the exiled French leader was receiving harsh treatment at the hands of his British captors. The doings of Napoleon and the long war in Europe had always seemed very far removed from Sarah's life in N'goe.

Mies leaned close to her. "I wish you'd told me you were Dutch."

"I'm not Dutch, Mies. My father was. I'm not English, and I'm not African, either. I don't know what I am."

"You have been here less than a day. You will feel more at home after a while. Much more at home than you ever did in your African village."

Sarah frowned. What right did he have to think he knew her so well—or where she belonged? She glanced at the other three and saw they were still engaged in animated conversation. Martín was laughing and arguing with Lord Ramsay. His face bore an expression of openness she'd never seen before, even during their best tutoring sessions. As if feeling her eyes upon him, he turned. His smile chilled, and all the warmth drained from his face. Sarah turned away, her eyes welling. What had she ever done to him that he should look at her with such coldness and hostility?

Martín focused his attention on Hugh and Lady Ramsay rather than on whatever Sarah and the Dutchman were whispering about.

He needed to hide his irritation from Ramsay. If Hugh guessed for a moment that Martín felt anything for Sarah—not that he did, of course—he would dig until he got to the bottom of the issue. Martín's teeth hurt at the thought. Becoming fodder for Ramsay's well-developed sense of humor was not something he wanted.

They'd just completed their meal when Hugh's mad aunt entered the dining room. Martín groaned inwardly as she drifted in with a pack of noisy dogs.

"Ah, Aunt Amelia, we're so glad you could join us," Ramsay boomed over the din of her barking dogs. He made brief introductions, and the men resumed their seats after the old lady took hers. Conversation ground to a halt. The only one who didn't seem to notice the deafening barking was Lady Amelia, who shared her food with her dogs and directed questions in her penetrating voice to the various people in the room.

"So, you are back, are you?" she asked Martín, her question surprising him. He wouldn't have thought she'd taken any notice of him the last time he'd stayed at Lessing Hall, a few years earlier. Her next words proved him wrong. "I certainly hope you will leave the servant girls alone this time." She paused in her tirade to give half the fowl on her plate to one of her baying dogs.

Martín pursed his lips and stared at his glass, turning it in restless circles on the table.

"I'm pleased to see you are decently dressed this time," the old witch continued in a ringing voice, fixing him with a quelling stare when he looked up. "After all, this isn't the—"

"Aunt Amelia." Lady Ramsay's soft voice was unusually penetrating. "Have you spoken to Cook? I believe she was not able to get those calf livers you wanted."

Martín met the baroness's cool blue eyes, surprised she'd decided to rescue him. Ramsay certainly didn't look as if he'd had any plans to stop the old lady. In fact, he looked like a man trying not to laugh.

"I cannot understand what the problem is," Lady Amelia groused, taking a tiny mouthful of food before placing yet another plate on the floor. "Why is it so difficult to procure calf liver?" She directed this question at her one-eyed nephew.

"Well, there is only one per calf, you know. Perhaps you could find some other part of the calf to feed to your pugs, something less exclusive—more common. Feet perhaps. Even ears."

She gave him a withering look before raising her quizzing glass, an even gaudier specimen than the one Ramsay wore. She turned her grossly magnified eye on Graaf, examining him for a long moment.

"You are Caroline Balfour's grandson," she stridently informed him, her stern look and inaccurate supposition causing the Dutchman's jaw to sag. Martín felt a flare of pleasure at the other man's discomfort. "I gather your grandmother has finally come to terms with your mother's shameless behavior at Lord Atherton's ball? There is no hiding that your brother inherited Atherton's ears."

Graaf opened his mouth. "Er—"

"I'll have you know we do not tolerate that type of nonsense here at Lessing Hall." Her eyes, usually a hazy gray, were like the sharpened points of rapiers.

"Uh—" the Dutch peer began.

Choking sounds came from Ramsay's direction.

Graaf opened his mouth again to say God-knows-what, but Lady Amelia had already lost interest in whoever she thought he was.

"I am going to go speak with Cook about the appalling lack of liver," she declared to nobody in particular, her eyes slewing back to her nephew, who appeared to be in actual physical pain.

She frowned at him. "Dyspeptic? I shall have Klemp make you a posset." She heaved her tall, thin form up from her chair and almost careened into the approaching footman, who was bearing a tray with several dishes she'd requested.

"You are too late. I have finished my meal, young man." She dismissed him with an irritable wave while several of her hounds nipped his ankles. She shot Martín a narrow look, as if he were somehow responsible for the deplorable liver shortage, and then sailed from the room.

The silence was broken only by the sound of Ramsay's choking and snorting. Martín glared at the red-faced baron and shook his head.

Ramsay saw Martín's disgusted expression, and the room shook with his laughter.

They retired to the library after dinner, where Sarah proceeded to thrash both Graaf and Ramsay at chess. Martín enjoyed watching her deliver the setdown to the arrogant baron.

"It seems you have learned a new lesson tonight, my lord."

The one-eyed man grinned at Martín's taunting. "Judging by your refusal to play Miss Fisher, you've learned the same lesson already." His green eye slid from Martín to Sarah, who was blushing, but smiling.

"I must be off," Martín said.

"But Lady Ramsay has readied a room for you here, Martín."

Martín shook his head at his mischievous former employer. "I have business on the *Scythe.*" He bowed to the baroness. "But I thank you for the kind offer."

The truth was that Martín wasn't comfortable staying in a house in which he had once been little more than a servant. Besides, several of the maids he'd bedded were still employed at Lessing Hall. He'd encountered one of the women, Susan, just before dinner. She was now married to a groom by the name of Caswell, a man Martín had once pummeled when he'd objected to Martín's association with Susan.

Susan had obviously been lingering and hoping to have a word with Martín. She was as fetching as ever, her green eyes sparkling and her lush figure enhanced by marriage and a couple of brats.

"Hello, Captain." She had the same welcoming smile.

"Hello, Mrs. Caswell." He'd hoped the use of her married name would dampen her ardor. But Susan had ignored his hint, and he'd only been able to escape unmolested due to the appearance of the wooden-faced butler, Gates, a man who hated Martín with a passion.

"Susan, Mrs. Porter is looking for you." The dour butler's eyes had been on Martín when he spoke, his expression as haughty as a lord's.

No, it was much better for Martín to remain on his ship.

He encountered Beauville just outside his cabin.

"Ah, Captain, do you have a moment to spare?"

"Of course, come in." Once inside, Martín poured them both brandies. "So, what is it, Mr. Beauville?"

"I wanted to tell you this past journey was my last."

Martín froze in the act of raising his drink. He lowered it, untouched. "What? Why?"

Beauville flushed and looked down at his own glass. "I am going to be married."

"Married?" Martín repeated, sounding like a startled parrot.

"Yes, married."

"To whom?"

Beauville's bemused expression shifted into something hard. "To the young lady at the Pig and Whistle."

Why did he look so accusing? "What woman?"

"The innkeeper's daughter, Mary."

Martín blinked. "The serving wench at the Pig and Whistle?"

Beauville's eyes narrowed at the word "wench." "Her name is Mary Simpson. She has agreed to marry me on the condition I give up sailing. Her brother died at sea, and she says she could never be happy always worrying about her husband." Beauville looked pleased with the idea that a woman cared enough to want to keep him safe.

"Congratulations, Beauville. She is a lovely woman and will make you very happy," Martín said, still unable to recall the woman in question. He doubted it would be prudent to admit that to the obviously besotted man across from him.

Beauville glowed.

"Will you be marrying immediately or will you accompany me to London to assist with the *Blue Bird* claim— although I doubt it is worth our time to pursue the matter given Graaf's connections?"

"We will not marry until after the banns have been read. I would be glad to assist with any other matters just so long as they are on land."

"So, what will you do? Become an innkeeper?"

Beauville laughed. "No, I do not have the temperament for it. I was hoping you might guide me in purchasing a small farm. I recall you own several properties of your own."

"I would be glad to help in any way I can." Martín was flattered Beauville would look to him in such an important matter.

They discussed a few pressing matters that always arose

when a ship came into port, and Beauville left a short time later. Martín poured himself another brandy.

Graaf had been very interested in the information that Sarah's father was Dutch. As if that somehow made a bond between them. Martín snorted at the snobbishness of the man. He realized he was squeezing his coat jacket tightly, as if it were the Dutchman's neck. As if the fact that Sarah might have Dutch relatives somehow brought Graaf and Sarah closer together and maybe meant she would be more inclined to accept his attentions.

Ridiculous!

Wasn't it?

Not that any of that mattered. Martín would hardly be moving in the same circles as Sarah, the Dutchman, and Ramsay once they got to London. Lady Ramsay would see to it Sarah was accepted wherever she went. Hugh and his wife might be unconventional, but the baron was connected to just about every powerful house in England. However, even the baron would not be able to shoehorn an ex-slave into the exalted company of the *ton*. Not that Martín wanted such a thing, of course.

He tossed back his drink, and poured another. He would have to find his own level in London.

Chapter Twenty-One

The three days at Lessing Hall passed too quickly for Sarah. Although she spent no time alone with Martín, she saw him most days and every evening at dinner. She loved those evenings, the wonderful conversation around the dinner table, and the after-dinner chess and cards. Lord Ramsay took it upon himself to teach her whist, and the games among the four of them—Lady Ramsay did not care for cards—were loud, raucous events filled with much arguing.

Sarah was a fast learner and felt pleased the evening she and the baron beat the two captains for the first time. It was amusing to see Martín repress his irritation at losing and even more humorous to watch the two men wrangle and try to pin the blame for their loss on each other.

By the morning of their departure Sarah felt more at home at Lessing Hall than she had anywhere since leaving her village.

Mies, Daphne, Sarah, and Rowena occupied the coach, while the baron and Martín rode beside it. Sarah was not surprised to see Martín was an excellent rider and looked as if he were one with his horse.

They stopped for lunch and a change of horses at a charming posting inn, making a very merry party, well acquainted and comfortable with one another by now. Even Martín resisted the urge to bait Mies, instead treating him with the same tolerant contempt he showed everyone except Ramsay.

The carriage reached the outskirts of London just as darkness was falling, and Sarah gawked in wonder as the coach rolled through street after street of the massive city. The buildings and the people seemed to get more attractive and well-tended looking the farther away they got from the river.

Davenport House—the family home of Lord Ramsay—was considerably smaller than Lessing Hall, but infinitely more elegant, something Sarah would not have believed possible.

When Sarah entered her sumptuous suite, she found an enormous tub of hot water and a maid already waiting for her. She left her clothing and hair decisions to the maid and was soon dressed and ready. Although Daphne had not said as much, Sarah assumed they would all meet in the library.

Sarah encountered Mies on the stairs.

"You look divine, Sarah."

She recoiled at his words and warm look. "Thank you, Mies. You look very nice, too," she replied coolly, hoping to halt the flow of fulsome compliments. The young Dutchman, with his limited wardrobe, was always the first down to dinner. Martín, by contrast, was generally the last, his time-consuming toilette requiring more time than either of the women's.

Daphne was still in her traveling clothes and leaning over a mass of books and papers when they entered the library.

"Oh, is it time for dinner?" Daphne frowned at the half dozen books that lay open. "I suppose I should leave this until later." She looked down at one of the open books and turned a page, as if she were considering sitting down.

"If you make haste I shall tell Lord Ramsay you will be down shortly," Sarah said, realizing only after she'd spoken how presumptuous it sounded to order the baroness about in her own house.

Daphne bit her lower lip. "Yes, I believe you're correct. Thank you, Sarah." She gave the books one last yearning glance before hurrying from the room.

Mies grimaced at the pile of books. "She has trapped me twice to discuss Spinoza. I have no clue what she is talking about. She is a brilliant woman—almost frightening." He shivered.

The library was not as large as that at Lessing Hall, but it seemed to have more novels. Sarah pulled down a new-looking volume titled *Pride and Prejudice*. She'd only read a couple of pages when the baron entered.

He glanced at the cluttered desk and smiled. "Did you have to chase her from the room at gunpoint?"

"Yes, but she will still be down before Captain Bouchard."

Ramsay chuckled. "How about a glass of something to tide us over?" he asked them. "We could be here for hours."

In fact, they'd only been chatting a few minutes when Martín joined them.

"Good Lord, Martín, how many men participated in the construction of that cravat?" Ramsay demanded. "Where in God's name did you come upon that design?"

"This is something I picked up from my French tailor in Cairo."

"I suppose it's a good deal better than *some* of the things you could have picked up in Cairo."

Ramsay and even Mies snickered.

Martín gave them a look of haughty contempt. "No doubt you will be seeing more of such stylish fashions now that France can again influence this benighted country."

"Gad, I hope not." Ramsay gave Sarah a sly wink.

"I daresay you wouldn't, Ramsay. Fashion is for the young, after all."

The baron laughed, delighted by the insult.

Martín turned his attention to Sarah. "This is a new gown, no?"

"Yes, Lady Ramsay had it made up for me out of one of hers."

Martín circled her in a way that disconcerted her.

"What are your plans tomorrow, Martín?" Ramsay's question diverted Martín's attention away from her, much to Sarah's relief.

"A lot of that depends on Captain Graaf," Martín drawled. He took the glass of wine Ramsay handed him. "What *is* our plan, Captain Graaf?"

Mies, who'd been peering out the library window onto the street below, turned at the sound of his name. "Tomorrow I will see Lord Bathurst."

Ramsay addressed himself to Sarah. "As for you, my dear, I believe you will not find it difficult to locate your uncles. They are Septimus and Barnabus Fisher."

Sarah stared.

"No, I am not a wizard. I sent a letter to my man of business the day you arrived at Lessing Hall. There was a message waiting for me here. Your uncles are very well-established bankers."

Sarah blinked, her mind spinning. "I'd thought they were merely wool brokers."

"They have—I believe the term is—diversified."

Sarah was still marveling at this shocking information when Lady Ramsay rushed into the library, and they all repaired to the dining room.

After breakfast the following morning, Sarah wrote her uncles and told them about the death of her father, her arrival in England, and her current residence with Lord and Lady Ramsay. She ended the short missive by expressing an interest in meeting such members of her family as were in town.

When she'd given the letter to Lord Ramsay to frank, she fetched her cloak and bonnet and went to meet Lady Ramsay, who'd invited her to go shopping.

"I must visit Hatchards. I have a long list of books I wish to order." She held up a piece of paper filled with writing as they took their seats in the stylish town carriage. "I am also in need of new clothing, as it seems I will be increasing soon."

"Oh, congratulations, Daphne!"

Her friend's ivory skin tinted. "Thank you. Ramsay and I are quite pleased. I *could* have worn the same garments I did four years ago, but apparently my husband instructed Rowena to throw them all out." She glared at her maid, who sat across from them. The older woman resolutely ignored Daphne, clutching her own long list of requirements.

"Rowena has my dimensions and will take care of my purchases, but we must get something for you, Sarah. You will need much more than what I have given you." Daphne held up a staying hand when Sarah opened her mouth. "No, I will not dispute the matter. I will become vexed if you insist on arguing about money. There is nothing I find more tedious. Well, except shopping for clothing." Her blue eyes, usually so vague and introspective, settled on Sarah and sharpened. "I shall buy you the clothing that is necessary for your first few weeks. If you argue with me, I shall buy you more."

Sarah laughed. "I will be delighted to accept your kind offer."

Daphne moved to another topic. "Ramsay tells me your uncles are quite important bankers. Indeed, Septimus was recently made Baron Danestoke. I understand they were involved in the sale of Napoleon's American holdings some years ago. I daresay they have many interesting stories. I shall give a dinner and invite them." She made a *tsk*ing sound. "I'm afraid we shall soon be flooded with invitations, many of them tedious, but necessary to properly launch you."

"Launch me—?" Sarah began, aghast.

Daphne ignored the interruption. "No doubt we shall be invited to whatever Mia Exley—that is Lady Exley—has organized. The Exleys mix with the most *interesting* people. I think you will enjoy their friends more than the stuffy people we shall be forced to invite. Ramsay's aunt, Lady Thornehill, is a terrifying woman and very much an ape leader. It is because of her that Hugh and I have not been entirely cast off by society." She pursed her lips. "I've been told I should be grateful for that."

Lady Ramsay's town carriage dropped them at the famous bookseller and took Rowena on to Daphne's dressmaker, where she would begin the dreaded shopping. Rowena reminded her mistress sharply that the carriage would call back for them in an hour.

It was a good thing the carriage came for them, otherwise Sarah believed they would have spent the entire day—and perhaps evening—in the bookseller's. As it was, they left with several packages and the promise of more to be delivered.

Daphne held an enormous volume in her lap as the carriage rolled slowly toward the dressmaker. It appeared to be written in German. "I cannot abide translations. One is so much at the mercy of the intellect of the translator. Even if the translators are adequate to the task, they frequently cannot keep their own opinions from coloring the translation. It is quite vexing," she murmured, pushing her glasses further up her nose.

Sarah smiled at her distracted hostess and took advantage of the lull in conversation to enjoy the view out the window. She did not believe she would ever take for granted the din and activity of London.

When the carriage stopped, Daphne looked up from her

book, confused. She frowned when she saw the dressmaker's shop. "Drat, I suppose we'd better go in. I shan't have any peace until Rowena gets what she wants."

Sarah enjoyed the next couple of hours greatly, even if her hostess did not. She was thrilled by the variety of fabrics and dress styles available. The women on Tenerife had said their shop was pitifully small and their designs outmoded, and now Sarah could see they'd spoken the truth.

Madam Saint Claire was a terrifying older woman who bullied Daphne and Sarah, but met her match in Rowena. The two women bickered endlessly over fabrics and styles. Sarah found their interaction amusing, but Daphne merely retired to a comfortable sofa and immersed herself in her book. As a result, Sarah became the battleground for the two women, her own preferences about color or style going completely unheeded.

After three-quarters of an hour of open warfare, Sarah found herself standing before a mirror in one of Madam's "ready-made" creations while the tiny Frenchwoman pinned and tucked the gown for alterations. Apparently the dress had been part of a trousseau for a young woman who'd subsequently eloped with someone other than her fiancé. As a result, Madam had been left with dozens of dresses and undergarments she was most eager to sell. It was Sarah's luck that the young woman had been almost as tall as she but somewhat larger. Sarah was speechless at the beauty of the garment.

The dress consisted of a crimson slip that was overlaid with beige lace. The effect was stunning. The red by itself would have been too garish, but the mere glimpse of it below the lace was subtle and elegant. The colors made Sarah's skin glow and her hair look more golden than she'd believed possible.

There was a lovely full train that gathered at the middle

of her back. The only embellishment was a broad beige velvet ribbon that ran beneath her bust and was caught up in the front by a lovely piece of jewelry that looked just like a cabochon-cut ruby set in antique gold.

"This can be ready tonight, *mademoiselle,*" Madam said, scrutinizing the gown in the mirror.

Sarah turned to Daphne, who was not paying attention. "My lady, will I need this tonight?"

Daphne's eyes gradually focused on Sarah. "Oh, how lovely! Yes, that is perfect on you."

Sarah flushed. "When do you think I will need this?"

"Take it for tonight. I'm sure Ramsay will come up with something. He never makes plans more than ten minutes in advance if he can help it," she mumbled, returning to her book.

"I suppose I will take it tonight, if that is not too much trouble?"

"It will be done," the Frenchwoman said. "Come, you must try on this ball gown. It was always too nice for that eloper," she added, gesturing to the gauzy confection one of the shop girls was bringing forward.

"My goodness," Sarah whispered. The beauty of the gown before her made the last dress look like a rag.

"Yes, my goodness, indeed," Madam agreed, helping Sarah into yards and yards of chiffon the color of a summer sky.

As Sarah regarded her reflection in the mirror, she was ashamed to realize how desperately she wanted this gown. She knew she shouldn't accept it from Lady Ramsay, but she could not help herself. It made her look beautiful. Or at least closer than anything else she had seen. She had to have it. The only thing she could think of as she stared at her reflection was the expression on Martín's face when he saw her wearing it.

* * *

Martín was not surprised by the reception he received at the offices for the Secretary of War and the Colonies. As he listened to the extended obsequies Graaf and the haughty English lord exchanged, he imagined he could hear the sound of his purse strings being cut and his pockets being riffled.

There would be no compensation for the capture of the *Blue Bird*—that much was apparent. He hid his irritation and focused his attention on the endlessly maundering Graaf.

"And so, my lord, it is with the deepest gratitude that I thank Captain Bouchard. Without his assistance I would not be in England." The Dutchman met Martín's eyes. He knew better than anyone how annoying it must be for Martín to witness his feting.

"Ah, yes. Captain Bouchard." Lord Bathurst looked at Martín as if he were a new type of beetle, one that he expected to classify in the dung category. "His Majesty is most grateful for your assistance as well as your discretion in the matter. The ship will be returned to his lordship's father, who—I'm sure—will wish to make arrangements to compensate you for your efforts on his lordship's behalf."

Martín looked from Bathurst to the Dutch lordling. Graaf gave him an uncomfortable smile; the Dutchman already knew his father would not be forthcoming with compensation of any kind.

"Thank you, Lord Bathurst, for your generous offer. I believe my first officer is in the process of compiling a list of expenses that he can present to, er, *his lordship*." Martín stood. He knew it was not his place to end the meeting, but he no longer cared.

"Er, yes, quite." The older man rose slowly, his smile uncertain as he transferred Martín from the beetle category to that of unstable chemical requiring careful handling and disposal.

Good. Martín enjoyed the uncertainty of others. He turned

to the Dutchman. "Tell me, will you be leaving directly for Amsterdam?" He'd hoped the meaning behind his question—when will you talk to your father about the money he owes me—was clear, but Graaf's answer demonstrated Martín's question was far too subtle.

"I believe I will stay for the duration of the Season. Perhaps I will see you at some of the entertainments?"

Martín merely raised his brows, the ludicrous suggestion not deserving of any response.

As he departed Whitehall, he couldn't help being grateful Graaf was now off his hands and out of Ramsay's house—and away from Sarah.

As to the matter of compensation? Martín snorted. He doubted he'd ever receive compensation for even the cost of Graaf's journey back to England. Not that such a trifling amount was of any interest. And it would not cover even a fraction of his costs for this last journey, all of which would be on his shoulders.

He raised a hand, and a dilapidated hackney rattled to a stop in front of him.

"Tattersalls," he ordered, climbing into the dark, filthy carriage.

He considered Graaf's last words to him—about seeing him during the Season. The man had been speaking in jest. Even with Martín's vast fortune, no hostess would entertain a man with his lineage. And if people did not know his true background now, they would certainly learn of it if he remained in London long enough.

The ancient vehicle rumbled along, and Martín considered the possibility of an ex-slave whore actually moving among the *ton*. He looked at the signet ring on his left hand. Its red stone winked at him in the dim light of the carriage, as if it were amused by his pretensions.

He was a fool.

He rapped on the carriage roof with his cane.

The vehicle slowed, and the small hatch slid open.

"Aye?" the grizzled coachman asked.

"I've changed my mind. Where is the best place to get a meal, a bed, and a wench?"

The old coachman smiled—a gruesome sight. "I've just the place for you, sir." The hatch closed with a snap.

Martín sat back against the tattered leather seat. Ramsay would understand when Martín didn't show up at Tatts. He would know where Martín had gone.

The cab stopped in front of a structure that looked very similar to the bank Martín had visited earlier in the day. In general, Martín did not hold with the notion of giving his valuables to strangers for safekeeping, but several years ago Ramsay had prevailed on him to deposit at least some of his money in such an institution.

Martín eyed the bland-looking building. Had the driver misunderstood his request? Or had he heard Martín's accent and decided to play foul with a Frenchie?

The hatch slid open, and the man gave him a toothless grin. "Here ye are, sir. The Cherry Pit. The finest place in all London." Martín gave him a skeptical look, but stepped out of the cab.

"The finest ladies in London, sir. Jes up that walk, knock on that black door, and they'll take care of ye."

Martín paid the man and mounted the steps. A bewigged and powdered lackey answered his knock.

"Good afternoon, sir. Please, come inside." He took Martín's hat and cane and led him up a flight of stairs before depositing him in a drawing room to wait.

Martín poured a drink from one of the decanters on a small table. He took a sip. It was quite fine brandy. A small shelf of books caught his attention, and he was reading the titles when the door opened. For a moment, he thought a young girl had entered the room. But as the woman came closer he saw that she wasn't a girl at all. In fact, he would place her age close to his.

"I am Mrs. Hensleigh. Welcome to the White House." Her voice was low for such a tiny thing.

"*Bonjour,* madam, I am Captain Bouchard." He bowed over her hand. "I am worried that maybe I came to the wrong place?" He smiled down into her upturned face. She wasn't merely the size of a doll; she also looked like one. Her guinea-colored curls framed a heart-shaped face with large blue eyes and small bow-shaped lips. She bore a remarkable resemblance to the porcelain doll he'd brought back for Ramsay's daughter.

But then she smiled, and he realized the only thing innocent or doll-like about her eyes was the color. The expression in them was as old as sin. "I believe you have come to the perfect place," she countered, taking a seat on the delicate settee and gesturing him to the wing chair across from it.

"This is the . . . Cherry Pit?"

"That is not my choice of name, but it seems to have stuck. Tell me—how did you hear of my establishment?"

"A hackney driver delivered me to your doorstep when I asked him to bring me to the finest establishment your city offered."

She smiled slightly. "We are unique; there is no denying that. But we are unique in a way that is not to everyone's taste. The women who work here do so of their own free will. We do not cater to men interested in virgins, nor are there any women here younger than eight and ten." She cut him a direct look from eyes like blue glass.

"I am not interested in young girls, and I certainly do not want a virgin." A sudden vision of Sarah intruded on his business negotiations. One virgin was enough to last him a lifetime.

"Excellent. Also, we do not allow any roughness. Any such behavior will be dealt with immediately."

"*Bien sûr*, madam. I do not enjoy beating women."

"I can see we shall deal exceedingly well, Captain. That is quite enough business for the present. Let us turn to pleasure. What is your preference?"

"Your best room, two girls—any but brown-haired—two bottles of your best red to start and one of this brandy, and a meal for three—unless you would like to join us?" He liked the knowing look in her eyes.

She gazed up from beneath blond lashes. "Thank you, Captain. I shall certainly keep your offer in mind."

Martín laughed at her coquettish look. It was designed to tease and put him in his place at the same time. She would not be joining him for bed sport.

Mrs. Hensleigh led Martín up two more flights of stairs to a suite that was capacious and decorated in shades of brown and gold. Fine carpets covered the polished wood floor, and the furniture was built for comfort as well as style. All and all, it was every bit as elegant as the rooms in Davenport House.

"This will serve me admirably. I will engage it for the foreseeable future. I would ask you to send word to my man and have him bring my things." He gave her the address of Davenport House. "Make sure whoever delivers the message is discreet."

"Naturally."

"I would have my bath and more brandy before my meal."

She inclined her head and left.

Martín went to the window and gazed out onto the quiet, empty street below.

It was better this way. He would mix with his own kind and leave Sarah to find hers. From what Ramsay had said, the woman was a member of one of the wealthiest banking families in England. No doubt they would see to it she met suitable men.

The last thing she would want was to bring to her rich relations an association with an ex-slave, not to mention the rest.

The door opened, and he turned away from the street and his thoughts. Two women stood in the entryway, a buxom redhead and a petite blonde. He breathed a sigh of relief. Both women were lovely and very elegantly dressed, and neither of them bore even a passing resemblance to Sarah.

The women stood aside as a parade of strapping servants arrived with buckets of steaming water for his bath.

Martín smiled. "Please, come in, *mesdemoiselles,* and let us become better acquainted."

Chapter Twenty-Two

Martín had moved his belongings out of Davenport House.

"Bouchard has taken rooms at Mivart's, I believe," Ramsay said at breakfast the following morning. "He does not like to be beholden to anyone."

For the first time since she'd met him, the baron was not his usual, smiling self. She hoped the two men had not quarreled. Martín often rubbed people—men, in particular— the wrong way, but she would have thought that wouldn't apply to the baron, who seemed to enjoy the younger man's abrasive company. In fact, Sarah believed he actively encouraged and taunted Martín into behaving badly.

For her part, Sarah was too choked with emotion to speak. She nodded and smiled, lifting a forkful of kipper to her mouth.

"I had hoped to learn what happened at Lord Bathurst's office." Sarah's face heated at Ramsay's inquiring look, and she hastened to explain. "Admiral Keeton promised Bouchard he would receive compensation for taking me back to England."

Ramsay added a shocking amount of sugar to his coffee. "I haven't spoken to him on the matter. Neither did I find out from Graaf what happened before he left."

Mies, too, was gone—a guest at the king's London residence, of all places.

"I shall send word to Martín today and invite him to the theater tonight, if I am able to secure seats at this late date."

Sarah squirmed under the baron's kind, knowing look.

Daphne, who'd been absorbed in the book that lay open beside her plate, fixed her husband with a long, bespectacled look before turning to Sarah.

"I daresay we shall see Bouchard in the coming days. In any case, we shall be busy. Tomorrow you meet your uncles."

Sarah had received an immediate response from her uncle Sir Septimus, informing her of their intention to call on Lady Ramsay. Because his brother was out of town, he begged to delay their first meeting until he returned to London. Sarah had been relieved. She needed a little more time to accustom herself to the sudden appearance of two wealthy uncles. And to decide what she would, and wouldn't, tell them.

True to his word, Lord Ramsay secured a box at the theater that night.

Even Martín's absence could not ruin Sarah's enjoyment in her first play. Not only was the play itself diverting, but the cream of London society stopped by their box. Lord Ramsay attracted people, mainly women, like moths to a flame.

Daphne, too, had her share of admirers, mainly scholars who'd been dragged to the opera by spouses or friends. Sarah watched with amusement as the beautiful blond woman engaged in a heated exchange with three elderly men and a boy who must certainly still be at university. Mysterious words like "Hegelian," "dialectic," and "hegemony," were enough to keep Sarah at a safe distance.

She was speaking with Lord Ramsay and one of his cousins when she felt a light tap on her shoulder and turned to find Mies.

"Good evening, Sarah." The Dutchman must have visited Bond Street as he was now dressed in well-tailored black-and-white evening clothes.

"Mies! What are you doing here?" she asked rather rudely.

He grinned. "I am likely to pop up anywhere now that I am no longer under house arrest."

"Yes, of course. But tell me, how was your meeting with Lord Bathurst?"

Mies glanced around the box. "Did Bouchard not tell you?"

"He moved out of Lord Ramsay's house yesterday."

Mies shrugged and held his hands out, palm up. "Well, you are now looking at a free man."

"I am glad for you, Mies." While Sarah could never approve of what he'd done, she did not approve of incarceration either. "Will you be going home soon?"

"I thought I should stay and experience the London Season while I am here. Also, I am scheduled to meet the regent and Princess Charlotte. Apparently they are determined to show me every kindness even though Her Royal Highness gave my cousin William the boot."

"What a horrible thing to say," she said, laughing.

"It is the truth. It seems they do not realize my father has long been estranged from his royal relations. In any case, I am the beneficiary of that ignorance, so I will stay for the introduction. Perhaps our paths will cross and we will be able to dance?"

"You wouldn't enjoy it, I can promise you that. I'm afraid I don't know a single dance."

He seemed to find that a welcome piece of news. "Perhaps Lady Ramsay will allow me to offer lessons—with the correct supervision, of course."

"I'm sure you have much more important things to do."

"I can't think of anything more important to me." His expression was dangerously earnest, and Sarah was glad the baron picked that moment to introduce her to one of his acquaintances.

Sarah found Mies's interest in her embarrassing. She'd understood his infatuation while they'd been aboard the *Golden Scythe*. After all, she'd been the only woman onboard.

But she'd hoped his feelings for her would dissipate when they left the ship.

She supposed she could not be so lucky. After all, her interest in Martín had not diminished with her increased exposure to new and interesting people. On the contrary, every handsome man she met just served to make Martín more attractive to her.

Pounding, agonizing pain. At first Martín thought the pounding was only inside his skull, just as it had been every morning for the past two weeks, but then he realized somebody was knocking on his door. He looked at the clock on the nightstand; it was almost noon. He felt the bed next to him and realized it was empty.

"What?" he croaked, the sound of his voice causing his head to ache even worse.

"Captain Bouchard, you have a visitor downstairs."

It sounded like Mrs. Hensleigh, or Venetia as he now called her. The door opened, and the diminutive madam entered. Her blurry form advanced on the bed. "You have a visitor," she repeated. "A rather impressive visitor. Six and a half feet, one eye?"

"*Merde*." Martín gripped his forehead with one hand, squeezing like a vise.

She chuckled. "I should not like to have him come and fetch me. He looks pleasant enough right now, but he has given you an hour to join him in the drawing room. I will try to keep him entertained, although he has already made it plain he is not interested in conducting any business."

Martín couldn't resist laughing even though it was agony. "He is besotted with his wife and only gets worse every day."

"Mmm, how wonderful for them both," she said wistfully. "I've ordered a bath, and Nicole and Francie will be along to help you. You will do as I ask, won't you, darling? I'd hate for the giant downstairs to come looking for you."

Martín grunted.

Taking that for an assent, she left him alone.

Martín lay back on the bed; he would get up when the two women arrived to help him. God knew he was paying them enough for little other than bathing, dressing, and undressing him every day. And for keeping mum about what *did not* go on in his suite every night. He suppressed the urge to weep like a little girl as he considered his predicament.

Just as in Freetown and Tenerife, he was unable to enjoy sexual relations with the two whores who were getting a fortune to attend to his needs around the clock. Just as before, he had only been able to get an erection when by himself.

When thinking of Sarah.

He turned on his side, burying his face in the rumpled bedclothes. After three days of it, Venetia had come to his room. She'd been polite, but firm. Was there something wrong? Did he need someone other than Francie or Nicole?

At the time he'd been too intoxicated and careless of how he might appear, so he'd told the tiny madam how he'd not been able to bed a woman since that first night with Sarah.

Martín had not been surprised when she had laughed at him. He would have thought it was a laughable matter if it hadn't been happening to him.

But then she had told him something he didn't want to hear: that he was infatuated with the annoying missionary woman.

Well, Venetia had used the word "love," as women were wont to do, but Martín had discarded *that* idea immediately. It wasn't love; it was infatuation. And while that was almost as bad, he had hopes the affliction would eventually go away. Already he had a difficult time recalling Sarah's face.

Well, except for the way she'd looked that time in the cabin, when he had given her pleasure and almost climaxed himself in the process. Or how she looked while teaching him to read. Or the cute way she scolded him for breaking another quill. Or the time when she'd held him at gunpoint on the deck of his ship.

"Enough," he yelled at his treacherous mind, wincing at the pain in his pounding head. So he remembered more about her than he'd thought—what of it? The memories would fade.

The door opened, and a troop of servants with steaming buckets marched through the room. He turned his face to the wall until the door closed again.

"Captain?"

He rolled over and grunted, taking a deep breath and swinging his feet to the ground. "*Mon Dieu.*" He was too wobbly to stand.

Small hands grasped his arms and helped him to his feet. Francie, the little blonde, stood beside him. "Come on, Captain, you've not got too much time. You don't want to keep the big gentleman waiting."

Nicole giggled. "My goodness, he's a big one. I don't think I've ever seen a man that tall. He's that pirate, isn't he—One-Eyed Standish? I read about him in the paper a few years back. I heard he was handsome but . . . crikey!"

"No more giggling," Martín ordered. The women pulled his shirt over his head and then shoved him toward the tub. He dipped a toe in the scalding water and recoiled. "Do you think I am a lobster?"

"Don't be a big softie; it'll feel good when you're in it." Francie pushed him with her small hands.

"Oh, is that true, *mademoiselle?* Perhaps you would like to join me?" He snaked his arm around her slim waist, and she squealed in his ear, causing him to jerk away. "In the name of God, Francie!" He slid into the tub, his head ringing from her high-pitched cry.

The women laughed, ignoring his complaints, scrubbing and soaping him while he lay like a corpse in the water.

"Lovely hair, isn't it, Francie?"

"Oh, aye." She massaged his scalp, almost making his headache disappear. Almost.

"Isn't it interesting that it's so much darker down here?" Nicole manipulated his flaccid member to show her friend his darker pubic hair.

"Enough," Martín roared. "Get out, both of you, out." He was pleased at the sound of their receding footsteps and giggling until he realized that now he'd need to finish bathing and dressing himself. Well, anything was better than a couple of nosy whores who poked and prodded him as if he were a side of beef. He gritted his teeth at the humiliation of his situation. And now here was Ramsay to poke his own big nose into Martín's business. "I'll bloody well tell him where to take his nose," Martín said, soaping himself so hard he winced.

Martín reached the drawing room just as it struck the hour and found Ramsay in the process of getting to his feet, his face determined.

"What do you want?" Martín asked, not caring how ungracious he sounded.

Naturally the baron merely laughed at his rudeness.

Martín ignored him and poured himself a glass of Venetia's fine brandy, exhaling with relief as the liquid burned its way down his throat. "Well?" he snapped, when the other man didn't answer.

"My wife sent me to inquire as to when you will be returning to Davenport House?"

Martín looked at him to see if he was in jest. Lady Ramsay detested him. She would be over the moon he had left.

"Barring your return, she wonders if you have any plans

to join any of her entertainments. You know how women are when it comes to having the right number for dinner and so forth."

Martín couldn't resist laughing at the blatant lie. Lady Ramsay could scarcely remember to *dress* herself for dinner. She was the last woman in the world to be interested in matters as mundane as seating charts and headcounts.

He took his full glass to the seat farthest from the baron. "I like it here."

"Yes, I can see why you would. Mrs. Hensleigh seems an excellent hostess. However, she did indicate that you might be—shall we say—lacking the requisite enthusiasm?"

Martín swore. "Am I not paying these whores good money to keep their mouths closed?"

Again the baron laughed. "Oh, come, Martín, she told me nothing. I guessed how it was. You do not look like a man who's been well serviced. You look like a man who can hardly stand his own skin. Even my wife, who barely takes notice of events such as war, famine, or plague, commented that you were behaving oddly during your brief sojourn with us."

"I do not know what you are talking about. I am behaving exactly as I usually do." Martín gestured to his person with one hand. "You see me, here. It shouldn't surprise you I am most at home in a whorehouse."

"No, that does not surprise me. What does surprise me is that I should have to rescue you from one. Again."

Martín was stunned. Never before had Ramsay mentioned the night they'd met.

"Come, my friend," the older man said, his voice suddenly gentle. "You cannot be afraid of one small girl?"

"You do not know of what you speak, *Lord Ramsay*." Martín threw back his drink and pondered the wisdom of having another.

"I know exactly of what I speak, although I can see you are somewhat confused. I came here today to tell you to act or miss your chance. Graaf has rarely left her side these past two weeks. He's also ingratiated himself with her uncles. Naturally they share much in common."

Martín felt as though he were looking through a veil of steam.

"Yes," the baron continued, relentless. "Graaf runs tame in their London house. I understand he is even teaching Sarah to ride. In any event"—he shrugged, as if suddenly bored with the topic—"here are several invitations." Ramsay stood and handed Martín a small bundle of cards. "One of those is from Lady Ramsay. She is hosting a dinner party, a small one. I expect she would appreciate a response from you if you can find the time." He smiled down at Martín while pulling on his gloves. "My wife has indicated your room is ready and at your disposal. Or, if you prefer, I can direct you to more appropriate lodgings. Either way, I'm certain you will make the correct decision."

Martín sat at the small desk after Ramsay took his leave. He looked at the cards he still held in his hand. Ramsay must have exerted pressure on his behalf. Who otherwise would invite a man like him to any function? Against his will, but too curious to resist, he opened the first card, a handwritten invitation from Lady Ramsay. The second, more formally printed, was an invitation to a ball in Miss Sarah Fisher's honor, to be held at her uncle's—Baron Danestoke's—house. The third was an invitation from Mia, the Marchioness of Exley. Martín's mouth twisted at the thought of being a guest of the Marquess of Exley. He wondered if the marchioness had told her starchy husband whom she'd invited to their house. Probably not.

Venetia entered without knocking. "Your friend has gone, I see."

Martín stood as she entered the room. "Yes, he has delivered what he came to deliver." He waved the stack of invitations at her.

Her lips twisted. "Oh, was that what he came to deliver?"

Martín resumed his seat after she'd taken hers, wondering what the woman wanted. He didn't have long to wonder.

"I've taken the liberty of having your bags packed."

"What? Am I in arrears?"

"You know you are not. But I think it is time for you to move to more suitable accommodations."

Martín shook his head. "Have I been such an unpleasant guest? Why would you cast away such a guaranteed source of income?"

"I have decided to put something else above profit."

He snorted. "Is that wise?"

"I doubt it. Still, I find I like you very much, Captain."

Martín raised his eyebrows. After all, he'd invited her to his bed numerous times. He'd told her she could name her own price, believing maybe she would be what he needed to break the wretched curse that held him. She'd rejected every offer.

"I do not mean as a lover," she said, easily reading his thoughts. "We would never suit each other in that way. We are too much alike, our pasts and expectations too similar. We neither of us believe anything good will come our way. And both of us are suspicious of anyone who appears to care for us." Martín met her gaze and saw the truth in her hard, doll-like eyes.

"But perhaps we are wrong, Captain. You are not so dead to your feelings as you pretend. I know this is frightening to you because I know how much *I* should dislike it. But I believe you cannot rid yourself of your emotions by drinking and whoring. Well, particularly not by whoring," she added, her smile mocking.

Heat crept up his neck. "What makes you think you understand me so well?"

She raised one delicate blond eyebrow. "You do not recall all you told me that night, do you?"

His face twitched at the memory of the night in question. Who knew the entirety of what he had said while in his cups? She did, apparently.

"I shall tell you what I did not tell you that night. I, too, was sold into this life." She nodded at his startled look. "Yes, the English not only sell Africans into slavery, but their own kind, as well. The market for young girls and boys always flourishes, a fact my three sisters and I learned to our detriment." She paused, her expression unreadable.

"My point in telling you this is to let you know that I *do* understand you. Better than anyone. You and I think we know what the world is, but we only know one dark corner of it. Your missionary isn't from our corner. Perhaps she is what you need. Or maybe you will tire of her once you finally possess her." Venetia shrugged, her outlook on the subject as practical as it would be on the matter of purchasing a joint of meat or a flagon of wine. "In either case, it ill behooves you to hide here, avoiding the situation. We might be whores, Captain, but we are neither of us cowards."

Martín was too stunned to speak. Kicked out of a brothel by a madam. Who would have thought it possible? He looked at the decanter of brandy and then set down his glass without finishing what remained.

"Can you recommend a comfortable hotel?"

Chapter Twenty-Three

Sarah stared at her reflection in the glass as her maid applied the finishing touches to her hair. She wore the sky blue ball gown Lady Ramsay had insisted on buying for her. The heavenly hue made her freckled, sun-browned skin glow and turned her mousy hair a golden honey brown.

The neckline was rather lower than she liked, but she knew it was modest compared to those of the dresses her contemporaries wore. She felt that her uncles, both somewhat conservative, would not approve of many of the necklines she had seen.

Sarah smiled at the thought of her uncles. Who would have believed such dry countenances could conceal such generous hearts? The two old bachelors had never found time to marry. As a result, they took a close interest in their nieces and nephews, and Sarah was no exception.

Sarah had learned much about her father in the few weeks she'd lived with his older brothers. Michael Fisher had been born late in his parents' lives, the youngest of six children.

"We all indulged him horribly, I'm afraid," her uncle Septimus admitted.

"Our parents allowed him to pursue his medical studies

even though they believed it no better than barbering. But they drew a line at his interest in Nonconformism and hoped Michael would grow away from such beliefs if given enough time," her uncle Barnabus explained, describing the family schism.

"He might have if he hadn't met your mother," Septimus added.

The three of them were discussing the matter after dinner one night in her uncles' vast house on Charles Street.

"Your mother strengthened his resolve. As a parson's daughter she had the courage of her convictions, and it was just the motivation Michael needed."

It was plain to see how much the two old men had cared for her father. Sarah also saw how much they blamed her mother for leading Michael Fisher into missionary work. She didn't have the heart to tell her uncles she was of the same mind as her parents.

She could not live in England.

At first, she'd been afraid she would become so enamored of the sparkle and glamor of London that she'd forget all about the promises she'd made to her parents. But it had taken only a few weeks for her to see this was not the life she wanted.

Although it had felt treasonous toward her uncles, who'd welcomed her so warmly into their lives, she'd not been able to resist meeting with the head of the missionary society that had funded her parents so long ago.

She'd explained who she was and what had transpired in her village and had then presented her idea of returning to Africa and resuming her parents' work.

The elderly man had looked at her with scorn on his haughty face before thoroughly rejecting both Sarah and her plans.

"I'm afraid we cannot help you, Miss Fisher. It is my

opinion you'd do better to apply your misguided enthusiasm to some more suitable cause, like acquiring a husband and children."

Another four meetings with different organizations had yielded similar outcomes.

If Sarah was to get back to Africa, it would not be with the assistance of a missionary society.

"There you are, miss." Cooper's voice pulled Sarah's thoughts from her failed ventures.

Sarah smiled at her maid in the mirror. "Thank you, Cooper, you are a miracle worker." She adjusted her gauzy wrap and collected her reticule, wishing she viewed her first ball with more anticipation. It was no use lying about the reason for her lack of interest. It was six feet of stubborn male beauty that went by the name of Martín Bouchard.

She arrived downstairs to find her Aunt Anna—the oldest of her father's sisters—waiting for her.

"You look lovely, Sarah," her aunt said, and then commenced to chatter on about the evening ahead. Her aunt had already married off her own daughters and had gladly accepted the role of chaperone, no matter how foolish that might be given the fact that Sarah had been on her own for several years. Still, it made her uncles happy, so Sarah accepted her aunt's offer, even though Anna was a rather frivolous woman and they had little in common.

Her uncles' carriage waited to take them to Exley House, the town house of the Marquess of Exley. A footman helped them into the luxurious vehicle, and she relaxed against the squabs while her aunt conducted a conversation that required no responses from Sarah. Tonight was not only her first ball; it was also going to be the first time she danced in public. That was if anyone asked her.

Although Daphne would have rather spent her days reading,

she'd been unflagging in her support of bringing Sarah into society, even going so far as to teach Sarah to dance.

Naturally the project had attracted the attention of Lord Ramsay, and the three of them had spent a good portion of the prior weeks in the large drawing room at Davenport House, which Daphne had converted into a ballroom. Daphne played the pianoforte while Lord Ramsay and Sarah danced. Ramsay was an exquisite dancer, particularly for such a large man.

"Years spent on board a ship," he replied when Sarah complimented his grace.

"Don't believe him, Sarah," Daphne called from the pianoforte, over which her fingers were moving smoothly even as she spoke. "He has all the skills of an accomplished rake."

"My wife would have you believe I did nothing but pursue women and my own pleasure in the years before I met her."

"I do not need your wife's word to believe that," Sarah assured the handsome baron, her acerbic comment drawing his wife's laughter.

Sarah did not imagine she could ever enjoy a ball as much as she had those afternoons with her two friends.

"You will be the toast of the ball, Sarah," the baron had assured her this afternoon after her last lesson, a particularly grueling session spent on the waltz.

"That is a well-intentioned exaggeration. Thanks to you and Lady Ramsay, I believe I will not shame myself, which is more than I ever hoped to achieve in such a short time."

The ball this evening was considered a highlight of the Season. Sarah knew Mies would not be there. Apparently he was busy with some function at Carlton House. Sarah had been relieved to hear it as he'd been spending entirely too much time haunting her uncles' house—and her.

Even though Mies was being feted by doting mamas and

royalty alike, he was still intent on gaining Sarah's attention. He'd even approached her uncles for permission to court her. Sarah had been furious and had told him so. She was almost five and twenty—she did not need anyone's permission to marry.

Her uncles, not unnaturally, were thrilled that a member of the Dutch aristocracy wanted to marry their niece. She hated to disappoint them, but she would never marry Mies. She liked him well enough, but she could never admire him. It pained her to think that she had such an unforgiving nature, but she could never overlook his past.

As was always the case when she thought of slavery, or practically any subject of late, a pair of gold eyes flashed into her mind. Sarah *tsk*ed in disgust. She should be glad he'd left Davenport House before she made a fool of herself.

Their carriage was one of the first to arrive at the imposing Palladian mansion, and she'd just removed her wrap and handed it to a footman when the tiny Marchioness of Exley came rushing toward her, a taller woman hurrying to keep up with her.

"Sarah, how lovely to see you." The exuberant woman embraced Sarah as if she were a dear friend.

Sarah blushed at the warm welcome. "Good evening, Lady Exley. This is my aunt, Mrs. Anna Dearing."

"Good evening, Mrs. Dearing, this is my cousin, Mrs. Rebecca Devane and she is dying to meet you. Do you mind if I steal Sarah away from you for a moment?" Before her aunt could formulate an answer, the smaller woman whisked her away. "I'm sorry if that was rather rude, but I simply *must* introduce you to my husband and I'm afraid Adam isn't good for more than one or two introductions per evening, and you will be his second."

Sarah laughed. "I'm honored, Lady Exley."

"Do not tell me you mean to stand on ceremony?" the other woman demanded, all but dragging Sarah toward the large drawing room. "We have consumed too much wine together and exchanged naughty secrets. I thought I told you to call me Mia?"

The marchioness was referring to the first time they'd met at Lady Ramsay's. They had indeed consumed too much wine and exchanged too many confidences. The small redhead was quite irrepressible, and even Daphne, usually the voice of reason, had laughed until tears sprang to her eyes at the marchioness's amusing gossip.

Mia Exley barely came up to Sarah's shoulder and was built like a fairy—a very sensual fairy. Her dress clung indecently to her small, shapely form. And she didn't merely walk; she flowed. Sarah knew she was older than she appeared and that she'd lived for many years in a harem; it was something of an open secret among the *ton*.

"Adam has been dying to meet you," Mia said, leading her toward a slim man standing by himself. "Adam, here is Miss Fisher." Several other guests turned their heads at the sound of her overly loud voice.

Daphne's description of the Marquess of Exley had been accurate: he looked like a marble statue come to life. He was also the most perfectly dressed and coiffed man she'd ever seen. What Daphne hadn't shared was how perfectly cold he was. It was easy to see how he'd come by his notorious sobriquet: the Murderous Marquess.

"This is my husband, the Marquess of Exley. But you must call him Adam." The marchioness smiled up at her husband, her face tilted toward him like a flower. He looked at his wife for a long moment before turning to Sarah. His eyes were an extraordinary pale blue that seemed to flay the flesh from her bones. Sarah wished she'd kept her wrap.

He bowed over her hand. "It is a pleasure, Miss Fisher. I understand you come to us from Africa. No doubt my wife will have much to discuss with you." As if he, personally, would have nothing to say to her.

"Adam, you are being obtuse." Mia hit him with her fan. Sarah could have sworn the marquess almost smiled.

"I'm afraid I must persist with my behavior. Exactly how am I being obtuse, my dear?"

"Sarah lived in *West* Africa; I lived in *North* Africa. They could not be more different. Also, Sarah lived with her parents, who were missionaries. Don't you think that sounds fascinating?"

"One can only imagine," Exley murmured, as if he put such information on a list somewhere between a tooth extraction and a trip to Lady Exley's milliner. The killing smile he bestowed on his wife would have been enough to make any normal person crawl under a rock. A small dimple appeared in the redhead's cheek, and Sarah realized she was baiting her austere spouse.

"Oh, look, here is Gabriel." Lady Exley transferred her attention to the young man who'd just joined them.

"Good evening, Mother."

"This is Miss Fisher, Gabriel. Sarah, this is my son, Gabriel."

His dark auburn hair and tilted green eyes would have proclaimed his relationship to Lady Exley even without an introduction. His charming accent, high cheekbones, and prominent nose must have come from his father, the deceased Sultan Babba Hassan.

He gave Sarah a warm smile and bowed. "I am very pleased to meet you, Miss Fisher. I understand you have recently arrived from the Gold Coast."

They were conversing about West Africa when Daphne and Hugh arrived.

"Sarah, my dear, you look lovely," Ramsay said, kissing her hand with a teasing smile.

"Captain Martín Bouchard," the butler's voice boomed behind them. Sarah started so violently she jostled the baron's arm.

"Steady on," Ramsay murmured.

"What a pleasure to see you, Martín," Lady Exley called out, greeting Martín with the same affectionate manner she seemed to use with everyone. Sarah shot a surreptitious look around the little group. The marquess appeared even more supercilious, Gabriel Marlington looked openly annoyed, and Daphne was as inscrutable as ever. Only Ramsay and Lady Exley seemed truly pleased to see the man.

Well, and Sarah.

Martín turned to Sarah after relinquishing Lady Exley's hand. "Good evening, Mademoiselle Fisher. It is a pleasure to see you looking so well." He subjected her to a piercing visual inspection. Heat and desire flared in her abdomen as his lips pressed against the back of her gloved hand.

"What a pleasant surprise," she murmured.

"An unexpected pleasure indeed," Lord Exley said, giving his wife an unreadable look before turning to greet his guest. "It's been a long time, Bouchard." The unspoken message being: not long enough.

Martín flashed a grin. "To me it seems like only yesterday, my lord." He turned to Mia's son and looked him up and down. "Well, look at you, boy—all grown up, eh?"

"Captain Bouchard." The younger man's exceedingly handsome face darkened, and he glanced at his mother. "If you will excuse me, I will go see what is keeping Eva." He gave Martín a narrow-eyed glare as he left.

Ramsay, predictably, burst out laughing. "Come now, Martín, you must behave. You are among civilized people here."

Martín smiled roguishly at his mentor.

The group split into smaller parts, and Sarah was surprised to see Martín move off with the Marquess of Exley. Rather than look annoyed, the reserved peer engaged in a quiet, but earnest conversation with the exotic captain. Sarah burned with curiosity. What could the two men possibly have to talk about?

"I'm sorry, Sarah. I should have told you he might be here tonight," Daphne said from beside her. "Hugh told me that he'd gone to see Captain Bouchard to deliver the invitation."

"No doubt he found him in some bordello or other."

Daphne neither confirmed nor denied Sarah's claim. "Coming here tonight is a big step for him. You must try to understand that this is a world he is completely unprepared for, no matter that he possesses the correct clothing and the only real requirement for membership—money."

"Until a short while ago I lived in a *jungle*."

"But you are a woman, and we are much smarter."

Sarah laughed at Daphne's quiet certitude.

"Captain Bouchard is very much like my two sons, Sarah. You cannot *tell* them what it is you want them to do. You must make them believe the idea was theirs to begin with. I expect he is rather intimidated by your recently elevated status. Don't be surprised if he is somewhat prickly."

"He was prickly before he learned of my family connections. He's behaved rudely from the first moment I met him."

"I believe that is his usual way of going on. He exhibited shocking rudeness when I first met him. When he wasn't actually going out of his way to taunt me, he was completely dismissive."

"That is exactly how he's behaved toward me."

"I doubt he has behaved *exactly* the same way toward you."

Sarah's face burned as she recalled three episodes when he'd been anything but dismissive.

"Daphne." Mia's voice came from behind them. "I must interrupt you two for a moment and introduce Miss Fisher to the Misses Manton and their brother, Viscount Danforth."

Mia stood with two elegant older women and a handsome younger man.

"We understand you are only recently come from Africa, Miss Fisher. We are most eager to hear all about your experiences," the taller of the two sisters said.

"You'll have to excuse my sister, Miss Fisher. If you don't have a care, she will have you trapped in a corner the entire evening, extracting every detail of your life," Viscount Danforth warned with a good-natured smile.

"I should be glad to tell you anything you like, Miss Manton. I, too, wish to extract some information from you."

"Oh? What kind of information do you seek?"

"Lady Exley told me you are associated with several charitable endeavors."

Miss Manton's eyes warmed. "Indeed we are. We are always looking to swell the ranks of our volunteers."

The dinner announcement interrupted their conversation, and Viscount Danforth offered Sarah his arm. "May I have the pleasure of escorting you to dinner, Miss Fisher?"

"Thank you, my lord."

They walked the short distance to the dining room, where the large table had settings for about thirty people.

"Hmm," he murmured, examining the place cards. "Here you are and here am I, right next to you. How pleasant!"

Sarah was seated when Martín appeared beside her, a sardonic gleam in his eyes. "It looks as if I, too, will have the pleasure of your company, Miss Fisher."

Sarah's treacherous nerves tingled at his nearness, and she caught the faintest whiff of his scent as he sat beside her. He looked spectacular. The only man in the room attired more elegantly was their host. Still, Sarah found Martín's muscular build and exotic looks far more attractive than those of the slim, supercilious peer. Martín, for all his faults—and Sarah knew they were legion—was never inhuman.

Arrogant, intractable, irascible, unpredictable, moody, and vain—but not inhuman.

It wasn't until nearly halfway through the second course that Sarah was able to turn away from the diverting and talkative viscount toward Martín. He was engaged in a lively discussion with the woman on his other side, the younger of the two Manton sisters. The woman said something that caused him to throw back his head and laugh. Jealousy clawed Sarah from stem to stern. It seemed he was fitting in quite nicely.

"I understand you came to England on Captain Bouchard's ship, Miss Fisher?" Danforth asked, pulling her attention back to him.

"Yes, the captain was kind enough to offer me passage."

"I've heard several stops along that route are quite lovely."

"Tenerife was particularly charming. Do you travel much, my lord?"

"No, I'm afraid I have not been much of anyplace. Now that the Continent is once again accessible, I expect we will eventually make a journey—my sisters and I."

"You are very close to your sisters, I collect."

He smiled. "Yes, they've been very good to me. My parents died when I was quite young, and they gave up their own lives to raise me."

"It must be wonderful to have siblings. I was close to several of the children in my village, but it is not the same, I think."

Naturally the mention of her village brought the subject around to Africa. They spent some time discussing life in the jungle before his attention was claimed by the attractive young woman on the other side of him. The cold look she gave Sarah made her realize she'd been monopolizing the handsome young viscount.

"You are monopolizing your dinner partner," Martín drawled in her ear, his words echoing her thoughts.

Sarah turned to face him directly. "Very well, Captain Bouchard, I shall monopolize you for a while." She was proud of how level her voice sounded in spite of the thumping in her chest. "I was just discussing the subject of siblings with Lord Danforth and lamenting my lack. Have you any brothers or sisters?"

His lips twisted. "More than likely, but none with whom I am acquainted. I was born a slave, Miss Fisher—the property of another man. The people at this table probably pay closer attention to the bloodlines of their horses or dogs than my owner paid to my lineage. But no doubt my mother, whoever she was, produced reliably, just like any other of his broodmares. I would not be surprised to learn I have more than a few siblings."

Sarah felt as though she'd been slapped; she couldn't think of anything to say.

Luckily, he didn't seem to expect anything. He raised a forkful of food to his mouth and regarded her with his unnerving yellow gaze as he chewed, swallowed, and then drank deeply from the ruby liquid in his glass. "Your relations are of far greater interest to me. How are you finding life as the member of such an august family?"

Was there anything she could ever do or say to shake the defensive look from his face? Why did he insist on viewing everything she said as an attack? Why could he not laugh with her as he had with Miss Manton?

"You could have met them yourself if you'd not disappeared," she said coolly.

He gave her an amused look before raising his glass to his lips. She stared at his full, sensuous mouth, slammed by the memory of it between her legs. The vision was so powerful, so . . . physical, it rendered her blind and deaf.

"Sarah?" He was peering at her, and his voice was hollow, as if it came from the end of a long corridor.

"I . . . I beg your pardon?"

"I said, surely your guardians would not welcome a visit from one such as me?"

His words worked like a magnet on her scattered thoughts, and Sarah gave vent to the sigh of irritation this topic deserved.

"It is inconceivable to me why your past as a slave should influence any forward-thinking person. It is the person who owned you who should be ashamed. I find it beyond irksome that you would ever think me, or a member of my family, capable of such thoughts. I am also disappointed you think learning I have *august relations* would change me. I am the same person as ever."

Martín merely smiled.

Sarah found his condescending smirk more than a little galling. She could no longer hold back the question that had been burning a hole in her mind for days. "And where have *you* been these past weeks?"

He laughed. "I, too, am the same person I have always been."

She jerked her eyes away from his taunting face and gazed sightlessly at the plate before her, unable to hide her misery. That was as good as an admission that he'd spent the past weeks in a brothel. She was a fool to care for him. His behavior proclaimed his feelings for her all too plainly: he had none. What had happened between them meant less than nothing to him. He'd hardly been able to get away from her quickly enough when they reached London, and now she knew he'd spent the entire time in the arms of another woman. Or several, more likely. The sour tang of bile flooded her mouth, threatening to choke her.

"Are you quite all right, Miss Fisher?" Lord Danforth's handsome brow wrinkled with concern.

She was making a spectacle of herself.

She blinked hard several times. "I must have inhaled a piece of pepper. I will be fine," she assured him, drinking deeply from her water goblet.

The meal lasted several hundred years. Sarah answered the viscount's questions and made the requisite inquiries, the entire time aware of the low rumble beside her that indicated Martín was engaged in conversation with his other dinner partner, oblivious to what his words had done to her.

Chapter Twenty-Four

Martín regretted the words even as they left his mouth. Once again he'd behaved like an obnoxious boor. He did not understand this urge to offend and disgust her. Why had he snapped at her so viciously when she'd asked about his family? Why did he have to tell her where he had been? In the past he had never hidden his behavior from anyone, but neither had he flaunted it as he did with Sarah.

"How long will you be in England, Captain Bouchard?"

Martín realized he'd not been paying heed to his dinner companion. "I have no fixed plans, merely a few matters that need my attention."

"Where will you go next?"

"I will go to Paris."

"Indeed, how exciting! You are French?"

Martín eyed the woman beside him. She was perhaps ten years older than he. Although she was by no means attractive, she had an intelligent sparkle in her wide gray eyes and a very engaging manner. The way her gaze roamed his face and body was suggestive. He wondered if the unmarried sisters of a viscount were permitted to engage in carnal adventures. He made a note to ask Ramsay about such matters when they were next alone.

"No, *mademoiselle,* I am an American."

Her expressive brows rose at this information.

"Oh, then you are recently our enemy. Tell me, are you the spearhead of some new invasion? An advance force of handsome men come to turn Englishwomen's heads?"

He smiled, amused by her provocative question. "I'm afraid I have little to do with my country. In fact, it would not be an exaggeration to call me an agent of your government as my ship operates under a British letter of marque and reprisal."

"Goodness! Does not your country consider you a traitor?"

"No, *mademoiselle,* they do not. In fact, my country does not even consider me a human being." He watched as the truth came to her, her eyes flickering across his face and features, as if suddenly seeing beyond his fine clothing.

"I see." Her smile, if anything, was warmer than before. Martín found her response intriguing. But not quite as surprising as her next words. "You must come to our house and visit my sister and me. Will you call on us, Captain? The Marquess of Exley is one of our greatest supporters and has told us of your association with Baron Ramsay. I understand you and the baron both have a great interest in the subject of slavery?"

Had the woman really not known of his past? Or was she merely prodding him to see if he would disclose anything of interest? Martín knew the women of Ramsay's class had nothing better to do with their time than shop and gossip, so it was entirely possible this woman knew a great deal about him. The last thing he would allow was a woman—any woman—mucking around in his past for her own amusement. He certainly had no plans to present himself at her house so she could wheedle gossip out of him.

"I have returned a number of people taken by the corsairs," Martín said, choosing his words cautiously. "Please remember I also make a considerable amount of money taking such vessels. I would never want to misrepresent myself as an angel of mercy."

Her eyes narrowed to pale gray slits. "Oh, I doubt you'd be mistaken for an angel of any kind, Captain."

Martín laughed, far more comfortable in the area of flirtation than that of slave emancipation.

Sarah was beyond grateful Lord Ramsay had claimed her first dance.

"I see you've made another conquest, Sarah," Ramsay teased, glancing at Viscount Danforth, who'd escorted her from the dining room.

Sarah rolled her eyes, eliciting one of his bellows of laughter.

"I know *that* look. My dear wife uses it on me at least once a day." He continued undaunted. "Danforth seems a nice young chap."

"I cannot concentrate on these steps and answer your questions at the same time, my lord."

"But that is the most important part of dancing, Sarah dear, keeping your partner amused. If you do it well enough, they will not care about their flattened toes."

"I have not stepped on your feet. Yet."

"See, you *can* speak and dance at the same time. Come now, what did that wretch Martín say to upset you so at dinner?"

She was disappointed her tantrum had been noticed. "Oh, he told me where he had spent the previous fortnight."

Ramsay laughed.

"It is not a laughing matter, my lord. Surely the man can find a more productive use of his time."

"Perhaps he only wants some guidance?"

"Not from me, he doesn't. He has made that abundantly clear."

"My dear Sarah, I believe you do not know how to read men as well as you think you do."

"I'm sure you are correct. Your wife informs me I should treat you all like children."

"My wife is as wise as she is lovely. But she neglected to mention you must also dispense with any attempt at kindness." He was no longer mocking. "Martín has no experience with it, is suspicious of it, and has no clue how to respond to it."

"But what of you, my lord? You have been kind to him."

"Yes, but I'm a man. With women it is different."

"So I see," she retorted, her eyes lingering balefully on the subject of their discussion: Martín surrounded by at least eight females.

Ramsay laughed.

"You are an absolutely dreadful man."

"I am laughing because you clearly have nothing to worry about."

"Are you mad? Look at him!"

"My dear Sarah, haven't you noticed the careful way he has placed himself?"

"Placed himself?"

"Yes, you silly girl. He is standing just where he may keep watch over you."

Sarah glanced back at the herd of women around Martín and met his eyes. She scowled, and he grinned in return.

"Martín is a complete stranger to kindness or tenderness. You scare the wits out of him each time you do or say anything nice. He has no idea what it means or how to respond. So he responds like an animal confronted in its den—he attacks. You must treat him badly. At least initially, until you get through his defenses."

"But that's—that's—"

"Childish? Deceptive? Cruel? Deceitful? Flirtation?"

Sarah missed a step, and Ramsay cupped her elbow, smoothly moving her back into formation.

It was all those things, she realized.

As if reading her thoughts, Ramsay gave her a knowing look. "Yes, it is war, my dear, and 'the rules of fair play do not apply in love and war.'"

Sarah considered his advice in between concentrating on her steps. What was the harm in employing his approach? After all, her previous efforts had proven worse than useless.

"Very well," she said as Ramsay led her off the floor. "I shall abuse him roundly at every opportunity. I shall mock and taunt him whenever possible."

"That's the spirit. You can begin now. He is coming this way."

"My lord." Martín gave Ramsay a suspicious look before turning to Sarah. "Mademoiselle Fisher, may I have the honor of this next dance?" His arrogant smile said the honor was all hers.

"What an unexpected pleasure it is to hear you count the quadrille among your myriad achievements, Captain Bouchard. Unfortunately, I am engaged for this next set."

His arrogant smile faltered, and his eyes slid from her face to her fan, which she'd deployed to cool her heated countenance.

He cocked his head to read her unfurled fan. "Very well, I claim the pleasure of the next set, which I see you still have free, and the first waltz, as the second is taken." Without waiting for a reply, he bowed abruptly and left.

"Four runs to you, my dear." The baron smirked, his green eye on Martín's stiff shoulders.

"I believe you are correct." Sarah shook her head. Who could have guessed that rudeness and a challenging manner would be so effective in making Martín pursue her?

The anticipation of dancing with him caused Sarah to slaughter the next dance. Luckily, Lord Danforth, her unfortunate partner, was as sunny natured as he was attractive. Why couldn't Sarah have lost her heart to such a man? Why had she become obsessed with an arrogant, domineering, changeable pig of a man? Why?

"You are frowning most fiercely, Miss Fisher. May I ask the cause of your displeasure?"

Sarah flushed and dragged her attention back to her attractive partner. "I am very sorry for the savage beating you've taken at my hands—or feet, rather," she apologized as he escorted her from the floor.

"Nonsense, I'm sure I'll be able to walk again properly in a few weeks. A month at the most. Would you like some refreshment? I'm limping in that direction in any case to find a splint and some sticking plaster."

Sarah laughed. "That would be lovely." She watched him walk away, grateful to see he was not in fact limping.

"Imagining yourself a viscountess, Mademoiselle Fisher?"

Sarah started and turned. "He's heir to an earldom," she corrected, forcing herself to ignore her pounding heart as she looked into Martín's eyes.

"What? Is poor *Mies* no longer in the running?"

"Mies is merely a younger son, not the scion," she pointed out, inwardly cringing at her repulsive words.

Martín's eyes widened, and he gazed at her with something approaching respect. "This is a side of you I've not seen before, Mademoiselle Fisher."

She sniffed. "I daresay there are many of my sides you haven't seen—nor are you likely to, Captain Bouchard."

He burst out laughing, his eyes shining with appreciation. "Oh, but the sides I *have* seen I have liked so very much." His words evoked a brief, but searing memory.

Danforth chose that moment to return.

"Thank you, my lord." Sarah snatched the glass from his hand and gulped it down.

"Are you feeling quite all right, Miss Fisher?"

"Yes, thank you. Have you met Captain Bouchard, my lord?" she asked, desperate to turn his solicitous gaze away from her beet-red face.

"No, I haven't. But Exley has told me a lot about him. I'm very pleased to meet you, Captain." Danforth smiled at the other man with genuine enthusiasm.

"The pleasure is mine," Martín murmured, his eyes narrow with suspicion. He shifted his gaze to Sarah. "As is the next dance." He offered Sarah his arm and led her away from the surprised-looking viscount.

"That was rude of you."

He shrugged.

"He was only trying to make pleasant conversation."

"I am not interested in pleasant conversation."

Sarah ground her teeth. He was impossible. She was grateful that the first dance she'd committed to did not allow for much conversation.

Naturally, he was an exquisite dancer. He moved far more fluidly than either Ramsay or Danforth, the arrogant angle at which he held his head making it obvious he was aware of his skill. Sarah refused to compliment him. Why swell his head any further? He was already receiving more attention than was good for him, and his presence was causing a frisson among the young ladies around them.

No other man in the room—not even Baron Ramsay, with his scar and black eye patch—exuded such dangerous, alien allure: Martín Bouchard was in a class of his very own.

Sarah collided with a broad, solid chest, and a pair of powerful arms came up to steady her. She looked up into the grinning face of the man she'd been contemplating.

"Mademoiselle Fisher, are you trying to start the waltz early? Is that why you are throwing yourself into my arms?"

He inclined his head apologetically to the couple beside them as they adjusted their steps to accommodate Sarah's fumbling.

"If only your manners were as polished as your dancing, Captain Bouchard. Don't you know that criticizing one's partner is not done?"

Martín laughed, and they didn't speak again until the dance was finished and he led her back to where Daphne was deeply in conversation with a man sporting a puce silk coat and clocks on his stockings. Words and phrases like *rights of man, materialism, and Diderot* clouded the air around the two philosophers like a haze of gnats.

"I shall be back to claim my waltz." Martín sauntered off like a man who'd conquered the world.

Sarah fumed and watched the dancers, trying to ignore the mind-boggling conversation occurring beside her.

She danced the next dance with the frigid Lord Exley and the one after that with his more gregarious stepson, Gabriel.

The redheaded young man had barely escorted her from the dance floor when Martín appeared beside her as if he'd sprung from the intricate parquet flooring. "You are no longer necessary, Jibril." He turned from the stunned, fuming younger man to Sarah. "I believe this dance is mine, Miss Fisher."

He led her away from Gabriel Marlington, who stood rooted to the spot, staring at Bouchard with a look that should have reduced him to cinders. Sarah didn't have the energy to scold Martín, nor would he listen if she did.

To say his hand on her side was distracting was an understatement. It wasn't merely his hand; it was the memory of the last time his hands had been on her.

"This is much nicer, eh?" His warm breath near her ear made her shiver.

Sarah ignored the comment as well as her body's annoying reaction and concentrated on the steps.

"Relax, Mademoiselle Fisher," he whispered. "Let me do the work instead of yanking me about so violently."

"Yes, you're quite the expert, aren't you, Captain Bouchard?" she asked waspishly.

He chuckled.

"I wouldn't have imagined dancing was a popular pastime at the places you choose to frequent, Captain."

"Oh," he said, pulling away slightly so he could look down at her face. "Tell me, what places and activities do you imagine me to enjoy, *mademoiselle?*"

"You willfully misunderstand me, sir. I don't spend any time at all imagining what you do. In fact, thoughts of you are something I actively suppress, should they occur."

"Oh, *mademoiselle,*" he said, giving her a look of mock lament. "Telling such untruths. Surely your father would be most displeased to find his teachings had so little purchase in his daughter."

Sarah bristled. "You have no idea of what my father did or did not teach me."

Again he laughed. "No, you are correct. I know nothing about missionaries and their teachings. I do, however, know something of the daughters of missionaries. Or at least one. I know you have spent a great deal of time thinking about me and what I do when I am not within your sight. I think you would very much like to know where I have been and who I have been with, eh?"

It took every ounce of willpower she possessed not to tread on his elegantly shod feet.

"You don't know the first thing about me, Captain Bouchard. You're too self-absorbed to know anyone but yourself."

"Shh, you are so vehement. People are beginning to stare, perhaps believing we are lovers, having a quarrel, eh?" He chuckled at the venomous look she gave him. "Come, let us not fight. Since the subject of my activities is not a topic for polite conversation, why don't you tell me what you have been doing?"

Sarah pursed her lips and stared at his chin, forcing her eyes away from his full lower lip.

"Very well, it appears you *do* want to hear what I have been doing, in great detail." He opened his mouth.

"Oh, shut up. I would prefer talking about anything else to . . . to . . . that." His shoulder shook beneath her hand. "Unlike some people, I have been visiting museums, galleries, booksellers, and other culturally significant places."

"Mm hmm, and what else?"

"I have been learning how to dance, ride a horse, and engage in proper dinner conversation."

"I noticed the first and last this evening. I would like an opportunity to observe the second."

"Why? So you may mock my efforts?"

"Do you fear my mocking?"

"Not in the least. Show up any morning you like and mock away. I warn you, however, we ride unfashionably early."

"We? You and *Mies?*" His light teasing tone fled, and his hand clenched on her side.

"Kindly stop mauling me, Captain. Yes, me, Mies, and my groom." Was that jealousy she heard in his voice or just the competitive instinct that any mention of the Dutchman seemed to evoke?

"Ah, you have the protection of a groom. Very good. Who knows what the good captain would get up to otherwise. Perhaps he would be overcome by the strength of his emotions and do something rash."

"Must you be odious every minute of the day?"

"Not without a great deal of effort. You dance much better when you are not thinking about your feet."

Sarah ignored his condescending observation, and they danced for a few moments in silence.

"You look very beautiful tonight," he said in her ear, his

voice husky, his scent more intoxicating than champagne. "This color suits you, the style also." His hungry look took in the low neckline, evoking both a desire to fling herself into his arms and a compulsion to box his ears.

She ignored both urges. "Tell me, Captain, where are you staying?"

"I am at a small hotel called Mivart's. Quite unexceptionable, I assure you. Perhaps you would like to come and have dinner? You could inspect my apartments and make sure they are respectable."

"I'm afraid that is impossible."

He grinned at her cool rejection, and Sarah realized the baron had been correct. Martín was much more comfortable with rejection than he'd ever been with any act of kindness. She sighed. How tiresome that she must treat him poorly in order to gain his attention.

"Why the deep sigh, *mademoiselle?*"

Sarah stared hard into his unusual eyes, hoping to catch a glimpse of what went on behind them. But they were as well guarded as the crown jewels.

She changed the subject. "Baron Ramsay said you had a property in the country, Captain."

"Has Ramsay taken the position of town crier?" He didn't sound amused.

"Why, is the fact that you own property some sort of secret? I understand it's quite common in this country."

"You are pleased to jest, *mademoiselle.*"

She shrugged rather than answered. Why not give him a little of his own back?

"I have not yet gone to inspect the estate. There are still several issues to talk over with Exley, who has been overseeing some matters for me."

"That is very kind of him." Sarah was more than a little surprised to hear the haughty peer would take an interest in an ex-slave's business.

"One would think him incapable of such kindness from looking at him, eh? But you mustn't judge by appearances, *mademoiselle*."

"No, I shouldn't; you are correct."

"Why do you sound so surprised? After all, I am correct about so much, eh?"

"If it pleases you to think so."

"*You* please me, Sarah." He spoke her name softly, his eyes darkening. Sarah looked quickly away, terrified she would launch herself into his arms and take whatever he wanted to give, not caring that it wouldn't be enough.

Thankfully, the music ended, and she was saved from her reckless impulses. They stood for a moment longer than was proper before the shrill laughter of a nearby woman broke the spell.

"Thank you, Captain."

He released her and stepped back; the moment had passed.

"The pleasure was mine." He led her back to her friends, bowed, and took his leave. Sarah stared at his broad shoulders as they disappeared from view, the pain in her chest making it difficult to breathe. She knew less about him and his feelings for her than she had the night they'd met. She was beginning to think she never would know him.

Chapter Twenty-Five

Martín was laboriously reading *Waverley* with both English and French dictionaries open before him when Ramsay called. The baron tossed his hat onto a nearby table and looked about the room, his gaze lingering on the cluttered desk.

"You seem to have settled in quite nicely."

"It lacks the amenities of Venetia's, but it will do."

"Daphne has kept your rooms ready for you," Ramsay said, helping himself to a glass of brandy.

"You meddle like an old woman, Ramsay."

"Somebody has to, my friend. When are you going to admit to yourself you want the girl?" He didn't bother to explain which girl he meant.

Martín's neck and face became hot. Ramsay, for a change, was not smiling.

Why bother with dissimulation? Besides, Ramsay would not stop until he got what he was after. The man was relentless.

"What can I offer her?" Martín asked, staring at the amber liquid in his glass and thinking back to the last time he'd argued with Sarah back on his ship, when she'd told him, in no uncertain terms, her opinion of him.

"Yourself."

"You have a good sense of humor, Ramsay. Unfortunately, I am not in the mood to be amused."

"You are behaving like a fool, Martín, a blind fool who cannot see what is right in front of him. The girl cares for you. She is sensible and makes up her own mind. Tell her the truth—she would not care about your past."

"But *I* care. Do you think I want her to know I was a whore? Do you think she would ever look at me the same way again? Even if she did, what would her family say? Eh? Do you think they will welcome an ex-slave, murderer, whore into their family with open arms?"

"Nobody will ever know about the murder, Martín."

"So you say, Hugh. But you don't have to build your life on lies and wonder how long such a foundation will last."

"So, tell me, then, what are you going to do, Martín? Keep running away, always afraid the past will catch you?"

Martín was so angry he was shaking. "It is easy for you to offer advice, *my lord*," he said, sneering the two words. "You are a bloody peer. Wealthy and connected to a family that goes back to the beginning of time. You were a slave for a few years but you were not born a slave because of the very blood that runs in your veins—because of who you *are*. You do not need to constantly worry you could become a slave again if the right people clapped hands on you. And, lastly, you were never sold to be some old man's whore."

"You know what the sultan's men did to me." The words were so quiet Martín hardly heard them. He looked at Ramsay and saw a chill in his usually warm eye. Yes, he knew what had happened to Ramsay in Hassan's palace.

The pause between them grew pregnant with a decade's worth of unspoken words and secrets.

It was Ramsay who broke it. "You cannot let what happened with d'Armand ruin your life, Martín."

Martín's head jerked up at the sound of the hated name.

"Your path has never been easy, my friend, but you've survived much worse than becoming an object of gossip. The people who matter—your crew, me, Daphne, Sarah,

Mia, Exley—they know your worth. If people judge you because of what was done to you, they are not worth knowing. You care deeply for somebody who cares for you. Do not leave her behind because you are in a hurry to run from your past."

"She doesn't want me. She wants the Dutchman."

Ramsay made a scoffing noise. "She does *not* want Graaf."

"Then why does she spend so much time with him?" Martín demanded, his gut clenching with fury at the thought of Sarah and the slaver.

"Because he puts himself before her? Because she pities him? Because she is bored?" Ramsay shrugged. "Who knows why a woman does anything?"

"Pity? Are you insane, Ramsay? The man is a peer on calling terms with the bloody king."

"You need stronger spectacles, Martín, because you appear to be blind when it comes to Sarah. She was raised by Christian missionaries, for God's sake. They believe in forgiveness above all else; at least the good ones do. Just because she has forgiven Graaf does not mean she doesn't pity him. And he *is* an object of pity—something you would realize if your vision were not so clouded. She was born and raised in Africa—do you think she could ever respect a man who would buy and sell the people she considers her own?"

"Then why does she defend him like a hen with a chick if I make even the smallest comment? Does a woman do such a thing for a man she despises?"

Ramsay shook his head and set his empty glass down with a thump. "I cannot stay and listen to such claptrap, Martín. Only an idiot would think she wanted anyone but you."

Martín stared at Ramsay's back as he stalked from the room. His former captain knew Martín better than any other person in the world. Could he be right? Would she be able to live with the truth if he told her? If the truth became public and the rest of the world found out?

Martín knew he could not outrun his past forever. With the war over, there would be more and more contact with his country of birth. One way or another the truth always came out. Would she be able to overlook what he'd once been? The things he'd done?

There was only one person in the entire world who could answer those questions. But he wasn't sure he could ask her.

Sarah was disappointed when Martín did not show up at her next riding lesson, or for the six after that. She'd been certain he would appear if only to display his own skill and mock her and Mies. By the time he finally did appear, she had given up looking for him.

She was fastening up her habit when Martín, seated on an enormous bay, cantered up. He stopped by Mies on his way toward her and muttered something she could not hear. While Sarah was no judge of horseflesh, she could see Bouchard's mount was something out of the ordinary.

"What a lovely animal," she said, when he came to a halt not far from her.

"Yes, he is one of a kind." Martín stroked the huge animal's neck, and the horse leaned into his touch and rubbed against his hand like a friendly dog. "His name is Pasha. He belongs to Ramsay, but today he gets a holiday from carrying such a giant brute on his back, eh?" The animal seemed to gaze at him with adoration. Martín gestured toward Sarah's horse. "Where did you get that sack of bones?"

"Not all of us require a mount fit for a king, Martín." She bit her lip, annoyed she'd let slip his Christian name. She was also unreasonably irritated by how perfect he looked in his riding clothes, from his highly polished boots to his fashionable high-crowned hat. Must he always look so irresistible?

She tore her eyes off his broad shoulders and powerful chest, only to find Mies had approached and was looking at her with narrowed eyes.

"Bouchard says you invited him to come and make sure I was offering adequate instruction." His face was as stiff as his words.

Sarah scowled at the grinning Bouchard before turning back to Mies.

"That is not how I put it at all. But now that he is here, why don't we all take a ride together?"

Martín tossed his reins to Mies, who caught them on reflex. He dismounted gracefully and closed the distance between them, waving away her groom. "Are you ready?"

Sarah nodded, and two big hands picked her up and placed her in the saddle with shocking ease. Her waist tingled as if his powerful hands still encircled it, and an exquisite tightness pulsed between her thighs.

Sarah couldn't escape the truth: she was a wanton. And the fact that such a realization did not upset her only served to underscore she was irredeemable.

He adjusted her stirrups and checked the girth, and Sarah couldn't take her eyes from his powerful leather-clad hands as they competently checked the saddle and straps. Hands that had been over her naked body. Inside her body. Hands that had brought her more pleasure than she'd known before or since.

"There. Are you comfortable?" He glanced up at her with a casual, inquiring look, oblivious of his effect on her.

She nodded, unable to speak.

As he mounted his monster of a horse, Sarah looked at Mies. His face was a mask of fury. This had been a very bad idea. Few men could associate with Martín and come away looking good, and Mies had already proven he was not one of them. She felt a surge of pity for the Dutchman.

"Are you ready, *mademoiselle?*" Bouchard asked her. He sat his horse as if he'd been born to it, his body graceful for all its size. He held the reins lightly in one hand, his other hand resting casually on a buckskin-clad thigh. A very muscular thigh.

She awkwardly guided her horse between the two men.

"Have you ridden in Hyde Park before, Captain?" she asked when it was clear neither man felt compelled to break the awkward silence.

"Not often. In general I have not had much opportunity to ride for pleasure. What of you, Captain Graaf?" Martín smirked across Sarah toward the smaller man. "You appear to have a decent seat. Do you hunt?"

The Dutchman's eyes were wary. "Yes, I hunt, although not so much these past few years while I have been at university. Why, do you hunt, Captain?" His skeptical tone said he already knew the answer.

"I take no pleasure in hunting defenseless animals. I prefer bigger game."

Mies's pale cheeks flushed a dull, angry red.

Sarah searched her mind frantically for a topic that wouldn't lead to open hostilities.

"What have you been doing for the past six days, Captain?" She gnawed her lower lip. Could she have demonstrated her infatuation any more clearly?

Martín's slow, lazy smile made her blush just as darkly as Graaf. "How nice of you to notice my absence with such exactitude, *Sarah.*"

"It is common courtesy, *Captain.* Some of us are interested in people other than ourselves."

He grinned at her shrewish tone. "I went to my property."

"Oh. You went there and back so quickly?"

"It was only a quick trip. I wanted to see the state of the house and what would be needed to make it habitable."

"You are planning to live there?"

"Perhaps," he drawled.

"I thought you were going to Paris?" Mies broke in, making Sarah realize she'd forgotten his presence.

"I am flattered by your interest in my future plans, *Captain*. But perhaps you are asking because you are concerned the payment you have promised will not find me? Do not worry, my man of business will forward any compensation he receives."

Judging by the way the color drained from Mies's face, the payment would not be forthcoming.

"Do you have to behave like such a toad?" she whispered angrily.

"No, I don't *have* to."

"If you have no objection, Sarah, I believe I will attend to some business that has been awaiting my attention," Mies said, not waiting for her reply before yanking his horse around and thundering back to the main path.

"I rejoice to hear he is attending to any business at all," Martín commented mildly.

Sarah stunned herself by laughing.

"There, that is much better."

"I am laughing because the alternative is to cry in frustration at your abominable behavior."

"Why? Because I ask Graaf to pay what he owes? Ask Ramsay if you do not believe me. He will tell you the code among *gentlemen*. By evading payment the Dutchman shames himself without any help from me. But, come, he is gone. Now we may talk of more interesting matters."

"Such as?"

"Me, you, my estate, your visit to my estate—to name only a few."

"Oh? Are you planning to entertain?"

He sighed. "Not for some time, I'm afraid. Oak Park is in need of a good deal of work before it is ready for guests."

"Oak Park. What a lovely name."

"Yes, lovely," he murmured, his eyes drifting to her mouth and then down her body and back. "Oak Park is not so far from Lessing Hall. I will invite Ramsay and his wife. They can bring their brats. I have an excellent trout pond and stream on the property, perfect for young boys looking for trouble. I would like you to see my house, Sarah."

Sarah looked away from his caressing gaze. What did such an invitation mean after weeks of ignoring her? Why must he be so awkward and unknowable? She realized he was waiting for a response.

"Naturally I would be pleased to see your house."

"Naturally." His smile was lazy and confident.

Martín considered his morning's work as he cantered away from Hyde Park. His feelings after seeing Sarah and Graaf were a mixture of relief and annoyance.

He was relieved to see that Sarah treated the Dutch nobleman with nothing other than friendly tolerance and annoyed that she treated Martín much the same way.

It had killed him to stay away from her after he'd learned she rode in the park almost daily with the Dutchman.

"You must go to Oak Park for a few days," Ramsay had ordered the day following the Exleys' ball, not that Martín had solicited his opinion. They'd been at Tattersalls, where the baron had just paid an outrageous amount for a pair of grays.

Martín ignored the suggestion, but that did not matter to the older man.

"You can see to the estate and also consider Sarah and how you will approach her."

"What makes you think I need to do either, old man?"

"Take Jenkins with you," Ramsay said, dismissing Martín's rude question.

"Jenkins is a fool. I can see to myself."

"A gentleman always travels with his manservant."

"I am no gentleman."

"You are to the people whose lives you now control. Oak Park is an impressive estate, Martín. Strive to live up to it."

He'd gritted his teeth at Ramsay's chiding tone.

"Take my curricle. It will be an excellent opportunity to put Zeus and Hades through their paces."

"Who?"

"My new horses." He gestured to the frisky grays, who looked as if they were ready to chew the arm off Ramsay's groom. "That is what I have named them." His smirk told Martín the names meant something. Something clever, no doubt. Martín refused to humor him by asking.

Instead, he'd humored him by leaving the following morning, taking the curricle, the horses, and Jenkins. He told himself he was going to escape Ramsay's nagging, but really he was going so he could figure out what he would do, once and for all. Or at least think about it.

Contrary to Ramsay's claim, Oak Park had looked less than impressive. Martín had arrived at twilight, and the old manor had looked dreary and ramshackle in the crepuscular light. He'd briefly considered turning around, but the late hour made such an impulse unwise.

The only servants in residence were an old man and his wife, remnants of a time when the house had been the country seat of a lord, the same man who'd lost it to the Marquess of Exley in a card game. Exley, in turn, had given Martín the estate several years back as a reward for risking his life and ship to save Lady Exley's son from his homicidal half-brother.

Exley had undertaken several major repairs when he'd

won the property, and he'd also begun construction of a new stable before he'd given the property to Martín.

Martín had funded the various repairs over the past four years but had left the key decisions to Exley. Until two weeks ago.

"My tenure as your factor is at an end, Bouchard," Exley had said. "You may keep it, sell it, rent it, or hire an agent to run it. What you may not do, however, is expect *me* to continue managing it."

This was Martín's first visit here in two years. Thankfully, the house proved more comfortable than it appeared. The old couple had been in the habit of keeping a room prepared in case Exley should visit, and Martín had enjoyed a comfortable night's sleep. He'd also enjoyed a simple but delicious breakfast of fresh eggs, meats, and homemade pastries the following morning. After eating his fill he'd summoned his two servants to the library.

The room was much smaller than the library at Lessing Hall, and the shelves were only half-filled. Even so, an excitement built in his stomach when he realized all these books were his and he could read them whenever he wished—albeit very slowly.

"I would like you to make the house habitable," he told the old couple, who'd shuffled into the room not long after breakfast. "Hire whomever you need to do the immediate cleaning, and I will consider suggestions for footmen, grooms, what have you. I shall see to the hiring of a cook and steward."

Mrs. Brownlee's steely gaze marked her as the leader of the pair. "Our eldest is a fine one with horses, Captain. Seeing as you'll have a grand new stable, you'll need a master and some grooms."

"Have your son come and speak to me this afternoon as I shall be leaving for London two mornings hence. If you should think of anything else that requires my attention, tell me before then."

"Leaving, my, uh, lor . . . Captain?" The old man repeated.

Martín frowned. Was the man still capable of functioning as butler, or was that another position he needed to fill?

"Very good, Captain," Mrs. Brownlee said, answering for her spouse as if reading Martín's thoughts. She dropped a curtsy and dragged her still gaping husband from the room.

Martín could not blame the old man for his confusion. It had been madness to ride such a distance for a stay of only a few days. He shrugged. What did he care if his servants thought him mad?

A set of double doors opened onto a flagstone court that overlooked extensive gardens. The prospect caught Martín by surprise, and he stopped, leaning against the stone balustrade to admire the view.

Exley had told him the house was an excellent example of an Elizabethan manor. As usual, Martín knew nothing of such matters. Apparently the house had once boasted one of the largest and most intricate knot gardens in England. What remained was only a wild tangle, barely recognizable but for the unruly box shrubs that enclosed it.

He made a note to find a gardener or groundskeeper who could deal with such matters. He'd be damned if he would own the best of anything and have it lying around in disrepair. He might be an ex-slave, murderer, whore, but he was as rich as a lord—richer. The wealth of several nations had flowed through Ramsay's hands during the war, and Martín had collected his share of it. This was not his only house. He owned two others, one on the coast of Italy and another in Shanghai. The baron had been adamant that property was the only thing that endured. So Martín had bought houses. Houses he'd never lived in and frankly had no desire to. But this house felt different. As he looked around at the lush, overgrown garden, Martín felt an odd sense of peace. Perhaps he could live here?

He closed his eyes to block out the ridiculous vision of himself as a country squire. What in God's name would he do in an Elizabethan manor house?

The annoying little voice in his head—strident today—had suggestions. Marry Sarah and bring her here, have children, build a life. Stop running from his past, from his fears.

He clenched his jaw against the hope that grew in his breast. It was best never to hope. The image in his mind was nothing but a fantasy—the kind of dreams that had kept him sane during his years as a slave.

As usual, the brand on his arm itched, an incessant reminder of the day the red-hot iron had burned not just his flesh, but something else inside of him.

Like the other slaves on the small plantation where he'd been born, Martín had been tattooed around his forearm when he was still young. He'd tattooed over that mark at the first opportunity, but, if you looked closely, you could still see the word "Bannock" beneath the newer ink. Bannock: the name of the man who'd owned him. His father, by all accounts.

Martín had run away when he'd learned he was soon to be sold. He'd been twelve or so, terrified at the thought of leaving the only home he'd ever known. He'd run without thinking and been caught before he'd even crossed the boundary of the plantation.

The beating that had followed had left him with a cracked rib and some bruises, but he soon learned that was nothing.

The second time he'd run, there had been no beating. Instead, his own people, the people who had raised him and cared for him, had been forced to restrain him as the Scottish overseer, a man named Clark, had lifted the large red iron from the fire. His arm had been too small a canvas for the brand, and part of the *R* was missing.

Martín turned away from both the memory of burning flesh and the sight of the ruined garden. He slammed the door behind him, as if he could shut his past in the ancient garden with the rest of the wreckage.

He drifted toward the big desk and absently opened the drawers. He found nothing but old papers, broken quills, and the odds and ends of someone else's life. He closed the drawer and dropped into the chair, lacing his hands over his stomach. Ramsay had been correct. Martín wanted Sarah, and the only way to have her was marriage. Her wealthy uncles would most likely fight it, and he couldn't blame them. He wouldn't want himself as a husband for a daughter or niece if he had one. Nobody's reputation had ever benefited by association with him.

Dread weaved its way from his stomach to his chest at the thought of approaching the two old bankers with his suit. Over and over he'd imagined simply carrying Sarah to his ship and sailing away. He could do it before anyone was the wiser. He pictured her sleek, long body and warm brown eyes, the drowsy, satisfied way she looked when he brought her to climax. Her petal-soft skin and how she responded to his intimate touches.

His groin ached at the memory of their few moments together. He tried to shift his pounding cock to a more comfortable position, but it proved impossible given his tight buckskins.

"*Merde.*" He drummed his fingers on the scarred surface of the desk. He was tired of relieving his needs with his fist like some green boy. His health—his very sanity—required she accept his suit.

Martín would take Ramsay's advice and leave his past behind. He would begin his life anew, and he would court her. While he did so, he would have Oak Park restored to some semblance of its former beauty so he would have something to offer her besides himself.

And if that wasn't enough to tempt her? His fingers stopped in mid drum.

Well, that didn't bear thinking about.

Chapter Twenty-Six

It was no exaggeration to say Olivia and Octavia Manton saved Sarah's life—or at least her sanity. Other than Daphne and Lady Exley, the two spinsters seemed to be the only women in *ton* circles who had interests other than gossip.

Sarah had not realized how much she missed her old life until a dinner party her uncles gave shortly before her birthday ball. She'd been seated between two handsome young men, one of whom had been uttering some rubbish about British policy in Africa. When he confused Cape Town with Freetown, Sarah had opened her mouth to correct him and then stopped. Not only would he not attend to anything she told him, but he would most likely feel insulted by the correction.

So, she'd bitten her tongue and let him continue.

That was the moment she realized that spending time in London—as enjoyable as parts of it had been—was not something she would want to do again.

That was the moment she realized that she missed Africa. Terribly.

It was not the grinding hardship or poverty she missed, of course, but the sense of purpose and, oddly, the sense of belonging. She'd always believed she was an outsider in

N'goe. Not until coming to London did she realize what being an outsider truly meant.

She now understood that what she'd yearned for all those years was a sense of who she was—where she came from.

What a shame she'd had to go halfway around the world to find out she never should have left. Still, the journey had not been without its benefits. She'd made many new friends and also learned about herself. Not only had she learned that she belonged in Africa, but she'd also learned what it was like to be in love. Of course she'd also learned what it was like to have her heart broken.

She told herself—over and over—that it was better Bouchard didn't love her. What would she have done if he'd asked her to marry him?—not that she'd really believed such a thing possible. Could she have stayed in England? Would she have been satisfied in her life as mistress of Oak Park?

No, she couldn't live the life of an English gentlewoman even if she was married to the man she loved.

Again, not that it mattered. The arrogant captain had shown no more interest in marrying her than he did in dancing naked in the streets of Mayfair.

She shoved the painful, unprofitable topic of Martín Bouchard from her mind.

No matter how little she enjoyed the social whirl, she'd determined to last through the remainder of the Season before telling her uncles she wanted to return to Africa.

So she'd continued to go to parties, wear lovely gowns, and make pleasant conversation. But she spent all her free time making plans and helping the Manton sisters at their Home for Displaced Women.

The Mantons had also introduced her to the network of people working for those who had no voice of their own in Parliament: slaves. Men like Paul Cuffe, a wealthy, mixed-race Quaker businessman who was organizing a journey to the coast of West Africa and joining the party as its captain.

Cuffe was primarily concerned with settling freed slaves in Freetown, but he'd been supportive of Sarah's plan to return to Africa and reestablish her parents' school. In fact, it had been Cuffe who'd given her the idea of the orphanage.

"A school is necessary, but many children will need someplace to live while they learn. Thousands have been orphaned during the slave raids, Miss Fisher," Mr. Cuffe had said one night at a dinner at the Mantons'. "They are, without a doubt, the most powerless and victimized group in Africa."

Cuffe's ship was set to sail only a few days after Sarah met him, so joining the Quaker's mission was not an option. But Sarah had donated her largely unspent quarterly allowance to his cause.

Sarah was ashamed to admit it, but she'd not been entirely disappointed that she wasn't leaving on the Quaker's ship. Not because she would miss the last part of the Season, but because of Martín. The handsome captain had emerged from wherever he'd been keeping himself and had begun to attend more and more functions.

A week after they'd ridden in the park, he'd shown up at a lively soiree at the Mantons' home. It had been fortunate that Mies, who'd become intolerably proprietary—offering for her hand not once, but twice—had not been invited. Martín, who'd been frustratingly scarce, had been seated beside her.

"I understand the upcoming ball your uncles are hosting is in honor of your birthday, *mademoiselle?*" Martín asked, ignoring the heated argument that raged across the table regarding a piece of labor legislation.

"Yes, it is, although my birthday is actually a day earlier."

"And what will be your age?"

"That is a rude question, Captain Bouchard."

"Only when the lady is older, or so I understand."

"But I *am* older. At four and twenty I am on the shelf."

"Shelf?" A line formed between his beautiful eyes. "What shelf?"

Sarah laughed. He spoke English so well that she often forgot it was not his first language.

"It is an idiom, a style of speaking that does not always mean what the words say. For example, down at the heels means to be experiencing hard luck. I am sure there are many idioms in French, but I cannot think of one right now."

Martín closed his eyes for a long moment and then opened them and smiled. "I have one. *Avoir du chien.* It says 'to have the dog,' but really it means to be a very attractive woman."

Sarah pursed her lips. "I believe you just made that up."

"No, no, it is true. I have heard it many times."

"But it is ridiculous."

He shrugged. "Tell me, what is 'on the shelf'?"

"It means to be past one's prime."

He gave her a look that seemed to burn the clothing from her body, and Sarah's heart pounded as if it would burst through her bodice.

"Now that, *mademoiselle,* is what I would call ridiculous. You are in your prime."

"Women in England are generally married before they are twenty," she explained, her voice oddly scratchy. She cleared her throat. "I am considered a spinster."

"You are young and fresh, like a flower whose petals are only now opening." His eyes settled on her bosom, which expanded and froze under his inspection. A slight smile flickered across his lips before he lifted his eyes. "And what of men? What is the age when they are put on a shelf?"

"Men are considered to be much like wines; they only improve with age."

He threw back his head and laughed.

Pride spiked in her fluttering chest; she'd finally made him laugh.

"But not all wines, eh, Sarah? Some go bad, I think?"

Her face heated, as it usually did when she was in his company. Whatever did he mean? She decided not to find out. "Tell me more about your house, about Oak Park. What do you do when you go there?"

"Mostly I authorize bank draughts. I am in the process of completing new stables, which is apparently more costly than building a cathedral." He gave her a dry look. "I feel as if I am single-handedly lifting England from its economic doldrums."

"All work and no play?"

"I did explore the house and grounds when it became freakishly warm one afternoon, warm enough that I could take a swim in the small pond."

Unbidden images of water sluicing over the hard, powerful contours of his body filled her head. Her breasts, which she usually did not notice, became heavy and full, making her bodice unbearably tight.

He leaned closer, his forehead creased with concern. "You are flushed, *mademoiselle*. Are you unwell?"

"No, no, I am fine," she said hoarsely. "I just find it rather warm suddenly."

Martín glanced around the table at the other guests. "They are certainly raising the temperature with their discussions."

"Yes, the Mantons enjoy a lively atmosphere," she agreed, glad he'd shifted his disturbing attention elsewhere.

Olivia Manton was scolding the Marquess of Exley on some point or other, and it was the first time Sarah had ever seen the haughty-looking man smile. Even his wife did not abuse him with the same enthusiasm as the two sisters. He appeared to blossom under their teasing and mockery.

"He looks almost human, does he not?" Martín observed, following her gaze.

"I believe this is the first time I've seen him smile."

"His wife makes him smile often enough." The not-so-subtle innuendo sent a pulse of heat straight to her clenched thighs. She realized Martín was staring at her with an odd, almost questioning look. She swallowed several times before she could speak.

"You know them quite well?"

"We spent quite a bit of time together on my ship several years back. It was a very tense time for Exley and his wife. I daresay all of us probably know *too* much about one another after such a close journey," he admitted, a strange twist to his lips. "But enough of that. I want to make sure I secure a dance with you for the night of your ball before they are all taken."

Sarah was nonplussed by this unprecedented show of interest.

"Perhaps another waltz?" he asked, as the silence stretched.

"Why ye—yes, if you wish."

A slow smile took possession of his sensuous lips. "A waltz would please me very much. For a start."

"I believe you enjoyed yourself this evening?" Ramsay asked, as they rode the short distance from the Manton party to Davenport House in Ramsay's luxurious carriage.

Martín hoped Ramsay was not going to start badgering him again about approaching Sarah's uncles. Luckily he was spared from answering by Lady Ramsay.

"Sir Cedric has expressed an interest in my last paper, Hugh. He wants to read it at the next meeting of the Philosophical Society."

"You have put my mind at ease, my dear. I had suspected Sir Cedric of making untoward offers to you. He was almost in your lap at dinner. He also had his elbow in your syllabub at one point." The man in question was an octogenarian with spectacles so thick they obscured his eyes.

Lady Ramsay appeared not to hear her husband. "I will have to change the portion of the paper that deals with Hume. I believe I was premature in my conclusions."

"Did Sir Cedric have the audacity to say that to you, my love? The brute! Shall I call him out?"

Lady Ramsay's eyes settled on her husband and came slowly into focus. "Perhaps I shall open the door to the carriage, and Captain Bouchard can shove you out?"

"Shall I tell the coachman to pick up speed first, my lady?" Martín offered.

Ramsay laughed.

His wife turned her disconcerting gaze on Martín. "I hope you are going to attend Miss Fisher's ball next week, Captain." It was not a question.

Martín looked from Lady Ramsay's face to her husband's. The baron gave a slight shrug of his massive shoulders, as if to say he had no hand in this. Martín never knew what the man told his wife. Probably everything, as besotted as he was.

"Yes. I have already claimed a waltz with Mademoiselle Fisher. Perhaps you will honor me by reserving a set, Lady Ramsay?"

"I shall be delighted, Captain Bouchard. You are a very accomplished dancer."

Martín reckoned she thought dancing his *only* accomplishment. He wondered if she, like her husband, felt he was worthy of Sarah. It was hard to tell what Lady Ramsay thought, unless the subject was some long-dead philosopher.

Thankfully the topic of Sarah Fisher was dropped, and the remainder of the short journey was spent discussing Martín's work at Oak Park.

Chapter Twenty-Seven

To Sarah's relief, her Aunt Anna took charge of organizing her birthday ball. Fortunately, Anna viewed the opportunity to organize a large party with pleasure. All Sarah had to do was decide on a dress and give Anna a list of guests.

Anna almost fainted when she saw the list contained a baron, a viscount, and a marquess. She was also thrilled to see Mies on the list. Every member of her family was hoping for a connection with Mies. Not only was he of the best blood and a relative to kings, but he was Dutch.

Anna was far less enthusiastic, however, about the inclusion of Martín Bouchard on the list.

"But my dear, who *is* he, really?"

"He is a friend. He brought me back to England without any expectation of remuneration or reward. And he freed me and the people of my village from Mies Graaf. Whom you *must know* was engaged in the illegal—not to mention revolting—business of slavery."

Anna waved this information aside as if it were a mere bagatelle. "Sarah, darling, I understand this captain was very kind and brought you home to us, but can we not simply *pay* him for his services? That is what one does with tradesmen." She saw Sarah's expression and stopped. "Oh, very well," she said, her natural inclination to avoid strife overriding considerations of status.

By the time Anna was finished with the list, the ball guests numbered no fewer than five hundred names. The dinner before the ball would also be enormous. There were to be two tables, each seating thirty. As much as she wished to sit next to Martín, Sarah could not bring herself to interfere with her aunt's seating arrangements.

Luckily, thanks to matters of precedence, she could count on being seated beside at least one person with whom she was acquainted.

Martín looked across the vast expanse of crystal, candelabra, and floral centerpieces to the table where Sarah sat with Exley on one side and some patrician fop on the other. He scowled at the sight and then sat back as the next course arrived.

Jellied trout.

God save him from English cuisine.

"Tell me, Captain Bouchard, is this your first visit to London?"

Martín turned to the attractive brunette on his left. It was no hardship; her exposed cleavage alone was worth the effort. She was married to a corpulent, older man who sat at the far end of the table. Her thigh was pressed against Martín's.

"No, Madam Redman, I have been here several times before."

"La, to think I have only just met you now." Her hand settled high on his leg. This was not the first time Martín had been the target of an unsatisfied wife—nor even the tenth. If there was one thing he knew about marriage, it was that unhappy wives were as sexually predatory as their spouses.

"I understand you are great friends with Baron Ramsay?"

"I am pleased to claim his acquaintance." Martín stifled a yawn and moved his leg.

For the fiftieth time, he cursed his decision to attend this wretched dinner. He'd known the ridiculous rules of precedence would mean he'd be as far from Sarah as possible, but Ramsay had threatened him.

"You are behaving like a fool," the older man had accused, catching Martín at breakfast one morning and commencing to nag when he'd learned Martín had not yet responded to the dinner invitation.

"And you are behaving like a nagging old woman. What concern is it of yours where I go or when?" he'd demanded, not caring how ungracious he sounded.

"Don't be a child, Martín." Ramsay had given him a good-natured smile in spite of his rudeness and plucked a piece of buttered bread from his plate. "It is a ball given in Sarah's honor. You are one of the few people she knows in London. Her family *honors* you by inviting you to the dinner. Must you have these things explained to you?"

"Here, take the rest of my meal." Martín shoved away the plate of food he'd been enjoying until Ramsay began lecturing him. "I am tired of making tepid dinner conversation. I am tired of being seated between daughters of impoverished peers or their bored wives. I am tired of being paraded as some sort of savage for the amusement of my betters."

"Welcome to the polite world, Martín. You know I experienced the very same thing when I returned several years ago. You are being inducted into society, and these things are part of the price."

Martín snorted. "I am only being 'inducted' because of your endless—" He stopped, unable to recall the English word he was searching for. He hit the table with his fist. "*Merde!* What do you call it?" he said in French. Getting angry always made his control of English slip. "Twisting of the arm!" he shouted, triumphant at having recalled the English phrase before Ramsay answered.

"I am only able to twist arms because of the dubious honor of being related to half the *ton*. I may have been born into this society, but I have never been part of it. I suspect Exley feels the same. But we have not left you alone, my friend, and you should not let Sarah feel alone. Go to the dinner and do the pretty—it will make her happy. And you like to see her happy, don't you?"

"If you were truly her friend, you would not want her to come within spitting distance of a man with my past."

"Are we going to have this tired argument again?" Ramsay didn't wait for a response. "When do you plan to speak to her uncles? You said you intended to do so two weeks ago, and yet you have done nothing."

"Will you never stop nagging? What is it to you when I speak to them? *If* I speak to them?"

"You are unbearable. And you will continue to be unbearable until you have confronted this like a man."

Martín threw up his hands, both figuratively and literally. "I will talk to them after the ball. It was too hectic for her with all the preparations."

"And you will go to the dinner?"

"I will go to the dinner. Now, will you go away?"

So, thanks to Ramsay's meddling and his own gutlessness, here he sat, removed from his reason for attending the dinner by an entire table and being fondled by an amorous stranger.

"You've known Lord Ramsay long?" asked the woman beside him—he'd already forgotten her name.

"Yes, we have known each other for many years. I began our acquaintance as a lowly member of his crew on the *Batavia's Ghost*." Martín hoped a reference to his less-than-auspicious beginnings might cool the woman's ardor.

"How fascinating!" Her heaving breasts put paid to his

hopes. He could see the notion of sitting so near such an enterprising savage was driving her into rut, as if Martín might lose control of himself and bend her over the table and take her right now. He smiled at the amusing image and glanced away from her chest toward Sarah's table.

She was looking right at him, a sweet smile on her face. For a moment it felt as if it were just the two of them in the huge room. And then the man next to her spoke and broke the spell.

Martín glared at the intrusive stranger. He could not recall meeting him, and he was sure he would have remembered. He was dressed like a Continental and possessed that certain something the English did not. He wasn't large, but he looked tall and well-formed. Glossy black hair framed a fine-boned face that wore an expression of jaded, world-weariness. Something about him made Martín uneasy. As if sensing Martín's concerns, the man looked directly at him and smiled, raising his glass in silent greeting.

"Do you know the marquis?" the brunette beside him asked, once again breaking into his thoughts.

"Who?" Martín asked rudely.

"The man who just raised his glass to you? He is the Marquis d'Armand, one of the many French refugees who've flooded the country since the Revolution. My husband says—"

Martín's brain spun like a child's top, tossing out random thoughts with dizzying speed. The Marquis d'Armand? Could it be another man with the same title? A distant relative of the old marquis? A not-so-distant relative?

Whoever he was, he was leaning intimately toward Sarah, a flirtatious smile on his thin lips. The handle of Martín's fork cut into the side of his hand.

"*Captain Bouchard?*"

The words came from a long way away.

"Captain? Are you well?"

He looked into the curious eyes of the woman next to him. "What?"

"You look as though you've seen a ghost. You've certainly become as pale as one."

His throat felt tight and thick, as if his stomach had migrated there. "What does your husband say, madam?"

She gave him an odd look, but seemed pleased to repeat herself. "He says most of them will have nothing to go back to after Napoleon granted their lands and houses to his supporters. I believe that is the case for the marquis. He has arrived only recently from America, where he is said to have some interest or other. Apparently his father lived there before the war."

"Is that so, madam?" Martín wrenched his eyes away from the man laughing and talking to Sarah.

So, this was d'Armand's heir? The son of the man Martín had killed.

Sarah bit back a groan. She'd been seated between the Marquess of Exley and her uncles' acquaintance from France, the Marquis d'Armand. She knew neither man well, and both of them looked dark and dangerous.

Exley turned to face her. "What a position of honor I find myself in, Miss Fisher, seated beside the lady of the hour." His lips twitched into what passed for a smile, and his beautiful eyes glinted like pale blue diamonds.

"Well, you are a marquess," she began, and then flushed at her gauche words. To her surprise Exley chuckled.

"I'm pleased to learn my title is good for something other than a moth-eaten robe and an uncomfortable chair." His ironic words were accompanied by a devastating smile that held surprising warmth.

"You are teasing me, my lord, and I deserve it. Thank you so much for coming to my birthday dinner."

"It is a pleasure, Miss Fisher. I'm going to take further advantage of my august title and claim a set. I am accounted something of an expert at Scottish reels."

"I look forward to learning the finer points, my lord."

She turned to the man on her other side. He was waiting for her.

"*Bonjour, mademoiselle,* it is a great pleasure to finally meet you. Your uncles have told me much about you." Something about the Frenchman's thin, smiling lips and knowing, dark eyes made Sarah's stomach clench.

"You are too kind, my lord. I understand you have only just arrived in London from America. Will you be staying long?"

"I am hoping there will be a reason to extend my stay." His heavy lids dropped suggestively.

Goodness! What had her uncles told the man to make him so eager? It certainly couldn't be her looks that had drawn such ardor. She was easily the most average-looking woman at the two tables. He must have somehow learned of the amount they'd settled on her yesterday, her actual birthday. No doubt she would soon acquire an entire throng of admirers. All except the one she wanted.

She glanced toward the other table. Martín was looking right at her. She smiled at him before recalling the baron's advice to ignore and abuse him. He smiled back.

"You know Captain Bouchard?" d'Armand asked, pulling her attention away from the only man in the room she wanted to talk to.

"It was his ship that brought me back from Africa."

"I understand he is an escaped slave." D'Armand's dark eyes were intense.

"I know little about his past, my lord. What I do know is that he rescued me and hundreds of others from a disastrous situation. To us, he was a miracle." Sarah turned away, wishing to let d'Armand know in no uncertain terms that the subject of Martín Bouchard's past was not one she would discuss with him.

The meal was extremely tiresome. Not only did he have to answer the incessant, flirtatious questions of the woman next to him, but he also had to fend off her questing hands beneath the table.

Martín couldn't even approach Sarah after dinner as her uncles spirited her away to the area where she would greet her guests. The best he could do was position himself against the French doors so he could watch her in the receiving line.

"Captain Bouchard."

Martín turned. "Ah, Captain Graaf." He made no effort to keep the irony from his voice.

The Dutchman sighed. "Can you not call me Mies? Or if you can't stomach such familiarity, at least call me Graaf. We both know I am not worthy of the title of captain." The skin beneath the younger man's eyes was shadowed, as if he'd not been sleeping well.

Martín took in the man's slumped shoulders and lined face and frowned. He'd already taken the man's ship and held him captive. What further sport could there be in humiliating such a weak, pitiful figure?

"Very well, Graaf," he said, unwilling to use his Christian name. He might feel pity, but he still despised the man and had no desire to become fast friends.

"Miss Fisher has added a new admirer to the growing list." Graaf jutted his chin toward d'Armand, who was also in a position to watch the receiving line.

Martín's chest tightened; just what the devil was the man about? "Do you know him?" he asked.

"I know *of* him. His mother was from Liège, a Belgian Lowland province famous for its wine. At least it was before

Napoleon took it in 1795 and then burned their vineyards so they would not compete with French wine." Graaf shrugged. "Anyhow, he spent several years in England after escaping the guillotine. Apparently his father was something of an embarrassment to the family and was banished to the Americas before the Revolution. D'Armand has only just recently returned from the United States. He has petitioned Louis for the return of his family lands. Who knows? Maybe he will end up back in his home. In either case, he will need money. I'm sure he wouldn't mind a rich bride to augment his family coffers." Graaf eyed the Frenchman with an expression of distaste.

"A rich bride?" Martín repeated.

Graaf gave him a look of surprise. "Haven't you heard Sarah's uncles settled an enormous amount on her for her birthday?"

"No, I had not heard that." And he did not like it. Especially when he considered how it would encourage every fortune hunter in London.

Martín did not want the Dutchman to see how much the news disturbed him. "And you, Graaf, when are you going home?"

"Oh, soon, I suppose." He cut Martín a bitter look. "You might as well set your mind at rest that you will not be receiving any remuneration. My family, I'm ashamed to say, has not a feather to fly with after this bloody war."

Martín lifted one shoulder. "I am a man of the world. I was never under any misapprehension."

"My father will actually have to pay to retrieve the ship. I'm sure you can imagine how eager I am to reunite with my family."

"Actually, I cannot."

Graaf opened his mouth, and then shut it, his face a fiery shade of red.

"But I know what you mean," Martín said. It would be churlish to use his unfortunate childhood as a weapon, especially when he had so many other sources of ammunition to use on the weak and useless Dutchman. "You can console yourself with the knowledge that you survived a deadly illness, a mutiny, and failed to sell several hundred human beings into lives of slavery. Not to mention saving Mademoiselle Fisher from an unfortunate fate."

The Dutchman's flush deepened. "You are correct on the first three counts. On the fourth, it was you, and not me, who saved Sarah. Actually"—he smiled wryly—"it was *Sarah* who saved Sarah, and held both of us at gunpoint in the process."

"You have the right of it, Graaf. Whomever she marries will be wise to keep the key to his gun cabinet well hidden."

Both men laughed.

Sarah glanced around the room, searching for the person who took up more and more space in her brain. There he was, talking to Mies of all people. What in the world could the two men be discussing without having their hands around each other's necks? Suddenly, they both looked in her direction and laughed.

Sarah whipped her head around and focused her attention on the two women who were next in the receiving line, smiling at some comment they made. Her face hurt from all the polite smiling. In all truth, the evening—the preparations, the hundreds of strangers, the ball—was more taxing than she would have believed possible.

She offered her hand to three more young women she didn't know and uttered some inane pleasantry.

Her eyes drifted back to Martín. Even from across the ballroom he radiated an irresistible magnetism. He was attired like every other man in the room, but his sun-kissed skin made him glow. He looked positively . . . edible. She flushed at the inappropriate thought and greeted the next person in line, a spotty young buck sporting an unfortunate yellow and blue waistcoat.

Dinner had been both strained and far too long. The Marquess of Exley spoke very little, and, when he did, the meaning behind his words was often obscure.

The Marquis d'Armand, on the other hand, was an engaging dinner partner as well as being both elegant and handsome. So elegant, in fact, that his sophisticated manner made Sarah want to run from the room. So, too, did the frequent and heated glances she intercepted from Martín—who'd been seated as far as he could be from her.

Sarah wanted to kick herself for not requesting that Aunt Anna seat him beside her in spite of her ridiculous notions of precedence. It was Sarah's party. Shouldn't she have some say in where her guests sat?

She pulled her eyes away from the object of her obsession and turned back to the endless line.

Martín returned his giggling dance partner to her clique of gigglers and made his way back to where Ramsay and Exley stood.

Ramsay grinned at him. "There, that wasn't as bad as you thought it would be, was it?" He was referring to the dance Martín had just completed with the mindless little idiot Ramsay had foisted upon him.

"I see you are denying yourself the same pleasure, my lord."

Ramsay chuckled, and even Exley smiled.

"That goes for both of you," Martín added before turning to search for Sarah in the crowd. She was dancing with Danforth. Well, at least she wasn't dancing with d'Armand.

"Fortunately for me, no mother would allow me within a

league of her daughter," Exley said, surveying the ballroom as if it represented the manifestation of his worst nightmare.

Martín snorted. "I no longer believe you, Exley. They are all too willing to thrust their daughters into the arms of a man of dubious background and questionable reputation."

"Cultivate a reputation as a murderer," Exley suggested, giving Martín his habitual icy stare.

Before Martín could formulate an appropriate response, Lady Ramsay and Lady Exley returned.

"Adam, have you not danced with anyone? Why must you and Hugh behave like such dolts?"

"Which of your questions should I answer first, my dear?" Exley asked. He met his wife's glare and sighed. "Will you do me the honor, Lady Ramsay?"

The baroness laid her hand on his arm, and the attractive pair went to take their places on the dance floor.

"Would you care to dance, Mia?" Ramsay asked.

Lady Exley looked up over a foot and a half to meet the baron's single green eye. "Good Lord, Hugh, what a stupid-looking couple we would make. Besides, I'm exhausted after only three dances. I expect it is due to my condition."

"Condition?" Martín repeated, and then closed his eyes at his own stupidity. "Er, please accept my congratulations, my lady."

"I believe I have embarrassed you, Captain Bouchard." The marchioness grabbed his arm and stood on tiptoe to peer into his face. "Is that lovely face of yours blushing?"

His ears grew even warmer.

Ramsay's laugh was audible even over the orchestra. "Good gad, you're a menace, Mia. Exley must be made of stone."

"Parts of him are."

Martín shook his head at their raucous laughter; the two never stopped talking.

He tapped his foot and looked at his watch. He would

dance with Sarah and then leave directly afterward. He needed to get away and consider the problem of d'Armand. He would have gone already but for the promised dance. As it was, he had to endure another quarter of an hour of Ramsay's teasing before the time came.

"Are you enjoying your birthday, *mademoiselle?*" Martín asked after they'd danced a quarter of the floor, his words abrupt to his own ears.

Sarah was light in his arms, her dancing much more smooth than it had been the first—and only—time they had waltzed.

"Everyone has been very good to me." Her smile was shy and un-Sarah-like. "I wanted to thank you for the lovely gift. I began reading it immediately."

Martín's gift was a book by a female writer named Jane Austen. It was the first book he'd ever purchased. It was also the first inscription he'd ever written.

"I am pleased you like it."

"It was very thoughtful."

"Bah! A book." He dismissed her thanks, embarrassed. "I'm sure you received much more interesting gifts. I'll swear that is a new necklace you are wearing. It becomes you." She wore a double strand of pearls around her long, graceful neck.

"Yes, it is from my uncles. It is lovely, but I do not love it as much as their other gift."

"What? *Two* gifts? You are being spoiled, I think. Tell me about this other gift."

"I am being terribly spoiled. My uncles gave me a horse of my very own."

"I am relieved to hear it. The mount you had in Hyde Park was a sorry excuse for an animal."

"You are too unkind to poor old Blossom. He was a lovely horse to learn with, but Banker is absolutely perfect."

Martín threw back his head and laughed. "Banker?"

"Yes, Banker. But enough of me, how are you enjoying the evening?"

"Very much. Now."

She flushed, and he could see his words pleased her.

"I—I wanted very much to be seated next to you at dinner."

"Oh?" he said, too surprised to say more.

"Unfortunately, I left the seating arrangements to my aunt, and she is very rigid in her adherence to precedence."

"You can hardly blame her for not wanting to seat an ex-slave at the head of the table."

Her hand tensed in his. "I wish you would not refer to yourself in such a manner."

"I speak the truth, and you should not forget that, *mademoiselle*. Don't tell yourself I am anything other than what I am." His words were harsher than he'd intended, but something about her trusting brown eyes made him impatient that she see him for what he was. And also afraid of what would happen when she finally did.

"You could just as truthfully describe yourself as a very successful sea captain who has saved thousands of lives."

Martín laughed at her vehemence, but was secretly pleased by her defense. "You misunderstand me, *mademoiselle*. I do what I do for money, just as your family engages in banking. But, come, let us speak of more interesting matters. Soon this dance will be over, and it will be unseemly of me to ask you for another. Perhaps we can argue more when we go for a ride in Hyde Park? I have the use of Ramsay's curricle, and I am told there is nothing exceptionable about such an activity. You will rest tomorrow, no doubt, but perhaps you are free the day after?"

Her smile was radiant. "I should like that very much."

"*Bien,*" he said, too pleased to say more.

They completed the dance in silence, as if neither of them wanted to inadvertently disturb the delicate spirit of détente that had grown between them. When he escorted her back to where Lady Ramsay stood, he was displeased, but not entirely surprised, to see the Marquis d'Armand approaching.

"I am here to collect my dance, *mademoiselle*." He spoke to Sarah, but fixed his cool, amused stare on Martín.

"My lord, I would like to introduce you to Captain Bouchard," Sarah said.

Martín gave him an abrupt nod. "D'Armand."

"Captain Bouchard, I have heard so much about you. I believe you knew my father . . . intimately." The Frenchman's eyes flickered over Martín in a way that made Martín's hands tighten into fists. "I look forward to furthering our acquaintance, but right now is not the time." He glanced from Martín to Sarah, his eyes narrow and reptilian.

Martín watched him lead Sarah away to the dance floor, feeling as though he'd just engaged in something particularly unclean.

"I don't like that man." Lady Ramsay's quiet words startled Martín out of his trance.

"Oh? And why is that, my lady?"

"I don't know," she admitted bluntly, never taking her clear blue gaze off the pair as they took their places for the dance. "Call it female intuition."

The suave Frenchman said something that made Sarah laugh. He took her hand, and it made Martín's skin crawl.

"I understand he is only recently arrived from America. Why do you think he has come to England, Captain?"

Martín shook his head slowly, unable to pull his gaze from the elegant nobleman.

"I could not say, Lady Ramsay." And he couldn't. The only thing he knew for certain was that no good would come of it.

Chapter Twenty-Eight

Sarah was stunned by the number of gifts that awaited her the morning after the ball. She knew that it was to curry favor with her uncles, rather than to celebrate her birthday, that most people sent presents.

After writing thank-you cards, she divided the gifts up into two groups: the few she would keep, and those she would give to the Manton sisters for dispersal at their home for women.

The only gifts she kept were those from her family and friends. As well as a ridiculously expensive brush and comb set she received from the Marquis d'Armand. The set was silver and set with stones that could only be sapphires. Sarah was going to talk to Daphne about the best way to return the gift without giving offense.

Her uncles seemed very interested in pursuing their acquaintance with the sophisticated peer, but Sarah was uneasy about the suave Frenchman's intentions. When he'd heard she'd received a new horse for her birthday, he'd been persistent about riding with her, until she finally told him that she rode in the park most days.

For once, she hoped Martín did not make an appearance at her usual morning ride. Martín's expression when she'd introduced them had looked almost murderous. More competitive instinct? For months she'd wished he'd showed some sign of jealousy with Mies, but d'Armand was a different matter entirely. She'd be happier if the two men never met again.

However, when Sarah arrived at the park the next morning, it was to find Martín already waiting for her—along with Daphne and Hugh.

"What a delightful surprise!"

"I had to see how your riding was progressing, Sarah," the baron said, smiling at her before turning coyly to his wife. "Naturally Daphne wanted to tag along when she heard I was coming. And then Martín insisted *he* come to chaperone the two of us."

Martín snorted. "I invited Lady Ramsay to ride with me, and her husband attached himself like a big burr," he clarified. "I am pleased you are here, Sarah. I thought you would be resting today."

"I told him you'd be here," Hugh said to Sarah. He grinned at Martín. "You should know I'm always right, my friend."

Martín rolled his eyes.

They'd just set off when a voice called out from behind them. "Miss Fisher!"

Sarah closed her eyes briefly before turning.

"I hoped I would find you here." D'Armand was mounted on a magnificent black horse that he rode with breathtaking grace.

"What the devil is he doing here?" Hugh muttered loudly. For once, Daphne did not chastise her husband for his bad manners.

"I'm afraid I may have mentioned I rode in the park most mornings," Sarah said beneath her breath before welcoming the man. "My lord, how nice to see you again. Have you come to ride with us?" She winced at the stupid comment. Why else would he be here?

His lips curled, and his dark eyes flashed her a warm,

intimate look. "I should love to," he said, either unaware of or unconcerned by her friends' disapproving stares.

"You have met Lady and Lord Ramsay?"

"*Enchanté*." His eyes swept the blond woman in a bold, almost provocative manner.

Daphne gave the man a look that could have frozen water.

The baron rode his giant horse between the Frenchman and his wife. "D'Armand." The usually amiable man radiated barely suppressed violence and—for the first time— Sarah caught a glimpse of the dangerous pirate who'd been so feared by corsairs and the French navy.

D'Armand looked amused by Ramsay's obvious hostility. He turned to Martín.

"Ah, Bouchard," he said, as though he'd only just then noticed him. He eyed Martín's red mare. "That is a particularly fine mount." His tone suggested it was too good for the likes of Martín.

"As is yours, d'Armand."

The Frenchman's smile grew. "The men of my family are excellent judges of cattle. My father, in particular, owned only the best animals. He was well known as a superlative breeder of livestock."

The silence was deafening. Martín's eyes had gone flat, and his face looked as though it had been chiseled from stone. Sarah looked at the faces of her friends. Just what was going on?

"Shall we lead the way, d'Armand?" Ramsay asked.

After what seemed like forever, the Frenchman spurred his mount forward.

Martín and Daphne waited beside Sarah until the other two men had gone ahead.

"Your ball was a fabulous crush, Sarah. Its success must have pleased your uncles very much. Are you quite recovered?" Daphne asked.

Sarah blinked. The baroness *never* engaged in idle chit-chat.

Sarah would have sworn Daphne didn't actually know how. Just who the devil was the marquis and what was he to Martín? And why would nobody tell her?

They spoke of the ball and other unimportant matters, all the while watching the backs of the two men who rode ahead of them.

Martín listened to the women's chatter, his eyes fixed on the slim, straight shoulders of the French peer. D'Armand sat his exquisite mount like a man born to it, as he had been. Why was he lingering around Sarah? Was it her money? Her connection to a powerful banking family? Revenge against Martín? Or all three? It would not be for Sarah herself. Such a man—a proud member of the French aristocracy—would consider Sarah's lineage far beneath him. Unless he could gain something from it, like money or revenge or both.

Ramsay and the marquis had reached a shady spot not far from the serpentine and pulled up.

"It looks like Ramsay wishes to talk for a while," Lady Ramsay said. "I would like a bit of a gallop. Would you care to join me, Sarah?"

Sarah looked from Lady Ramsay to where the marquis was in conversation with the baron to Martín.

"Go with Lady Ramsay," Martín urged, ignoring her questioning look. "I will join you soon."

"But—"

"Our business will not take long. Ramsay and I will find you." He could see she wanted to argue with him but did not wish to offend Lady Ramsay.

Martín waited until the women had cantered away before guiding his horse over to the two men. The tension between them was palpable. He turned to his friend. "You should go and see to the ladies, my lord. I will handle this."

Ramsay opened his mouth, as if to disagree, but then closed it. He gave Martín an abrupt nod and turned his horse.

"What elevated company you keep, Bouchard." The Frenchman smirked as Ramsay rode off. "I know Ramsay realizes you were a whore, but does Miss Fisher? Her uncles? The people who dined and danced with you at her ball?"

"What do you want, d'Armand?"

The marquis's thin lips curled unpleasantly, as if it irked him to speak to a man he considered no better than chattel. *His* chattel.

"Were we standing on different soil, I could have you stripped, whipped, and hung by the neck until dead, and nobody would stop me."

"But we are standing *here*, d'Armand, and on *this* soil, slavery is not legal."

D'Armand chuckled. "Are you a barrister now? How . . . quaint."

"What do you want?"

"What do I want?" One black brow arched. "That is simple. I want my property back. All of it."

"Do you think to take me by force?"

The nobleman laughed. "You rate your worth highly, Bouchard, too highly. To me you are just another of my father's breeding stock." His eyes flickered up and down Martín's body, a darkly amused glint in them. "I would hardly have sailed halfway round the world to collect a bull."

"Then what do you want?" Martín repeated.

D'Armand saw Martín's clenched fists, and his smile grew into a grin. "I have something that might interest *you*—two things, as a matter of fact. One of them looks remarkably like you." He withdrew a slim silver case from his exquisitely cut riding jacket and extracted a rectangle of white paper. "I will be at home to you tomorrow at three o'clock. That will be the only time I will ever receive you through the front door." He held out the card. When Martín reached out to take it, d'Armand let it flutter to the ground.

Martín watched the Frenchman disappear before dismounting and picking up the card. It listed an address not far from Davenport House.

He stared at the card without seeing it. D'Armand had something that would interest him? Two somethings? What could he possibly have that would interest him? Most likely the man thought it necessary to lie to him in order to lure him to his house for the purpose of killing or capturing him. Martín could have told the nobleman he didn't have to resort to subterfuge to get him alone; he would gladly meet him anywhere, anytime.

He'd not wanted to face his past and all the humiliations associated with it, but now—now that his past had come for *him*—he felt nothing but relief.

Tomorrow he would take Sarah for a curricle ride. He had worried it was too soon to press his suit with her, especially as she was now a rich, independent woman. But d'Armand's presence had taken the difficult decision of what and when to tell Sarah completely out of his hands.

Martín tucked the card into his coat pocket and mounted his horse. He felt a hundred times stronger than he'd felt in months, as if a crushing weight had been lifted from his shoulders. He felt . . . liberated. Laughing out loud like a madman, he turned his mount in the direction of his friends and urged it into a gallop.

Tomorrow afternoon, years of worrying, wondering, and waiting would be over.

Sarah was ready a full quarter of an hour before Martín arrived in Ramsay's elegant curricle with two magnificent grays in harness.

He smiled down at her. "Please forgive me for not helping you into the carriage, but I'm afraid these frisky devils require all my attention," he apologized, while a groom assisted her into the stylish vehicle. There was no avoiding his big body on the narrow bench, and their legs pressed against each other from hip to knee.

"Are you ready?" he asked, his face close enough to hers that she could smell his intoxicating cologne.

Sarah nodded and gave a strangled yelp as the vehicle leapt forward, hurtling toward the busy intersection.

"They're fabulous!" She clutched her hat, which was threatening to fly away even though it was secured under her chin.

"Ramsay is a fine judge of horseflesh. Zeus and Hades are his most recent pair."

Sarah laughed. "Named after feuding gods? How like him."

"Named for gods, are they? I could see he was proud of his cleverness and wanted me to ask, but I refused to give him the satisfaction. You must tell me, who are Hades and Zeus and why were they feuding?"

Sarah entertained Martín with whatever tales of Greek mythology she could recall as they wove their way through the busy streets.

"Those fellows sound more like sailors than gods," Martín commented, tooling the carriage through the park gates and turning off the congested carriage path. "In fact, some of those stories sound remarkably like Ramsay."

"Yes, he would make an excellent Zeus. And you—" Sarah broke off when she realized what she was about to say.

"Yes?" He slowed the horses and turned to face her, giving her a quizzical glance.

"Oh, nothing."

He laughed. "Sarah, you must know by now that I will have it from you no matter what the cost."

"It is nothing, really. I was merely going to say you would make an excellent Ares to Lord Ramsay's Zeus."

"And who is he?"

"He is Zeus's son, the god of war."

"Why do I remind you of him?"

She bit her lip. Why had she begun this ridiculous conversation?

"Sarah . . ."

"Fine. You look remarkably like Lord Ramsay's painting of Ares."

"Have I seen this painting?"

"It hangs in the lower gallery at Lessing Hall, just beside the enormous sculpture of Artemis."

"You mean the naked woman with the bird?"

How like him to recall a naked female, even when she was made from marble. "Yes, her."

Martín was quiet for a moment, his eyes narrowing as he tried to recall the painting. He suddenly snorted. "The naked man with the serpent?"

Sarah flushed, looking away from his diverted expression. "Yes. That one."

His body shook. "That is the one which has a leaf covering—"

"Yes." Her cheeks burned.

"Hmm. No, I do not think there is a resemblance," he concluded.

She cut him a sidelong look. "He is your height and build, your noses are almost identical, and even his hair is the same color."

"Yes, that much is true, but I would need a much larger leaf."

Sarah's mouth fell open. "Captain Bouchard!"

He laughed. "Oh, come, can you not call me Martín? After all, we have spent months together on board my ship, danced together, ridden together, and now . . . discussed leaves together. Besides, you have used my name before."

She heated all over at the memory. "Very well, but you must stop talking of . . . leaves." Not that it would stop her from recalling the last time she'd seen him naked and aroused. She had to agree about the leaf.

He guided the grays onto a small pull-off that was separated from the main path by a cluster of trees. He turned to her, his body pinning her against the bench seat's low back. His chest blocked the carriage path from view.

"I have wanted to talk to you alone for quite some time, Sarah."

"Oh?" she said, her voice breathy.

"You sound surprised?"

"I am."

"Then you are not as clever as you seem. Come, look at me." He stripped his glove from his hand and took her chin, holding her so she could not avoid looking at him. His Ares-like features softened, and his full lower lip curved into a gentle smile as his thumb stroked her chin.

"I want you, Sarah." He pulled her close and feathered a kiss over her lips, his wicked mouth teasing and licking and nipping until Sarah's head was empty of any thought but wanting him. It had been so long since he'd touched her. His thigh was a hot, hard barrier between them, and she was vaguely aware of a hand sliding around her waist.

A low moan broke the silence, and she realized with a shock that it had come from her. His answer was to lift her onto his lap and pull her tight against his chest while massaging her back.

"I think of you constantly." He took her hand and lowered it over the hard ridge straining against the front of his breeches.

Sarah thrilled at the proof of his desire for her, and her hand tightened around him. Her body *ached* for him.

"God that feels good," he groaned into her throat. "No other woman can make me so hard, Sarah. I can think of nobody but you—even when I am with another woman."

She jerked her hand away from him as though she'd been burned. "What?"

He reached up to stroke her face, his eyelids heavy and drowsy, but she slapped him away.

"Are you telling me that I'm interfering with your . . . your . . ." Sarah couldn't bring herself to say the word.

Undeterred, he lightly bit her chin. "It is true that my amorous activities have suffered," he admitted, kissing her lower lip.

Sarah gasped and pulled away. "How *dare* you?"

A small line formed between his hooded eyes. "What? I am telling you other women no longer arouse me, no matter how skillful they are with their bodies or what they do to pleasure me. I can only think of you. What is so bad in speaking the truth?"

Sarah felt as if her corset had been drawn too tight; but she wasn't wearing a corset. The words "other," "women," "skillful," and "pleasure" whirled in her head. He had been with other women? Women who had tried to pleasure him with their skillful bodies? Her mind exploded.

"Let me go this instant!" She put her hands against his chest and pushed, but it was like trying to shove a block of stone. A warm, infuriating block of stone. She shoved harder. "Let. Go. Of. Me."

"Eh?" Dazed golden eyes looked back at her.

His obliviousness enraged her. "How *dare* you handle me so in public?" She ignored the nagging voice inside her that said she'd been perfectly happy to grope him in public *before* he'd mentioned other women. "What if somebody saw us?"

His shoulders rubbed against her as he shrugged. "So what if they did? You care so much for the opinions of others?" His eyes, which had been dark with desire, narrowed, and his expression shifted from amorous to . . . annoyed? Hurt? Angry?

Good!

"How could I not care? I have a family—people who will be harmed by my actions. What would they think if they heard about us? What would any *decent* person think if he or she learned I was behaving no better than a common *whore?*"

The words "common" and "whore" were like a sharp stick to his groin. Martín shoved her off his lap, and she landed with a soft thump on the seat beside him. The expression of fury and horror in her eyes was a damning judgment of everything he was—everything he'd done. He must have been *mad* to think he could ever tell her the truth!

He met her furious stare and laughed unpleasantly. "How could such a lowly one as me ever hope to understand what goes on in the minds of *decent* people? *Decent* like Graaf, I suppose, or perhaps d'Armand, eh? He has been sniffing about you, too, has he not? A slave trader and a slave owner—what elevated suitors you have." He raked her with a nasty look. "I humbly beg your forgiveness for touching your person and heaping shame on both your family and the great banking house of Fisher. I can only hope your *decent* family and friends never learn of this disgusting tussle. I, for one, wish I could forget the entire episode." He snapped the reins, and the curricle bolted forward. "I will take you back to where you belong. To Graaf, eh? You are two of a kind— two *decent* people. I wish you a happy life—you deserve each other."

She hit him in the shoulder. Hard. He wasn't prepared and the reins slipped, causing the curricle to jerk wildly and the skittish horses to bolt across the narrow carriage path.

"Are you mad?" he roared. It took all his strength to pull the horses up in time to avoid running down a man on horseback. Martín tipped his head apologetically at the man's raised fist.

"Don't ever raise your voice to me," she yelled back.

"You almost got us both killed." The curricle shot between the massive pillars, scattering pedestrians and generating a hail of furious looks and angry voices. Martín ignored them all and aimed the horses toward the Fisher mansion. He glanced at Sarah. She'd drawn herself up so close to the end of the bench, she was in danger of falling off.

She met his look with a sneer. "You are an insensitive pig who treats women like objects. Graaf is worth a dozen of you. At least he behaves like a gentleman and considers the effect of his actions on those around him."

Martín let out a string of curse words harsh enough to strip barnacles off a ship's hull. Had the woman forgotten how she'd met the Dutchman and what he'd been doing?

"If you esteem him so much, perhaps you should marry him."

"Perhaps I will accept him the next time he asks," she flung back.

Martín gripped the reins so tightly, the horses danced nervously to the side. The curricle swerved in front of an oncoming phaeton, causing the other driver's mouth to form a terrified O. Martín twitched the reins, and the skittish grays darted out of the way at the last minute. Even so, the wheels of both vehicles brushed against each other with a high-pitched squeal.

"He has asked you to marry him?"

Her eyes narrowed to vicious slits, and he barely recognized her.

"Twice. Unlike you, he does not treat all women as though they are common tarts. Have you ever, for even one second, thought of anyone but yourself? Have you ever given any thought at all to how your actions—your carousing in brothels—might hurt those around you?"

"My actions?" he shouted, too stunned to think of anything more articulate.

"How *dare* you raise your voice to me?"

Her yell caused the horses to shy and jump, and Martín adjusted the reins and bit down on his tongue. Hard. They traveled in hostile silence as he struggled to gain control of his behavior, if not his emotions. The streets passed in a blur. It wasn't until he neared the turn to her uncles' house that he felt calm enough to resume the argument.

"*My* actions? What about your actions? You didn't object to me when you came to my cabin and *begged* me to take you." Martín pulled up sharply in front of her uncles' house. "Nor did you complain back there when you had my cock in your hand."

"You swine!" She launched herself at him in front of two stunned footmen.

Martín grabbed her flailing hands as she beat them against his chest, holding them easily while he looked down at the two gaping servants.

"There is nothing to alarmed about. Miss Fisher is not herself. Perhaps if one of—"

"Unhand me," Sarah snarled, yanking her arms from his grasp and flinging herself from the curricle. Her skirt caught in some part of the carriage mechanism and yanked her back when she tried to storm up the stairs. The two footmen hastened to assist her, but she slapped away their hands and then, enraged beyond bearing, pulled on the garment so viciously a loud ripping noise split the air.

She looked from her shredded dress to Martín. "Now look what you made me do. I could *never* love a man like you! Go back to all your skilled *women*—I never want to see you again! I *hate* you!" She flung a tattered scrap of skirt at him before sprinting up the steps and disappearing into the house.

Martín realized he was standing and lowered himself back onto his seat. He stared at the closed door at the top of the stairs. Should he go after her? But no, it would be a disaster to pursue her. Besides, what would he say?

He drove the team slowly away from the house, his head a bit dizzy. How had a day that started with such promise turned so quickly into a nightmare? He took a deep breath and exhaled slowly. She hated him?

Relief vied with despair that he'd not poured out the truth about his past. He should be grateful to have learned her true feelings before he'd pathetically laid his past and heart at her feet. Whom had he been fooling? He was no country squire; he was a privateer, a sailor who belonged on his ship. He had greatly enjoyed his life before *she* had come along. He would enjoy it again. He would forget her, even if he had to visit every whore in existence. He was healthy, wealthy, and free—what was there not to like about his life?

Thinking of freedom made him recall the meeting he had today with the Frenchman.

Ah, yes, d'Armand. Martín's savage grin startled a passing coachman so badly, he jerked the reins to his team and would have scraped the side of the curricle had Martín not quickly guided the grays to safety.

D'Armand could only be here for one reason: revenge. Did he think, foolishly, to reestablish his father's claim of ownership and drag Martín back to New Orleans? Or perhaps he thought to blackmail him? To threaten to expose Martín's past to Sarah or her uncles unless Martín did his bidding?

Martín smiled grimly. Whatever he planned, it wouldn't matter. Martín could no longer be threatened or blackmailed with anything because he no longer had anything to lose.

Chapter Twenty-Nine

D'Armand's town house was a four-story stone monstrosity. A footman wearing lavish burgundy and black livery answered the door and made Martín wait in a small anteroom. Threadbare carpets, dusty green silk wallpaper, and three battered fan-backed chairs filled the small chamber. D'Armand must have rented the rooms and not been able to afford anything better. Martín smiled at the thought.

He was examining the only painting in the room—a rather dark landscape that took up most of one wall—when the footman returned.

"The marquis will see you now." He led Martín up another flight of stairs to an ornate set of double doors at the end of the hall. An enormous, brawny man stood on either side of the double doors—d'Armand's protection, no doubt. Martín ignored them both and flung open one of the doors without waiting for the footman.

The furnishings in this room were far superior to the one he'd just left. Rich brocades draped the windows and gilt bergère chairs; delicate settees and tables crowded the plush Aubusson carpet that spanned the room. The walls were crammed with paintings, and yet more were propped up in stacks around the edges of the room. A full-length picture of a man dressed in court clothing hung above a console table heavy with crystal decanters.

"You recognize him?" D'Armand's voice called from the other side of the room.

Martín looked into the face of the dead marquis, a face that had haunted him for years. He was just a man in rather silly clothing. A vain, self-indulgent man.

"He was not so young and prosperous looking when I knew him."

The marquis chuckled. "No, he was in a rather bad way after my grandfather banished him to the savage hinterlands."

Martín turned away from the image of the long-dead marquis.

D'Armand sat behind a large desk. A tall, thin, black woman and a young boy stood beside his chair.

The room shifted and began to darken from the edges inward. Martín blinked his eyes to sharpen his hazy vision, but the woman and boy shimmered and receded. He steadied himself against the wall with one hand.

"*Valerie?*" His voice was the ghost of a whisper.

The marquis's laugh was rich yet unpleasant, like a lavish banquet that had begun to spoil and decay. "Ah, I see introductions are not entirely necessary." D'Armand gestured toward Valerie, a woman Martín had not seen in over a decade. "Why don't you introduce your son to his father, my dear?"

Martín didn't need an introduction. The boy's eyes alone would have told him whose child he was. He was the very image of Martín at that age. Valerie murmured something to the boy, and he came forward and executed a graceful bow.

"*Bonjour, monsieur.*" He spoke with d'Armand's more proper French accent.

"*Comment t'appelles-tu?*" Martín asked his son.

"*Je m'appelle* Gaston, *monsieur.*"

Martín couldn't tear his eyes from the boy. He was slighter

and darker than Martín, and he had his mother's impassive expression and air of calm. Martín looked from his son to the man who claimed title to him. He strode toward the marquis, his vision red. He distantly heard d'Armand yell something, and the two brawny men entered the room, armed with pistols.

"They will kill the boy, Bouchard."

Martín stopped, his breathing like thunder in his ears. Good God, how could this be?

"Step back, Bouchard."

Martín shook off his shock; now was not the time to give in to emotion.

He turned to d'Armand. "The boy does not have to hear any of this. We can discuss the rest in private." Martín knew it was probably pointless to try to protect the child; d'Armand had no doubt gone to great lengths to educate him as to his place in the world. Even so, Martín would be damned if he'd play the Frenchman's game in front of his own son.

D'Armand shrugged and spoke to the boy in French. "Go back to your quarters, Gaston." When the woman moved to follow, he shook his head. "Not you, Valerie. You will stay here."

Her expression remained unchanged, and she made no attempt to demur.

Martín waited for the door to click shut behind the boy and the two guards before he spoke. "How much?"

D'Armand laughed. "Oh yes, you are a rich man, now. I have heard much of the great Captain Bouchard. Tales of your daring deeds and how you are driven to free slaves." He flicked an impatient look at Valerie. "Sit."

The woman sat, not taking her eyes from the floor. She'd not looked at Martín since he'd first entered the room.

D'Armand poured himself something from a fine crystal decanter on his desk, not bothering to offer any to the two humans over whom he claimed legal title.

Martín looked at Valerie while he waited for the man to get to the point. She was even lovelier than she'd been a decade ago. Judging by her expression, she was just as unknowable. Martín had made love to her—had sex with her, really—dozens of times, but had never had a conversation with her. He had never even heard her speak, although he assumed she spoke one of the many West African dialects. Perhaps Sarah might know her language and be able to talk to her.

Oh God. Sarah. Martín briefly closed his eyes, as if he could shut the door between Sarah and what was happening in this room. When he opened his eyes, he said to d'Armand, "This is the last time I ask—what do you want?"

"Very well, I will get to the point." D'Armand stood and walked around to the front of his desk, hitching up a hip and sitting on it, his glass dangling from long, white fingers.

"You have nothing to offer me that is not mine already, Bouchard. Under the law, everything belongs to me, including your body and your life." The Frenchman's voice was conversational, but Martín heard the steel beneath it. D'Armand took a sip from his glass and then strolled forward, not stopping until he was a mere foot from Martín.

Martín thought about reminding him that he referred to American law and they were now on British soil, but he was sure the man already knew as much. He remained quiet, letting things unfold. If d'Armand thought to goad him, he would fail. Martín had been goaded by the best. Ramsay himself was enough to drive the average man mad; Martín could listen to the Frenchman without losing his temper.

D'Armand's dark eyes glowed with contempt and pride and . . . anger. Yes, he was angry. Whether he was angry because Martín had known his degenerate father or angry because Martín had escaped, he could not say. Perhaps it was some of both. Perhaps it was something else entirely.

"I already have your son, and soon I will have your possessions and the woman you love."

Martín's startled gaze flickered from d'Armand to the woman who still had not spoken. D'Armand saw the look and smiled, the action doing nothing to soften his cruel expression.

"No, not her, you fool. I already have her. I'm speaking of *Sarah*. Sweet, sweet Sarah." He looked at Martín's expression and gave a laugh of genuine amusement. "Oh yes, I can see you love her; so can everyone else. Everyone except you and her, it would seem. How cruel and blind love is, eh?" He enjoyed whatever it was he saw on Martín's face. "Tell me, how do you think your beloved will respond when I tell her about your son and how he was begotten?" The smile slid from his face.

Martín refused to give this man what he wanted.

"Don't worry," d'Armand taunted. "You will not lose her completely. I will make her my wife—her uncles will see to that. Already our men of business meet to discuss the details of our union. In spite of her humble origins, I will do her the honor of making her my marquise." He began to pace in circles around Martín, each circle smaller in circumference, each circle bringing him closer.

"You will be able to see her after we have married, provided you continue to produce more healthy offspring like fine young Gaston. You will have the privilege of watching Sarah flower as I initiate her into the pleasures of the flesh."

Martín began to unravel, and visions of the Frenchman's head, disconnected from his body, filled his mind. He repressed his fury and took a deep breath, forcing himself to ignore the red haze of rage already clouding his vision. Killing the man where he stood would only create more problems.

As if reading Martín's mind, d'Armand turned away abruptly, sauntered to the decanter, and refilled his glass.

"I understand you and Valerie used to put on quite a show. I can't blame you for that." He turned and cast a look at the woman, who appeared as distant as the moon. "She is quite magnificent when it comes to pleasuring a man . . . or a woman."

"What do you want?" Martín once again forced the words from between clenched teeth.

D'Armand stepped close enough that Martín could feel his hot breath and smell the brandy. His pupils were tiny black specks. "I want what belongs to me. I want what you *stole* from me. I could seize you right now, throw you in a sack, take you back to New Orleans, and mete out whatever punishment I deem fit." His words came out a flat, dangerous hiss. "I would be within my rights to do anything I wish, and you *know it*. The laws of this country might forbid me from taking any of you back where you belong, but laws are brittle and easily broken, and they serve those in power. The blood of kings runs in my veins, Bouchard, and you are a runaway slave whore."

"None of that matters to a man's liberty under English law." Martín glanced at Valerie. "Or to a woman's liberty."

"Ahh, that might be true. But what will *English law* do when they learn you are also a murderer?"

Martín's head jerked up.

D'Armand's reptilian smile grew. "Ah, yes, now I have your attention. English law will not look so fondly on your presence here when they learn *who* you killed. They take the murder of a peer very seriously."

"How do you know?"

The Frenchman flicked a dismissive hand. "What does it matter?"

"You have no proof of anything."

D'Armand made a *tsk*ing noise. "Oh, Bouchard, you have been away a long time. Many things have happened in so many years." He pivoted and went back to his desk, drawing out a folded sheaf of papers with an official-looking seal. He waved it in front of Martín's face.

"The authorities here will not stop me from taking you back when they see this."

Martín reached out a hand, stopping d'Armand in mid-rant.

"What? You wish to look at this? What good would it do you? There are no pictures." D'Armand laughed.

"I can read."

The Frenchman's eyebrows inched up his forehead. "Has someone been teaching you tricks? How precocious." He advanced on Martín. "Of course you may see it, not that it matters. You will find yourself on a ship heading back to New Orleans before you can even blink. You killed a peer, Bouchard, not some sailor in a bar fight. I could have had you clapped in irons already."

D'Armand resembled a snake in speed as well as demeanor, and the papers were a white blur that made a *crack* like the rapport of a gun when they struck Martín's face.

Martín lunged, but was stopped by something hard pressed against his sternum.

"You. Killed. *My*. Father," d'Armand whispered, pushing the gun into Martín's chest. "He might not have been much of a father, but he was the head of my family. A family that can trace its lineage back to Charlemagne. And you?" He shook his head, hatred rolling off him in waves. "Now. Step *back*."

Martín recognized the white-hot rage in the other man's eyes and complied.

The Frenchman tossed him the papers, took a step back, and tucked the pistol into the back of his breeches, where it must have been all along.

Martín looked at the mass of copperplate writing before extracting a pair of spectacles from a pocket on his coat. His eyes quickly found the word *murder,* and he read enough to know the Frenchman had somehow found out what had happened that night.

"I would exercise this warrant right now, but your friend Ramsay has already told me he will know where to look if anything untoward happens to you. He is a truly powerful man and related to half the English peerage. I prefer not to dodge him and his annoying band of associates all the way back to New Orleans. I could hand this paper over to the right person, and you would find yourself in the deepest cell in Newgate. But lucky for you, Bouchard, I will not tolerate having this matter dragged before the courts—either here or in New Orleans." D'Armand's sneer deepened, and he leaned back against his desk, crossing his arms.

"Particularly when there is a better, quicker way of settling the issue. I have the right to avenge my father in a duel. When I kill you, it will be a matter of honor. I will lose your stud services, of course, but I suspect you would have proved intractable and ultimately . . . unprofitable."

"And what will I get for killing you?" Martín asked.

D'Armand laughed. "So much fire! I can see why my father enjoyed making you kneel." He raked cold eyes down Martín's body, the look calculated and insulting. "You will not kill me, but I will still make you an offer. I will give you your deed."

Martín snorted. "That is unnecessary. But you will give me Valerie's and the boy's." He would take her and Gaston away from d'Armand with or without the papers, but their lives would be far easier if they had them. Martín turned to the woman. "Are there any others?" he asked, not bothering to explain what he meant.

She gave d'Armand a long, inscrutable look before shaking her head.

"I will want their papers and your word you will release them into Ramsay's care—no matter what happens. In exchange, I will deed everything over in advance, and you will not have to wait to get your hands on my ship and my property. If you do not agree, you will get nothing. I will deed it all away to Ramsay, and you can try to fight *him* for it."

D'Armand's breathing quickened, and Martín wondered if the man would shoot him right now and be done with it.

But d'Armand wanted his pound of flesh, so he shrugged. "Very well—but I will give the warrant to the authorities here. If you live, I will not have you go on with your life as if you've done nothing wrong. No, you *will* be punished for what you did. That is the only offer I will accept."

So, there it was. He would have to kill d'Armand, grab Valerie and the boy, and leave England immediately after the duel. That would mean he couldn't—

"I said *very well* to your terms. Do you agree to mine?" d'Armand said when Martín made no response.

"I agree."

"Excellent. Now, how do you prefer to die?"

Martín would have liked to choose fists, but knew that would not be an option: d'Armand wanted blood and death. "I choose pistols."

Again, d'Armand shrugged, as if it didn't matter one way or another. "I assume Ramsay will be your second?"

The last thing Martín wanted was Hugh getting involved and telling his wife, who would no doubt tell Sarah. "No. The Marquess of Exley will second me."

D'Armand's eyebrows rose. "Such august friends you have. Oliver Chenier will call on Exley, and we will meet in the morning, before first light."

"I will require some time to get my affairs in order."

D'Armand's mouth twisted. "Such an important man of business. Very well. The day after tomorrow and no later. I have no desire to waste any more time on you."

Martín ignored the insult, instead thinking about Exley's nosy little wife. "I do not want this matter sullying my friend's house. Exley will call on your man. Now, I want a few moments with Valerie. Alone."

The only sign that the Frenchman was annoyed at being ordered around by his slave was a very slight flaring of his nostrils. "By all means. There is no spiriting her out of the house—I have more men than you have seen. In any case, I have the boy."

Martín ignored the threat and went to sit across from the woman. He waited until the door closed behind d'Armand before he spoke.

"How old is he?" he asked in French, looking into a pair of dark eyes he recalled well.

"He is thirteen." Her voice was low and sultry and fit her person.

"You have had no others?" He could not believe d'Armand would have resisted his base urges.

She looked down again. "There was a girl. He sold her a year ago."

Martín stared. "Good God—she could not be more than—"

"Yes."

Martín was not surprised; after all, his own father had sold him. Here was yet another man who treated his own children like livestock.

"D'Armand needs money—he is barely one step ahead of the law himself."

"I am sorry I never came to find you after I escaped," Martín said, speaking words that had caused him shame and grief for over a decade.

She gave a laugh that chilled him. "You were in no position to save anyone—not even yourself."

"I could have tried," he persisted.

"And how is that? Did you know it was the marquis who bought me?"

"No, but—"

"You knew nothing and could do nothing, Bouchard. You were given a chance to escape and you took it. I would have done the same as you. Besides, you could not have known about the child."

He hadn't known, but he should have guessed. Madam Sonia had not been shy about putting them together.

"Do you know how d'Armand found out it was me who killed his father?"

But Valerie was not interested in small talk now any more than she'd been fifteen years earlier. "He will kill you." She spoke the words with a quiet certainty that made every muscle in his body tense.

Martín bristled. "I am no mean hand with a pistol."

"It doesn't matter what you choose. He has killed many men. That is all he enjoys—killing. Blades, pistols, it does not matter; he is a killer."

Her stoic acceptance of d'Armand's superiority with weapons was annoying, but Martín chose to ignore her lack of faith in him.

"After I kill *him* we will have to leave immediately. You can never go back home. You know that?"

She stared at him with her unnerving, dead eyes. "I have no home."

"I have a property in Italy that will be suitable. I have money. You will not want for anything, and neither will the boy." Again she shrugged, the gesture so fatalistic it made him boil inside. "Do you have no desire to escape him? Or have you come to enjoy his attentions?" He knew the question was cruel before it left his mouth.

This time he saw an expression: raw hatred that made him recoil. "Only death offers an escape. Had I been stronger I would have killed Gaston, the girl, and myself long ago. But I was pitiful and weak."

Bile rose in his throat. How could she survive such bleakness? How had the boy survived? Martín would not rest until he found her daughter.

"I will find your girl. Even if he kills me tomorrow, I will leave instructions and money. I know men who will rip the world apart for her. They will find her, buy her freedom, and bring her to you."

She laughed, the sound so bitter and hate-filled, Martín felt as though she'd raked her nails across his face.

"You will only need a shovel and a little patience to find her."

Martín stared.

"He sold her to his nearest neighbor. She was only there a few months before she died of some disease that killed everyone on the plantation. I begged him to wait, to—" Valerie stopped abruptly, her face once again impassive, as though she'd never divulged such unbearable horror. That was when he realized she was little more than a beautiful shell, a vessel with nothing other than hate to fill it.

He stared at his hands, which were clenched so tightly his knuckles were white. As white as the man who claimed to own him. A hand like delicately carved ebony covered his clenched fists, her touch cool and as light as a feather. He looked up, stunned by the comforting gesture. But there was no tenderness in her face; she was not seeking to comfort or to be comforted.

"I will attend tomorrow, as I have done several times in the past. It arouses him to have an audience to his violence. He likes to display his skill and take me after." Her hand fell away. "See that our son is cared for."

Martín's head throbbed with rage. He wanted to grab and shake some anger into her, but he could see she had already retreated back into herself.

He stood. "Make sure the boy is ready to leave when this is finished. And yourself, too."

Adam de Courtney, the seventh Marquess of Exley, looked at Martín without speaking. For the second time in one day Martín found himself looking at a person who gave away very little. With Valerie, it was because she had nothing left to give. With the marquess? Well, who knew what the man was hiding?

He had listened to Martín's story without asking a single question or making even one comment. When Martín finished, he rose and poured them each a second glass of brandy.

Exley resumed his chair, his posture so rigid it made Martín sore just looking at him. The marquess took a sip of brandy and met Martín's eyes.

"I saw d'Armand shoot at Manton's some years ago. He lived in London for a while before he went to America. I shot against him on four occasions."

Martín hated to ask, but he had to. "And did you best him?"

Exley gave Martín the arctic stare that made it so difficult for some members of the *ton* to forget his notorious nickname.

"We run even as of our last match."

Damn! He should have chosen blades.

Exley took a sip and gave a slight smile, as if he could hear Martín's thoughts. "He is even more dangerous with a short sword."

Martín nodded and sighed. "You will second me?"

Exley's bizarrely pale eyes blinked at the question; Martín thought it might have been the first time he'd seen the man exhibit even mild surprise. "I would have thought you'd ask Ramsay."

"Ramsay has been acting like an old woman since his

marriage. He would tell his wife, and she would find some way to stop me."

Exley sat as still as a cat, his cold stare enough to make any man jumpy. "And you believe I will not tell my wife?" he asked, both his expression and his tone incurious.

"If you recall, I once helped you keep a matter of some importance from Lady Exley. You owe me."

"Ah, I see. Giving you Oak Park was not enough to clear the ledger?" He did not wait for an answer to his sarcastic question. "I will act as your second, and I will not tell my wife."

Martín suddenly felt weak with relief. Exley might be an uncomfortable man to be around, but at least he was straightforward and not overly emotional. Unlike Ramsay. Martín grimaced at the thought of the mercurial ex-privateer learning about this duel.

"As your second it is part of my duty to urge you to seek reconciliation. I will only ask you once, Captain Bouchard. Is there no other way out of this?"

"No. He wishes to kill me. Whether it is for the money or for revenge"—Martín shrugged—"I don't know."

"Very well," Exley said, unperturbed. "If you kill him, you must have plans to leave the country immediately. And if you don't kill him? Well, you must still have plans for the woman and boy."

"I have agreed to sign over my ship and properties—including Oak Park. In exchange for that he has agreed to free Valerie and the boy. If he kills me and seems unwilling to keep his word to me, offer him money. I have a great deal of money tucked away, far more than d'Armand can possibly know about."

Exley grimaced. "It is a wretched coincidence we only took care of the deed to Oak Park recently."

Martín would have called it something far worse. "Let's hope he doesn't get anything from me."

Exley's blank stare said what he thought of such wishful thinking.

"Ramsay knows about the money I have hidden and he will help you . . . after, if I am no longer able." Martín's mind spun as he tried to consider every eventuality. "Put the boy and the woman on Ramsay's ship. I will leave Ramsay a letter and ask him to make arrangements to take them to one of his foreign properties. He will protect them." Martín looked into the hard, pale face across from him. "You will see to this for me, if I am gone?"

"Yes, I will see to it. You should go now," the marquess said, opening a drawer and taking out a sheet of paper. "You have matters to see to, and I must send a message to d'Armand's second."

When Martín reached the door to the study, he turned around to thank the man for his help. But Exley was already bent over his desk, the scratching of his quill moving across paper the only sound in the large room. Martín swallowed his words of thanks and quietly left the room.

Exley was correct; he did have matters to see to. One of those matters was a letter to Sarah.

Chapter Thirty

Sarah closed the door to her Uncle Septimus's study and leaned against the glossy brown wood to catch her breath. The meeting with her uncles had not been as bad as she'd feared. In fact, her uncles had seemed almost resigned to her plans. Her Aunt Anna on the other hand, had been appalled.

"You're going to do *what?*"

"I'm going back to Africa to build a school and an orphanage," Sarah repeated.

The older woman's eyes were wide and almost crazed. She turned to her elder brothers.

"Can you not do something? She cannot do this foolish thing if she has no money to do it."

Septimus smiled, and Sarah's heart hurt at the pain she saw in his eyes.

"We settled her inheritance on her outright, Anna. We did not want to use the promise or the threat of money to make her stay. It was our hope she would remain in London, but Barnabus believed she would probably wish to return to Africa. She is, after all, from there, Anna."

His words had made Sarah blink. Her staid, proper uncles—the same men who'd wanted her to marry Mies—had believed all along she might leave?

The realization that they had believed such a thing yet

treated her so lovingly had made her weep. Indeed, she was still crying. She brushed the back of her hand across her damp eyes and straightened away from the study door.

The deed was done, and she had told her family. The only thing left to do now was to finalize her plans. She squared her shoulders and strode toward the smallest sitting room, an unused chamber that she'd claimed as her sanctum.

Sarah's mind went from the meeting she'd just left to her immediate future. She'd already set her plans in motion. Paul Cuffe had helped her, and the Manton sisters had promoted her cause among their wealthy donors. She had acquired—

"Miss Fisher?"

Sarah squeaked and spun around.

A footman was behind her. "I'm sorry, miss. I didn't mean to startle you. A letter came for you." He held out a thick cream envelope.

She looked at the envelope and froze. She knew only one person who possessed such bold, almost outrageous hand-writing.

It was from Martín.

Her eyes swept over the writing again and again, as if to convince her brain they'd not misled her. She reached out to steady herself against the wall.

"Are you all right, Miss Fisher?"

Sarah looked up from the envelope and gave the footman a reassuring smile. "Yes, thank you, Charles." She watched the man depart before making her way down the hall on legs as unsteady as a toddler's.

Once inside the soothing, mint-green sitting room, she practiced breathing deeply while staring at the letter in her hands. His handwriting looked bolder and more confident since she'd last seen it; he'd been practicing.

Why had he written instead of coming to see her? It could not be good.

She swallowed several times, forcing back her fear.

Was she going to merely sit here and stare at it?

"You're a big girl, Sarah," she muttered.

She pulled open the heavy cream envelope and spread the pages before her; there were four of them.

She took a deep breath and began.

"My Dearest Sarah,"

Her heart fluttered. She was his dearest? Hope sprouted and grew inside her as she stared at the loving salutation. Was it possible—

"Just read the letter, Sarah," she scolded herself.

"My Dearest Sarah,
   I have tried to speek to you many times of the way I feel about you. Each time my eforts have ended in failure—or at least in a bad argument. I do not no why this happens. But I think may be a letter will be best."

Sarah's lips twitched at the small errors. How hard it must have been for him to write this letter—and yet he'd done it. What an amazing man he was. Six months ago he could do no more than write his name and now—

A drop of water hit the page, and the words *Dearest* and *Sarah* blurred and mingled into a small black puddle.

"Oh, drat!"

She blotted at the stain with her finger and smeared the words below it. She muttered and pulled her handkerchief from the sleeve of her morning gown and dabbed at her eyes.

It took her several minutes of sniffling before it was safe to resume reading.

"The story of my past is not fit for the drawing rooms of London. When you met me I only wanted

*one thing in my life: to hound, herry, and capture
every slaver that crossed my path. Well, and maybe
I wanted to dress in fine clothes, eat good food, and
enjoy the company of women, two. But, in any case,
I could not forsea a life where I was not a privateer.*

*And then I met you. You tot me to read and write
and you opened a hole new world to me.*

*Of course I still burn to capture slavers, but I am
no longer a slave myself. You freed me, Sarah. But
then you enslaved me, two.*

*When I lerned about your rich and powerful
family I new I was not the man for you."*

Sarah crumpled the pages in her fist. "Foolish, stupid,
arrogant, idiot man! Why do you think you know what is
best for me without even asking?"

She scowled at the wrinkled paper and smoothed the
sheets flat.

*"I new you were ment for better things, but I culd
not stay away. And Ramsay, he nagged me and
nagged me to tell you the truth and let you decide.
(You no how bad he can be.) He said I culd marry
you and we culd live happily at Oak Park."*

Sarah grinned. "Well done, Hugh!"

*"I started to beleev him. But then my past cot up
with me, just as I was going to tell you the truth.*

Oh, Sarah, what a terrible truth it is.

*I will try to keep my story short, and not just
becus my hand is cramping, but becus it is not a
happy story or the kind of thing a gentlewoman
should here."*

"Foolish, stupid, arrogant, idiot man! Can you really be so blind when it comes to me?"

Sarah realized she was squeezing the pages as if they were his neck. She took a deep breath and released her death grip on the unoffending pieces of paper.

"My father was John Bannock. The Bannocks had been in French held territory for sevral generations. They once owned huge tracts of land, but had lost most of it threw gaming and bad stuardship. My father was the last of his line.

Well, except for me, I suppose.

I never knew my mother. She died when I was born.

My father was a gambler and lost everything when I was somewhere between ten and twelve. He had to sell everything: his house, cattle—both human and animal—and all his land.

I was young and stupid and scared and ran away when I herd I was to be sold. The first time I ran and they cot me, it was a beating, the second time, I was branded a runaway."

Sarah sucked in a breath and held it, her heart pounding in her ears. *Branded?*

Oh, Lord.

Sarah closed her eyes, but tears leaked out anyway.

When she had no more tears left, she opened the letter again.

"Bannock sold me to a brothel."

Sarah's vision clouded, and it was several minutes before she could reread the sentence again. *A brothel?* The man sold a little boy—his own son—to a brothel? She felt as if somebody had kicked her in the chest. *Good God.* Did she want to know what came next?

Her face heated at the thought. If Martín had survived it—only a mere *boy*—surely she could read about it? Or was she really as fragile as he believed?

She gritted her teeth and turned to the next page.

> *"Life at Madam Sonia's was far better than I could have hopped for. Even then I had a love of fine clothing and Madam saw to it that all who worked for her were dressed better than any other brothel in a town which had many.*
>
> *I lived above the stables with an old man named Etienne Bouchard. Bouchard had forgotten more about horses than I would ever learn. He was a meen old bastard, but he tot me all he cud before he died. I had no last name and was called only Martín, which was a name I pikked for myself after a story I once herd. So when the old man died I took his name, thinking I wood also take his place.*
>
> *I loved caring for madam's horses and I foolishly believed life would go on that way. But of corse things changed."*

Sarah closed her eyes, terrified to read what had happened next. How had he survived?

> *"I was sixteen or so when Madam Sonia told me it was time to take up my reel job. There is no way to say this that is polite, Sarah. I became a whore."*

Sarah looked up from the page and blinked. A whore? But . . . he was a man.

> *"You are such a sweet innocent Sarah. I hate to be the one to take your illushuns, but the truth is*

*some women are willing to pay for the pleasures of
the flesh, Sarah, just like their male counterparts.
And, of course, some men prefer men or boys. But
that was not my purpose. Not at first. At first I was
used to provide more . . . exotic entertainments.
Some of these involved other slaves—other whores."*

Sarah's hands shook as she lowered the letter to the dark
green velvet settee. She stood and began to pace the room in
restless circles, lacing and unlacing her hands as Martín's
words bounced and ricocheted endlessly in her head.

His past—his life—was unimaginable to her. Who could
do this to another human? What kind of person could buy
and sell others? Her hands curled into fists. Who could use
others in ways that not only violated common decency, but
the very heart and soul of another human being? They'd taken
physical love from him and made it commerce. No wonder
he spent his time in brothels. What else did he know?

Fury coursed through her and tempered her pity into rage.
She marched back to the divan and snatched up the letter.

*"Not long after Bouchard died, Madam Sonia
moved me to the howse. That was also when I first
met Valerie—the mother of my son."*

"*What?*" Sarah's voice was so shrill she didn't even recognize it as her own.

Sarah reread the last sentence.

It said the same thing.

He had a *child?* She collapsed back against the settee and
read the words over and over. Why had he never told her?
She felt as if a giant, black pit had opened inside her.

Was he married?

Sarah cursed herself for even wondering such a thing.
What? Was she actually hoping he'd fathered a child *outside*

of wedlock? She ignored the howling pain in her chest and picked up the letter with numb, clumsy fingers.

"Madam bot Valerie off a slave ship. She was maybe a little older than me, a dimond hidden in a dung heep, far two butiful to waste on common labor. She spoke hardly a word—at least no English or French—and we never even talked to each other."

Sarah stared at the words in gape-mouthed astonishment. How could they be married if they'd never spoken? Her head felt light and dizzy—as if it might come detached from her neck and float away.

She turned the page.

"Madam Sonia had many slaves but Valerie and I became her most popular attraction. To say it now makes me sick. I shuld have refused—may be we both shuld have. But we were yung and skared and without any power. And to refuse wood only leed both of us to wurs things, and we both new it.

I don't know how many men and women paid to sit in a darkened room and watch us, but Madam was nothing if not a good bisnesswoman. She whipped her buyers into a frenzy and drove our value to the roof before finally selling both of us to the hiest bidder: the Marquis d'Armand bot us."

"That *bastard!*" Sarah startled at the curse word and bit her lip. She stared down at the page, the name swimming before her eyes and the hatred she'd felt in the park that morning now making sense. Why had nobody told her? How could a man like that even show his face in decent society?

She glared at the letter and resumed reading.

*"The man I speak of was the current marquis's
father. D'Armand was notorius in New Orleans for
his debachery and when Madam told me the marquis
had bot me, I paniked. D'Armand sent men to take
Valerie away furst—and I never saw her again.
D'Armand was to take me, but I ran.*

*I wasn't ignorant of what went on between men
and boys at the brothel, Sarah, but I did not want to
live my life that way, being given to whoever wood
pay for me."*

"Oh, Martín," she whispered, staring blindly at the pages
before her.

*"I tried to escape the very night I fownd out but
I had no money, no nowledge of anything outside
the doors of the brothel, no friends other than those
trapped inside. I acted impulsively and it was beyond
stupid.*

*The marquis lerned of the escape and must have
baulked at the notion of purchasing such an untamed
animal. To convince him, Madam drugged me and
invited the marquis to sample me while I slept."*

"Oh God," Sarah murmured, her head bowed. For the
first time since she'd begun reading, she seriously considered
stopping. Half an hour ago she'd believed Martín Bouchard
to be an arrogant, confident, wealthy, beautiful man whom
she loved and who did not love her in return.

And now?

Well, he was still all those things—especially arrogant—
but he was also unspeakably damaged.

But he had written this letter to her. It showed he must hold
her in some esteem—mustn't he? Perhaps, just perhaps . . .

She picked up the pages.

*"The old man wasn't satisfied. He told Madam
he wanted compliance, not drugged and sleeping.
Madam told me I would have one last chance to
please d'Armand. She then pointed out there were
other buyers waiting behind him. I new what she
meant. Ether way, I would end up kept by some man.
I could not live that way, Sarah, do you understand
me? I wood do anything to escape. Anything. And if
I culd not escape, I wood rather die."*

Sarah's eyes began to brim over, and she dashed her tears
aside. She turned to the last page.

*"I pretended my spirit had been broken, that I
had axcepted my fate. The old man came for me
wearing a sly smile and making witty comments
about how much he had enjoyed our prior
engagement but how he was looking forward to an
eager participant.*
*When he came toward me I flung him away and
told him I would not submit. He became enraged and
came after me again. I pushed him back but he wood
not stop coming at me. The last time I pushed him he
stumbled and struck his head on a piece of furniture.*
He did not get up.
*So, you see, I killed him, Sarah. I did not mean to,
but the fact is, I did. And I could not be sorry."*

Sarah bit her lower lip until it bled.

*"I injured myself jumping from the bilding and
alerted my captors in the process. It was then that I
encowntered Lord Ramsay. You know how Hugh is,
he can be stubborn. He wood not let them take me.
When Madam Sonia lerned what had happened in*

*her own brothel, she was glad to be rid of me and to
take his help. Ramsay arranged for the marquis's
body to be found in the reckage of his carriage—just
another victim of the poor roads in the area.*

*The rest of the story you no. I became one of
Hugh's crew and worked my way up to have my own
ship. With every year that passed I worried less and
less about discovery. But the feer was always with
me and I cannot say I was surprised when d'Armand
showed up in London.*

*My past had finally cot up with me—just as I was
hoping to leave it behind and start a new life with
you, Sarah."*

Sarah stared at the letter, but saw Martín's beautiful
face. "Why didn't you tell me all of this before? Why?"
she whispered.

*"D'Armand showed me that my dreem of
marrying and settling down was foolish. There is no
place for me in England, Sarah. And I knew you
would never want to leave your family and the life
you were bilding for yourself heer."*

"You idiot!" she yelled at the top of her lungs.

Feet thudded outside the sitting room, and the door flew
open. Her uncles' staid butler stood in the doorway.

"Miss Fisher, is something the matter?" he asked, his eyes
flickering around the room.

Sarah's face burned. She must look and sound like a lu-
natic. "I'm fine, Sedgewick. I apologize for startling you."

There was a long pause as his eyebrows crept slowly up
his forehead. "Very good, miss," he said, bowing before quietly shutting the door.

Sarah looked at the page. There were only a few sentences left. How bad could it be?

"When I met with d'Armand I larned he didn't just want justice for his father's death, he wanted revenge on me.

It shuld not have surprised me that Valerie had a child, but I am ashamed to admit it did. His name is Gaston and he is thirteen years old, Sarah. He is very handsome and looks much like I did when I was his age."

Sarah's lip twitched at his unconsciously vain comment.

"D'Armand holds title to him and Valerie and the only way to free them is to fight for them. I cannot leeve her a second time.

But that is not all. D'Armand has somehow learned the truth about his father's death and I have been accused of murder. Any man who captures me will receive a substantial reward if he returns me to New Orleans to stand trial.

I am a fugitive, Sarah. I tell you this so you will understand why it is best for you if I go. I also tell you this because it is possible I will not leave—that I will die. If that is so, I would prefer you to know the truth in my own words.

Tomorrow I will meet d'Armand and we will dule for the freedom of my child, his mother, and myself and I will—"

Sarah grabbed the other sheets of paper and looked at each; there was no date anywhere on the letter. She lunged to her feet, and the pages fluttered from her limp fingers.

A duel? Had it taken place yet? Was it about to take place?

How could he do this to her?

"You arrogant ass!" Sarah ran for the bellpull and yanked it so hard the heavy velvet rope came off in her hand.

A duel? His son? What of the woman? Was he to marry her now? Why had nobody said anything to her? Surely Hugh would know, and if Hugh knew, Daphne must know. Why had none of them told her?

She stared at the sheets that lay scattered on her uncles' expensive carpet, and fury blossomed inside her. How dare Martín make not only his decisions, but hers as well?

The door opened, and a footman stood in the doorway, his gaze dropping to the bellpull in her hands. "Yes, Miss Fisher?"

"Send word to the stables. I'll want my uncles' post chaise made ready."

The man's eyes flickered to the late afternoon sky outside the sitting room window.

"Post chaise, Miss?"

"Yes, post chaise."

The young man hesitated.

"Do not worry. I will speak to my uncles. You will not get in trouble."

The lines of worry on his forehead dissipated. "Very good, miss. Can I tell the coachmen how far you will be going?"

Sarah gathered up the sheets of paper before turning a grim smile on him. "Tell him our journey could be as short as Davenport House or as long as Eastbourne."

Chapter Thirty-One

Martín wasn't really surprised when he opened the door to Exley's carriage and found Ramsay waiting inside it. The carriage was lighted with a small lantern, but Martín didn't need to see Ramsay's face to know he was angry.

Martín turned to Exley, who raised a slim, black-gloved hand.

"Don't bother scowling and scolding, Bouchard. Ramsay did not hear about it from me."

Martín dropped onto the seat beside the smaller man. Ramsay took up the entire opposite bench, his knees almost at his chin, a fact that also wouldn't improve his humor.

"How did you find out?" Martín asked.

Ramsay's face shifted into the hard, unemotional mask that usually scattered men in all directions. Martín had to admit he did not appreciate being the recipient of such a murderous expression. Here was yet another man eager to kill him.

"Chenier shot his bloody mouth off all over town. Imagine my surprise when I learned from a *stranger* at Brooks's that my bloody protégé was going to fight a duel."

Martín smiled at the word *protégé*.

"I don't know why you have that obnoxious smirk on

your face, Martín, but you're not too big for me to thrash it off you."

"You are not my father, Ramsay," Martín snapped, bristling at the other man's tone.

"No, but I'm the closest damn thing to it." The baron leaned forward, until their faces were only inches apart. "Do you think I rescued you all those years ago and then put up with your shenanigans for more than a bloody decade just so you could throw your life away on a whim?"

"This is no *whim,* you stubborn, dog-headed—"

"Bull." The word was soft, like the sound of a razor-sharp dagger being slipped from its leather sheath.

"What?" Ramsay and Martín both said at the same time.

Exley gave them a chilling smile. "*Bull*-headed, not dog-headed." The marquess waved his hand. "But that is neither here nor there. As much as I would enjoy watching you two squabble and pull each other's hair, we don't have time." He looked from Martín to Ramsay. "If Bouchard wins, he gets two deeds—the woman's and his son's. If Bouchard loses, d'Armand gets everything he has but has still agreed to tender the two deeds. Correct?" He looked at Martín.

Martín nodded.

"Now, you expressed some concern about d'Armand's honoring his word." Exley's skeptical tone told Martín what he thought of the outrageous notion of a gentleman peer not honoring his word.

Again Martín nodded.

"So, to encourage his compliance you would have me offer him something that is in Ramsay's possession."

Martín turned to Ramsay. "He's talking about the—"

"I *know* what he's talking about, Martín," Ramsay burst out, his tone pure acid. "Are you mad? You are going to your death and doing paperwork on your death walk." He made an almost feral sound. "And you have a son?" Martín nodded, and Ramsay's face creased into pleading lines. "You have a son and yet you would risk your life before you can ever get to know him? You don't need to do this, Martín. Let me talk to the man. I will make him listen to sense. And if I cannot, I will know somebody who can. You forget—I am not without friends and influence."

"I have not forgotten your connections, Ramsay, but this is *my* matter to handle. It is a matter of honor."

"You will give up a chance to know your son on a *matter of honor?*"

"You do not understand! I am doing this *for* my son, Ramsay. D'Armand will never release him otherwise. Not as long as I'm alive."

"We can *make* him, Martín! He cannot compel you or your son to leave British soil against your will—you *know* that. We can stop him if we just take our time and handle this correctly." When Martín didn't respond Hugh asked, "And what about Sarah? Are you doing this for her, too?"

Martín flinched at the sound of her name.

Ramsay saw his chance and pounced. "Does she even know about this? Have you—"

"I have written her everything she needs to know, my lord."

"But have—"

"D'Armand has a document—something that will force the British authorities to send me back—from a New Orleans magistrate accusing me of the murder. He has probably already given the document to the authorities here. You know they will not let me go free. And you *know* what will happen if I go back."

Ramsay's mouth sagged open, and the carriage compartment became as silent as the proverbial grave.

"How did he find out?" the baron asked, his voice subdued.

"Perhaps he bribed somebody who was at Madam Sonia's that night? Maybe even *she* sold him the information—you know she will do anything for money." Martín shrugged. "What does it matter how he found out? You see now why I must do this? I must get my son to safety *now*, while I still can."

"It was an accident, Martín. You and I will go to the authorities. I will tell—"

"Tell them what, my lord? You weren't *there*. The only two people in that room were a wealthy, powerful marquis and an adolescent slave whore. Who do you think they will blame? Besides, the minute I set foot in that country . . ."

"Fine. But if we can learn where d'Armand got his evidence, then we can find the person and make him or her recant. If we—"

"If, if, if." Martín shook his head. "It is time to face the truth, Ramsay. It was inevitable that someday the secret would get out."

"'Three may keep a secret if two of them are dead.'"

Martín and Ramsay both turned to stare at the usually laconic Marquess of Exley.

"What did you say?" Martín asked.

Exley gifted them with one of his rare smiles. "Benjamin Franklin."

Ramsay opened his mouth to resume his nagging tirade.

"Hugh." Martín almost never used his friend's first name, and the word closed the big man's mouth faster than he could have imagined. "I am honored by your friendship, truly, but this is my affair. I ask you as a friend, please let my decision stand. Please?"

Hugh's single green eye burned, but he nodded. "Fine. It is your neck. Go ahead and shove it in the noose. I will say nothing more—to you or anyone else." He flung himself against the back of his seat with enough violence to make the entire carriage rock.

Exley sighed. "I beg you not to wreck my carriage,

Ramsay. I have only just purchased it, and it makes my wife excessively happy." He glanced at the box Martín was holding and extended his hand. "I will have a look at those, Bouchard."

They spent the remainder of the journey watching Exley inspect the two dueling pistols, which Martín had commissioned some years ago from a Brazilian gunsmith. He'd fired them in the past, but never for dueling. Dueling was not a pastime men like him engaged in.

The light was just breaking when they reached the appointed spot on Hampstead Heath. There was a light rain falling and the morning held a chill. They were the first to arrive, followed shortly afterward by a very crotchety doctor in a gig large enough to haul at least a half-dozen bodies.

D'Armand arrived a quarter of an hour late to make his point: he would not be punctual for a slave. His carriage had seen better days, and the crest of the d'Armands—a blending of their coronet with some type of vicious-looking bird—was so faded it was almost unrecognizable. A liveried servant hopped down and opened the door. First d'Armand and then his second exited. The servant reached into the darkened coach and handed out a third person.

"What the bloody hell is she doing here?" Ramsay demanded in a booming voice.

D'Armand looked up at the sound of the baron's bellow, his lips twisted into a contemptuous smile.

Martín glanced at the unreadable, beautiful woman and then looked away. "Valerie told me he always has her accompany him."

"Why, the pompous arsehole," Ramsay muttered, loud enough for all to hear. Martín, Exley, and even the grim-visaged doctor chuckled. Laughing might be inappropriate, given the fact that Martín would soon be dead, but Ramsay's comment managed to settle the pitching, churning sensation that had dominated his stomach for the past thirty-six hours.

D'Armand's second approached the Marquess of Exley, and they stepped off to one side. Hugh joined them, deliberately looming over d'Armand's man, as if to make his presence felt.

Martín turned back to where d'Armand and Valerie stood beside the open door of the carriage. The woman wore only a light cloak, and Martín couldn't help thinking she must be cold. Not that you could tell from her face or posture, both of which were rigid and motionless in the hoary dawn light.

D'Armand opened an ornate metal box that sat on the floor of the carriage and extracted a pistol that was impressive even from Martín's vantage point. Why had both he and Martín brought pistols? Would they each use their own weapons? He shrugged away the thought. He knew nothing about duels, Exley would handle such matters.

Valerie stood staring at the horizon while the Frenchman saw to his firearms. When he'd finished checking the guns, he said something Martín could not hear.

The woman went to him, and they stood face-to-face for a moment before he leaned closer to say something, or perhaps to hear something.

Martín knew what would happen even before the woman's arm snaked around d'Armand's side, her hand reaching into the carriage. She turned to Martín as he began to run, his mouth open but no sound coming out. She smiled, the first smile he'd ever seen on her face, and it transformed her already beautiful face into something truly transcendent.

D'Armand's body jolted in such a way that Martín knew he wasn't the only one surprised by her sudden, almost unholy look of joy. She stepped back from the Frenchman, holding the pistol he'd just finished inspecting.

"Noooooooooo!" The word was torn from Martín's throat,

and his body moved with agonizing slowness, as though he were running through water.

The Frenchman looked at her hand and then threw back his head and laughed.

Valerie raised the gun and pulled the trigger. Without even hesitating, she stepped past his staggering body and picked up the second gun.

Chapter Thirty-Two

Martín marched up and down the deck of the *Scythe* looking for something or someone to criticize. He was aware of his mood—bad—but felt no compunction to do anything about it.

His eyes swept the deck, searching for his first mate, a man called Butkins. Butkins was new and highly recommended by Ramsay to fill Beauville's place.

Not only did Martín have to adjust to a new first mate, but his second had also decamped. Daniels had taken an offer from Beauville of all people. Martín had left Oak Park in Beauville's hands, providing the Frenchman and his new young bride with a home and an immediate position.

To repay him, Beauville had stolen Daniels to act as steward. Not that Martín had ever felt any particular attachment to Daniels, or even liked him. In fact, the man had annoyed him more often than not. But it was the principle of the matter that counted.

Martín paced and brooded about the duplicitous nature of men.

That subject naturally led him to his new, and apparently invisible, second mate. A man whose surname was, laughably, Newman.

Martín had only caught a glimpse of Newman as he'd

scuttled on board at the last possible moment and darted below deck.

"Mr. Newman is, er, well, he's very ill, Captain," the idiot Butkins had reported when Martín had questioned him on the matter.

A sailor who got ill before his ship even left port? It could not be a coincidence. It had to be some manner of farce—most likely perpetrated by Ramsay. Yes, Martín smelled the influence of Ramsay the same way a mouse could smell cheese.

"Butkins!" His bad mood was made even worse at having to yell such a stupid name.

Feet pounded the deck behind him, and Martín turned.

"Uh, Captain Bouchard?" The shorter man slid to a halt mere inches from his face.

Martín took a step back. "Where is the elusive Mr. Newman?"

"Uh, Mr. Newman?"

"Is it your intention to begin every sentence with 'uh' and follow with a repetition of my own words, Butkins?"

"Uh . . . that is, no, sir."

Martín waited.

"Mr. Newman is below deck, sir. He is . . . uh . . . not well. Or so I comprehend, sir."

"Mr. Butkins, I am sure it is not necessary for me to point out to you that we are now well under way. At this point in the voyage, at least in my *humble* experience, it is customary for the second to give his captain a thorough report on trivial matters such as tonnage, cargo—things of that nature." He smiled down at the smaller man, who wilted away from him as if Martín were a noxious gas.

"Uh . . . that is, begging your pardon, sir—"

Martín held up his hand, rather than wrapping it around the other man's neck. "I am going to my cabin, Mr. Butkins. I want you—without speaking another word to me—to have

Mr. Newman sent directly to my cabin, no matter what the condition of his health."

Martín stormed down the stairs, stopping only to check on Gaston, whom he'd installed in the same cabin Graaf had once occupied. Martín cracked the door and waited until his eyes adjusted. The boy was fast asleep, his chest moving slowly and deeply. Martín watched for a few moments before closing the door.

His son was a very good boy, although far too quiet. He was also, understandably, torn with grief over his mother's death. But Gaston's reticence was not just the result of grief; it was that of a boy who'd lived his entire life balanced on the edge of a precipice. Martín knew the feeling well and could only hope Gaston would come out of his shell now that he was no longer under d'Armand's warped influence.

Martín opened the door to his cabin and froze. A man sat slumped over his desk.

"Who the devil are you?" Martín demanded.

The figure sat upright, but did not turn.

Martín strode forward and yanked the chair around. "I said—"

The man's hat tumbled to one side, and brown hair spilled around a pale, freckled face.

"*Mon Dieu!*"

"Hello, Martín." Sarah stood and took a step toward him.

He took a step back. "Where did you come from?" he asked stupidly.

Her lips twisted into a bitter smile—an expression he'd never seen on her face before.

"I boarded the ship along with everyone else and hid until we were under way."

"Are you mad?" He spun around. "I must turn the ship back and—"

"It's too late, Martín."

He turned on her. "Did you not read my letter, Sarah? I

am wanted for murder!" He lowered his voice. "People might guess you are with me—your uncles, for one. As it is, I will have to take you to Lessing Hall and tolerate Ramsay's meddling if he is to help shield you from scandal."

"He already knows where I am. So does Daphne; so do my uncles. And yes, I read your letter. I don't care that you are an accused murderer."

"You don't know what you are saying."

She crossed her arms, but her lower lip trembled, making her brave stance a lie.

"Tell me you are glad to see me this instant or I will go directly to the crew berth and hang my hammock."

Martín was on her in an instant. He gripped her upper arms. "You have a hammock? Tell me you have not been below with my crew." His gut clenched at the thought of her in a roomful of randy, partially clad sailors.

"I have *not* been below with your crew." She pulled away from him, her eyes blazing. "When will you realize the only man I'm interested in bunking with is *you?*"

Martín blinked.

She waved some crumpled sheets of paper in the air. "How *could* you?"

"How could I *what?*"

"How could you send me this letter?"

He squinted at the wadded ball of paper. "Why? What is wrong with my letter? Are there mistakes?"

She made a sound not dissimilar to that of an angry badger. "I'm not talking about the grammar, you idiot! I'm talking about the letter itself. How could you?"

"I did it for you. I told you already—I do not want your reputation to suffer."

"I don't *care* about my reputation," she yelled back, just as loudly.

The cabin door opened a crack, and Jenkins looked through the narrow gap.

"Are you all right, miss?" he asked, his beady eyes flickering toward Martín and just as quickly flickering away.

"What the—" Martín began.

Sarah smiled sweetly at the little man. "Thank you, Mr. Jenkins, I'm fine."

The door shut with a crisp *click*.

Martín swung around. "Who does he think he is? Does he think you need protection from *me?*"

"Don't try to change the subject, Martín."

"But—"

"You were so worried about my reputation suffering. Didn't you think about me? About how I would suffer without you?"

Martín opened his mouth and then closed it. And then opened it again. "You would?"

"Of course I would!" She threw the crumpled paper at him, and he caught her wrist, holding it gently.

"You would?"

"You must be the stupidest man alive."

He opened his mouth.

"No, shut up. You've already had your chance. Now it's my turn." She pulled her hand away and crossed her arms. "I'm here because of you, and I'm not leaving—that is"— for the first time since entering the cabin her confidence seemed to falter—"unless you don't want me?"

Martín groaned and cast his eyes toward the ceiling before shoving her onto the padded bench and taking the seat across from her.

"Who helped you with . . . this?" He waved his hand, unable to find the words.

"You mean this?" She ran both hands down the sides of the mannish coat she wore, the gesture emphasizing the very unmannish body beneath it. "Are you telling me you don't recognize it?"

Martín looked away from her delectable body, which

was—inexplicably—clad in the same clothes she'd worn the first day they met, and massaged his temple as if that would somehow assuage the swelling in his pants.

"Martín."

"What?"

"Look at me."

He looked up and found her standing in front of him, her right hand at the top button on her coat. She opened the button with a practiced flick.

Moisture flooded his mouth, as if he were a starving man confronted with a banquet.

Her finger released a second button.

He swallowed. He should stop her and see to getting her off this ship. But maybe he could wait a moment and do so after she—

"I am a woman grown, Martín. Or haven't you realized that?" She flicked another button open.

Her expression was serious, and he realized she was waiting for an answer.

"Uh—" He cleared his throat, his eyes already on the next button. "I have realized that."

"Good. Then you should know I like to make up my own mind, just like an adult. So, I want you to ask me a question."

"A question?" Martín couldn't seem to pull his eyes away from the button—the third to last. Her hand came beneath his chin and tilted his face up.

"Martín?"

He blinked. "You want me to ask a question?"

"Ask me if I want to stay with you."

He groaned. "Oh, Sarah. I don't think—"

"Ask me, Martín." Her face became stern—it was her Egyptian queen expression.

He gazed into her beautiful brown and gold and green eyes. "Do you want to stay with me, Sarah?"

Her features shifted from serious to shy and girlish, her cheeks tinting a rosy pink. And then her fingers resumed their journey.

"Yes, Martín, I do."

She released the last button and gave a slight shrug. The movement pulled the jacket open and exposed what she wore beneath: nothing.

Martín's hands did what his brain would have told them to do if it hadn't stopped functioning some time back. They slid around her waist, the feel of silken skin beneath his fingers causing his cock to throb.

"My God, Sarah," he groaned, kissing the gentle swell of her stomach, thrilling at the quivering muscles beneath his lips. Her hands wove into his hair, pulling him closer.

He tongued her navel while his hands traveled the distance from her slim waist to cup a small breast in each hand. Her gasp of pleasure was enough to drive him insane, but he forced himself to explore her as slowly and thoroughly as he had done in his mind many times beyond counting. He stood and took a step back to admire the beauty of her.

"By God, you look good in those breeches. It seems almost a pity to take them off." He drank in the sight of her long neck, erect nipples, and narrow waist and the way her slim hips stretched the male garment, making it more seductive than all the black lace he'd ever seen.

He gave her a gentle push and then sat back in his seat to admire her. He stroked a hand over his straining erection and smiled at her wide-eyed fascination. The sudden slackening of her lips made him even harder.

"You like to watch me touch myself?"

She nodded.

"Then you will strip for my pleasure."

She gasped and flushed a charming shade of pink.

Martín smirked and spread his thighs to shift his pounding

organ. "Remove the coat and then unbutton your breeches," he ordered, "slowly."

Her eyes remained fastened on his hand as he languidly stroked his aching groin. She lifted a hand to remove the coat, and it brushed against an erect nipple.

Martín stopped breathing, his eyes riveted to her hand as it drifted from her breast to her stomach, finally stopping at the top of her breeches. She ran one finger beneath the loose waistband of the garment, back and forth. Back and forth.

The hand stopped, and he looked up. Her lips were curved in a way that told him she was beginning to take pleasure in teasing him. He thrilled at her wicked expression, a look he'd never dreamed of seeing on her face.

She began the agonizing process of freeing each button, and the strain of watching her and waiting was a divine torture. When she reached the last button the flap parted, exposing a curly tangle of light brown hair: she wore no smallclothes beneath.

Martín lunged, picked her up by her hips, and tossed her onto his bed.

She gave a girlish laugh, her face flushed, her eyes alight with the joy of what she was doing to him.

"You like to make me hard, to make me suffer?"

Her brown eyes darkened, and he pulled off her heavy shoes, rolled down her stockings, and yanked off her breeches, pushing her thighs wide as he dropped to his knees. He stroked the long, smooth planes of her legs, holding them steady as she tried to squeeze them together. He gazed at what lay open before him.

"Oh, Sarah," he breathed, "I am going to make you scream."

The groan that burst from her when Martín took her into his mouth was the most primal noise she'd ever made. A low chuckle rumbled up her body while his lips and tongue began to do things that made rational thought impossible.

The sight of his sun-bleached curls between her thighs was almost more arousing than what he was doing down there.

Almost.

The fine navy coat he still wore stretched across his powerful shoulders as he leaned closer. His wicked tongue touched a part of her so sensitive she fell back on the bed, powerless against the sensation rippling through every part of her body. Several times he brought her to the brink of something immense, but each time he shied away, leaving her oddly frustrated and increasingly angry.

She reached down and grabbed two fists of hair, gripping his head tightly so he couldn't move away again. "*Martín . . . please.*"

He laughed softly, triumphantly. In the minutes that followed, she suddenly understood why.

Her words begged, but her strong hands commanded. Her need for him, for release, pulsed against his tongue, and he used every bit of skill he possessed to make the experience last. Her uncontrolled shuddering caused a fierce surge of possession inside of him. She was his. At long, bloody last, she was his.

He stroked her thighs and looked up the length of her sated body, the long, white lines of her once again reminding him of that ancient Egyptian queen.

She made a small noise. "Martín?"

"Yes, my love?"

She opened sleepy, sated eyes. "You're still wearing your clothing," she accused. "I want you to take it off. All of it."

Her words caused a strange sensation in his stomach. Was it possible he was nervous to disrobe before her? He'd never before felt a twinge of nervousness or embarrassment when it came to showing his body or bedding a woman. He'd exhibited himself in every possible position to more strangers than he cared to remember. How could he be shy, now?

"Martín."

"As you wish." His words were husky at the need he saw on her face. He began to unbutton his coat.

"Do it slowly." She propped herself up against some cushions and made herself comfortable.

He slowed his movements to a crawl, removing first his jacket, then his waistcoat, and finally his neckcloth, tossing all three over the chair.

She raised her eyebrows when he stopped. "You are still wearing far too many clothes, Captain Bouchard."

"I see I've created a monster." He sat down and lifted his booted leg. "If you would have me naked, you must serve as my boot jack. Unless you want me to call Jenkins."

She scrambled off the bed and then hesitated.

"You won't be able to do it from over there." He waved the tip of his boot beckoningly. "Come closer. Closer still," he encouraged, until she stood beside his leather-clad ankle. "*Bien.* Now, straddle my leg."

Her mouth fell open, and he couldn't help laughing. "Perhaps we are moving too quickly," he said, lowering his leg.

"No!" She lifted one foot over his leg, facing him, squirming at the odd position.

He shook his head with mock sadness. "Oh, Sarah. I despair of ever shedding these troublesome breeches. You must turn the other way." He twirled his fingers in the air to illustrate.

"You mean turn my *bottom* to you?"

He nodded slowly. For a moment he did not think she would do it. But she took a deep breath and turned quicker than he would have thought possible.

Amusement, triumph, and other emotions better left

unidentified surged through him at the sight of her rounded
bottom. He raised his leg until the soft leather of his boot
gently bumped her mound.

"Oh." She gave a little hop.

Martín laughed. "*Pardon, chérie.*"

"If you insist on being odious, I will let you remove your
own wretched boots," she threatened, not bothering to turn
around.

"Grip the boot with both hands, one under my heel, and
then pull." He raised his other boot and placed it on her surprisingly fleshy bottom. Martín did not believe he had ever
seen a prettier picture. He gave a slight push.

"Oof." She stumbled forward, dropping the boot to catch
her balance on the side of the bed.

"Come, come," he chided. "There are two of them, remember?"

The second boot came off without any struggle or com-
mentary. She flung it to one side and leapt onto the bed,
grabbing a large cushion and wrapping her arms around it,
clasping it to her middle.

She noticed his measuring look and squinted back at him,
aping his severe expression.

"You shan't see any more of *me* until I see all of *you*."

Martín resumed his disrobing, making the performance
as dramatic as she seemed to want.

Her expression when he pulled off his smallclothes was
comical.

She stared at his erection. "It's just as I remembered it."

Martín laughed. "What? Did you think I might have
changed it for another?"

"Why are you still wearing your shirt? Off," she commanded, making an imperious gesture.

He pulled his shirt over his head and threw it on top of his
other clothes. Her eyes ran up and down him in a way that
made his stomach clench. And then they stopped on his arm.

Her smile drained away, and her eyes brightened with unshed tears.

"What is this?" he asked, cupping her smooth cheek in his hand, stroking away a tear with his thumb. "Why are you crying, Sarah?"

She reached out and traced the burned ridges of the brand with a slim, sensitive finger, her touch searing him. He grabbed her wrist and held it, forcing her to meet his eyes.

"It happened a long time ago, Sarah. There is no need to weep for me."

"Foolish man. I'm not crying for you—I'm crying for the little boy who endured this." She kissed his chin. "Now tell me about the duel."

"I understand why she killed d'Armand, but why did she kill herself?" Sarah asked sometime later, shaking her head.

"I have thought about that a thousand times since." He shrugged. "All I can think is that she had no desire to live. I think her life—the harsh, unrelenting servitude—had simply driven her mad." His expression was beyond bleak. "I should have seen what she planned to do—I should have guessed from the deadness in her eyes."

Sarah did not know what to say. How could she ever guess what had been between the two?

"How is Gaston?"

"It is difficult to say. He is a very quiet boy who has been taught to hide his emotions. He is behaving as if nothing has happened."

"He must miss her terribly."

Martín nodded, his beautiful eyes unreadable and distant.

Sarah didn't want to ask, but the words came unbidden. "Did you love her, Martín?"

The question seemed to pull him back to the present. He smiled at her and took her hand. "No, *chérie,* we were never in love. How could we be? Both of us were forced to do those things with each other. We never even spoke until the day I went to d'Armand's. I didn't know of Gaston's existence until that day. Her life must have been one of constant terror. I think she only had enough love left in her to free Gaston from d'Armand's grasp."

"We will have to be gentle with him, Martín. He is just a little boy—our little boy, now."

Martín gave her a look that made her stomach fall out and then lowered his mouth over hers, kissing her with a ferocity that made her gasp.

He suddenly stopped. "You know I cannot live in England? At least not until I can address the issue of d'Armand's accusation against me?"

She nodded.

"That might never happen. You understand, Sarah? I might live the rest of my life with the threat of arrest over my head."

Again she nodded. "I didn't want to live in England, anyway."

He pulled away in surprise. "You didn't?"

She gave an exasperated sigh. "How could you think that kind of life would satisfy me?"

He grinned.

"What?" she demanded.

"Oh, nothing."

She crossed her arms. "Martín—"

"Oh, very well. I was just going to say that I should have remembered you are a woman who needs a cause in her life, whether it is trading your virtue to an unscrupulous captain to save the lives of mutineers or teaching a man to read."

She looked at him uncertainly. "Is that a bad thing?"

He shook his head, suddenly serious. "I don't know, but I am the same. I wanted to settle and live the life of a country squire, but I think that deep down I knew I would not be happy. I can never stop what I do, Sarah. It is almost like I *must* do it."

She laid a hand on his arm. "You do not need to explain, Martín. I think your calling is a noble one. It is a big part of why I love you. Besides, it will fit well with my own plans."

"What did you say?"

"I said your plans would—"

"No, before that."

"You mean when I said 'I love you'?" She caressed the mark on his arm that was as much a part of him as his beautiful eyes or muscular body.

He grabbed her so tightly that he squeezed all the air from her lungs.

"Yes, that was it," he muttered.

"Martín?" she gasped.

"*Oui?*"

"I think perhaps I should breathe for a few moments."

He released her abruptly. "*Mon Dieu!* I have hurt you?"

"Don't be silly. You merely squeezed me a little. That doesn't mean you should stop holding me."

He slipped one arm around her and pulled her down on the bed beside him, and she rested her head on his chest.

"When I saw you in my cabin I believed that meddler Ramsay was responsible," he said, his voice rumbling beneath her.

She laughed. "It was Mr. Beauville who actually arranged most of it. Lord Ramsay knew about my plans, of course. After reading your letter I went to find Daphne. She told me Hugh had taken a quick trip to Eastbourne, ostensibly on some ship-related business. Once I told her what had happened, she was furious and came with me to find him. She gave Hugh a very bad time, I'm afraid."

Martín crowed with laughter. "Ramsay deserves all the abuse he gets. I'm stunned he was able to keep his mouth shut about everything. He is terrible at keeping secrets. As for Beauville . . . That rascal. I never would have thought he had it in him."

"I think Mary may have changed him."

"Eh?"

"Mary, his wife."

"Oh. Is that her name?"

She slapped his arm. "How could you forget? They are living in your house, Martín."

He grunted again. "Perhaps not for long. He has saddled me with that idiot Butkins. He may need to be punished."

She sat up and glared at him. "You wouldn't."

"I might," he demurred, regarding her from beneath heavy lids.

She shoved him in the chest, which did nothing except elicit a tiny smile. "Perhaps you will need to persuade me to show mercy. I think you know how."

"You are incorrigible. Has anyone ever told you that?"

He rolled his eyes. "People seem to tell me almost nothing else."

"I did. I told you that I love you," she argued, staring at his mouth—which had given her so much pleasure a short time ago. Her inner thighs heated, and she couldn't look away.

His eyes opened a crack. "What did you say? I could not hear you."

"You heard me," she said, still distracted by thoughts of his wicked mouth.

"Remind me."

"I *said* I love you."

A smug smile curved his lips, and his eyes opened infinitesimally wider. "That's what I thought you said." He frowned. "Why are you coloring?"

When she didn't answer, he took her face in his hands. "Sarah?"

She jerked her chin from his hand. "I am *not* coloring."

He laughed and pushed her back on the bed. "I believe

we've discussed this problem once before." He rubbed her stomach as he spoke, and Sarah resisted the urge to purr at his touch.

"What subject?" she asked, not really caring. His wicked, knowing hand stroked her pelvis in the most distracting manner.

"About the daughters of preachers and how they should not lie." His hand slid up her stomach and cupped a breast. His lips curved into an oddly possessive smile as he took her breast into his mouth.

She gasped and arched against him.

He released her nipple and studied it. "You have beautiful breasts." He spoke with the authority of an expert.

"You've seen many, I collect."

"Yes," he agreed absently, switching to the other breast and thumbing her nipple.

Sarah laughed even as jealousy seared her. "You aren't supposed to admit that."

He pulled his eyes away from her hardened nipple with visible effort. "Admit what?"

"That you've seen many women's breasts."

"Oh." He turned back to her breast, clearly finding it more stimulating than her conversation.

Sarah sighed.

"Why do you sigh like that?" The words were muffled by the nipple obstructing his mouth.

"Shut up." She dragged her hand over the ridged muscles that ran down the side of his rib cage, stopping when she reached his compact hips.

"Mmm." He pushed against her, pressing his fascinating hardness on her leg.

Sarah stroked his hip, her hand inching around to the front, until she could feel springy hair at the base of his sex.

"Touch me, Sarah," he murmured, reaching between them

and taking her hand, guiding it to his satiny hardness and curling her fingers around him. He pushed into her fist and then drew out again, repeating the motion slowly and rhythmically.

"Yes, just like that," he praised, groaning as she tightened her hand around him. She could feel the tightly controlled passion in his thrusts, each one harder than the last.

"You will make me spend before I even get inside of you." His lips moved against her neck, the words creating an unbearable tightness between her legs.

He ran his hand down her stomach, stopping at the damp tangle of hair, dipping a finger into her and drawing a ragged breath at what he found.

"You are so wet for me." He slid a finger inside. "Do you want me in here?" He pushed deeper before pulling out again, his finger dragging across her most sensitive place.

Sarah spread her legs in answer and he stroked, leading her quickly to that place she was beginning to crave.

"You are greedy," he said, adding a second finger. The surprise of it drew a gasp from her.

"Shh." He caressed her neck with his tongue, nibbling the taut column of her throat while his thumb moved in languid circles around the sensitive bud he knew so well. He covered her with his body, stroking yet another wave of pleasure out of her while his knees nudged hers farther apart. "I cannot wait any longer, my sweet," he whispered, entering her in a slow, hard thrust. He held her in a grip like iron, his body controlled as he worked her deeply and thoroughly.

Sarah rose with him, wrapping her legs around his waist and tightening, the motion drawing a loud groan and several rapid thrusts before he cried out her name.

He froze for one long moment before collapsing on her chest, shuddering while he spent and filled her with heat.

Her hands ranged over his skin, damp from his efforts,

the slickness making the exploration of his contours even more exciting, the weight of his big, warm body a pleasure she could not live without. She caressed his back, arms, shoulders, her right hand resting on the brand before moving to his roughened jaw.

He murmured something too soft for her to hear, kissed the palm of her hand, and then fell asleep.

Chapter Thirty-Three

Martín woke with a start; for an instant he thought that he was in the rooms he kept at Venetia's. He looked through sleep-crusted eyes and saw he was in his cabin.

He'd been having a dream. Sarah . . . He propped himself up and surveyed the cabin, his heart in his mouth until he saw her discarded clothing on the floor.

She was real. She had been here.

But where was she now?

He yanked his banyan from his wardrobe and tied it around his waist before striding to the cabin door. The knob twisted beneath his hand, and the door pushed against him.

Sarah stood in the doorway, her arms burdened with a large tray.

"Here, I will take that." Martín lifted the tray from her hands and stepped aside to allow her to enter.

"You are most kind, Captain."

Martín was pleased to see she was wearing feminine garb again. But he would keep her other outfit in his wardrobe for his own viewing pleasure.

He set down the tray and frowned. "You are not to fetch your own food. I have a crew for that purpose."

She came closer, until they were almost touching, and

then placed her hands on his chest, giving him a light push that sent him into the padded booth behind him.

"It just so happens it *pleases* me to serve you. Besides, I would prefer not to receive your crew in a state of undress. And I wanted to let you rest. I believe you greatly needed it." She flushed, as if recalling how he'd exerted himself.

He caught her around her slim waist and pulled her into his lap.

"Sit nicely and stop your squirming," he chided. "I want to kiss you."

"But your food will get cold."

"Mm hmm," he murmured into her neck. He ran his hands over her body to assure himself she was really here. She slipped her arms around his neck and lowered her hot mouth over his. Her clever tongue darted between his lips and teased. *Mon Dieu!* She was a quick study. He shifted her delicious bottom so she could feel his excitement.

"Oh, Martín," she whispered against his mouth, their hot breath mingling while they stared into each other's eyes. "You have the loveliest eyes I have ever seen. They are the color of a falcon's—gold."

A strange heat suffused his neck and face at her words.

She gasped and took his face in her hands. "What's this? Have I made you blush?"

"Nonsense," he grunted dismissively, and scooped her into his arms before striding the few steps to the bed. She laughed and beat her fists uselessly on his chest.

"Martín! You must eat—you need to keep up your strength."

"Do I look as if I am lacking strength?" He threw her onto the bed before pulling at the belt that held his robe closed and shrugging it from his shoulders.

Her eyes settled between his legs, and her pupils flared.

"No, you do not look as if you lack strength," she admitted, sitting up and deftly tucking her knees beneath her before reaching out to wrap her hand around him, the action ripping the breath from his chest. She slid her hand up his shaft, and he closed his eyes. Her touch was inexpert, but the effect was like nothing he'd ever experienced.

"Mmm," he murmured, thrusting into her tight grasp. "That feels so good, Sarah."

The amount of stroking it took to bring him to an incredibly powerful climax would have been embarrassing if it hadn't felt so damn good.

"My God!" He collapsed on the bed beside her, breathing raggedly for several minutes before opening his eyes.

"That was wonderful, Martín." She was gazing at him as though he were some kind of magician because he had spent himself in her hand.

He laughed weakly. "I'll wager it was even better for me."

She shook her head. "You don't understand. It has been agonizing knowing I have been the one having all the pleasure."

"Surely not *all* the pleasure?" he challenged, recalling the sensation of burying himself deep within her. The flush that crept up her neck told him she knew what he meant.

"Perhaps not *all*. Now then," she said, becoming businesslike. "You sit here, and I will bring something to sustain you." She sprang off the bed before he could stop her and began to bustle around his small cabin. She placed some food on a plate and felt the coffee pot. "Merely warm," she muttered.

"Ring for another." He turned onto his side and propped his head in his hand.

She looked at him with eyes that seemed to devour him. "No. I cannot bear that you should need to put on your robe."

He laughed. Clearly she did not recall the first time

he'd had her in his bed, when the meddlesome Daniels had interrupted his pleasure.

She handed him a cup of lukewarm coffee and sat on the bed beside him. "Why are you frowning?"

He plucked at her dress. "I hate that you have covered your magnificent body."

Her cheeks darkened. "Here, eat." She pushed a piece of cheese between his lips. Martín chewed and swallowed, his eyes never leaving hers.

"What? Are you tired of me already? Hoping to choke me?"

"I could never tire of you, Martín."

The fierceness of her words caused him to look away.

"I shouldn't make such outrageous claims, *mademoiselle*."

"Martín."

He turned back to her. Her brown eyes were soft and dark. "I would not give myself to you if I did not mean it to be forever. I love you. I don't care if you don't love me—it is enough that you want to be with me, that you . . . desire me. And if you tire of me—" She shrugged. "Well, I will deal with that if it happens. I give myself to you with no ex-pectations other than we enjoy each other."

Why did it feel like looking over a steep, dangerous cliff even to contemplate uttering three small words? When had he become so craven?

"I will never tire of you." His voice was so thick with emotion he could hardly recognize himself. "*Dieu aide moi!*" He grasped her shoulders. "I love you, Sarah." He spoke the words quickly, eager to get them out now that he'd made the decision. "Do you hear me? I *love you*." The dazed, hungry expression on her face sent a wave of crip-pling relief through his body. "I will make you my wife at the first opportunity. Until that time, I will not let you out of my sight."

She smiled at his harsh words, and he looked away, unable to hold her loving gaze for very long.

"We will marry immediately after we arrive in Paris," he said. "I shall have gowns made for you by the best dressmaker in the city." He imagined her swathed in the finest silk. And then he imagined stripping such gowns off her body.

"I should like to see Paris one day."

"Eh?" he asked absently, her choice of words attracting his attention. He squinted, suddenly suspicious. "Why are you smiling like that?"

"Like what?"

"Like you know something I do not."

"Because I do."

"Sarah . . ."

"We are not going to Paris, Martín."

"What?"

"I said, 'We are not going to Paris.'"

"*Mon Dieu!*" He pushed up off his elbow and faced her. "We are not even married and already you want to defy me. Why do you not want to go to Paris? *Every* woman wishes to go to Paris."

Her eyes narrowed at the words "every" and "woman" together.

He held up one hand. "Fine. *I* wish to go to Paris. Besides, it is our first port of call, and we should marry as quickly as possible."

"Why?" She reached out and circled one of his nipples with a single finger.

Mother of God. He grabbed her hand and stilled it. Where had she learned such teasing tricks? "I am a father now, Sarah. I cannot have my son know we are living in sin. We must marry immediately if we are to set a good example for

Gaston." He strove to say the ridiculous words with his old arrogance, but her laughter told him he'd failed miserably.

"We can go to Paris later, after you've delivered your cargo."

"What cargo?"

She stood and sauntered toward his desk, casting a wicked look over her shoulder. "You'll just have to live with me in sin until we reach Tenerife. I've already notified the DuValle sisters we shall be stopping there. I expect the preparations for our wedding are well under way."

Martín felt as if he had plunged his head into the eye of a particularly savage storm.

"What do you know of my cargo?" he repeated, leaving aside for the moment the more unnerving issue: that she'd planned their marriage without him. Such behavior exhibited a degree of high-handedness he couldn't help but admire, as much as it terrified him.

"It is *my* cargo."

"What?" He seemed to be saying that a lot.

"I am your employer, Captain Bouchard. Butkins holds the ship's manifest proving the truth of my words."

"Butkins?"

"Butkins would tell you, if you asked him, that you are taking me and my cargo to Freetown." She settled onto the bench at the table and smirked across at him.

Martín scrambled off the bed and went to stand before her.

"What the devil are you talking about, Sarah?" She gazed into his navel, her lips curving into a slow smile. He took her chin and tilted her face. "The hold of my ship is full of cording and other supplies for a warehouse just outside Paris. I arranged the deal myself."

Sarah shrugged, and her eyes drifted down again. His cock—duplicitous organ that it was—betrayed the true contents of his brain by standing at attention. She looked from his erection to his face, openly grinning now.

"I'm afraid Lord Ramsay offered your merchant more appealing terms, which left you with an empty hold. Fortunately for you, Mr. Beauville knew I was looking for a ship, and he spoke to Butkins. Your first mate made an excellent deal on your behalf. You should be thanking him, rather than scolding him for his silly name."

Martín gaped.

"That is an attractive expression," Sarah observed.

Martín closed his mouth. He'd been outmaneuvered in just about every possible way. What was the use in arguing? She had always been diabolically single-minded in her pursuit of what she wanted. It appeared that she now wanted him. He began to smile and froze. It would not be wise to capitulate too quickly to the woman before him.

He assumed a haughty expression. "May I ask what kind of cargo I *am* transporting?" he asked, not caring if the hold was stuffed with potatoes or unicorns or ladies' undergarments.

Her hands slid around his waist, and she rested her face against his stomach, her hot breath teasing the head of his cock. *Good God.*

"Supplies for the orphanage we're going to build in Freetown." She spoke the words into his stomach while depositing little kisses on his skin, carefully avoiding the part of his body least able to hide its enthusiasm for her actions.

"We?" He gasped as her tongue probed his navel in a most distracting manner. Martín could not recall any other woman paying such close attention to his navel. Wisely, he did not share that information.

"Mm hmm." The sound vibrated through him, and she took a mouthful of taut, sensitive skin on his lower abdomen and sucked hard.

Martín swallowed. "That sounds like . . ."—the sucking paused—"a splendid plan," he continued hastily.

He felt her lips curve into a smile against his skin, just before her tongue resumed its voyage. He buried his hands in her tangled hair and sighed; perhaps an orphanage was not such a bad idea. "Yes, I can see it: Captain Bouchard's Home for Youths," he experimented, his voice catching on the last word as her questing tongue reached its ultimate destination.

Her mouth paused. "*Wayward* youths," she amended, her next actions very wayward, indeed.

Epilogue

Martín made his way from the docks on foot. He was not surprised Sarah had not met the ship—it was almost dark, and he himself had not believed he would make it back to Freetown today. He gave the soldier who stood sentry duty outside Admiral Keeton's office a friendly nod. It was not the same man who'd stood there a couple years ago, but then Martín was not the same man, either.

As he walked the short distance to the house he shared with Sarah, Gaston, and a constantly shifting number of orphans, Martín couldn't help recalling his first walk down this same street.

The bordello where he'd spent such an unfulfilling evening was still in business—not that Martín had been inside it since that night.

No, it would not be worth his life to visit the German madam and her ladies—even if he *had* wanted such a thing. Martín had a home of his own now; he no longer needed to seek it in a bordello.

The original orphanage he and Sarah had built was filled to bursting, and the expansion was almost completed. Sarah would not be satisfied until every child who needed a home had care and love until he or she was able to find a permanent family.

Martín was proud of what she'd done over the past two years. Even though his name had been cleared—thanks mainly to Ramsay's tireless work—and he could live any-where he wanted without fear of his past, Sarah still wanted to stay in Freetown. He did not care where they lived, as long as Sarah and Gaston were there with him.

"Papa!" Gaston's voice pulled him from his musings. The sight of his handsome son brought a smile to his face. The gangly youth was running toward him at full speed, as if some devil were on his heels.

"Papa!" Gaston repeated, screeching to a halt in front of him and obstructing Martín's progress.

Martín laid his hand on the boy's heaving shoulder, yet again overjoyed by what a fine son he had.

"Take a moment and catch your breath," he advised, looking into eyes that were almost the same color as his own. Gaston, for all his horrible childhood, was a sunny, good-natured boy. He had taken to Sarah like a person de-prived of air. While he had clearly loved and respected his mother, Valerie had cared for the boy's mind and body, but she'd had very little left of herself to give for his soul.

In Sarah, Gaston found a mother who loved him as if he were her very own flesh and blood and was able to show her affection. Sarah, Martín had learned, had endless love in her heart.

The thought made him swallow, his throat dangerously tight all of a sudden.

"Well?" he asked when Gaston's chest stopped heaving.

"It is Sarah . . . the baby . . ." he began.

Martín didn't wait to hear the rest; he flew past his son and toward the front door of their two-story white-washed house even before Gaston could complete his sentence.

"Sarah!" The word was ripped from his throat as he bounded up the stairs. When he reached the bedroom they shared, it was to find Sarah in bed, her pretty face tired, but her eyes shining with joy. In her arms was a small bundle.

"You're here," she said, the relief in her voice clear.

"What is this?" He strode to the bed and dropped down beside her, his heart still pounding. "I leave for only a few weeks, and you take charge of everything without me. I thought we had a month?"

"She was impatient—just like her father." Sarah held out the bundle, and Martín saw a tiny little face. "Your daughter, Captain Bouchard."

Martín looked into a pair of big brown eyes just like Sarah's, and his heart expanded until he thought it would explode. "*Mon Dieu,* she is a beauty!"

Sarah gave a tired chuckle. "Take her. Hold your daughter, Martín."

Martín looked at his hands, big, scarred, rough hands that were twice the size of the tiny person his wife held out toward him.

Sarah laughed at whatever she saw on his face. "Take her, my love."

Martín could not believe how weightless the bundle in his hands was. He looked up and found Sarah staring, tears in her eyes. He frowned. "Why are you crying?"

"Because you look so beautiful holding our daughter." She looked over his shoulder, toward the door, and smiled, waving her hand in a beckoning motion. "Come in, Gaston—why are you out there in the hall?"

Gaston came to stand beside them, his dark gold eyes on the small being in Martín's hands.

"Her name is Grace," he told Martín.

Martín's eyebrows shot up. "She told you that, eh?"

Gaston smiled. "I held her last night, just after she was born," he declared proudly, sharing a smile with Sarah.

"Gaston will make an excellent big brother," Sarah

confirmed, squeezing the boy's hand, the affectionate gesture causing him to blush furiously.

"So, Grace, is it?" Martín asked Sarah. "I don't recall that name as one we discussed."

Sarah's eyes slid to Gaston. "It was Gaston's choice."

Martín looked from Sarah to his tall, strapping son and smiled into his anxious face. "Grace is a good name, son."

Gaston smiled, but then his forehead wrinkled with concern. "She was born without teeth, Papa."

Martín laughed. "Don't worry, she is her mother's daughter—she will get teeth soon enough."

"Martín . . ." Sarah warned, shaking her head, a rueful smile curving her lips.

"Shh," he said, rising from the bed, his daughter still in his arms. "You need your rest, my dear. Gaston and I shall take Grace for a while." He leaned forward and kissed Sarah's forehead. "I love you, Sarah."

"I know you do, Martín. I love you, too."

Martín looked from his wife to his son and daughter, the emotion in his chest almost too much to bear. He'd thought he was a free man but, somewhere along the way, he'd become enslaved without even realizing it. This time it was chains of love that bound him, and he never wanted to break free.

Author's Note

Thank you so much for reading *Scandalous*!

As this is a historical romance novel and not a treatise on the subject of slavery, my references to the subject are, by necessity, brief.

If you find the topics of slavery in the British Isles or the Slave Trade Felony Act of 1811 or the West Africa Squadron interesting, I highly recommend you delve into the wealth of primary information available for free on various university websites. Of course there are also thousands of secondary sources on the subject.

If you are looking for a definitive monograph on the topic of slavery, there isn't one; the subject is simply too mammoth. It is one of the most written-about topics in the field of history, and the wealth of scholarship is impressive and well worth exploring if you wish to learn more.

Although I don't directly reference the *Somerset v. Stewart* case (1772), I do allude to it when Martin tells d'Armand he is free while on British soil. This was a *highly* controversial case that was interpreted in a myriad of different ways and was by no means an iron-clad protection for slaves who found themselves in Britain.

While the case was a boon to the abolitionist movement, the liberty of a freed slave was still subject to the caprices of local authorities. Slave-takers often operated with impunity, and many freed slaves were kidnapped, resold, and never escaped bondage, no matter how illegally they'd been seized or how public some of the cases became. Keep in mind that Britain did not formally abolish slavery until 1833.

Mies Graaf is a character from a fictional branch of the House of Orange.

Please read on for an excerpt from
the next novel in Minerva Spencer's Outcasts series,

Notorious

London, 1817

Drusilla Clare plied her fan, using it for its intended purpose—cooling—rather than its expected purpose—flirting. After all, who would flirt with her?

"Dru, you're doing it again."

At the sound of her name, she looked at her companion. Lady Eva de Courtney should not, by all rights, have been sitting beside Drusilla in the wallflower section of the Duchess of Montfort's ballroom. Eva wasn't just one of the most beautiful debutantes in London this Season, she was also one of the most exquisite women Drusilla had ever seen.

But Eva was also proof that a hefty dowry and a gorgeous person were not, alas, enough to overcome a fractious personality or notorious heritage. Or at least her mother's notorious heritage. Because it was a well-known fact that the Marquess of Exley's first wife and Eva's mother—Lady Veronica Exley—had not only been a ravishing, mesmerizing beauty who'd driven men of all ages insane with desire and yearning, she had also been barking mad.

Eva, reputed to be every bit as lovely as her dead mother,

had neither the desire, nor the charisma, to drive anyone mad. Except perhaps her stern, perfectionist father.

"What, exactly, am I doing?" Drusilla asked Eva, who had pulled a lock of glossy dark hair from her once-perfect coiffure and was twisting it into a frazzled mess.

"You're frowning and getting that look." Eva thrust out her lower jaw, flattened her lips, and glared through squinty eyes.

Drusilla laughed at her friend's impersonation.

Eva's expression shifted back to its natural, perfect state. "There, that is much better. You are very pretty when you laugh or smile."

Drusilla rolled her eyes.

"And even when you roll your eyes." Eva's smile turned into a grin. "Come, tell me what you were thinking when you were looking so thunderous."

Drusilla could hardly tell her friend she'd been wondering when Eva's gorgeous but irritating stepbrother, Gabriel Marlington, would make an appearance, so she lied. "I was wondering if Lady Sissingdon was going to fall out of her dress."

They both turned to stare at the well-endowed widow in question.

Eva snorted and then covered her mouth with her hand. Drusilla couldn't help noticing that her friend's previously white kid glove now had something that looked like cucumber soup—one of the dishes at dinner—on the knuckle and a stain that must be red wine on the index finger. Drusilla could not imagine how Eva had managed to acquire the stains as she had not been wearing her gloves to eat.

Eva's violet-blue eyes flickered from Lady Sissingdon's scandalous bodice back to Drusilla, and she opened her mouth to speak, but then saw something over Drusilla's shoulder.

"Gabe!" She shot to her feet and waved her arm in broad, unladylike motions.

Drusilla slowly swiveled in her chair while Eva attracted not only the attention of her stepbrother, but that of everyone in their half of the ballroom. Drusilla knew she should remind her friend to employ a little decorum—it seemed to be her duty in life to keep Eva out of scrapes—but her heart was pounding, her palms were damp, and her stomach was doing that odd, quivery thing it seemed destined to do whenever Gabriel Marlington entered her orbit. Something he'd been doing on an almost daily basis since the beginning of the Season when he'd begun escorting his sister—and, by extension, Drusilla—to every function under the sun.

He stood near the entrance to the ballroom as the major-domo announced him. His name—as always—sent a frisson of excitement through the crowd. The women in the room—young, old, married, widowed, or single—raised their fans or quizzing glasses, the better to watch him.

The men, also, took notice of his arrival. Especially the clutch of younger men who slouched near the entrance as if they were undecided about whether they should remain at the ball or leave to engage in some vile masculine pursuit. The men closed ranks as Gabriel walked past them, like a pack of wild dogs scenting a larger, more dangerous predator.

One of the group, Earl Visel, a man with perhaps the worst reputation in London—if not all of England—said something to Gabriel that made him stop.

The two men faced each other, Visel's cronies hanging back as their leader stepped closer to Gabriel. Visel and Gabriel were, Drusilla realized, both tall, broad-shouldered, narrow-hipped men, although Visel was pale, blue-eyed, and blond while Gabriel was golden, heavy-lidded, and flame-haired.

Whatever Gabriel said to Visel put the men behind the earl into a flutter, their gabble of voices audible even over the noise of the ballroom. Visel was the only one who seemed unconcerned. In fact, he threw back his head and laughed.

Gabriel ignored Visel's laughter and scanned the crowd just like the Barbary falcon he resembled, his full lips curving into an easy smile when his eyes landed on his sister. His gaze kept moving, and Drusilla couldn't help noticing how his expression turned to one of mocking amusement when he saw her. She told herself his reaction was entirely natural, especially since she had done everything in her power to provoke and annoy him for the last five years.

She also told herself that she disliked him because he was everything she despised in the masculine species: arrogant, too attractive for either his own or anyone else's good, assured of his superiority, and so accustomed to female adulation that he would never even have noticed Drusilla's existence if she hadn't forced him to.

But she knew she was just lying to herself.